NWA

We hope you enjoy this book. Please return or
renew it by the due date.

You can renew it at www.norfolk.gov.uk/libraries or
by using our free library app.

Otherwise you can phone 0344 800 8020 -
please have your library card and PIN ready.

You can sign up for email reminders too

Shirley Mann is a Derbyshire-based journalist who spent most of her career at the BBC. Her first novel, *Lily's War*, was inspired by Shirley's mother, who was a WAAF, and her father, who was in the Eighth Army. Her second book, *Bobby's War*, is about a young ATA pilot.

Bobby's WAR

Shirley Mann

ZAFFRE

First published in ebook in the UK in 2020
This paperback edition published in 2021 by
ZAFFRE
An imprint of Bonnier Books UK
80–81 Wimpole St, London W1G 9RE
Owned by Bonnier Books
Sveavägen 56, Stockholm, Sweden

A CIP catalogue record for this book is
available from the British Library.

ISBN: 978-1-83877-222-2

Also available as an ebook and in audio

1 3 5 7 9 10 8 6 4 2

Typeset by IDSUK (Data Connection) Ltd
Printed and bound in Great Britain by Clays Ltd, Elcograf S.p.A.

Zaffre is an imprint of Bonnier Books UK
www.bonnierbooks.co.uk

To our daughters, Sarah and Jayne – they are proof of the lasting impact of the groundbreaking work done by ATA women pilots

Prologue

1942

The cow's huge black eyes stared impassively from its position at the front propeller of the Tiger Moth aircraft. Roberta, Bobby for short, stuck her tongue out at it, but it carried on chewing. The aircraft was being rocked by the skittish movements of the twenty or so Friesian cows that had raced across the field to examine this enormous bird that had seemingly fallen out of the sky.

'Hah, fallen, my foot,' Bobby told her sceptical audience, 'it was skilfully landed despite cross-winds and the fact that this Moth's nose is high on landing.'

She pushed her thighs together and winced. She needed to reach the hedge – and quickly – but she scanned the herd and they showed no sign of moving.

'Shoo,' she yelled at the crowd around her, but still they did not react. A farmer's daughter, she had no fear of cows, but she gave them enormous respect. She breathed in sharply and tensed her stomach. She should never have had that last cup of tea.

Bobby glanced at her watch. Time was marching on and she was only in Lancashire. She had to get to Oxford before nightfall.

She waved her arms frantically at the crowd of four-legged admirers and then froze mid-wave as a human face appeared in the middle of the herd. A brown-haired, freckled man in RAF uniform was gently pushing the cows out of the way. Once other uniforms appeared, the cows backed off, sensing defeat. The coast was finally clear and Bobby was able to unstrap herself and jump down to the ground.

'Blimey, it's a girl!' the freckled young man exclaimed. 'You're surely not on your own, darlin'?'

Bobby gave a very curt nod and said, 'Excuse me one moment,' and walked with great haste towards the far side of the hedge. She crouched down and heard guffaws of laughter from the other side of field.

Roberta Hollis never blushed, but there was a rosy tinge to her cheeks when she emerged from the hedge, rearranging her uniform.

'Now gentlemen, I thank you for your assistance, but could I ask you to move out of the way while I take off?'

'Not so fast,' a blond-haired lad said, standing with his arms folded in front of the wing. 'We abandoned perfectly good pints in The King's Arms and came to check you were OK. We want an explanation.'

'Have you never seen a female pilot before?' Bobby looked in exasperation at her watch. She did not have time for this.

'It's the ATA,' a Scottish voice said from the back from the group.

'What's that when it's at home?' the freckled one demanded.

'Air Transport Auxiliary – the "glamour girls". They deliver planes,' the Scot explained patiently.

'Interesting as this aviation history lesson is,' Bobby butted in, 'I've got a delivery to make and need to get to Oxford by nightfall.'

She looked up at the fading sun and pushed past the 'sentry posts' to her plane.

'Does that mean . . . you . . . fly . . . these things on your own?'

'Yes, now you have to let me leave. As you're here, you can get me started, this ground is rougher than it looked from the air. You can wing walk me over the ruts.'

'Good job we've been specially trained in this war by the RAF or we'd never have known how to do that,' one tall man muttered as he moved to hold the wing tip, ready to walk it forward to keep it steady.

'And you,' Bobby added, pointing to another one with dark hair, 'you can swing the prop. Watch for my thumbs up.'

Bobby mounted the wing and climbed into the aircraft, hurriedly buckled the four straps around her and started the cockpit checks. 'OK!' she shouted to the dark RAF man at the front. He turned the prop several times and then stepped away, shaking his head. She was concentrating too hard to even notice the stroking of chins and amazed expressions she was leaving behind as she taxied down the field, scattering the cows once again.

Tutting to herself, she swore never again to drink more than one cup of anything before she set off. That was another lesson she had learned.

On the ground, the crowd of men stood with their mouths agape, watching the wings soar into the air, the tail kept impressively steady, and the small aircraft with a woman at the controls disappear into the October sunshine.

Chapter 1

It was almost dark when Bobby reached Bicester airfield near Oxford. She knew the route but had only just made it in daylight. A tall girl with burnished auburn hair that bounced as she walked, she went first to sign in at the control tower and then made her way across the airfield to the WAAF quarters, her heavy parachute on her shoulder. She cut a striking figure as she strode across the airfield but, at the age of twenty-seven, Roberta Hollis was oblivious to both the stares and the nudges that followed her in her distinctive blue uniform. Her complete concentration was on the job in hand.

Roberta had no time to think about the strange path that had led her to the Air Transport Auxiliary – the distant father, the troubled mother or the cold atmosphere of the brick farmhouse in Norfolk. There were so many problems at home that she had learned to ignore over the years, knowing that one day she would have to deal with her fractured family, but today was not the day. She had a tight schedule to tackle and, once again, she needed to ignore the haunting thoughts that engulfed her whenever she had a spare minute. Fortunately, the relentless time-tables left her with few enough of those, and that suited Bobby just fine. 'First Officer Hollis, signing in,' she told the WAAF on the front desk.

'No beds, I'm afraid. You'll have to make do with a mattress on the floor,' the WAAF said, and pointed her in the direction of a wooden hut to the right of the office.

Bobby sighed. She had been up since six and had delivered four planes to different locations around the country. All she wanted was a quick supper and a warm bed.

An hour later, after a very lumpy cauliflower cheese in the NAAFI, she had her wish.

'You can use mine,' said a sleepy WAAF, climbing out of her bunk. 'I'm on duty tonight.'

Bobby delightedly pushed the three 'biscuit' mattresses together and smoothed back the sheet and rough blanket to climb in. She was so tired she could have slept on a tailfin, and within ten minutes, she was fast asleep, unaware of the constant stream of WAAFs who came in and out of the hut, either going to or returning from a shift. They ignored the lump in the bed until one of them noticed the dark blue uniform with its distinctive gold braid hanging up next to the bunk.

'She's one of those ATA pilots.' She nudged her friend who turned around to look.

'Personally, I don't care if she's the Queen of Sheba, I'm so tired. I've been on duty for more than ten hours and I didn't even get a break.'

Another girl handed them both cups of cocoa that had been warming next to the black stove in the middle of the room for latecomers, according to custom.

They sipped gratefully.

'Oh, that's better,' one of them said. 'So that's one of the "glamour girls" is it?' She put her head on one side assessing the curled up, snoring figure in the bed. 'She doesn't look very glam.'

'I heard they get invited to all the parties and are treated like goddesses,' another chipped in. 'It must be exciting, though, being up there in the sky.'

'Bloody dangerous if you ask me. No radar, no radio and no gun to shoot back,' her friend commented, shaking her head in awe.

They finished their cocoa, got their washbags and went to the ablutions block to get ready for bed. They could not wait to tell the crowd of girls in the washrooms that they had a real-life ATA girl in their hut, which led to a constant stream of WAAFs peering round the door to examine the snoring figure of Bobby, tucked up in bed, and pointing in amazement at her uniform hung up behind it.

Unaware of all the attention, Bobby slept like a log, waking only when the morning tannoy went off. She stretched luxuriously like her family's farm cat, Perry, but then her mind immediately switched into gear and she bounded out of bed, ready for another day of heaven knows what.

She was into her second year as an ATA pilot after a whirlwind of training, classroom lessons, trial flights and nights spent peering at her instruction manuals in the dim light. Each level left her breathless and exhilarated and endorsed her belief that flying was the only thing she wanted to do. She completed her training at White Waltham with dedication and determination, gaining her first qualifications. She knew she was good, but she also knew that it would only take one unexpected storm, a barrage balloon or a moment's lack of concentration to add her name to the list of dead ATA pilots that was posted far too regularly. She also knew that to waver would not only put her life in jeopardy, but also the reputation of women pilots, that was already fragile to say the least.

Only last week, Bobby and her friends in the ATA had gathered around a copy of *Aviation* magazine in outrage at the words written by the male editor:

There are millions of women in the country who could do useful jobs in war. But the trouble is that so many of them insist on wanting to do jobs which they are quite incapable of doing. The menace is the woman who thinks that she ought to be flying in a high-speed bomber when she really has not the

> intelligence to scrub the floor of a hospital properly,
> or who wants to nose around as an Air Raid Warden
> and yet can't cook her husband's dinner.

Bobby brushed her teeth furiously at just the memory of that quote, using the dregs of a tin of baking powder. There was a notice above the washbasins warning that there was only a tiny cup of water per girl and she measured out three drips into her mouth to rinse with. Nobody dawdled in the freezing cold ablutions block so she dressed quickly, unearthed her bowl and her 'irons'– the knife, fork and spoon – as well as her metal mug from her bag and ran over to the NAAFI to grab some porridge, hesitating over the tea urn to work out her chances of finding a toilet en route. She shrugged her shoulders in resignation, only half filling her mug and sat down to look at her notes, trying to second-guess her aircraft for the day. She hardly noticed the curious glances of the men and women on the long tables in the room, concentrating on getting the piping hot porridge down her as quickly as possible. Bicester was an Operations Training Unit and although it was under Bomber Command, fighters did not fly from there. Bobby had heard rumours of collapsing field drains that would sometimes cause pitted holes, and as thorough as ever, even though she had arrived safely the night before, she decided she would like to walk the runway to scan the surface before she took an aircraft off the ground from there.

Bobby glanced at her watch. She had to hurry so swished her 'irons' in the soapy water by the door, like the WAAFs around her did, before running to the locker room to pick up her overnight bag, her parachute and the precious bar of chocolate that kept her going on long flights. She then raced across towards the operations room to receive her 'chits' – the list of deliveries for the day – clutching her blue Ferry Pilots Notes, the Bible of every ATA pilot, with its comprehensive instructions on how to fly a dazzling array of planes. Bobby mentally ran through the list of possible aircraft she might face that day. She had flown nineteen different types so far. She looked up at the sky, where the clouds were moving fast. ATA pilots were not supposed to fly above the clouds, which always caused problems in a country like Britain where the weather was so variable. She hoped she would not be assigned to a Walrus. They were so lumbering with minds of their own and a pain in strong wind.

Outside the office, on the side of the runway, were a line of Spitfires and Mosquitoes, used for training. The ground crews, or Erks as they were known, were all working fast to get them ready for flight. It was the ATA's job to get planes to where they were needed – and fast.

She recognised a blonde girl holding two small blocks of wood on a piece of string around her neck coming towards her. The girl raised her hand in greeting.

'Bobby, I didn't know you were here.'

'Daphne! You been here all night?'

'Yep, arrived by transport late last night. Had to sleep on mattresses on the floor. I can tell you, my neck really hurts. Those 'biscuits' parted company at three this morning and left my backside on the floor.'

Daphne was a petite girl from Lancashire whose feet sometimes failed to reach the pedals. She carried small blocks of wood around with her to attach to the pedals so she could reach them, but she was an excellent pilot.

'Get any sleep?' she asked Bobby.

'Yes, some kind WAAF left me her bed and it was still warm, so I was nice and toasty.'

'Lucky you,' replied Daphne, 'I was frozen. But I suppose I was lucky to get a mattress and staying in the WAAF huts does mean we save the quid for overnight accommodation, which always helps, doesn't it? Are you back at Hamble tonight?'

'Well, who knows, I suppose it'll depend on what those darned clouds decide to do,' Bobby replied, looking up dubiously.

Hamble was the headquarters where many of the ATA girls were based. There was a good feeling of camaraderie on the days when there was a group of them grounded by bad weather, known as 'washout days', but more often than not, the pilots got held up somewhere round the country, staying in hostels, WAAF huts, inns and sometimes in train stations. It was not always a comfortable life and their timetables were relentless, so they frequently felt like ships that passed in the night.

'You Roberta Hollis? Here are your 'chits', an operations manager said as Bobby and Daphne arrived at the ops room. 'You'd better get going. You have four today.'

The ATA pilots took turns to be operations manager. This was a nightmare job involving ridiculous logistics getting pilots and planes where they were supposed to be, and although she did not recognise the tall, dark girl behind the desk, Bobby gave her a sympathetic smile and took the top sheet from the huge pile of 'chits' the girl was holding.

Bobby scanned her list – a Swordfish to White Waltham, a Barracuda to Kemble and an Albacore to Woolsington, then a Moth back to Hamble.

She was not yet qualified to fly the faster single-engined planes like the Spitfire but she had gone through the instructions so many times in her head, she believed she could have flown one blindfold. She was just longing to get to the grade when she would be able to pilot one of those Spitfires; the aircraft ATA pilots loved above all others.

'Well, the plan is to get back to base and my own bed tonight,' Bobby called over her shoulder to Daphne as they struggled out onto the airfield, with their parachutes and tiny overnight bags. 'But we'll see how that works out. Remember what they told us in training – England doesn't have a climate, it has . . .'

'WEATHER!' they both shouted together, laughing.

'See you in the restroom if we get back in time, then,' Daphne said, but Bobby was already checking through her notes to see how the Swordfish behaved in high winds.

Bobby stared up at the sky, threatening the clouds with fury if they got too thick or started to run too fast. She did not want to get stuck again tonight and pleaded with them to behave before running over to the Met Office to check the forecast.

'I haven't been back to base for three nights,' she told the good-looking Met officer behind the desk. He had nice eyes, she thought. 'Please tell me it's going to be fine in Newcastle this afternoon.'

He glanced down at his charts, shifted a few papers and then his face cleared.

'Yep, you should be OK. Just don't go anywhere near the west coast.'

Bobby looked scornfully at him. He was not that good-looking, she decided. 'I do know my east from west, you know.'

She strode quickly along the edge of the runway, narrowing her eyes to check the surface and then, satisfied that no new holes had appeared, went over to the Swordfish and walked round, appraising it. An engineer was making final checks.

'Ah, got a girl, have we? Well, I've just fixed this aircraft, don't you go breaking it.'

'You're only saying that because I'm a girl!'

He paused for a moment before he walked clear of the wings. 'Actually, do you know what? I'm not. It's usually the men who get them damaged in the first place.'

Bobby laughed and mounted the aircraft, settling herself into the pilot's seat. She took her helmet off, shook out her hair and prepared to concentrate fully.

She got her maps out, her compass, protractor, ruler and pencil. She had ten minutes to prepare but had done the route from Bicester to White Waltham before, and the one from there to Kemble, so it was just the third one up to RAF Woolsington on the north-east coast that she was unfamiliar with. She drew straight black lines to give her the most direct routes she would need to follow with the four different aircraft, noting the landmarks en route, then she checked the handling notes. It was the second Swordfish she had flown that week, so she was quite familiar with its foibles and she settled into the seat happily and put her helmet back on.

Bobby carried out her pre-flight checks going through the HTTMPPFGG – hydraulics, trim, tension, mixture, pitch, petrol, flaps, gills, gauges, otherwise remembered as 'Hot Tempered MP Fancies Girls', and gently eased the throttle to start taxiing. Her shoulders relaxed. It was just her and the aircraft and that was exactly how she liked it.

As she took off, she began to sing.

Chapter 2

The clouds, for once, behaved as the textbooks dictated and Bobby arrived back at her Hamble-le-Rice digs in good time to wash her hair and iron her shirt for the next day. She shared the accommodation – a large country house with a sweeping gravel drive – with another ATA girl, Sally, a blonde who towered above many of the men they came across. Amy Johnson's flight from Croydon to Australia in 1930 had inspired so many well-off girls to learn to fly and many of them had been first in line to join the ATA. Sally was among them but her rebellious character meant she loved to fly close to the wind – in the air and on the ground. The daughter of an aristocrat, she came from a very advantaged background which meant she was used to getting her own way and often scandalised the other girls by diverting her delivery routes to go for luncheon with friends, or making sure she arrived late at a delivery site in order to stay over for a glamorous party. There was no schedule she could not break, no excuse too implausible for her to use with her superiors. She had announced on the first day that rules were meant to be flouted, a pronouncement that had made all the other conscientious girls rear up in protest. Sally only shrugged at their shocked expressions, adding that she had every intention of finding herself a rich, titled husband by the end of the war and that the ATA would give her a status that would impress even an earl.

Bobby walked into the large kitchen that had a huge pine table in the middle, copper pans hung up around the edges and a black Aga on one side; a status symbol that had always given the cook, Mrs Hampson, the chance to boast to the whole village about having four ovens. Unfortunately, that boast had been scuppered by the fuel shortages and she was having to manage on just one ring of an old cooker, a fact she never wasted a chance to complain about. The blackout curtains were pulled and with no supper to prepare, the cook and two ladies from the village who helped out were scurrying about having a good clean up while the owners of the house, Colonel and Mrs Mason, were out visiting friends. Mrs Hampson smiled at Bobby; she liked this one, she was nice, not like that hoity toity one who treated all the staff with disdain. She approved of Bobby's tidy room and the fact that she did her own ironing.

'I'll do you some supper if you'd like, miss,' she said, putting down her Mansion polish.

'It's OK, Mrs Hampson, I can make a sandwich, just tell me what I can have.'

'There's actually some Spam left in the fridge from the weekend. And I think there might be a bit of chutney from last summer in the scullery.'

'That sounds wonderful,' Bobby told her, grabbing a plate from the dresser. 'Is Sally in?'

'Not that I know of, but she only talks to me when she wants food, so how would I know?'

Bobby smiled and got on with making her sandwich. She was delighted that for once, she might be able to have the bathroom to herself. Sally was an entertaining housemate but she always took over when she was there, making getting ready into an elaborate ritual centred around herself.

The kitchen was a better, and warmer, place to eat than the cold dining room so Bobby perched on a high wooden stool to have her supper. The two middle-aged ladies stood around nervously until Bobby smiled at them, at which point one of them set about scrubbing a pan with crushed eggshells and the other dripped out cold tea to wipe down the worksurfaces. Mrs Hampson meanwhile got on with boiling scraps of soap with bits of herbs to make new bars, a task she undertook every week. Bobby recognised the routine as one she had watched so many times in the kitchen at home in Norfolk but took note of the different herbs that Mrs Hampson used so she could tell her aunt on her next visit.

Once she had eaten the last crumb, Bobby handed her plate to Mrs Hampson's outstretched hand with a grin and made her way down the cold corridor towards the stairs. The large windows on this side of the brick house faced north, so always felt cold, and she could understand why the Masons had decided to offer rooms to the war effort after their two sons had signed up to join the navy – the empty halls were eerily quiet and the Masons must have wanted some life back in them. Bobby and Sally had separate rooms with mahogany dressing tables and a yellow silk eiderdown on each bed. In Bobby's room, there was a big window that looked out onto a large front garden, bordered by beautiful white rhododendrons that, in the spring, railed against the greyness of war. In the corner of her room, there was a cream wicker chair with a plump tapestry cushion that, if Bobby had ever had the time, promised to be a lovely place to curl up and read a book.

Bobby took a moment to look around at the solid structure that had stood steadfast through the changing times of the Great War, the lively 1920s and the Depression. The building exuded calmness and sometimes Bobby had trouble remembering that there was a war going on outside its solid walls. The cheerful photographs in silver frames on every possible surface around the house were witness to a tranquil family. Bobby loved its peacefulness and could not help but compare it with her own home in Norfolk that always seemed to echo with ghosts from the past.

Sally and Bobby normally ate with the colonel and his wife but they were an elderly couple who were used to eating in silence and after a while, the grandfather clock's tick overwhelmed the stillness and Sally would catch Bobby's eye for them to make their escape back to Hamble or to the local pub. But this evening, in the empty house, there were no such constraints and Bobby raced upstairs with a pan of hot water to wash her hair in Amami shampoo over the basin. She looked longingly at the bath but the whole household was only allowed five inches of water a week and that meant she avoided, as often as possible, having to bathe in the Mason's used water. With her hair barely rinsed, Bobby tipped forward to towel it dry, which always took a long time because her hair was so thick. Eventually, she ran down the stone front steps to pick up her bicycle and cycle the short distance down Satchell Lane back to the ferry pool restroom.

It was a dark route and with no lights allowed during blackout hours, Bobby pedalled as fast as she could trying to ignore the dark shadows in the shrubbery on either side. Like all the girls when they were cycling, she wore her trousers and a cap, tucking her hair up underneath, and put a cigarette in her mouth to look as masculine as she could to ward off any unsavoury characters who might be lurking. She heaved a sigh of relief when she arrived at the airfield.

Hamble had become a cosy haven for the ATA female pilots. The girls entertained themselves through games, sewing, playing cards and writing letters, or listening to the radio that someone had won in a raffle. They had hung up blankets and material to make it warmer, but it was a constant battle to keep the heat in, especially when the athletic types like Christine insisted on having the windows open. There were some fresh flowers in a vase on the table by the door and the sweet aroma of the late autumn blooms pervaded the room. The blackout curtains were drawn, showing the flecks of white paint that represented the scrawled names of all the girls who were stationed at Hamble. Bobby could just spot where she had written hers with pride on the edge of the one on the left, the letters finished off with a triumphant swirl. The dark polished table in the middle of the room showed signs of discarded thin writing paper, a game of backgammon, and a book that was turned over to save the page, and all the girls, including Sally, were huddled together in one corner, chattering excitedly.

Daphne looked up.

'You made it. Just in time. We're planning a night out. You up for it?'

'OK,' Bobby smiled, still not sure about this new social whirl which, since she was unused to living in a group, always made her a little nervous. She moved over to join them and squatted on the floor next to Daphne, tucking her legs under herself. Sally grinned at her and squeezed her arm.

The girls received a constant flow of invitations from RAF men desperate for some female company and completely intrigued by these young women who commanded reluctant respect for the job they did. The pilots, who usually flew just one type of aircraft, were privately in awe of the ATA womens' ability to fly so many different planes at a moment's notice. Nearly always the products of families where women were very firmly in the kitchen, they felt uneasy in the presence of such competent girls and often over-compensated with bad jokes that very soon wore thin with the ATA women. But the invitations kept coming and, unbeknown to the girls, the pilots vied with each other to see how many ATA girls they could get to their party, totting up the results on a board in the officers' mess at Gosport. The reward for the winner was a large whisky. Innocent of the significance of their presence, the girls just saw a night out as an appealing prospect.

'We've been asked over to the Instructors' party. Should be good,' Sheila said. She was new to the ferry pool and was very excited that her new status gave her a power her mousy-coloured hair had denied her at previous social events.

Bobby patted her own hair, which had gone a little wild on the cycle ride over, into place, wondering whether she had enough time to dash to the toilet to try to tame it.

Daphne answered that question before she had time to ask it. 'A driver's picking us up in ten minutes, so who's got a comb?'

'Anyone got any face powder?' Sally asked the room. They all ignored her. She had moaned all week about breaking her compact when she was forced to tip her wings to avoid a sudden rise in the Chilterns. The sudden movement had sent her makeup bag flying across the cockpit of the Swordfish she was flying, sending a flurry of powder all over the instruments. She had not been popular with the ground crew who had to clean it, but no one was crosser than Sally, who had been first in the queue on the day the note went up in the NAAFI announcing the arrival of a rare supply of face powder. It had made her late for signing in but, clutching her powder, she had taken the telling off with a triumphant smile. The others had never bothered with any face powder to begin with.

The party was being held in the mess at Gosport and as soon as the double doors opened to herald their arrival, Sally, who was leading the way, was manhandled towards the piano and hoisted up onto the top of it. A young RAF pilot was cheerfully banging away at the keys, playing 'Let's All Go Down the Strand,' looking up delightedly at the attractive girl in front of him.

Daphne smiled at Bobby and then pushed her from side to side so they both swayed in time with the music, linking arms with the other girls who had gathered next to them.

The men moved forward quickly to offer the newcomers drinks and then pushed their way to the bar to be the first to put their orders in. Sally was enjoying every minute of being the centre of attention and when two beers were handed up to her, she cheerfully took a large gulp of each, wiggling her hips in time with the music.

Daphne leaned over to Bobby. 'This beats the Old King's Head at home,' she said, taking a sip of her drink.

Bobby did not have time to reply because she was swept up by a tall squadron leader, who whirled her onto the tiny dance floor and twirled her round until she was dizzy.

* * *

It was seven o'clock when Bobby's shrill alarm went off the next morning. The ATA started their shifts at nine o'clock in the winter but they had been told they would not be flying until midday as low cloud and heavy rain were forecast, however, when she drew back the curtains in her digs, the sky was clear.

She knocked loudly on Sally's door. 'Up you get, the skies are clear.'

'Damnation,' Sally muttered, grabbing her wash things and pushing past Bobby to head towards the small bathroom at the end of the corridor. Bobby followed her, but Sally was already staring into the mirror above the basin and pulling her face from side to side.

'Ugh, this is not a pretty sight,' she moaned. 'I thought we weren't supposed to be flying this morning or I wouldn't have had such a good time.' She smiled wanly at the memory of dancing in the middle of four men who were all cheering her on.

Bobby tried to smile sympathetically but remembered Sally accepting several beers while she and the others kept to one.

'You deserve those bags under your eyes,' she laughed tentatively, beginning to enjoy this new camaraderie and pushed Sally unceremoniously out of the way to rinse her toothbrush in a tiny drop of water so it was ready for the toothpaste.

Her mouth full, she listened to a catalogue of Sally's conquests from the night before, but once she had spat the toothpaste out she said, 'I don't know how you do it, Sally. I couldn't have drunk what you did last night and fly today.'

Sally looked pleadingly at Bobby and said, 'Please get me out of it, I don't think I could see the runway.'

Bobby shook her head in despair.

The two girls grabbed some breakfast and cycled off at speed to the Hamble.

* * *

For once, Sally was looking worried. The reality of flying with a hangover was not one any of them could countenance. The

ATA had started as a civilian organisation for male pilots to ferry RAF and Royal Navy warplanes between factories, maintenance units and front-line squadrons, but then Pauline Gower, an established pilot with her own air taxi business, used all her influence and determination to establish a women's section. Sally had approached the job initially with arrogance, but now even she was starting to feel a keen responsibility not to let her hero – or the good name of the ATA – down.

Bobby and Sally had joined the other girls, who were tucking into their porridge when Patsy, a plumpish girl with brown hair, came into the NAAFI. She was one of the most experienced pilots and had been in the ATA for longer than any of the others, having learned to fly out of Blackpool where her father owned a golf course.

'They need an ops manager, anyone fancy it?' she said to them with a trace of a Lancashire accent.

In a blink of an eye, Sally put her hand up. 'I'll do it.'

Bobby looked quizzically at her.

'I can't do much mischief behind a desk,' Sally said, before standing up to follow Patsy out of the room.

Ten minutes later, the girls stood in an orderly queue to await their instructions for the day from Sally, who had positioned herself behind a large desk, piled high with 'chits' for the waiting pilots. When it came to Bobby's turn, Sally, with a wink, gave her three flights telling her one had been dropped because of the change in the weather. The first was a Wimpy to Sherburn.

'You'll have to stand up to see anything over the cowling,' Sally warned her. Bobby checked the rest, a Swordfish, known as a Stringbag, to Silloth and a Hurricane to Abingdon and she hurried to the Met Office for an up-to-date report.

The first run went without incident but by the time she landed at Silloth, the weather had worsened and as she approached the runway she was irritated to see the clouds suddenly thicken so visibility became poor. This was the sort of landing she hated the most, when she could not see other planes' approaches, and she was nothing but a small dot without a radio to warn of her approach. It was only when she got to about a hundred feet from the ground, that she was able to see the runway and her eyes narrowed while she scanned the skies to make sure there were no other planes coming in. The view in front of her was clear and she sighed with relief, bringing the Stringbag to a stop in front of the control tower. Time was running out and she raced out of the Swordfish to go to the Receipt and Despatch Office to get everything signed and then she ran out to the Hurricane. She looked in dismay at about ten sheep that were munching the grass under the fuselage.

'Shoo!' she shouted at them. She shared her father's opinion that sheep were the stupidest animals, and certainly, these sheep hardly looked at her and carried on chewing.

She ran up to them with her arms outstretched, shouting. One in front of her looked up disdainfully, so she swore at the lot and that seemed to do the trick. Frustratingly slowly, they meandered out of her way to a patch of grass at the other side of the runway and out of harm's way. She checked her watch: it had cost her valuable minutes. Climbing into the cockpit, Bobby did her checks quickly and started to taxi out, but then the ground staff suddenly indicated she should change runways.

Oh, for heaven's sake, she thought. She looked at her radiator temperature, it was overheating and she was ten degrees above the safety level. She delved into the back of her mind for a solution and then remembered advice they had all been given once by an experienced instructor. Hoping he was right, she crossed her fingers that the slipstream would bring the temperature down. Luckily, her tactics worked and she moved to another runway to make her take off. After that, it only took one hour fifteen to get to Abingdon but then she had to wait for a Fairchild to come and pick her up. She stood shielding her eyes against the setting sun, watching for it to appear in the sky, but by the time she spotted it circling it was nearly last landing time, and just as it started its approach to the runway the 'Unserviceable' sign went up and Bobby knew she would have to stay the night.

Bobby's life was one long list of aircraft, time constraints and weather problems, but it did mean she had little time to think, and the one thing Roberta Hollis, with the haunting memories of her strange upbringing and even stranger family, did not need was time to think.

* * *

Mathilda Hollis shaded her eyes against the weak November sun as she followed the path of a plane that was flying above Salhouse Farm, her home on the outskirts of Norwich. It vaguely occurred to her that it could be her daughter at the controls, but she shrugged her shoulders and carried on with her scissors, deadheading the one autumn rose that she had left. She looked round wistfully at the former rose garden, that was now planted with potatoes. Flowers were yet one more luxury she was deprived of by this war. She kept looking fearfully back at the red-bricked farmhouse she supposed was her home, nervous as always that she was doing something wrong.

There was little sign of the dimple-cheeked, dark-haired beauty who had pierced the sangfroid of the reserved Andrew Hollis just before the Great War broke out. This was a deflated woman whose clothes hung off her once nicely-rounded figure and who wafted through the garden like a ghost, disconnected from the ground around her. In the privacy of the warm farmhouse kitchen, the cook, Mrs Hill, explained to any new staff that Mrs Hollis was 'not well', a term the family used to explain Mathilda Hollis's distant stare, but everyone in the village knew that she had been like this since she had struggled to give birth to twins in 1915. In a dark bedroom on a cold April day, the last vestiges of that joyous young woman had been obliterated by the death of her and Andrew's new-born son. The hurriedly summoned vicar had grabbed some water from the jug on the washstand to christen the child with the name Michael. Just a moment later, the doctor shook his head sadly and Mathilda heard a loud scream. She did not realise it came from her own mouth. On the other side of the room Mathilda's sister, Agnes, was holding the other twin, a daughter, Roberta, who started to cry lustily.

From that moment, Mathilda seemed to slip back into the shadows, leaving her sister in almost sole charge of the little girl. Agnes often thought that Roberta's loud and relentless cries were simply to remind the family she was still there. Dressed as always in a pale grey, threadbare dress, with a buttoned-up collar, Agnes stood by the latticed drawing room window, watching the diminutive figure of her younger sister in the garden. She felt the usual mix of gloom and concern and frowned at the sight of Mathilda meandering next to the rose plant, clipping an odd stem randomly. Agnes bit her lip, hoping her fragile sibling would remember not to cut herself.

It was a bright, early winter's day and seeing a couple of men walking slowly past the stone gate at the end of the drive, Agnes thought back to another day in November 1919 when her brother-in-law had led a sparse group of village men home from the Great War. *So much has changed*, she thought, *and yet not nearly enough*.

Chapter 3

Bobby stood at the bottom of the drive to Salhouse Farm. She hesitated and then took a deep breath. This was her first trip home in weeks and she felt the familiar thumping of her heart at the sight of the large rambling eighteenth century building that always brought with it feelings of dread.

The long, straight, gravel drive was guarded by two pillars with a round stone ball on the top of each one. Bobby had walked the short distance from the bus stop in the village to the farm. Once she got to the gate, she assessed the state of the farm in front of her. Everywhere leading up to the house looked overgrown and unkempt, a far cry from the pristinely-maintained farm of her childhood. The farm had always used local labourers but now most of them had been called up, some never to return, leaving only essential workers and a few Land Army girls, who had been drafted in when Bobby signed up.

She looked towards the porch where, in 1919, she had fidgeted as a four-year-old in a stiff, new calico pinafore with a shiny yellow ribbon in her pigtails. She had been told the man who was going to arrive at the farm at ten to four that afternoon was her father. With no idea what a father should be like, she had relied on her story books, that always depicted them playing with their children, teasing and comforting them. Roberta had spent hours with her knees tucked up on the sitting room window seat imagining the moment when her very own father would return from the war, but once the sparse troop of men finally arrived, she was puzzled to see a stooped man peel off from the little group of bedraggled soldiers, looking nothing like the heroic figure she was expecting. His clothes were dirty, and his threadbare kitbag was thrown heavily over his bony shoulder. Bobby had wanted to hop up and down, but it soon became apparent that her daydreams of being tossed in the air by a delighted father were likely to be dashed, so she stood as quietly as the rest of them. The young child had vaguely registered his hair, which was exactly the same colour as her pigtails, but when he passed, he stopped to pat her on the head.

Bobby closed her eyes for a moment, leaning gently against the pillar, feeling a constriction in her throat. It had been an unnatural childhood, she thought. Her father had practically ignored her and every time she tried to climb up onto her mother's knee for a cuddle, the lap had been cold and her mother's arms had gone rigid on either side of her upright body.

'The mistress is like an Easter egg with its sugared almonds taken out,' Bobby remembered hearing Mrs Hill whisper to Archie. That description was still sadly apt, she thought.

Every time her mother saw her, she would gasp and then stare at the space behind Bobby, as if seeing a spectre from another world. It left Bobby with a feeling of crushing guilt that she had been the surviving twin and therefore to blame for all her family's distress. Aunt Agnes disguised any feelings behind that high-necked collar of hers and as far as Bobby could remember, while her aunt had performed all the essential parenting, there had been no show of affection there either.

Bobby marched determinedly up the drive, wondering when the chilling memories would ever fade, but then her frown broke into a smile as she spotted Archie the foreman, who had been with the family since he was a lad, coming round the side of the house.

Catching sight of her, Archie waved in delight, remembering the child who had flinched at nothing during her childhood.

'Bobby Hollis, 'bout time you turned up. Too busy winning the war to visit us poor country folk, are you?'

Bobby quickened her step and ran up to him to be clasped in an engulfing hug. Archie was a bull of a man with a mop of curly brown hair and a face that bore witness to a lifetime spent in the elements. He was strong and completely reliable and had dedicated his life to the family with a loyalty he might otherwise have given to a wife.

'Oh Archie, it's so good to see you. How are you? How's . . . everyone?'

He smiled at her hesitation. 'Your father's as . . . he always is . . . and your mother's in her own world. Agnes, is, of course,' he said with undisguised admiration, 'holding the fort.'

'Oh Archie, what would this family do without you?' She glanced at her watch. 'Oh, darn it, I'd love to stay for a long chat with you, Archie, but I'd better go in. I said I'd be here an hour ago but I had to wait for the taxi aircraft to get me to Bircham Newton and then it took ages to get a bus.'

'You get along,' Archie said, 'or you'll miss your dinner. They're waiting for you.'

Bobby groaned dramatically then grinned at him before going towards the house. She stopped with one foot poised on the step that led to the back-kitchen door and turned instead towards the little plot with iron railings at the side of the barn. In the plot were five or six marble headstones, all bearing the name Hollis. One was smaller than all the others with a stone angel, arms outstretched benevolently over the grave beneath. Above the grave was a large oak tree that had witnessed solemn funeral processions over three generations, none more sombre than the one for

Bobby's twin brother, when the whole village had gathered in their black Sunday best to watch the tiny coffin being lowered into the ground. Bobby turned towards the tree, spreading her fingers against the weak winter sunlight to form shadows like the fingers of the branches above, which were pointing accusingly at the grave below. She then turned around so that the tendril shadows pointed towards her and shivered.

'Hello, Michael,' she whispered, feeling the familiar inner conflict that always engulfed her when she confronted her twin's death and her own survival. 'I'm sorry I haven't been to see you for a while. It's been busy.' She stopped, as ever, not sure how to continue. 'There's a war, you know, like the last one when father was away. You'd have been in it, I suppose.' The thought struck her that her brother might not have survived this war and she gasped. It was like losing him twice.

Her hand clutched the cold, black railing around the grave, her knees weak and then she reached out to touch the headstone, willing it to give her the strength to go up to the house.

The huge open sky of Norfolk spread above her. Her mind felt as vast and as empty. Bobby looked back at the grave and took a moment to gather her thoughts.

The farm had always been a fixed point in her life but everywhere she looked, it seemed the buildings were looking down at her in disappointment, like the rest of the family. It was only when she had joined the ATA, that she had felt accepted on equal terms. When she was flying, she could escape the suffocating atmosphere of her home and she looked longingly at the unlimited horizons above her – how she yearned to be back up there rather than about to face the blank emotions of her family.

Chapter 4

Bobby went in the back door, stopping to pat Shep, the old sheepdog who slept there throughout the year, in summer's heatwaves and winter's frost, forcing everyone to step over him. He raised his head in weary greeting and then went back to sleep.

'Hello, Mrs Hill, I'm home. Sorry I'm late.'

'Well, you've just about made it, it's good to see you,' said the cook, who had known Bobby since birth. Rachel, the maid, was standing next to her smiling with delight to see the one person in the family who always had time for a chat with her. Her childhood polio had left her with a limp, allowing her to escape being called up. She had worked at the Hollis farm since the age of fourteen and felt more at home in the warm kitchen there than in the bleak rooms of her own home where her elderly, widowed mother complained about the unfairness of life from dawn to dusk.

'How are you both?' Bobby asked, giving Mrs Hill a hug.

'Trying to make a gallon out of a pint as usual with this war,' Mrs Hill moaned, waving her arms around the kitchen. 'If these shortages go on much longer, I'll be so emaciated, this pinny will go round me twice.'

Bobby caught Rachel's eye and they both smiled, looking sideways at the ample figure of the middle-aged cook in front of them who was trying unsuccessfully to pull the strings of her white pinny tighter.

The kitchen was a large room with a window looking out onto the rows of vegetables that had replaced flower beds. All over Britain, flowers were frowned on as being an unnecessary luxury and the garden that had been the pride and joy of the young Hollis bride, had been given over to vegetables as part of the national 'Dig for Victory' campaign. The family was able to use some of the produce of the farm but the authorities were becoming stricter about how much they could supplement the decreasing rations that the nation was expected to live on and Mrs Hill found it a constant struggle to create interesting meals out of the miserable supplies of Spam, reconstituted egg and tiny amounts of cooking fat, with an occasional rabbit bagged by Archie from the fields. If she sometimes 'adjusted' the books as she called it, she was not going to apologise to anyone, let alone those men in their bowler hats with notebooks tucked under their arms who turned up on the farm from time to time.

As she had done since childhood, Bobby had hopped up onto the draining board, preferring a cosy chat in her favourite place in the house to braving the atmosphere in the dining room, when the door opened and Aunt Agnes came in, her shoulders back and her head held high as usual. Here was a woman who had been trained to walk with books on her head to improve her deportment. As a child, Bobby had checked regularly to see if the books were still there.

'Roberta! About time. You're late, it's past one; you'd better get in there. Your father's been grumbling about you being late for the past twenty minutes.'

Bobby shrugged at Mrs Hill, who gave her arm an affectionate pat. Aunt Agnes scrutinised her niece, sizing up the smartness of her uniform, belied by the mop of auburn hair that was tumbling loose around her shoulders. She watched Bobby bite her bottom lip and recognised the same nervous tendency she had seen in her as a little girl. Smiling to herself, she ushered her niece out through the kitchen door towards the formal dining room.

The winter sunshine that burst through the enormous bay windows overlooking the garden almost blinded Bobby for a moment. The room looked the same, just a little more tired around the edges after three years of war. The patterned drapes had been supplemented by hastily-made blackout curtains and the three tapestry armchairs were frayed. There was a large, oblong oak dining table in the middle surrounded by high-backed chairs. Only two of the chairs at one end of the table were occupied, making the room look cavernous and empty. The fire was not lit and the room felt cold, despite the weak winter sun.

'Ah, Roberta, finally,' the austere tones of her father greeted her.

'Hello, Father, Mother, how are you?' Bobby sat down in her usual place further down the table and looked around at the familiar walls and furniture. These rooms had always seemed to echo with the unspoken thoughts of her family and, even now, she knew the words that would come out of her mouth would bear no relation to the thoughts in her head. Aunt Agnes came in behind her and put a warmed-up plateful of macaroni cheese in Bobby's place, sitting next to her with her own dish of rice pudding.

'Eat up,' she said, 'we've all eaten and are on dessert. You're looking a bit thin.'

'Oh, thank you, Aunt, that looks lovely. How are you, Mother?'

Mathilda Hollis looked nervously at her husband before speaking. It had been so many years since she had ventured to express an opinion of her own, she had almost forgotten how. 'I'm fine, dear. Yes, f—'

'How's flying?' her father butted in, ignoring his wife. Mathilda sat back, relieved to have the attention shifted away from her. 'We seem to be getting a lot more coming overhead these days. Are they keeping you busy?'

'Yes, very.' Bobby thought about telling them all about the fourteen different types of planes she had flown in the last fortnight but decided, as usual, to keep her silence to avoid criticism or comment or worse, a lack of interest.

'How's the farm doing?' she asked.

Mathilda Hollis's glance was darting around the faces at the table. She should have been delighted to see her daughter, but it always brought back so many painful memories of the year spent in the gloom of the bedroom above, engulfed in a grief so piercing in its cruelty that she had almost lost her mind. Even now, when she looked at Bobby, she felt a need to put her hand to her breast to stop her heart from breaking.

'The cattle got a terrible price at market this morning with those damned controlled prices,' her husband was saying. 'Do you know how much I had to sell them for, Mathilda?' His wife tried to look interested but immediately felt the panic that rose in her stomach with every word he had uttered since he came home from the war.

The fact that she had committed the arch sin of not providing him with a male heir was exacerbated by the irony that there had been one, almost within reach, but she had killed it with her ill-shapen womb. It was all her fault and now she did not know the value of a cow.

Agnes came to her rescue as usual. 'I'm sure you got more than you did last month,' she said. 'That was the lowest price this year.'

'Well yes, I suppose I did, but it was small consolation. I've nurtured and fed those animals and I'm hardly getting my money back. Of course, if Bobby had stayed at home, I wouldn't have had to employ Jed. He can hardly walk with that leg of his. That would have saved me some money and those Land Army girls are less than useless. I wish I'd never spent money on those flying lessons.'

Bobby interrupted to halt this habitual direction of conversation. 'So, Father, have you heard about El Alamein? We've finally got the Germans on the run.'

It was the one topic that would get her father away from the dire finances of the farm and the selfishness of his daughter and it worked like a charm. He spent the rest of the meal taking great delight in regaling the family with the shortcomings of Rommel and Bobby relaxed, finally feeling on safe ground.

Mathilda Hollis could hardly finish her rice pudding and looked glumly at the watery contents of her bowl, stirring it absent-mindedly with her spoon, letting the conversation go over her head. She so wanted to join in but had forgotten how. She tentatively reached out her hand for a moment towards Bobby, but then when her daughter looked up, she withdrew it quickly.

The rest of the meal went painfully slowly and Bobby could not wait to get out into the cold, fresh air after luncheon to escape the stifling atmosphere of the house. Every subject she brought up with her father seemed to prompt a fiery debate between the two of them and after spending ten minutes trying to persuade him that women were just as capable as men at piloting planes, she had given up and turned on her heels to leave him. She stood on the front porch and took a deep breath to calm down but then she spotted her aunt hurrying towards the woods, clutching a small posy. She looked curiously after her and then saw Archie, looking in the same direction, his garden fork in his hand.

'Archie?' she called. 'Do you know where she's going?'

'It's none of our business to be honest, Bobby, we should respect her privacy. Now if you're at a loose end, come and help me dig this patch over before the frost.'

Bobby jumped down and went into the barn to grab a set of overalls to put over her uniform. This was the one thing about going home that she loved – getting her hands dirty.

Archie continued to dig the soil. He had his suspicions about Agnes's forays into the woods but he kept them to himself. He was painfully aware that everything that woman did interested him. He dug harder and deeper to take his mind off her. Bobby worked silently and happily alongside him until the heavy macaroni cheese had settled in her stomach.

'Bobby, Bobby, are you there?' She heard Harriet's voice from the driveway.

Dark-haired Harriet Marcham was a whirlwind who had breezed through Bobby's detachment like a puppy determined to be loved. She had followed Bobby slavishly since the day her heroine had marched between two boys at the village school who were teasing Harriet, twisting their arms so that they were powerless, and therefore rescuing her. Harriet had looked through her tears in grateful surprise at her saviour and from that day on, Bobby's strength and unerring sense of right and wrong had won Harriet's undying loyalty. While the rest of the school shunned this strange child with auburn pigtails, who seemed to have none of the usual need of friends or approbation, Harriet had immediately appointed herself as Bobby's defender and number one admirer.

'Ah, there you are,' Harriet said, coming towards the barn. She was in the blue WAAF uniform that reflected her grey eyes and the heavy Oxford shoes that she had worn since 1940 when she joined Bomber Command. 'Hello Archie, can you spare this farmhand for a minute?'

Archie grinned and took Bobby's spade off her, watching with pleasure as the two girls went off arm in arm. When they got around the corner, the small frame of Harriet flung her arms around Bobby's waist, taking her breath away.

'So, how are you, where have you been, how long are you staying, why haven't you written?'

When she paused for breath, Bobby broke in, laughing. 'Fine, working . . . all over the country and only tonight. There, does that answer all your questions?'

'Humph,' Harriet replied, unimpressed. 'Well, you still haven't said why you haven't written. It was only because my mother ran into Mrs Hill in the queue at the butcher's that I even knew you were coming. So, how's everybody? How's the ATA? Had any time for gorgeous men?'

'Whoa!' Bobby said, putting her hand gently over her friend's mouth. 'Look Harriet, first, can you come back for supper? Please say yes, I can't bear another meal where I have to put up with father's lack of interest, mother staring into space and Aunt Agnes's probing. Please, please . . .'

'Nope, I'm due back at Coltishall in fifteen minutes, I had to bike really fast before my shift to catch you and tell you off for not writing. Oh, and I just wanted to tell you about Gus Prince.'

The undisputed leader of the pack at the village primary school, Gus Prince had been the best at sport, the most popular boy in school and the one all the girls fell in love with. All except Bobby, that was, she was too interested in trying to beat the boys at every possible sport to be interested in playground gossip.

'Oh, I had such a crush on him!' Harriet went on. 'We all did. Well, all except you and it was you he liked. That used to make me so mad! Do you remember those arm-wrestling contests you and Gus used to have across the desks?' she said. 'You were the best in the school at it, even he couldn't beat you.' She paused and then gave a deep sigh.

'Sometimes he did win,' Bobby said, rubbing her arm with the memory. 'But get on with it, Harriet, what did you have to tell me?'

'Oh, well, I haven't seen him for years and then just the other week, I found out he's a pilot. Just think, Bobby, he might turn up at Coltishall. I could be the telephone operator picking up his signal. Wouldn't that be the perfect romantic reunion?'

She paused dramatically and was pleased to see Bobby waiting for the next piece of information.

'Anyway, I only managed to find out that he'd become a pilot because I interrogated Helen at the surgery. Her mother's in the same Red Cross group as the cleaner at the Prince's house. Apparently, even his mother doesn't know where he's based – I saw her last week in the greengrocer's and went straight in there and asked her. She had no idea! Now isn't that a mystery. Do you think he's a spy?'

'Oh Harriet, you're hilarious. No, of course he isn't. He's just a pilot like Billy Wade and Frank Abbot.'

'Hmm,' Harriet said, and then touched the side of her nose, knowingly.

'You'll see, he's going to do something amazing. I always said he was just the cleverest, most gorgeous man and,' she clutched her heart and raised her eyes to heaven, 'one day, who knows, maybe we *are* destined to be together.

She thought for a moment. 'That is, if I don't run off with one of those Americans, I've heard they're quite something and could be over here soon. Oh, and then there's Gerry, he's an engineer and definitely "The One", well, this week. Oh, he's lovely.' Harriet's love affairs were legendary, and she fell in love on a regular basis. Bobby had trouble keeping up.

Bobby glanced at her watch and said, 'I thought you had to go.'

Harriet grabbed her friend's arm and looked fiercely at the watch on her wrist. 'Oh hell's bells, is that the time? I'm going to have to pedal at double speed.' And with that, she gave Bobby a quick hug and raced off down the drive towards her bicycle that she had flung onto the verge. 'Can you get out to the Dun Cow tonight after supper?' she shouted back. 'I'm off duty at eight so could meet you there, oh and Roberta Hollis, comb your hair before you come. You look a mess!'

Bobby smiled after her, shaking her unruly hair in defiance. Harriet never gave up her attempt to make her friend into a respectable female. As far as Bobby was concerned, *her* job was to try to keep Harriet Marcham out of trouble but sometimes, that seemed like a full-time occupation.

Once Harriet had left, Bobby grabbed her bike and cycled off to the nearby airfield where she had learned to fly. Strangely, it had been Harriet Marcham who had first put the idea of flying into her head years before when they had both been at Lonsdale School for Girls in Norwich.

One Sunday afternoon, the girls had been allowed out for their usual prescribed walk and Harriet and Bobby had headed for the fields on the outskirts of the city.

Bobby had been swirling round trying to emulate the skylark above her when she had suddenly flopped down into the grass.

'What's up?' Harriet had asked, a little alarmed.

'Oh, I don't know, I just sometimes feel this earth is too . . . too . . . I don't know, *flat* for me.'

'What in heaven's name are you talking about now?' Harriet sat down next to her.

Bobby lay back and shielded her eyes against the late spring sun. She pointed up towards the skylark soaring above them. 'Look at that skylark. It's completely free, while I'm stuck down here with a family that doesn't communicate *and* in a school where the only thing that matters is how much Shakespeare you can recite. It makes me long to be up there swirling around in the clouds.'

'Oh well, maybe you should learn to fly like that woman pilot I'm named after, what was her name? Harriet Qu . . . erm, Quimby, that's it!'

Harriet lay back triumphantly but Bobby grabbed her by the shoulders and yanked her up again. 'What pilot? You were named after a pilot? A woman pilot? Flying planes? Tell me more this instant.' She glared at her friend but Harriet just shrugged.

'I don't know, my father heard about her and thought it was a nice name, that's all.'

From that moment, the idea became an obsession that occupied every moment of Bobby's spare time and she scoured the library for books about aviation. Over the last year at school, she learned about farms in America and South Africa where they were using planes to fertilise the fields. Slowly but surely, she constructed the case to present to her father. The confrontation between them had taken three days of an unusually reasoned argument by Bobby. On the first day she told him that it would take longer by tractor to spray the fields with pesticide, then she gave him figures that proved it would be more efficient to do it from the air, and on the final day she triumphantly revealed that there was not one man on the farm who had expressed any interest in learning to fly. Her father was a man who was only swayed by practicalities and once he realised he could find no flaws in her argument and exhausted by his relentless daughter's determination, he finally gave in and agreed to arrange some lessons with an old friend of his at the price of twelve shillings and sixpence each.

The first time she had sat in the pilot's seat she had felt a shiver permeate through her body. It was as if the part of her life that had been missing was there in the controls in front of her. All she had to do was reach out to them and they would belong to her and she would belong to them. She had found home.

At that moment, everything had slotted into place and for the first time in her life she felt she was in the right place, doing the right thing. She worked hard to achieve her licence, spending every possible moment at the airfield, either in the aircraft or in the control tower, watching the planes take off and land, noting the position of the wings, the speed and the operation of the undercarriage on landing.

Bobby looked around at the weeds that were beginning to grow on the edges of the tarmac. The planes had been commissioned into service and the large runway felt eerily empty. Her reverie was disturbed by footsteps behind her and she turned to find Group Captain Turner approaching her from the redundant control tower.

'Hello Roberta,' he said, delightedly. This young woman had been his best pupil. From the day she arrived, swinging herself into the cockpit, eschewing with a dismissive 'Pah' the ladder he had provided for her, she had absorbed the lessons with enthusiasm and dedication. He remembered watching her take her first solo flight, watching from below but somehow not being as nervous as he was with his other trainees. He had been confident that here was one pupil he could trust. When she joined the ATA, he had not been surprised; it was the perfect job for her.

'Hello Group Captain Turner.' She held out her hand to give the formal handshake he expected. 'It's sad to see the old airfield unused.'

'They're coming with the camouflage next week, it's going to be a dummy one,' he told her. In many parts of the country, and East Anglia in particular, the authorities were using every ploy possible to confuse the enemy. Bobby shivered, looking over at the nearby houses. They would be increasingly at risk if the airfield on their doorstep was being used as a decoy.

'I hope you're reading those Pilot's Notes thoroughly,' he went on. 'I heard of an ATA pilot being killed last month.'

'Yes, don't worry, I study them every night.'

Archibald Turner nodded approvingly. 'You make sure you do; I just don't want to lose my best pupil. Now, if you've got a bit of time, I'd love to go over some of the aircraft you've been flying with you.'

The two walked companionably to the control tower and spent a contented hour doing what Bobby loved best – talking about aeroplanes.

On her way home from the airfield, Bobby fingered the golden wings on her ATA tunic. When war broke out in 1939, her father had been furious – at the reneging on promises that the Great War would be the last-ever conflict; that fuel shortages meant no more aerial crop spraying, and then on top of all that, his daughter, already a spinster in the making, had heard a BBC radio appeal for women pilots and was mounting a campaign to be allowed to join the Air Transport Auxiliary. Every time she raised the issue, he countered with the fact that the more useful thing she could do would be to find a husband who could take over the farm. His insistence only made her more determined to thwart him and one suitor after another was given short shrift as she refused to give in to her father's demands, dismissing without compassion the stream of young men who attempted to take her out, scorning their limited horizons. Bobby Hollis was completely focused on her own goal, which had nothing to do with walking down the aisle and becoming someone's wife. In 1942, in desperation, she informed her father that unless he agreed to let her join the ATA, she would never look at any man ever again.

Chapter 5

'You're late,' she accused Harriet, spotting her friend peering round the door at the Dun Cow.

Harriet crept in, looking round her nervously. The bar was full of farmers, old men and some other people in uniform.

'Did you really walk in here all on your own?' she said, sidling in to join Bobby. 'Didn't people stare at you?'

Bobby shrugged. 'I've no idea, I didn't notice, but I got fed up with waiting outside in the cold for you.'

'I know, I'm sorry, but you'll never believe who I've just bumped into.'

Bobby sat back. She knew her friend would spend the next half hour slowly revealing details about an encounter that she was determined would have an impact on Bobby and it was a waste of time to try to rush her.

'OK, but first, I'm parched. Let's get a drink,' Bobby said. 'I suppose I'll have to go to the bar, will I?'

'You certainly will, I'm not going,' Harriet replied, her eyes darting around the room in embarrassment.

Bobby sighed with resignation, refused the coppers that Harriet had pushed towards her and headed to the bar. The men parted for her, universally gratified that their wives and daughters were not brazen enough to drink in a bar without a male escort like Andrew Hollis's wayward daughter. Others, strangers to the village, scanned Bobby's uniform with puzzled expressions.

When Bobby had picked up the two halves of cider, the two factions of men closed ranks and a low whispering began. She ignored it and went to the corner table where Harriet was sitting forward, fidgeting with excitement.

'So . . . I was coming round the corner,' Harriet said conspiratorially, 'by the school, you know where the old tree was cut down last year, the one we used to climb and Pauline nearly fell . . .' she paused, seeing Bobby's look of impatience, anyway, who do you think was coming in the other direction?'

Bobby gave an appropriately quizzical look.

'It was . . . Marie McGill!' Harriet finally said with triumph.

'Marie, as in "you must pronounce my name with a French accent", Marie?'

'Yes!' Harriet exclaimed. 'She looked as if she was in such a hurry heading for the bus stop. She only had a small bag with her and I have to say, was wearing the dowdiest brown coat I've ever seen. She always used to be so fashion conscious and smartly turned-out. Do you remember how awful she was to you about your hair, your clothes ... actually, just about everything about you? She really was horrid. Anyway, she shuffled past as if she didn't want anyone to recognise her.'

'Did you speak to her?'

'No, she didn't give me the chance.' Harriet thought for a moment. 'In fact, she almost veered into a bicycle to avoid me, I think. She always hated us both, well, you mostly. I think she felt threatened by you because you didn't treat her like she was the queen of the castle like everyone else did. It drove me mad how she used to constantly jabber on in French just because she had a French grandmother. She thought she was the bee's knees. She used to spend every summer over there, didn't she? Somewhere in Normandy I think. Oh, I loved that day when you talked back to her in French. Do you remember?' Harriet raced on, not pausing for breath – or an answer. 'Anyway, I couldn't believe it! You were almost as fluent as she was. She was so shocked. Mind you, we all were.'

Bobby took a sip of her drink.

Andrew Hollis's announcement that he would teach his daughter French had come as a surprise to everyone. Generally, he took scant interest in the female members of his family, but when she told him a girl at school was fluent, he seemed to be galvanised into action with a competitiveness that was equalled by his headstrong daughter. The lessons took on a regimented routine that helped Bobby progress rapidly in the French language. During those lessons, she started to suspect how much her father had fallen in love with France where he was based as a soldier, and for the first time, she had glimpsed a different man beneath the uncompromising veneer she had come to expect.

Harriet finally ran out of breath, at which stage Bobby reached out and put her hand on her friend's hand and said, 'She never bothered me, you know. All that bullying went to waste to be honest. I didn't like her, so it didn't matter what she said.'

Harriet looked with undisguised admiration at Bobby. She really had never been sure whether she totally understood Roberta Hollis. It flummoxed Harriet that Bobby did not need anyone's approval.

'So, tell me the news,' Bobby finally said to Harriet, a request that unleashed an hour and a half of titbits of interest about the long stream of men that Harriet had been out with, the exhausting shift patterns of a WAAF, the deprivations of the NAAFI, where the food was definitely getting worse, with everything tasting of carrots or cabbage and the depressing belief that the war was going to go on until they were both old maids.

Bobby started to giggle and Harriet's face lit up. 'Oh, it is good to see you behaving like a normal person!'

'I *am* a normal person,' Bobby protested.

'No, you're not; you're Bobby Hollis, but you're wonderful, and I love you to pieces.'

'Do you know, Harriet, it wasn't until we were at Lonsdale that Marie nearly succeeded in her bullying campaign?' Bobby suddenly confided, leaning forward. Harriet reared up in surprise.

'I thought you were always impervious to her nastiness.'

'Yes, I was. All those comments about my hair, my freckles and so on just went over my head, but then we all started the "curse", do you remember? For the first time, I felt out of control, my hormones were all over the place and nothing made sense. It was then that Marie's jibes finally got through and I would go to bed in tears.'

'I had no idea,' Harriet began, but then added, 'Oh, no, I do remember, that was when I took you in hand and made a lady out of you. Well, I tried.'

'Hmm, well, you failed there, but I did appreciate your efforts – all that brushing of my hair and making me put it in rags to curl it.' She fingered her hair. It was so thick no curl had ever taken over from the natural waves, but Harriet's cajoling had made Bobby realise, for the first time, what it was like to have a friend.

With two ciders inside her, Bobby was feeling quite mellow. 'Do you know, coming home always makes me feel a bit too pensive. I'm so happy when I'm up in the air with other things to concentrate on, but coming home always makes me think, and I'm not sure I like it.'

'Oh, yes, thinking . . . personally, I've always thought it's overrated! I just act first and think later and that, Bobby, is exactly how I got into trouble again this week. Let me tell you about it . . .'

* * *

At the farm, Bobby's father was also doing some thinking. He sat in the gloom in his study with the blackout curtains drawn. The farm was struggling to make ends meet. There were constant demands from the government to provide more food, but the supply of feedstuff was getting more scarce and the profit margins were narrow.

In front of him was a letter from the War Office inform-ing him that his land to the east of the farm was to be used to house German prisoners of war. His knuckles clenched and his expression hardened. A survivor of Passchendaele, his memory of the steel helmet and the desperate face beneath it holding up a bayonet to his chest haunted his dreams every night and he was not a man to forgive easily. He had battled with the men from the Ministry, but his objections had been overruled and the first batch were due to arrive next week.

He stood up and went over to the gas lamp in the cor-ner to read the fine print of the instructions about what housing they would need. He had restored the lamp to reduce the electricity bills, but to be honest, it was really hard to see by it and his eyes narrowed to read the long list of demands, feeling fury rising in his chest. His equanimity had not been helped by the argument he'd had with his daughter over women pilots. Every time he saw her, she seemed more difficult, more belligerent and infuriatingly more stubborn. Agnes could have told him that they were traits Roberta had inherited from him, but that comparison never occurred to Andrew. Instead, he was mulling over an idea he had had after meeting Archibald Turner at the country club the previous week, which might just provide a way to protect the farm's future. The idea was purely to his and the farm's advantage and seemed like a very practical solution; the fact that it would prompt even more anger from his daughter did not occur to him.

Chapter 6

The winter was a relentless round of aircraft deliveries and Bobby had no time to dwell on the lingering suspicion that her father was plotting something. Her days off were spent sleeping or reading up on aircraft and as Bobby was not in the habit of indulging in introspection, she pushed all thoughts of her family out of her mind. After flying a Wimpy to Staffordshire in late March, 1943, she was exhausted and was even grateful to bag a bunk in a freezing cold hut, but before she fell asleep, she checked her logbook. The last few pages were a mass of pencil scribbles, impossible timescales and technical notes for herself. She liked to go over them each night to remind herself of things that might be useful when she was flying the same aeroplanes again, although when she looked at the list of craft she had flown over the past month, she noticed there were hardly any repeats.

She flopped onto the flock-filled pillow, sniffed and wondered whether she had a cold coming. A cold was a casualty of war, not an illness that warranted time off curled up with a hot cocoa and a hot water bottle; the pilots simply carried on with streaming, red noses, struggling pathetically into freezing cold planes, shivering and sneezing. Bobby sniffed again; she definitely had a dry throat.

The girl in the next bed turned over, opening one eye to glare at Bobby.

'Sorry,' Bobby whispered. She glanced over at her uniform, hung up on a hanger. There was an inspection due when she got back, and before she went to sleep she systematically went through all the items in her head. Ticking each item off, she stopped suddenly when she came to her hat. Her skirt was hung up in the wardrobe at Hamble but when she envisaged the top shelf where the hat should have been, she could not remember having seen it for ages.

Where the hell is my hat? she thought with a jolt, sitting up again. She wracked her brains to try to think when she had last had it. It had been over a month ago. A helmet was the usual headgear the pilots wore but they had to keep their hats spruced up and clean to wear for church parade and official occasions and the last time she had worn it had been for a funeral for one of the male ATA pilots who had been killed when his engine failed on landing. She remembered wearing it then because, seeing his distraught widow and two children standing behind the coffin, she had lowered her head under her hat so no one could see she was crying, but after that, for the life of her, she could not remember where she had put it.

Bobby felt panic rising; the punishment system in the ATA was not nearly as stringent as in the WAAF, but losing a piece of your uniform was a chargeable offence. Her heart started to race and she pulled her knees up to rock backwards and forwards while she went through every possible place where she might have left it.

Keeping a clean record was a prime objective of every ATA pilot and Bobby had tried not to make any mistakes, but it was uncomfortably true that she had concentrated her efforts on getting the essentials of flying correct, consigning worrying about her formal uniform to the bottom of her list of priorities.

With the pragmatism that defined her, Bobby eventually shrugged her shoulders and lay back down to go to sleep, reasoning that it would either be at Hamble or, heaven forbid, she had lost it somewhere. She told herself that if she was going to get any sleep, she had to believe the hat was safely at the back of the wardrobe at Hamble.

* * *

Back at base on the south coast, some of the girls were plotting. It was going to be Bobby's birthday shortly and Sally, Daphne and Patsy were debating whether they should hold a party for her.

'I think she'd like it and it would do her good to mix a bit more,' Patsy said.

'I'm not sure, she does seem to like to keep herself to herself a lot,' Daphne said thoughtfully.

'Nonsense, everyone loves a party, even Bobby,' Sally butted in, leaning forward to grab a pencil and piece of paper.

'You just want an excuse to dress up and flirt,' Patsy said, leaning forward to pinch the pencil from her.

'Of course I do. Hands off, I'm doing the list,' Sally protested, holding the pencil in the air out of Patsy's reach. 'I know everyone, you don't.'

'All the men, you mean,' Daphne interrupted.

'Why would we bother having anyone else at the party?' Sally laughed and started to write down a list of RAF pilots' names.

* * *

Bobby got back to Hamble and after a fruitless search, went to the adjutant who sent her to see the commanding officer, Margot Gore. Standing outside the CO's office on a bright April morning was not the way Bobby wanted to start her 28th birthday. Her nose was still red and she was sniffling uncomfortably. She took a large breath, knocked and went in. Margot was sitting behind her desk and smiled when Bobby came in.

'Hello Bobby, what can I do for you?'

'I've, umm, lost my hat and the adjutant said I had to come and see you.'

Normally, Margot was very informal and would ask the girls to sit down but, on this occasion, she just frowned and bit the end of her pencil, leaving Bobby standing looking very sheepish in front of her.

'It'll have to go to the Accident Committee, you know that?' she said. 'Our uniform is part of who and what we are. I'm sorry, Bobby, but I have to report you.'

Bobby nodded, more miserable than she could have believed possible. Her CO looked at her in disappointment and waved a hand for her to leave.

Bobby knew this would be a black mark against her and if the committee decided, as she feared they might, to make an example of her, it could cost her dearly, both financially as well as damaging her reputation, which had been spotless to date.

* * *

That evening, Bobby walked slowly into the mess, her head lowered. Her cold was making her feel especially miserable and she was only wasting time before she could go to bed. As she opened the door, a huge cheer went up and she stopped in her tracks.

In front of her were Sally, Patsy and Daphne, all looking very pleased with themselves. They had decked the room out in paper streamers and on the wall opposite the bar, there was a handwritten 'Happy Birthday' sign.

Behind the girls were about ten men in uniform who Bobby did not know, all clapping happily at the chance to put the war to the back of their minds and have a good night out.

Bobby looked round in horror. A party was the last thing she needed or wanted. She was feeling ill and was far too distracted by the uncomfortable conversation she had had with Margot Gore earlier that day.

Sally moved forward and swept her towards the men. 'We thought you deserved time off for some celebration,' she said, pushing a drink into Bobby's hands.

'This is Wally, he's just dying to dance with you. Someone put the gramophone on and let's get the dancing going.'

Bobby stood awkwardly in front of Wally, who at the age of twenty-two, suddenly felt intimidated by this tall, older woman in front of him.

'W . . . would you like to dance?' he murmured, tentatively reaching his arms out towards her as Glenn Miller's 'American Patrol' started up.

Bobby hesitated; she really did not feel like dancing.

Sally came up behind her and fiercely took her arm, steering her momentarily away from the embarrassed Wally.

'Come on, Bobby, lighten up a bit, everyone's gone to quite a bit of effort to make a nice do for you. It might be helpful if you tried to enjoy it a bit.'

Bobby looked around at all the expectant faces. It was the first birthday party anyone had ever organised for her and she suddenly felt ashamed that she was such a reluctant participant.

'Of course, I'm sorry,' she said, suddenly, making an effort to brighten her face. She took a large swig of the drink, which slid down her throat in an instant. It helped to ease her sore throat. She turned back to Wally, who was suddenly captivated by the beautiful smile in front of him and took courage enough to whisk her away into a lively dance.

By her third drink, Bobby was surprised to find she really was feeling better and enjoying herself. She had two days off to look forward to and the hearing about her uniform wasn't until the following month, so with her usual equanimity she decided what would be would be and there was nothing she could do about it, so she may as well let her hair down a little.

Towards the end of the evening, she went over to the little group of girls who were standing by the bar.

'I'm sorry I was such a misery guts,' she said. Bobby paused, it did not come naturally to her to open up and share the possibility that she might have failings but with three drinks inside her, she decided she would risk ridicule.

'I've lost my hat and now there's a hearing in a month.'

She looked around at the group of girls waiting for sarcasm or superiority but she saw nothing but sympathy and understanding. Patsy leaned forward and patted her arm.

'Oh Bobby, no wonder you were so fed up, but all in all perhaps this was exactly what you needed. A good party is a great way to forget your miseries.'

Bobby looked around at the little group and felt a surge of affection she had rarely felt before.

'Thank you all for going to so much trouble,' she told them, and then, 'To be honest, that's the first birthday party I've ever had.'

Daphne looked horrified. With five brothers and two sisters, her whole year was an excuse for celebrations and birthday parties were a regular occurrence in her household. Even Sally looked surprised.

Patsy spoke first, 'Do you know what then, Roberta Hollis? We'd better get on and make sure it's one you never forget.' And all three of them grabbed her by the arm and dragged her back towards the dance floor.

'Gentlemen,' Sally called out, 'I think this young lady needs to have the birthday bumps. Apparently, she's never had them.'

The men whooped with delight and scooped Bobby up in their arms to throw her up and down in the air.

'How many times?' one yelled to Sally.

'Never you mind,' Bobby panted as she landed back into the outflung arms, 'but I think that'll do. I'm exhausted!'

They gently placed her on the ground and then all gathered around her to sing, 'For She's a Jolly Good Fellow'.

Bobby felt tears appearing on her cheek. For the first time in her life she was part of a community and she could not believe how good it felt.

* * *

The following month, Bobby paced up and down outside Margot Gore's office, knowing that, at any moment, Margot would receive the telephone call from White Waltham where the Accident Committee were meeting. Her palms were sweating. The girls had all wished her good luck that morning and their genuine concern had helped her face the day, but the possibilities of the various forms of punishment kept flashing before her eyes. She kept trying to reason it was only a hat, she had not damaged any aircraft, disobeyed any ground instructions or been guilty of 'lifting the arm' – drinking too much – so surely, the punishment could not be too severe. Could it?

The door opened and Margot came out. She gave Bobby a severe look and then her face relaxed.

'Fined one and ten pence,' she said.

Bobby heaved a huge sigh of relief and moved out of the way to let Margot past.

'Oh, and you have to pay for another hat,' Margot called back.

'With pleasure!' Bobby said quietly.

Chapter 7

Night-time bombing had started and Bobby was working harder than ever with relentless schedules to make
sure the RAF had aircraft in the right places at the right
times. At the end of May 1943 she sent in her logbook to
the commanding officer as usual and was delighted when
Margot Gore put her forward for more training.

She turned from the post up on the noticeboard in
excitement to Sally who was also scanning the list.

'Sally, we're going to White Waltham. Spitfires, here we
come!'

Sally grabbed her by the arm and swung her round, nar-
rowly missing the wall. 'High-flyers, that's what we are.
Oh, what a dream. Next, it'll be the heavy bombers like
Wellingtons. Oh, and Bobby, just think, we can get to
London from there. Right, I'll find out what parties are on.'

'But we'll be far too busy cramming for the tests,' Bobby
said hurriedly.

'We'll just see about that,' and with that Sally linked her
friend's arm and made her waltz down the hallway.

White Waltham was just outside Maidenhead and was the headquarters of the ATA. Walking down one of the corridors, it seemed an age since Bobby had come for her initial interview and she paused for a moment outside the door with the revered Senior Commander's name on it. Reaching out her hand and tracing the letters of Pauline Gower's name, she remembered the day of her practical test and interview at the beginning of 1942, when she had shivered with trepidation on a bench outside this very office waiting to be called to her aircraft. She had had to sit on her hands to stop them twiddling nervously, knowing that her experience as a pilot was very limited, with only some crop spraying to her name. Bobby looked across at the training rooms with those familiar desks where they had all learned about Morse code, navigation and plotting. She remembered the steep learning curve that had taught her how to plan her route using golf courses, railways, churches and roads, instead of radios or navigation equipment. Then there had been that all-important interview with Pauline. To begin with, Bobby had almost frozen in fright at being in front of the woman who had taken on all opposition to make sure women were given the same status as men in the ATA, but then Pauline Gower smiled at her encouragingly and she had relaxed. She had not known that Pauline was delighted to see a serious, more mature young woman applying to join, so was willing her on to succeed. Aircraft production was being stepped up after the destruction of so many aeroplanes during the Battle of Britain and the demands on the ATA were relentless, so they needed pilots like Roberta Hollins, the head of the ATA had thought, stamping her application form with the word 'Accepted.'

Bobby knew how far she and women in general had come in the last few years. Without the war, she thought, crop spraying would have been her only expression of freedom; the rest of the time, she would have been expected to pursue ladylike activities, help her mother in the garden or attend the most tedious cocktail parties. She sent a prayer of thanks skyward for a leader like Pauline and, she ruefully admitted, for a war that had opened new opportunities to girls like her. As a child, she had stopped in wonder to stare upwards on the rare occasion that a plane flew overhead, astonished at its speed and ability to soar above the clouds and here she was, flying aircraft all over Britain. It seemed like an impossible journey in such a short time. Dawdling outside Pauline's room, Bobby heard a chair scraping inside and scuttled away before the door opened, unwilling to be found hovering in the corridor like a star-struck schoolgirl.

* * *

The advanced training week at White Waltham went quickly and with a head spinning with information about the more advanced single-engined aircraft, Bobby sat in the exam room nervously twiddling her pencil. She had successfully completed the practical tests without any problem but the written test demanded an in-depth knowledge of a huge number of aircraft, weather patterns and navigation risks and by the time the exam was over, she had bitten off the end of her pencil in consternation. She raced straight to the library to check what facts she had written down and heaved a huge sigh of relief that most of them seemed correct. She just hoped the examiners agreed with her.

The next morning the results were announced and both Sally and Bobby had passed their Class II exams and even Sally was relieved. Amid the glasses of gin and tonic, the parties and her lengthening list of romantic conquests, Sally was surprised to discover how satisfying it was to do a real job and to do it well. However, she reasoned, the exam results did offer a very good reason to celebrate.

'Bobby, if you're a good girl, I'll take you to London tonight and we can finally have some fun,' she announced as they got back to the room they were sharing in their digs.

Bobby was planning an early night; she had been working really hard, spending her evenings in the library, swotting up on the new categories of planes and was exhausted, but Sally had other ideas.

'Don't argue,' she said, putting her hand up to stop Bobby's protests. 'There's a new revue at The Windmill and I've found two men who'll take us.

Bobby looked at her aghast. 'But the Windmill has nude dancers!'

'So?' Sally replied, taking off her bra to reach for a new silk one.

'Well, when you put it like that,' Bobby smiled shyly, trying not to stare at the naked body in front of her.

'Anyway, the dancers don't move, you know that. It's all really tame, actually. I've heard there are going to be striptease joints opening up in London soon,' Sally added knowingly.

Bobby thought for a moment. Society was changing too fast, she could hardly keep up with it. She suddenly giggled when she thought of how her father and Aunt Agnes were going to deal with this new, modern world.

Sally was using a shoelace to try to curl her hair into the fashionable roll, but suddenly turned round, 'Tell me Bobby Hollis, have you ever even kissed a man?'

Bobby sat back and thought.

'You haven't, have you? You actually haven't.'

'I have!' said Bobby indignantly. 'I've been kissed by lots.'

'Yes, but have you ever really kissed them back? Wanted them to devour you, possess you . . . love you?' Sally asked, and for once Bobby was stumped. She had been out with men but their inept fumblings had left her cold.

'Well . . .'

'Oh hell, we do have a long way to go, my girl,' Sally said. 'OK, we've got ten minutes, they'll be here soon. Get a move on.'

Bobby glanced at her dishevelled hair and jumped up in a panic.

'Help, move over, I need to brush my hair.'

* * *

Ten minutes later, the girls raced down the drive to find a black car waiting for them. As they arrived at it, a pilot with freckles and curly brown hair wound down the front window.

'Come on you gorgeous females, we'll have to get a move on if we're going to get there in time. They have shows all day, but we need to get there for the half past seven one.'

Sally strategically put herself in the back with Joe, a dark-haired pilot she had been chatting up earlier that day, so Bobby had no option but to get into the front, next to the curly-haired driver. He had a nice strong profile and unfairly long eyelashes for a man Bobby thought, Sally's words ringing in her ears.

'I'm Harry,' he announced taking his right hand off the wheel to shake hands with her.

'Bobby,' she replied, suddenly embarrassed. 'Um, are you going to The Windmill too?'

He turned towards her and seeing her hesitation, smiled. 'Too right, wouldn't miss it for the world,' he told her.

Bobby looked earnestly out of the window. She was horrified that she would be sitting next to a man looking at naked women and wished she had questioned Sally more closely before committing to this adventure.

Harry chatted easily all the way to London, not noticing that the young woman next to him was answering in monosyllables. They arrived at a crowded Piccadilly and the boys dropped the two girls off and went to go and park the car. Bobby looked up at the domed entrance and saw the words 'Revudeville' in large letters. She immediately read the word as 'Rudeville'. She checked the name again, realised her mistake and felt her discomfort growing. Once she and Sally had handed their coats to the cloakroom attendant, Bobby let rip.

'Sally, how could you? I can't sit next to a man while there are naked women on the stage!'

Sally reared up in mock horror. 'Oh Roberta Hollis, I didn't realise you were such an innocent baby! Well, it'll do you good to let your hair down a bit. This is 1943, not 1843,' she went on, 'and we're not living in the Victorian era. You'd better get used to it. You can't have it all your way. You're a pilot in a man's world, you can't now pretend you don't want to be a liberated woman.' And she turned away to smile flirtatiously at Joe, who was waiting for them in the foyer.

Bobby fingered her lapel nervously as the little group made their way to the front of the stalls, just behind the orchestra.

'I managed to get the best seats,' Joe whispered to the little group. He touched his nose. 'It all depends on who you know.'

'And who do you know?' Sally asked, placing her bag and gas mask under her seat.

'Just look carefully at the little blonde on the front row,' he replied with a satisfied smile.

Bobby had never felt out of her depth but at that moment she found herself checking the exits hoping there would be an air raid and she could escape. But she caught sight of the sign at the side of the stage, 'We never closed', the proud boast of the theatre that it had kept open throughout the Blitz and every air raid since.

I'm doomed, Bobby thought miserably, hunching her shoulders in case there was anyone in the theatre who might know her. It suddenly occurred to her that if she were to die here in these plush seats, everyone in Salthouse would know she had been at a racy performance of unclothed women with a man. She groaned.

'Shh', Sally said from beside her. 'Just relax and enjoy it.'

Bobby missed the first part of the performance, spending the whole time examining her feet, but then a pianist came on and started to play some American tunes and she watched in surprise as her toe started to tap. She looked up and gasped.

The women were all over the stage behind the pianist with large strategically placed feather fans. They were standing like statues, a stance insisted upon by Lord Cromer. She looked critically at them, they were no more risqué than the Greek statues she had seen in books at school and she began to wonder if her own body would look as good in such a pose, and then she shifted in her seat.

'Sorry,' Harry whispered, 'Did you say something?'

'Er, no, no, I was just enjoying the music.'

He tucked her arm in his and patted it. 'Good, I knew you'd enjoy it.' And he sat back in his seat with a smile on his face.

After that, Bobby was surprised to find she enjoyed the show very much. There was dancing, singing and some wonderful acrobatics, all the time with the backcloth of the girls with the fans, which just became like part of the scenery.

After the show, the four of them retired to the Fitzroy Tavern just on the corner of Windmill Street. Its dark wood and etched glass windows provided a cosy meeting place for crowds of theatre-goers and it was obviously a place Sally had been before. Sally confidently led Bobby to a corner seat, while the boys got them each a port and lemon. Sally looked with satisfaction at Bobby's enthralled face.

'So, you enjoyed it, then, did you, Miss Prim?'

'Yes, OK, Sal, I did enjoy it, just don't ever tell my father I went there,' Bobby said grinning.

Sally looked at her with approval. A girl whose own selfish gratification had always been her first concern, she was strangely enjoying helping Bobby discover the delights of society – and, if she had any say in it, the delights of men too.

Joe and Harry pushed their way through the throng towards the girls and Bobby realised how thirsty she was. She gulped at the drink Harry handed her.

'Careful, it'll be your turn to dance on the piano if you keep that up,' Sally said, laughing.

'Oh help, no, that's your party trick, not mine,' said Bobby, putting her half-empty glass down quickly, feeling she was in a strange land where she did not know the rules.

There were some WAAF girls standing next to them, wearing flat shoes and blue uniforms. They looked with superiority at the two girls in the corner and then whispered amongst themselves.

'They think you're socialites,' Harry whispered. 'You know, not in uniform so must be too rich to do anything useful in the war.'

Sally looked over towards the little group and nudged Bobby. 'So, it's back to delivering Spitfires tomorrow,' she said loudly. 'I can't believe the next course we do will be to fly Manchesters. I bet you boys don't fly anything that big, do you?'

Harry and Joe played along and shook their heads in wonder. 'I envy the ATA,' Joe said helpfully. 'You get to fly so many different planes and we normally stick to one. You girl pilots are amazing.'

Bobby and Sally watched with a certain smugness as the little group of girls looked first shamefacedly at their drinks and then with undisguised admiration at the two girls in the corner.

The four of them burst into giggles and Bobby looked up at Sally, who was enjoying every minute of their triumph. She had to admire her style and felt like a country hick next to this glamorous woman. Harry offered to buy Bobby another drink and she accepted eagerly, feeling it was perhaps time for her to join this modern world.

Chapter 8

One of the advantages of being in the ATA was a roster which allowed the pilots thirteen days on and two days off. It should have given Bobby the option of travelling home on a regular basis, but she knew she had been avoiding going back to Norfolk. Each time she was due to travel home, she found a new excuse to escape her home's library-type atmosphere where everyone whispered and tiptoed around the obvious estrangement of the couple at the head of the household and somehow the weeks turned into months. One Friday night in November, 1943, she had finally given in to her aunt's cajoling and had promised to go home but this time it was the weather that came to her rescue. Bobby arrived at Prestwick in Scotland just as the fog started to engulf the airfield and she grinned, hugging her parachute to herself, feeling her shoulders drop with relief. She could put off making a trip home for a little longer. After a fruitless attempt to find a bed in a WAAF hut, she faced either a rug on a wooden floor or she could venture out of the airfield and find a cheap hotel. Bobby decided to play hooky.

She headed for the hotel closest to the airfield, moving her heavy parachute onto her shoulder. It was a dingy, back street hostelry and she had to turn sideways to get herself and the parachute in through the narrow door. At the far end of a dark corridor was a wooden desk with a large red book open on it. The word 'Reception' was written on a piece of card propped up against an alabaster lamp with a tasselled green lampshade, but the lamp was not lit.

'Hello,' she called out into the gloom.

A banging noise came from behind the desk.

Bobby peered nervously towards the noise; perhaps this was not such a good idea.

The two-way door from the kitchen swung open and a man wearing a dirty apron and with a chef's hat falling over one eye, came out.

He looked astonished to find an unaccompanied woman in his hallway. 'Can I help you?' he said suspiciously, turning on the lamp to examine her more closely.

'Ahem, I'm in the Air Transport Auxiliary and I have just flown from the south coast. I need a meal and a bed for the night.' Her voice started off confidently, but started to waver by the end of the sentence.

'You on your own?'

'Um, yes. We always travel on our own. We're pilots.'

'And I'm Winston Churchill,' he snorted in reply.

She pointed to the golden wings on her tunic and stood up straight.

'Do you have a room, my man, or not? I only came here because it's the nearest hotel to the airfield. I need to get an aircraft back tomorrow morning.'

Bobby's knees were beginning to wobble.

He wiped his hands on his stained white apron and moved across to the reception desk, turning the red book towards him and examining its columns.

'Well, yes, I suppose I do have a room, but just be aware, young lady, we'll have no shenanigans here. I don't know exactly what you are, you look smart enough, but you never can tell.'

'I can assure you I am perfectly respectable,' Bobby said, bridling with indignation.

'Hmm, well we'll see about that, but tea's at six, it's vegetable pie tonight and breakfast is at seven. We serve porridge. You pay up front.'

By now, Bobby was thoroughly regretting her impulse.

The man showed Bobby to her room, which made her heart sink more than ever. It was a grim mixture of dark, flowery wallpaper and a deep red candlewick counterpane. There was one dim lamp that would be impossible to read by and the freezing cold bathroom was at the end of a long hallway with a daunting number of doors that could hide murderers and rapists behind them. She almost changed her mind and turned around to get the night train home but, glancing at her watch, realised with a frown that she had missed it.

The man left and, within a few minutes, a knock came at the door and a young girl stood there with a faded towel for the guest.

'I'm sorry, miss, um sir, um, sorry, I'm not sure what to call you, you look so important,' she said.

'Bobby is fine,' Bobby replied, taking the towel with a smile. She was about to close the door, when the girl stopped her.

'Oh, I couldn't call you that,' she said breathlessly. 'I'm sorry, um . . . but are you really one of them women pilots?'

'Yes, I am,' Bobby replied, beginning to feel better.

'Oh my,' the girl said, her eyes opening wide. 'My da had never heard of them, but I have, you fly planes and everything, don't you?'

'Yes, I do,' Bobby said, relaxing slightly.

'Well, I never, wait until I tell the girls at the factory about this.' The girl turned on her heels with a delighted grin and went off down the corridor.

Bobby slowly closed the door and admonished herself. She was so used to being ignored by her family, it had never occurred to her that she was a lone female and, as such, she was supposed to be chaperoned at all times, by a father, a brother or a husband. She was putting herself at risk by behaving as if she would be taken on an equal footing by other men or even, she realised, some women.

Her independence had often got her into trouble, but her father's insouciance had strangely led her to believe she could do anything, go anywhere and be anyone.

Bobby, with all the pragmatism that had shaped her life, settled down on her bed to have a nap. It had been a long day. However, her dozing was soon interrupted by chattering in the corridor.

She listened intently. They were talking about the airfield and it sounded as if they were service personnel.

'Oh help,' she thought, 'how do I explain this to a gang of officers?'

Deciding that brazening it out was the best defence, Bobby brushed her hair and went downstairs for supper. She walked into a room with brown curtains where about six tables were all covered with slightly yellowing table-cloths and bore small vases of dried flowers. The chairs were covered in maroon velvet, but the seats were shiny from years of seated diners. The room smelt of vinegar and was empty apart from one table with three pilots chattering in the corner.

She groaned inwardly. *I should have known better*, she thought. *It's the nearest hotel to the airfield. How could I have been so stupid?*

'Evening,' she said with her nose in the air, passing their table.

They looked up in surprise at this stunning, tall woman in uniform.

'Bobby, Bobby Hollis!' one of them exclaimed.

Bobby stopped abruptly and looked back, peering at the good-looking one with blond hair in the middle. He looked familiar.

'Gus? Is it Gus Prince?'

'Yes,' he said, standing up. 'What ... on earth are you ... er doing here?' He was immediately struck by the same awkwardness he had been afflicted with as a blushing nine-year-old boy. At school, while all the other girls giggled and vied for Gus's attention, auburn-haired Roberta Hollis had totally ignored him and to the young Gus, that was irresistible.

Bobby shrugged her shoulders and with the honesty that had impressed him as a young boy at primary school all those years ago said, 'I'm playing truant.'

The three men burst out laughing.

'Aren't you going to introduce us to your friend?' a tall Scot said, standing up as well.

The introductions were made and another chair was pulled up for her by the waiter who could not decide whether he was impressed by this woman or appalled that a girl should be walking alone into the dining room. He knew his mam would be horrified that women were taking on men's jobs.

'So, you're in the ATA?' Gus said, looking at the gold wings on her uniform.

'Yes, I am,' she replied, waiting for his reaction.

'That's just great, I always knew you would do something amazing.'

Basking in praise was a new experience for Bobby and she glowed, not realising the effect her golden red hair and green eyes were having on all three young men in front of her. She looked out of the corner of her eye at the boy she had known from school and appraised him from an adult perspective. Noticing the good-looking features that had so captivated Harriet, she was surprised to feel a slight frisson of interest.

Gus sat back, listening to his friends trying to impress the female pilot in front of them. He felt that old jealousy rising in him. She had been such an oddball at school, always sitting on her own munching an apple at lunchtime. He remembered with shame how he had darted around the playground, trying to casually send the football in her direction, to no avail. She had simply moved her feet without looking up from her book. Used to undisguised attention, it had driven the young boy wild and years later, sat in a dining room in Prestwick, he had a premonition that nothing had changed. Bobby's tension eased as the men quizzed her about different aircraft, the effect of weather on the wings of the different Hawkers and how ATA pilots' days were structured. Visibly impressed by her knowledge and the schedules she outlined, they looked with admiration at the girl in front of them. For the next two hours, the four chatted like equals, discussing aeronautics, weather and comparing notes about the uncomfortable conditions of their individual war existences.

But all Gus Prince wanted to talk about was how he could date this beautiful woman.

Chapter 9

Bobby's dreams in the lumpy bed were untroubled, but Gus Prince spent the night tossing and turning in his room, tantalisingly just along the creaky landing from Bobby on the first floor. He shifted onto his side, opened his eyes and checked his watch. It was moving painfully slowly. Gus moaned in frustration and turned onto his other side, facing the wall, but visions of Bobby's beautiful face kept appearing in front of his eyelids. He clamped them shut, he did not need this distraction in his life. Gus had consigned the girl with auburn pigtails and a freckled face to a childhood memory but the stunning woman who had chatted so naturally across the table in the shabby dining room that evening had taken his adult breath away. At two o'clock in the morning, he knew his youthful crush had not diminished one bit; by three o'clock, he knew she was like no other girl he had ever met and by three forty-five, he realised he was completely and utterly smitten.

He raced down to breakfast the next morning but there was no sign of Bobby. The proprietor complained bitterly about her demand for an early bowl of porridge.

'I don't know who she thought she was, Miss High and Mighty,' he moaned as he spooned congealed oats into Gus's bowl. 'Girls should stay where they're supposed to be and that certainly ain't flying planes, taking men's jobs.'

He looked for support from the young man in front of him, expecting male solidarity, but none was forthcoming.

Gus was looking wistfully at the chair where Bobby had sat the night before.

* * *

Meanwhile, Bobby was already in the air. She had been picked up by a Fairchild taxi aeroplane and was on her way to the south coast. With another day and a half left before she was due back on duty, she intended to spend the time going through her notes and getting some washing done.

'Barrage balloons,' the call came back from the cockpit. 'Brace yourselves.'

There was a universal groan from the three passengers in the back. They all hated barrage balloons; they appeared out of nowhere if an enemy aircraft was in the area and at 1,500 feet, their purpose was to force planes to fly higher by giving them huge obstacles they could fly into. Filled with helium, their rubber skins were silvery grey in colour and about sixty feet long and twenty-five feet wide, like the torso of an enormous elephant. Their steel cables were barely visible and many a time Bobby had been forced to bank suddenly to avoid one. All the pilots complained that while the balloons might cause damage to the enemy, they put Britain's own pilots at huge risk as well.

Bobby tightened her seat belt and clung onto the side of the aircraft just as the Fairchild took a dip to the left. She fell against the small window on her left and jarred her shoulder, taking a sharp intake of breath.

'Sorry about that. The sun's in my eyes and I only saw the cable at the last minute,' the pilot called back. An older man in his late fifties, Bobby did not know him, but had spotted that he had one arm shorter than the other and suspected he had had polio as a child. She knew there were several men with disabilities who had ended up in the ATA after being rejected by the RAF. They were all good pilots and often with more experience than most of their fellow pilots, they grasped the opportunity to get behind the control panel of an aircraft.

Bobby recovered her position and stared out at the clouds above them. These moments as a passenger were rare and, rubbing her sore shoulder, she allowed herself to daydream about the previous evening.

She had been delighted to see Gus, noticing that the gawky boy had grown into a rather good-looking young man.

Maybe I should relax a little more and have a bit more fun, she thought, thinking of Sally's advice, but then, as usual, her mind went to the possible list of aircraft she would have to fly that week and her concentration became totally absorbed in her job.

However, as Christmas came and went amid long lists of deliveries and bad weather, a letter arrived that suddenly brought her personal life into sharp focus.

Dear Roberta,

We were sorry you could not join us at Christmas as I had a proposal I wished to discuss with you. I have decided as you have reached the age of twenty-eight and are as yet, still unmarried, that it would be beneficial to the family for you to be settled. While your mother and I are aware of your love of flying and your role in the ATA, we feel it is about time that you thought about your future after the end of this terrible war, and that of the farm.

For this reason, I have agreed with my friend, Group Captain Turner, that you should marry his only son, Edward. He is a little older than you, but a fine upstanding man who works in the War Office.

We will arrange everything from here for your next leave.

Your mother and aunt are well and we are managing to produce some crops with careful management.

Your loving father.

Bobby read and re-read the letter, in stunned silence. She was absolutely livid and stomped around the bedroom, stopping every few steps to re-read the peremptory words.

'How dare he?' she seethed at the window.

'The nerve of the man,' she shouted at the curtains.

'If he thinks I'm giving in to his commands, he's got another think coming,' she finally announced to the whole room and sat down heavily on the bed. Bobby stared at the embossed notepaper and then tore it up into tiny shreds and threw it in the waste paper bin with a certain amount of satisfaction.

But Bobby knew her father's scheming could not be dismissed as easily as a bit of paper and she fell back onto the pillow to stare at the ceiling, looking for inspiration on how to deal with this incredible proposal.

She cast her mind back to a day at the airfield when Group Commander Turner had introduced her to his son, a tall man in a pin-striped suit and black, shiny shoes, who looked completely out of place amid the flying suits and overalls. She seemed to recall he had stuttered when he was introduced to her, looking down at his feet. *He must be at least forty,* she thought.

Bobby Hollis had no intention of being steered towards a marriage she had no interest in and was quite prepared to take on her father, her mother, Group Captain Turner and any other bumbling son he or her father pushed in her direction.

She wrote to Harriet, thinking that maybe her worldly friend might, for once, be the one to help her. She was so incensed she forgot to mention she had met Gus until she had signed her name at the bottom. For a moment, she wondered whether to tear up the letter and start again, but she was due on duty and if she wanted to get this note off to the post room, the gossip about meeting Gus would have to wait.

Dear Harriet,

I hope you are well and that you're behaving in the WAAF. How many men have you been out with this week? Do you still fancy that engineer – Gerry, was it? – or have you moved on to the next victim? How's it all going? Did you notice it was Christmas? I certainly didn't.

Harriet, I know you won't believe it of me but I'm in a complete dither. My father has sent me a letter telling me I must marry some old chap who's the son of Group Captain Turner! I think I met him once, he seemed such a civvy and OLD! You have to help me.

What am I going to do? Are you around the weekend after next? I've decided a trip home is well overdue. I'm going to have it out with my father and I may need moral support.

Love Bobby

P.S. Flying is wonderful, as always – who needs a man?

* * *

In a wood-panelled office in Whitehall, Edward Turner let out a loud expletive. His secretary on the other side of the wall looked up in surprise. Mr Turner was a complete gentleman and the bespectacled Miss Mavis Arbuckle had never heard him swear in all the years she had worked for him. She shook her head, wondering what had prompted this sudden outburst but glanced at the clock and hurriedly went back to the squiggles of shorthand notes that had to be transcribed for coding by four o'clock.

Edward got up jerkily and went over to the window to stare blankly at the light-coloured stone wall beyond. He had his father's letter in his hand but quickly screwed it up with vehemence. He looked down at the crumpled piece of paper.

'He has to be kidding,' he said out loud. 'I'm thirty-two years of age, I can make my own bloody decisions thank you very much, Father.'

The suggestion in the letter that Edward might like to marry the daughter of his good friend, Andrew Hollis, had been short and to the point. His father said very little else apart from the fact that he believed it was about time Edward gave some consideration as to how he was going to carry on the family name.

Edward's childhood had been a typical upper-class round of Latin, healthy, muddy sports and a series of nannies who had been too busy coping with the daily needs of three boisterous boys in the large, Victorian home to have any spare time to offer cuddles or affection. His father had covered himself in glory with the RFC, the precursor to the RAF, in the Great War, but he disappeared every afternoon to his beloved airfield, oblivious to domestic affairs, leaving the young boys to their tutor. His mother was involved in 'good works', too concerned with raising money to help the poor of the parish to notice the three sons who gave her a headache. Edward was the eldest of the three brothers and had been the first to be turfed out to board at Eton once he was old enough. Edward immediately had to hide the crushing homesickness in stifled sobs under the bedclothes at night to avoid being bullied. He learned to button up all feelings with the top fastening of his Eton classic dress shirt and stiff collar but then his father, in a bid to toughen up this quiet, studious boy, agreed to sailing lessons on the Thames. From then on, Edward spent his holidays on the south coast, battling waves and winds and it was during these holidays that he discovered he had a true love of danger.

When he was approached at Cambridge by a strange man from the government, Edward threw caution to that wind he loved so much and agreed to accept the chance to live a precarious life abroad feeding information back to his home country. Edward Turner discovered he only felt at ease with himself when he was facing danger, living out of a small bag and surrounded by genuine people who had no idea what a six o'clock cocktail looked like. But when war broke out, he was called back to serve in Whitehall, sitting unnaturally behind a large mahogany desk and attending endless, boring socially enhancing soirées. His quiet manner, added to his experience in Europe, gave him an invaluable advantage and he became embroiled in a life of strategy meetings and reports. It did not take long for him to be invited to act as an advisor to a dazzling array of high-ranking titles and influential people.

Edward banged his fist on the table. He had avoided the clutches of many a young woman who had picked him out at Foreign Office functions; escaped the advances of debutantes put in front of him by his mother, and categorically refused to have anything to do with the nieces of friends of his family for years. He had no intention of being inveigled into a relationship now.

Reaching into the bottom drawer of his mahogany desk, where he kept a small silver flask of brandy for emergencies, he took a swig. As the warming liquid slid down his throat, he cast his mind back to a gawky, auburn-haired girl he had spotted once at the airfield near his home before the war began. She was a child, for heaven's sake.

* * *

The following week, Bobby sat on the packed train and closed her eyes. It had been a frantic time with endless deliveries all over the country and she had learned more about her own native land than she had ever thought possible, recognising places from the air by roads, rivers, railway lines and tall spires. She switched her mind to Norfolk and made herself remember all the positive things about going home. She envisaged the snowdrops that would soon be coming through on the top meadow, imagined being treated to one – or maybe two – of Mrs Hill's scones, being brought up to date by Aunt Agnes about her parents and teasing Archie. But then her mind turned to her father. His letter had made her more furious than she had been in years and she was determined not to be intimidated by his cold, matter of fact manner or his assumption that she would comply with his instructions. For a brief moment, Bobby wondered whether she could appeal to her mother but knew that would be a waste of time; her mother would never have the courage to question her husband.

Bobby opened her eyes to stop thinking about the confrontation to come and looked around at the service people on the train to take her mind off it. They were all clutching their travel warrants. As a civilian, she had had to pay for the one she was holding in her own hand but acknowledged there were other perks that more than made up for that one disadvantage. The recent decision to allow ATA pilots equal pay, for example, uniquely put women on a par with men. In celebration of her pay rise to £6 a week, Bobby had started to send her uniform to the drycleaners. She looked again at the service people around her, more pityingly this time. She was not part of the 'saluting brigade' as she called them, and therefore was not subject to the same number of rules and regulations that her fellow passengers had to suffer. That autonomy gave all the ATA pilots, especially the women, a status that was envied and when she arrived at Norwich, she strode confidently down the platform, aware that the hordes of uniforms parted to let her pass, staring at her with curiosity. She had almost reached the front of the building when a woman in spectacles with a fox fur around her shoulders patted her on the shoulder.

'Excuse me my dear, could you tell me the way to the powder room?'

Bobby looked flummoxed.

'Oh, I am sorry, dear, I thought – with that uniform – that you worked for the railways. I do beg your pardon.'

There was a guffaw of laughter from behind Bobby as she stared at the lady who tottered off to find another uniform to ask. Archie was standing waiting for her, next to the farm cart and one horse.

'Hello high-flying Bobby Hollis, are you waiting to clean the station toilets or are you going to come home?'

Bobby grinned at the tall figure of a man standing next to a small cart and stopped to pat the horse affectionately.

'Hello Archie' she giggled. 'Oh take me home. It's certainly never boring being in the ATA. Come on, let's get going, I'm dying for one of Mrs Hill's scones; she promised she'd save some rations to make some. Anyway, how are all those nephews and nieces of yours?'

'Growing fast, but not as fast as you. I swear you are even taller.'

Bobby launched herself into the cart and settled next to him. He was right, she almost reached his shoulders now.

'What news of everyone? Sorry I couldn't get home for Christmas.'

'Life goes on,' Archie replied. 'Your father's struggling with the ledgers without you.'

'Good,' said Bobby fiercely. Her father was not her favourite person at the moment.

Archie looked sideways at her. He knew exactly what she was talking about but, as usual, his discretion was complete.

'Not found a nice pilot to put the hounds off the scent?'

'No, I'm going to have to beg the next man I see to marry me to save me and whisk me away from marauding group captains' sons!' She laughed as Archie nodded in understanding. Nothing was a secret from Archie.

As they turned the corner, they passed old Walter, who was trundling along to his fields, a hessian sack tied round his middle as usual.

'There's a prime candidate, I could stop and ask Walter if you like? He could do with a nice wife,' Archie suggested with a grin.

Bobby looked at Walter, disappearing in the distance. She clasped her hands to her breast with dramatic longing and then turned back round and chuckled.

'You always cheer me up, Archie,' she said but the whole time she had been eyeing up the reins, dying to take hold of them, and eventually Archie gave in to the inevitable and handed them over to her. She immediately chivvied the horse on to a faster trot. 'Oh well, you're probably right. I'll just have to sacrifice myself and become a wife to an old man and dedicate my life to fetching his slippers every night.'

'Hah, fat chance,' chuckled Archie.

As soon as they pulled up outside the farmhouse, she gave him a peck on the cheek and swung herself off the cart.

She slowed her pace as she passed the burial plot near the barn on her left. On every leave, she always took a moment to visit the tiny grave of her stillborn brother. She looked up at the farmhouse; her father could wait.

Approaching the iron railings that enclosed the plot, protecting the souls within from goodness knows what, Bobby looked round for something to place on the graves of her grandparents and her unknown twin. She found some hellebores growing next to the barn and plucked off the pale white heads to make little posies. She knelt for a moment next to the tiny mound of soil and glanced at the white headstone just under the angel's feet. 'Here lies the body of Michael Hollis, who died before a life was granted to him. May God help him rest in peace.' Her heart suddenly jumped and she felt a shadow cross her body. It made her shiver and yet gave her comfort as shadows always did. A brother would have saved her from this fate of a marriage she did not want. Bobby got to her feet, sent a quick prayer asking for help skywards and marched into the house.

She strode straight into her father's study.

'Father, you cannot do this.' She had not even stopped to take off her fur-lined boots.

Andrew Hollis looked up from his desk where he had been going through his accounts. It had not been an edifying task. He glared back at his daughter, who was standing in front of him with her hands on her hips, legs apart. Her red hair seemed to be on fire.

'Someone has to secure the future of this farm,' he said calmly.

'Well, why can't I do that?'

'Because you're a girl,' he retorted, going back to his ledger.

She stepped forward and bent over his large book. She put her hand over the figures to stop him reading them.

'Nonsense, of course I can. I'm as good as any man and you know that. I'm not just marrying some man to provide an heir for this place.'

'Well, he's coming for supper tonight, you can tell him that yourself,' her father said, pushing her hand away.

'No!' she protested. 'But has he . . . I mean . . . does he know about this crazy idea?' she stuttered.

Her father shrugged. 'Probably not, but he'll see the sense in it. He's been too busy to find a wife and you're a good catch.'

Bobby was so indignant she could not speak properly; all she could manage was a loud 'Hah!' before storming out of the room, all her prepared replies forgotten in her anger.

Bobby refused Aunt Agnes's pleas to change out of uniform. She believed the trousers and boots gave her an authority she felt she was losing fast with every minute she was back at home and with bad grace, she stalked into the drawing room at ten to seven as instructed, Aunt Agnes hurrying in her wake. The room was a typical large farmhouse sitting room with random pieces of furniture dotted around the marble fireplace with a solitary log smouldering in the grate. On the mantlepiece above it, were black and white photographs showing austere ancestors sitting primly on high-backed chairs. The room had been dull and oppressive when Mathilda married Andrew and it had been the first place she had insisted on decorating, mainly to eradicate all of his mother's overdone, Victorian style that had made the room seem like an outdated parlour. Mathilda had introduced the primrose wallpaper, the light tapestry armchairs and the contrasting green carpet and curtains, and had clasped her hands in glee when it had been finished, prompting her young husband to take her up in his arms and swing her round.

Now there was a different woman sitting on the edge of the armchair. Mathilda Hollis always seemed as if she were constantly looking for an escape from the room. Her eyes darted from left to right and she would hold her breath whenever the stranger who was her husband started to speak.

Rachel had unearthed some old sherry that had been hidden since before the war and was beginning to pour the dregs of it into the best glasses on a silver tray in the drawing room. Andrew Hollis was standing by the fireplace with his chin tilted upwards, telling his wife that she needed to keep better control of the household budget. Mathilda had started to play with the lace on the back of her chair nervously. She looked up in relief when it seemed that Bobby was about to speak, but then the door knocker sounded. Bobby looked around in alarm, her suitor was early.

Rachel put down the sherry bottle, checking to see if there was any left and went to answer it.

They all heard her gasp.

'Ma'am, sir . . . There's a . . .' She stuttered, coming back into the room slowly.

Andrew Hollis tutted in exasperation and went to push past her. He stopped suddenly in his tracks. In the doorway was a tall, young man with a head of deep auburn that mirrored the hair of both Bobby and her father.

'*Je m'appelle Michel*. Excuse but I not know where to go.'

Mathilda Hollis's face suddenly lit up like a flash of lightening and she ran towards him.

'Michael, Michael, my son!'

Chapter 10

'Who is he?' Mrs Hill held a stunned Rachel by the shoulders at the entrance to the kitchen. 'Speak, girl.'

'I don't know what he said. Well I think he said ... he spoke in broken English ...' her voice tailed off into a whisper. 'I think he said he was Mr Hollis's son.'

Mrs Hill smoothed her pinny over and over. She shook her head from side to side in wonder.

The door knocker went again.

'Oh, for crying out loud. Don't stand there like an idiot,' she urged Rachel, who was standing with her arms uselessly at her sides. 'Go and answer it, it'll be Mr Turner. Oh, and the pie's burning.' She rushed to the other side of the kitchen, grabbing the old oven gloves from the pine table on the way.

When Rachel showed Edward Turner into the drawing room, he raised his eyebrows in surprise. A tall, dark man, he had deep brown eyes and sleeked back hair with a fringe that flopped in defiance. He wore a pin-striped suit and the shiniest shoes Rachel had ever seen. He surveyed the room, his practised eyes taking in the scene in front of him. The blackout curtains were pulled around the bay window at the front and the sherry glasses were half filled, but the rest of the scene was like a melodrama. Mrs Hollis was clinging dramatically to a young man standing by the fireplace in a woolly scarf and old jacket. The jacket was covered with dark stains. Edward peered at them concluding they looked suspiciously like dried blood. Mr Hollis was staring at the young man's auburn hair and was as white and still as the alabaster statue of the Roman emperor next to him. Roberta was sitting up straight in an armchair by the fireplace. He took a second look, surprised. The figure in front of him was a long way from the youngster he had met at the airfield before the war, no longer a fresh-faced, awkward girl but a woman, looking remarkably – he almost smiled – like a heroine in a film. Another woman, she must be a relative, he decided, was standing by the window, clutching the curtain.

Bobby looked round at her family in total disarray and realised it was going to be up to her to take control.

'I'm so sorry, Mr Turner, but there has been an unexpected turn of events and we have a visitor from France, Monsieur . . . um, Michel.'

She looked round for help but did not receive any. Her family looked as if they were frozen in time.

She ploughed on. 'He has only just arrived, but we suspect he has a story to tell and we probably need to hear it. I wonder if we could postpone this dinner until another day.'

'Of course, of course,' Edward said quickly. 'I can come back another time.' He started to back out of the room, almost relieved. His father had insisted on this ridiculous charade and Edward had finally agreed on making just one visit and one visit only to stop his mother taking to her bed in hysterics. But, looking at the fraught face in front of him, he reluctantly admitted, he was intrigued. She was rather lovely but, stubborn to the core, Edward was not going to give in to his father just because of a pretty face. He concentrated on the scene in front of him. His war work had taken him down routes he could not share with anyone, but his training took in the dried blood stains, the three auburn heads and the young man's haunted stare.

After several years of rising to a higher and higher position, Edward had almost forgotten what it was like to feel that surge of excitement that was so shallowly buried behind the lapels of the Whitehall suit. The scene in front of him resurrected some of those feelings and it made his brown eyes twinkle.

'May I ... um ... call tomorrow?' he asked in the halting speech he had adopted as part of his bumbling persona. He had to do some checks and then come back to find out more. 'I may be able to be of some service. As you know, I ... um ... work for the government.'

'Yes, yes, do,' Roberta said, shuffling him out of the room.

As she walked him down the hallway, she looked at him properly for the first time. He was not as old as she remembered and, she reluctantly acknowledged, he did have rather nice eyes. It was a shame he was so shy and socially inept.

With an unexpected tinge of regret, she opened the front door. 'I'm so sorry, Mr Turner, we're not sure what's happening here. We may be a little clearer tomorrow. Please do come for luncheon when I'm sure things will be calmer.'

'I don't want to intrude but I fear . . . I'm afraid the authorities will need to know about this,' he said, reluctantly letting go of her proffered hand to walk down the steps to his sleek, black car.

Roberta paused for a moment in the corridor, holding the doorknob to the drawing room with her right hand, which suddenly seemed hot and clammy.

She took a deep breath and walked back into the room. What had she come home to?

'*Eh alors*?' she asked the young man, who finally managed to extricate himself from a sobbing Mrs Hollis and steer her carefully into a chintz covered armchair.

'I can speak the English,' he said. 'My mother . . .' He looked towards Andrew Hollis, who blanched. 'She teach me before she die. She always tell me to come to find you.'

'Your mother was . . . Nicole?' Andrew whispered. 'She is dead?'

'*Oui*,' the young man said quietly.

Bobby's father slumped in the armchair on the other side of the fireplace opposite his wife, who had not taken her eyes off the Frenchman. She had stopped sobbing, but her shoulders were still shaking.

Bobby rang the little silver bell on the walnut side table sharply. It made Aunt Agnes jump. Rachel appeared immediately from the other side of the door where she had been trying to listen.

'Rachel, would you take my mother into her bedroom and get her a drink please. Do we have any of that marrow brandy left?' she added as an afterthought.

'I think there is some at the back of the kitchen cabinet,' Agnes said in a weak voice.

'Good, it's nothing like the real thing but it might help.' Bobby went over to the silver tray and downed two of the glasses of sherry, holding on to one glass for any brandy that might be found. She passed a third glass of the precious sherry to her aunt, who drained it in one gulp, while watching the events unfolding in front of her in silence.

Rachel's eyes were wide as she scanned the room in front of her. She eventually stepped forward to help Mrs Hollis out of her chair, but she struggled to move her dead weight. Agnes put down her empty glass and went to help. They both ushered Mathilda out of the room.

Mrs Hill was hovering in the hall. She took over from Rachel on one side and with Agnes on the other, they gently steered Mathilda towards the stairs. Rachel ran into the kitchen to search the cupboards.

In the drawing room, Bobby looked from one man to the other. She was sure the large grandfather clock in the corner was ticking louder than usual.

At last the young man spoke. 'I am sorry, I know not what to do.'

Bobby's father had had his head in his hands but looked up at the French voice. 'You had better tell me from the beginning – *le début*,' he said faintly.

'I will begin at the end and perhaps you will understand why I had not the choice. May I sit?'

'Of course,' Bobby said, waving her arm towards a hard-backed chair near the rosewood sideboard.

Her father looked up in surprise. He had forgotten she was there. 'Roberta . . . perhaps you should leave?'

'No, father, I think I need to hear this.'

He had no strength to argue.

'I am with . . . *La Résistance*,' Michel said, looking behind him nervously out of habit. 'It is safe to speak, yes?'

Andrew Hollis nodded slowly.

'We were 'elping . . . someone . . . leave. They were to meet a plane on a field near our village in Normandie. It all went very wrong.' Michel paused, wincing in pain at the memory. 'Somehow, someone, oh I do not know, the

Germans were waiting for us. They know we were going to be there. We come out of the bushes; we shine our torches when we hear the motor of the plane. They shoot all my friends. They shoot the person who was to be rescued. They fall on me, I hold her. Bang bang. She . . . dies, here, in my arms.'

He looked down at the stains on his jacket and fingered them incredulously, shaking his head. 'They all die, my friends . . .' He looked round helplessly, hoping for someone to wake him from this nightmare. His eyes blurred with tears.

Bobby ran over to him, knelt down on the green, swirly-patterned carpet and gently took his hand. 'It's OK, it's OK. You're safe now.'

He looked down, searching for some reality. He found it in a familiar face that was before him, the same colour hair, the same features. He put his hand out to stroke her cheek. She reached up and covered his shaking hand with her own. The connection between them was palpable.

Michel's eyes glazed again, the room in front of him replaced by the scene he had left behind in France. 'I had nowhere to go but the plane door – it was open, an arm leaned out, the motor still runs. I just reach and the hands pull me in. We take off, there is gunfire everywhere. I look back, there are all my friends on the ground . . .'

He started to sob and Bobby stood up and encircled him with her arms. She looked desperately towards her father. His normally erect figure was slumped, his eyes staring into the distance as if he could not focus on what was happening in front of him, but Bobby's next words made him start and he looked up.

'I don't think we need to know any more tonight,' she said.

He nodded, putting his head back in his hands.

She pulled the young man to his feet and rang the bell again but Aunt Agnes was already coming through the door.

'I will take him to the spare room and get some clothes from Archie for him,' she said calmly, 'and then he can have some pie and warm milk. I have asked Rachel to make up a bed for our guest, and Mrs Hill is warming a hot water bottle for him.'

Andrew had not moved but Bobby looked gratefully at her aunt. Agnes moved forward to take hold of the young man, who glanced back with wide eyes as he was led out of the room.

'Merci, merci, merci,' he uttered.

Once he and Agnes had gone, Bobby turned back to her father. She had never seen him lose control but at that moment, he stared wide-eyed at her then flung open his arms in despair.

'What do you expect me to do? What? Oh, for Christ's sake, what?'

'It's all right, Father, we'll talk in the morning. Oh, no, Edward Turner is coming tomorrow,' she remembered.

'I can't think tonight, I just can't,' Andrew Hollis muttered and stumbled towards the door.

Bobby collapsed into the armchair her father had just vacated and leaned back, closing her eyes to shut the world out. Her thoughts were jumping all over the place and none of them made any sense.

'Oh, do be quiet,' she told the grandfather clock, which was smugly sounding the supper hour and she flung herself out of the chair, grabbing her discarded glass on the way.

I need brandy, Bobby thought, her head already spinning from the sherry, and went into the kitchen clutching her empty glass. At that same moment, Aunt Agnes brought Michel in behind her to have his supper and milk. The two redheads were haloed in the gaslight.

Mrs Hill gasped. 'It's the shadow. It's come to life.'

Bobby turned around to look at Michel; it was just like looking in a mirror.

Chapter 11

The following morning, Bobby was crossing from her bedroom to the bathroom when she saw her father standing staring out of the landing window. He was still in his dressing gown, which was unheard of so long after sunrise.

'Father?' Bobby said quietly.

He turned around, his face as pale as the white wall behind him. His tall body crumpled and he felt for the wicker chair behind him. He could not look at his daughter.

'Father, are you all right?'

'No, no, no, I'm very much afraid, Roberta, that I'm not.'

Bobby edged forward. She felt very uncomfortable and in vain looked around for help.

'I don't know what to say to you ... or your mother,' her father started. 'I had no idea that Nicole ... it was such a long time ago ... I never thought I would get back alive.'

Bobby had never in her life had a cosy tête-à-tête with any of her family, let alone her austere father, and she had no idea how to deal with the dejected figure in front of her. She started to creep away but he called after her.

'Can you ... your mother ... will you ever be able to forgive me?' He buried his head in his hands and his shoulders started to shake. Bobby was stricken. This was her father, the man she had battled with for years, the one who was able to infuriate her more than anyone else. There had been times when she had hated him. But now all she wanted to do was reach out her arms and fold them around him.

Her father's muffled voice whispered to her.

'I have to explain. You have to understand. I had had a letter from Agnes telling me about Michael's death. I was given compassionate leave. I was billeted at a house. It belonged to Nicole. While I was there she had a telegram to say her husband was missing in action, believed killed. We were both distraught ... that evening, we had some wine ... Oh, Bobby, how can I ever face your mother again?'

She took a step towards him. 'I don't know what to say,' Bobby said, 'but if he is ... your ... son, then we have to help him.'

'Yes, yes, of course,' Andrew Hollis stood up, glad to have found something he could do.

'Thank you, Bobby.' For a brief moment, they looked at each other and Bobby saw tears in her father's eyes. She fought for breath.

He stretched out his hand towards her and she moved forwards to clasp it. It was the first time the father and daughter had ever reached out to each other.

He abruptly withdrew his hand and said in a more controlled voice, 'I'll get onto it, um, have you seen your mother?'

'I think she's downstairs sorting out some clothes. Father, I don't know how to say this but, she does seem to have come to life this morning,' she added.

'Do you think so? It would be wonderful to see her as she used to be . . .' he tailed off, slowly making his way along the landing towards the stairs.

* * *

'Hello, hello, anyone at home?' Harriet peered through the kitchen door. It was normally such a scene of activity, but today it was unnervingly quiet. On the wooden table in the corner, next to the wash-house, was an old jacket with stains on it. The breakfast things had been cleared but were waiting to be washed.

Bobby came through the door, in a pair of overalls and a man's shirt. Her hair was a mess, Harriet noticed with a despairing sigh.

'Oh Harriet, it's so wonderful to see you. I know, I know, I look a sight.'

The two girls collided as Bobby rushed forward to give her best friend an especially strong hug, feeling the need of her support and unquestioning love.

'Yes, you do,' Harriet scolded as she stepped back to assess her friend. It was rare that Bobby was demonstrative, and she did indeed look very pale.

'It's great being so near at Coltishall,' she said. 'I can sneak out. I'm on nights as usual so probably should be sleeping, but . . . hell's bells, Bobby, you do look a mess.' She stopped and raised her hand towards Bobby's unruly hair. Bobby ducked out of her way, not in the mood for a telling off about her appearance.

Harriet gave in and changed tack. 'OK, fill me in. Do we have a strategy to put into operation to prevent this marriage?'

Bobby took hold of her friend's arm and pulled her out of the kitchen towards the vegetable plot, glancing behind her conspiratorially, but then suddenly stopped in her tracks. 'Won't you get into trouble for sneaking out?'

'Nah, I do it all the time. Anyway, what about this Turner man?' Harriet asked impatiently.

'Never mind him,' Bobby replied, and then stopped to add, 'although, I can't make my mind up about him. He seems such a twit but he is better looking than I remembered. But no,' she went on determinedly, 'we have a new problem.'

She steered Harriet towards the bench on the corner of the vegetable plot and they both sat down. Briefly, she explained to Harriet the events of the previous night. For once, Harriet kept quiet and let her friend finish.

'So, who is this Frenchman?' she finally said.

'I'm not sure . . . but I think he may be . . . my . . . half-brother.'

Harriet reeled. 'Your what?' she asked incredulously. 'But how . . . ?' Bobby could see her friend's mind working at double its normal speed. 'So . . . your father?' She had always been terrified of Andrew Hollis; he seemed so fierce.

'I spoke to father this morning,' Bobby said. 'He was absolutely broken and could hardly look me in the eye. He said something about Michael's death, being given compassionate leave while he was in France. Then he rambled on about some woman, Nicole, he was billeted with; she heard her husband was missing, he'd heard about Michael and . . . oh, I don't know, something must have happened between them. I mean, what about my mother, Harriet? What does it say about their marriage? Is this why they're so cold with each other? You just wait until you see Michel, you'll see what I mean.'

At that moment, as if on cue, an auburn head popped out of the kitchen door behind them. It was Michel. He was dressed in an old pair of overalls.

'*Excuse moi*, I look for your mother, she has clothes for me, she say. I am so sorry, I sleep. I not wake up.'

Harriet stared at the young man with her mouth open. She looked from Bobby to him and back to Bobby.

'Of course,' Bobby said. 'She is on the landing, at the linen cupboard.'

'*Merci, merci,*' Michel said on his way back in. Harriet stared after him and then blurted out, 'He is your twin,' and then stopped herself. 'I mean, he's your double, he has to be your brother. And his name, it's almost the same.

'I know, I know. I just don't know what to do, my father seems to have a son who's popped up from nowhere, my mother doesn't even seem to have registered the implications of all this and now is convinced that this is Michael come back to life and, oh hell, we have Edward Turner coming for luncheon. Oh God, I could do without that. He talked about having to let the authorities know.' She finally stopped to breathe.

'This is incredible,' Harriet said, pacing up and down, then she reached over to look at Bobby's watch – somehow, she always forgot to wear hers. 'Dammit, I have to get back to base, before they miss me. I so want to stay and see what happens next, this is so exciting. Oh, Bobby, what are you going to do?'

Bobby was feeling anything but excited. Her stomach had sunk. 'I don't know, I just don't know,' she slumped and looked so forlorn that her friend put her arm around her.

'I mean,' Bobby went on, 'Aunt Agnes told me stories about how my mother changed overnight when Michael died but the sight of this grown man seems to have ignited something in her. I've never seen her so animated. I . . . I really don't know how to deal with it. Oh, and Harriet, you mustn't breath a word of this to anyone.'

Harriet nodded and Bobby leaned her head on Harriet's shoulder and then suddenly remembered she had still not told her about her recent meeting with Gus Prince.

'Harriet, I meant to tell you . . .' she started, but Harriet was already jumping up and heading down the path, with a backwards wave.

'Gotta go, Bobby, I'll write – and make sure you write back! I want the next instalment! And keep your chin up.'

Bobby slowly got up and went into the house. She hung around in the hallway, watching the closed study door but then she heard her mother calling her from the small drawing room.

Her mother's face was flushed and her eyes were bright. Bobby noticed how pretty she looked.

'So, we have to prepare a proper room for Michael,' she said, fiddling with the photographs on the mantlepiece. 'He must have his own room now he has come home. I've got Rachel to clean the front one with the bay window. There is a lovely view of the farm from there. I have put out all his things for him.'

Bobby looked aghast. 'But they're baby things –and his name is Michel, not Michael' she said. Her mother's face crumpled as she realised her mistake.

'Oh Bobby, I get so confused sometimes,' she whispered, looking frightened, then waved her hand in the air as if to dispel the fog that surrounded her thinking. 'Of course, of course, I knew that, but you're right that he will need something to wear. We must search the attic and find him some clothes.

'Isn't it wonderful?' she reached out her hands to Bobby, who had no choice but to take them and hold them.

* * *

Luncheon was a disaster. Mrs Hill had tried her best, but Rachel had been too busy cleaning the blood out of Michel's clothes and looking after this strange young man to help. With all the extra visitors, rations had to be eked out carefully and Mrs Hill had been forced to scrape off the burnt edges of the previous night's pie to make enough food for them all. Andrew Hollis sat in silence, staring at his food and Mathilda Hollis fussed over Michel like a mother hen.

Bobby sat opposite Edward Turner. For the first time, she was able to look at him properly as he made polite conversation with her aunt. Edward had a natural easiness and she began to suspect the bumbling visitor who had backed out of the room the night before was nothing more than a front. He seemed to dominate the room, somehow, in contrast to her father, who looked like a shrunken man this lunchtime, and she looked at the tall, imposing man with more interest. He was certainly intriguing, she decided.

'We're so sorry you were not able to stay for supper last night,' her aunt was saying, looking round in vain for some help from her sister and brother-in-law. With some hesitation, Bobby butted in and tried to explain, in as vague a way as possible, how Michel had come to be at Salhouse Farm the previous evening. Aunt Agnes looked at her gratefully. Meanwhile, Edward was attempting to match up the family's story with the one he had discovered in an early morning phone call to the office. He skirted round the information he had received from a senior intelligence officer during that phone call. He did not mention that the pilot who had carried out the operation, was a local Norfolk man who belonged to 161 Squadron, a small unit that operated by moonlight, ferrying secret agents and pilots in and out of France. He did, however, tell Roberta and Agnes – no one else seemed to be listening – that Michel's story had been corroborated by the pilot of the aircraft that had carried out the mission and that enquiries were now in place to establish how they would get Michel back to Normandy.

At this, Mrs Hollis looked up.

'Oh, no, no, he is not going back. This is his home,' she said decisively, piling more potatoes on the young Frenchman's plate. Michel stared in front of him with the same haunted expression he had had since he arrived.

Bobby and Edward Turner looked at each other. For a second, their eyes met and Bobby shivered, taken aback at the intensity of their gaze. Edward turned brusquely away.

'Michel has a very important job to do and his unexpected appearance here gives us an opportunity we need to make the most of,' he told Mrs Hollis in a professional manner. 'I'm sure he will be able to come back again once the war is over – if he wants to. In the meantime, he must not be seen outside this farm and his presence must be kept a secret.'

Once the meal was over, Mr Hollis retired to his study and Mrs Hollis commandeered Michel to find him some better clothes. Aunt Agnes hesitated, reluctant to leave, but her sister demanded her help.

Edward Turner turned to face Bobby at the empty table. There was an uncomfortable silence for a moment before he said, 'I will have to take this matter further, Miss Hollis.'

'Please, call me Bobby.'

'Very well . . . Bobby . . .' he smiled inwardly and coughed to regain his composure. 'We have to get Michel back to France. Umm . . . we need more information on what happened and . . .' he stuttered, 'there is dangerous work to do there. There is obviously a close link between you and Monsieur Bisset,' his face scanned her hair, which was billowing out around her head like an untamed autumnal leaf pile. Taken aback, he tried to make himself concentrate and went hurriedly on, 'He's not in a good state, mentally, and we need him to have as much time as possible to recover from what has obviously been a very traumatic experience. We'll organise for him to have medical care but we're relying on your family to keep him here, in a calm environment, until we've made arrangements. I realise you need to go back to Hamble but with your skill in French, we're hoping you can explain in his own language that he has to get strong and go back as soon as possible.'

Roberta nodded. It was strange but it did not surprise her that this man had done his homework and knew she spoke French.

'We ... um ... will talk to your CO. It has been suggested you may be able to help in other ways.'

Bobby was puzzled but the man in front of her suddenly seemed to be so much in control, she did not dare question his authority.

It was only as he was leaving that he addressed the reason he had come to the farmhouse in the first place. 'I suggest ... um Bobby ...' he paused at the informality between them and then went on, 'that this is neither the time, nor the place, to discuss our fathers' r-ridiculous plans for our future together.'

Bobby was astonished to feel a moment's disappointment but kept her face smiling and nodded.

Edward went slowly down the front steps from the porch, talking to himself angrily. *I refuse to fall for this woman; I will not give father the satisfaction,* he thought and promptly put Miss Roberta Hollis out of his mind.

The rest of Bobby's day was spent trying to contain her mother's excitement and gently talking to Michel in French, to reassure him and prepare him for whatever lay ahead.

Michel was hardly eating and his clothes seemed to hang off him. Bobby tried to talk to him and took him up to the top attic room where she had played as a child. She suddenly stopped as they reached the top wooden step under the eaves and clutched her chest. A picture came back to her of an isolated little girl sitting playing under the skylight and from the shadows came the memory of her imaginary playmate. She had forgotten all about 'Boy', but it was this figure from her imagination who had provided her with companionship from the day her father came home from the Great War. For several years she would trot around the farm with her hand outstretched to clasp a hand only she could see, having endless conversations with him and sharing her innermost thoughts. Eventually, Aunt Agnes was able to gently convince Bobby that she was going to have to let go of her imaginary friend. The teasing at school by Marie and her cronies had become relentless and Bobby had finally been forced to admit that it was not normal to talk to shadows. The night when she knelt by her bed to say her prayers and then told 'Boy' she could no longer talk to him was the only time in her childhood that Roberta Hollis had cried.

Bobby shook herself, smiled wanly at Michel behind her and leaned down to move the little cars and farm animals that were still scattered over the wooden flooring. She cleared a space and spreading out the old blanket that had been gathering dust silently motioned to Michel to sit down. She leaned forward and gently moved a piece of hair that had fallen over his eyes.

'Tell me about your life, *ta vie*, in France,' she whispered. Michel looked at her but seemed unable to speak. Eventually, eliciting no response, Bobby lay back to look up through the skylight to get inspiration from the pale blue skies with whirling clouds above her, as she had always done. Michel sat next to her, his arms clutching his knees, rocking backwards and forwards. Bobby sat up again and softly stroked his arm. Bit by bit, warmed by the rays of sunshine that shone into the room from above, she felt the tension in him relax and after a haunting silence he began to speak.

'I live in a small town in Normandy, it is just my father and I now my mother has . . .' He stopped and suddenly looked her in the eyes. 'You know, she called me Michel because she knew my . . . your father . . . had lost a son with that name and she wanted me to have a connection with him.'

Bobby nodded, encouraging him to go on.

'At that time, she think my French father was dead and she never see him again. Then my French father, Raoul, he come back. He know everything. He has been my real father, I miss him so much.'

He paused to wipe his eyes then went quickly on.

'We have help in the house, her name is Claudette. She is very pretty,' he added, as an afterthought.

'France has been terrible since the Germans came. My father and I, we help our country – just small things – but then the things get bigger and it is all too much.'

He buried his head in his hands and Bobby sat and waited while he regained control. All over the world, there were young people like Michel – and her – who were being asked to perform incredible tasks that only a few years ago would have seemed impossible. She understood how he felt overwhelmed by the responsibility that had been forced on him.

'Shhh, there's no need to speak. I know how you are feeling,' she told him. 'We are all out of our depth.'

Michel looked at her quizzically.

'That means we're all being asked to do things that we don't think we're capable of, but believe me, Michel, somehow we find that strength. We aren't the only ones who are finding this war almost impossible but what is the choice? We want our countries to have the freedom to live as we want to and to do that, we have to search deep within ourselves to do our own little bit that might, when added together, be enough to save us all.'

He took a deep breath and slowly nodded, absorbing her words one by one.

She went on. 'You have your own family and now you have us. We are somehow bonded together by our looks, if nothing else, and with that connection, we can help each other. I lost my brother, Michel. You will now be my brother.'

It took a moment for Bobby to realise she had just become an older sister. No one had ever needed her before and her breath got caught in her throat as she absorbed the warm glow that rushed through her body.

The young man leaned forward and hugged Bobby hard. Also without brothers and sisters, he had never known this sort of support and he grasped at it like a drowning man.

* * *

Later that evening, Bobby decided it was time she, too, reached out for help and her first thought was Aunt Agnes.

'What are we to do?' Bobby asked her when she cornered her aunt on her way to her mother's drawing room with a tray of tea.

'I think my priorities are caring for your mother and keeping your father fed,' she said. 'He's hardly eaten anything since Michel arrived. I will try to keep Michel calm and just make life as mundane as possible until it's decided what should be done with him. You'll go back to flying planes.'

Bobby took the tray out of her aunt's hands, laid it on the oak side table and gave her a hug, pleased to have her practicality to lean on.

Her aunt brushed her off. 'Nonsense,' she said. 'There's a war on and our little dramas are nothing compared with what some people are suffering.'

Bobby looked closely at her aunt. She suspected Agnes had her own story, but she was not a woman to share her feelings and had already closed her mouth tightly in that familiar tense line that brooked no discussion.

* * *

On the Sunday morning, Bobby took a pale Michel to the grave of her twin and told him in a mixture of French and English, the full story of the little brother, Michael, whose death had dominated her life. She told him about how, because of her parents' grief for a longed-for son, she had never felt a mother's hug or a father's pride in her achievements. As she stopped, not sure how to go on, Michel laid his arm on hers and gave a little squeeze. It unleashed a need to talk that Bobby had never experienced before.

She looked from the grave of her brother, Michael, that she had talked to all her life to the real life figure of Michel standing next to her and she began in a torrent of English to explain about her childhood. Michel stared hard at her trying to understand what she was saying.

'I have always felt so guilty, Michel, guilty that I'm the one left alive *and* that I am a girl. Father wanted a boy so much. I've tried to do everything a boy would have done but it's never been enough.

Bobby put her hand on the marble angel in front of her. She was struggling with this new feeling of vulnerability.

'You see, I've never allowed myself to feel anything, not really. I have to achieve – all the time – I have to be the best, the bravest, the most capable, because to show emotion would somehow be weak.'

And then, as if in defiance of that statement, she felt a tear on her cheek followed by the warmth of Michel's hand taking hers. It was a moment that gave her companionship like nothing had ever done since 'Boy' had left her life. She leaned against him and for a moment the two auburn heads were intertwined.

Chapter 12

As ever, Bobby's schedule meant she had to push all the drama of the weekend behind her as the RAF began bombarding Berlin and aircraft were needing to be replaced at a rapid rate. It left her little time to mull over events while she raced up and down the country, delivering aircraft after aircraft to where anxious RAF pilots were waiting to take off into battle. After one particularly long trip to Staffordshire, Yorkshire and East Anglia, Bobby arrived back at Hamble just before dark to cycle in the pitch black back to her digs with Colonel and Mrs Mason. Without lights, Bobby always waited for about ten minutes before she pedalled off at a fast rate to allow her eyes to adjust. She normally paused on the front drive to appreciate her good luck in being placed somewhere so comfortable but tonight she was so tired, she just raced straight into the kitchen to ask Mrs Hampson for a Spam sandwich for supper and then went directly up to bed. Before she snuggled down, she read a letter from her aunt telling her that Michel was slowly building up his strength but was hardly speaking. She added that some officials had been visiting Michel and bombarding him with questions. Bobby felt a deep unease and rubbing her tired eyes, she made herself write a reply asking for more details and then scribbled off a quick letter to Harriet finally remembering to tell her about the chance reunion with Gus Prince. Bobby knew how Harriet would savour that particular piece of information and could not wait to meet her friend again to have a proper gossip about the popular young boy who had turned into such an attractive pilot. Then she pulled the covers over herself, grateful for the silk eiderdown rather than the sheet and rough blanket that WAAF had to suffer. She went down further in the bed in an effort to block out the snoring she could hear from Sally next door. The Spam churned around Bobby's stomach and she found it hard to sleep, tossing and turning for what seemed like hours, so much so that she was surprised to be shaken awake in the morning by Sally.

'Come on, sleepyhead. You'll be late.'

'I didn't sleep,' Bobby replied, blinking and trying to erase the visions of her shrunken father and her over-excited mother that had plagued her dreams.

'Well, you took some waking so you must have got some shut-eye,' was the unsympathetic response.

Both girls washed and dressed speedily and ate a quick breakfast before grabbing their overnight bags to cycle to the airfield operations room in time for nine o'clock.

The late winter starts were a welcome relief on cold, frosty mornings but they did put the pilots under a great deal of pressure to get their deliveries done before dark. Bobby preferred summer timetables when they were up and running by six.

She scanned her 'chits' – a Hurricane to White Waltham, a Harvard to Worthy Down and then – she looked again to check . . . yes, her heart lurched – a Spitfire to Colerne.

Oh, why today? she thought. *I've been waiting for this moment for a year and now, when I have so much to think about, I finally get a Spitfire. It's almost not fair.*

She completed the first two flights, going through the motions automatically, but when she arrived at Worthy Down she felt her knees going weak.

She walked onto the airfield trying to look more confident than she felt. She was clutching her blue Ferry Pilots Notes and her fingers were white from holding them so tightly.

She tried to clear her head of the drama from the weekend.

You have to concentrate, you have to concentrate, she told herself fiercely and then she saw it – a shiny new Spitfire with an engineer's legs visible under the wings.

This is what being in love must be like, she thought, her heart pounding.

She walked past a couple of stunned ground crew emerging from the aircraft next to the Spitfire. They stood watching her, wiping their greasy hands on rags.

The rest of the engineer's body emerged. 'They said it was a girl pilot,' he said, 'you ever flown one of these before?'

Bobby hesitated; she was aware the nearby men were listening intently. They were all looking at her and she was almost tempted to lie, but eventually decided to come clean.

'Nope, first time.'

There was a gasp from the men behind her. She firmly placed her helmet on her head and swung her parachute into the cockpit.

'I'll be fine,' she said to the engineer, waving her Pilots Notes.

'Oh, *great*, she's got a little book,' one of the ground crew said. 'That'll do it then.'

The raucous laughter followed her as she clambered up the wing, but she gave them all as cheerful a grin as she could muster. Settling herself into the pilot's seat with her parachute as a cushion beneath her, she looked round the aircraft. There was not much room and she looked for somewhere to put her overnight bag, eventually pushing it behind her where the radio would normally have gone and hoped the valuable chocolate in her bag would not melt. She compared the instrument panel with the diagrams in the notes – so far so good. There were about forty controls to watch, including sleek, black dials. Bobby reached up and pulled the canopy over her head. She took off her helmet for a moment and shook her auburn hair out. She caught sight of the image in the Perspex above her and said to the reflection: "Bet you never thought you'd be flown by a girl. To be honest, I never dreamed I'd be here either, but I'll have you know, this is what I was born for.' The reflection grinned back at her. She replaced the helmet.

Brakes on? Fuel on? She focused, remembering her training.

She gave a 'thumbs up' signal to the ground mechanic but she was not sure he had seen her. 'Ready,' she called through the screen but her voice broke into a hoarse whisper so she shouted again, with more confidence.

'Ready!' She tasted the fumes and got the familiar knot in her stomach that always accompanied the first throaty roar of an engine and oh, the Merlin sounded magnificent. She felt the power surge through her, waved to the ground crew and then she was taxiing towards the runway.

She opened up the throttle and taxied from side to side to enable her to see over the long engine cowling and then felt a kick in her back as the aircraft roared into flight.

Oops, it's much more responsive than other planes, she thought, easing the control column forward to reduce the climb rate and increase speed. She selected the undercarriage up option and experienced a liberation she had never felt before. It was as if the Spitfire was delighted to be freed into the air at last and was playing with her. It was like flying a butterfly, it was so light and, she realised, able to turn on a sixpence.

'Let's remember who's boss,' she scolded. The airspeed indicator showed 150mph – this was no sluggish Walrus. Once in the air, Bobby looked out at the landmarks beneath. She wondered if anyone was looking up towards the small aeroplane in the sky. How surprised they would be to know it was a girl at the controls.

'Let's see what you can do,' she said out loud and tested out some stalls, tried out the flaps again and the landing gear. She did not want to forget to drop the undercarriage and pancake on the runway at Colerne in front of everyone. She tried out some of the controls to see what the aircraft was capable of but one thing she never wanted to have to touch, she thought with a shudder, was the metal crow-bar on the left side of her seat. It was there to help her open the canopy in an emergency.

She felt an enormous responsibility to get everything right on behalf of female ATA pilots who were determined to prove to a male-dominated, sceptical world that women were as capable as men but there were accidents, including her heroine, Amy Johnson, who had bailed out into the sea in bad weather while delivering an Airspeed Oxford. She had never been seen again. Some of her own friends had also been killed – girls and men. War was taking aircrew, but pilot error, weather and aircraft malfunction were also taking ATA friends she had shared cigarettes, jokes and a drink with. Without radar or a radio, she was completely alone up there and the thought made her sit up straight, straining with concentration.

'I'm going to have to go home soon to sort all this mess out,' she told the skies around her, 'I can't die now. Who else would deal with it?'

With that in mind, and the reputation of women pilots at stake, Bobby's concentration was complete for the journey to Colerne.

She checked her altimeter – 1,800 feet and not long to landing. She checked the view below her. Yes, there was the landing strip. She thought back to the Ferry Pilots Notes and remembered that the wheels unfolded inwards, unlike the Hurricane's that unfolded outwards and descended to 800 feet, slowing her speed to prepare for the approach. She selected the landing gear down option and then the grass sped beneath her and gradually, she touched down. She checked her radiator temperature gauge with satisfaction – 110 degrees.

The landing checks took her longer than usual, mainly because she did not want to get out of this perfect piece of machinery. All her worries about Michel and her family had seemed to evaporate with the clouds when she was flying. Eventually, she reluctantly climbed down.

An RAF mechanic had marshalled her in and he moved the chocks into place without looking up.

'Thank you,' she said.

He reeled up at the female voice, banging his head on the undercarriage to see a woman pilot shaking out her curls in front of him. He rubbed his sore head.

'Bloody hell, oh, sorry miss, I was just thinking what a great landing that was – and it turns out to be a girl!'

Because he was smiling in admiration, Bobby added, 'That was my first Spitfire.'

'Well, you could certainly teach some of the male pilots a thing or two, good on yer, girl.'

Bobby glowed with pride and walked towards the control tower to sign off and get transport back to the station.

'Bobby, Bobby Hollis.' A call from behind her pulled her up sharply. It was Gus Prince, on his way out to a waiting aircraft.

'We do keep meeting in the oddest of places.'

Bobby was surprised by how pleased she was to see his handsome face grinning at her. It occurred to her that Sally, with her insistence that she looked up from her Little Blue Book occasionally to notice men, may have opened a Pandora's Box in Bobby's life. She was not sure how she felt about that – especially if it meant losing control.

Gus, however, was delighted. Bobby Hollis had been in his thoughts far too much since they had bumped into each other in Scotland and then there was that really strange business in France he had wanted to ask her about.

'How's the family?' he went on, at a loss to say anything meaningful.

A cloud came over Bobby's face. 'It's a bit complicated. Anyway, what are you doing here?'

'Just helping out with training some sprogs,' he pointed with his thumb at the impossibly young men standing by some Hurricanes.

'Come on, sir,' said one of them. 'We need to get these circuits and bumps done. You promised us a pint tonight if we don't do a pancake landing.'

'Coming,' Gus shouted back.

He turned to face Bobby again.

'We need to catch up.' He leaned forward and whispered, 'I need to talk to you. I brought a French chap back from a pretty awful mission a while ago. He asked me where your father lived. It was all really odd.'

'Sir!' a ground crew engineer was calling him over.

'Gotta go, new crews – they need take off and landing practice.' Gus kissed Bobby on the cheek, aware that everyone on the runway was staring in admiration at this pilot who knew one of the 'Attagirls'.

Bobby called after him. 'I'm at Hamble, get in touch . . . asap . . . I need to know more!'

Chapter 13

The days passed and Bobby had heard nothing from Gus and now fog was preventing them all from flying. She was curled up in the armchair in the corner of the restroom assigned to the women ATA pilots at Hamble but had read the same paragraph of her book twice now. In front of her, she had a letter from Harriet, which demanded more information on both meetings with Gus before she went on to enthuse about her current boyfriend, Gerry. She then spent the next page telling Bobby off for courting trouble by wandering into strange hotels on her own adding that, really, she should take more care. Bobby smiled at the admonishing tone of the letter and then looked out of the window for the umpteenth time to peer towards the buildings opposite, but the visibility was so bad, all she could see were mists swirling towards the dark shadows of their gable ends. She put her book down and glanced around the now familiar room. It had a mix of upright chairs and armchairs, a few tables and a couple of vases filled with snowdrops, shedding some brightness into the dull day. Patsy was full of cold but had spread out a pillowcase on the floor and was bent over it, with pins in her mouth, marking out the seam points. She was carefully making a blouse out of the material and had already unpicked some lace from a nightie to put around the collar. Sally was sitting at one of the tables, putting her makeup on as usual.

'I'm starving, when's dinner?' Patsy said, sniffling. She moaned constantly about being hungry and always regaled the girls with stories of her mother's Lancashire hotpot. 'How come I never get a fever? They say you're supposed to not be hungry when you have a fever? I only ever get colds, and they make me hungrier than ever.'

She coughed over her pillowcase. 'I'm never flying a Moth again, they're so cold. I feel so ill. Why can't they put canopies on them?'

They all nodded in sympathy. The winds up in the sky were penetrating and no matter how many layers they wore under their uniforms, everyone hated flying the open-topped Tiger Moth that was normally flown at no more than sixty miles per hour, meaning that the cold journeys took longer than in other aircraft.

This was the third day that the weather had halted all deliveries and the girls were bored.

Bobby found the inactivity made her brain whirr. She was cross she had not heard from Gus and her letters from Aunt Agnes were perfunctory and minimalist in their information. Bobby hardly knew what was going on. She could not fathom how Gus had become involved and she was unable to find out any more information or to exert any influence over the next steps and she hated it. All she knew was that Michel was very weak and not talking very much. Her father spent all his time in the study and the only one who had found a new lease of life was her mother, taking charge of looking after Michel with more purpose than anyone had seen for years. Bobby huffed with frustration.

'I know I should be pleased to be in this warm room, but I am so fed up with not doing anything,' Bobby said. 'I wish they'd let us go against the Germans – I'd love to fight.'

'Oh, I'm quite happy doing deliveries,' Patsy replied, talking through the side of her mouth since it was holding two pins. She took the pins out so she could talk more easily. 'Think of those Russian women flying in combat against the Luftwaffe, they are going down like ninepins, *and* it's freezing up there . . . they only have to touch the side of their cockpits and their skin burns off. That's what you call *real* cold, I suppose.' She sniffed.

There was a knock at the door and an orderly came in carrying a teleprinter message. They all looked up expectantly, but the message was for Bobby.

Party at officers' mess, Gosport, tonight. Bring friends. Gus.

She felt a mixture of relief that the mystery she had been pondering might finally be resolved and irritation that Gus just assumed that she would be available.

'There's a party tonight in Gosport. Anyone want to go?' she announced to the room.

That news galvanised them all into action. Sally said she knew someone who would come and pick them up, Patsy reached for the aspirin, her cold suddenly miraculously improved and then started to pack up her sewing. Bobby decided to file her nails after all. Daphne, who had been absorbed in cutting out a peppermint cream recipe from the newspaper, suddenly looked up, her eyes bright with excitement. Unlike other services, the ATA girls were allowed to wear their own clothes when off duty and they eagerly chatted about how they were going to make the most of the occasion.

'Well, this blouse won't be ready,' Patsy said, holding up her morning's work that still looked remarkably like a pillowcase. 'I'll have to wear my old one, which is almost threadbare, and I suppose I could wear that blue skirt.'

'I used to have a lovely one with pleats in,' Daphne put in. 'Do you remember when we were allowed pleats and men had turn-ups on their trousers?'

'Nope,' Sally said with a laugh. 'Can't remember that; it was in another lifetime when we had yards and yards of material to waste.' She grabbed the pillowcase. 'Just think

Patsy, if we all lived on cabbage for a week like they want us to, this would make blouses for all of us.'

Patsy giggled and helped herself to another carrot biscuit from the table.

Bobby and Sally went back to their digs to get ready. The huge rooms were freezing cold, but there was often a little fire in the drawing room, where every evening the girls were invited to join their hosts in a small glass of homemade elderberry wine. Colonel and Mrs Mason were delighted to have chatter in the house once again and fussed over the girls like long-lost daughters. Mrs Mason, in particular, loved the novelty of having girls in the house and was always offering to help them with their hair or suggesting lending them one of her scarves or a handbag to go with their outfits. Sally and Bobby's rooms both showed signs of their previous masculine inhabitants through the sparse and functional furnishings. There was a picture of the Masons' two boys on Sally's dressing table and she had already suggested to Mrs Mason that the particularly good-looking elder son, a high-ranking naval officer, should write to her. The rooms' huge windows normally looked out over the garden but today, the fog hung low on the horizon. Unlike Sally, Bobby had not bothered to put her feminine stamp on her room, and she delighted in its space and sparseness. There was a small bedside cupboard and two shelves above the bed. On them were books about the Boer War, the Napoleonic Wars and naval ships but, once Bobby had squeezed them along, there was just enough room for her aviation books. On the other side of the room, there was a wooden chest of drawers that she could use for her clothes. The one small mirror on the bedside cupboard just about allowed her to see to do her hair and pinch her cheeks to put some colour in them.

'Want some soot?' Sally asked, coming in carrying a small pot of grey dust. She nudged Bobby out of the way to use the mirror and smear it on her eyelids.

Bobby peered from behind Sally, examining the results.

'No, thanks. I never bothered before the war when I could have used a proper colour, so I don't think I'll start now when all that's on offer is a bit of grey dirt.'

'Suit yourself,' Sally replied, moving on to the dish of beetroot she kept for lipstick.

'This makes a nice change, doesn't it?' Bobby said, pushing her blouse into her skirt. 'We don't often get a night out all together, do we? We're normally stuck somewhere round the country on our own. It's nice for us all to have the chance to kick up some dust on our own doorstep.'

Sally passed over the little pot of ash to her. 'Here you are,' she laughed, 'here's some dust to start you off.'

Bobby gave in and used her little finger to spread some ash on her eyelids. They did look bigger, she decided. 'I just hope it stops raining; I don't want to look like a corpse!'

'There's a car waiting for you girls,' Mrs Mason called from the bottom of the stairs.

They both grabbed their coats and as an afterthought, Bobby put on a splash of Soir de Paris perfume with a shrug. She may as well enjoy this, she decided.

The girls were in a giggly mood as they piled into the car with the RAF pilot to go to Gosport round the coast. He had already picked up Daphne and Patsy in Hamble itself. His name was Paul and he was quite good looking, with sleek brown hair. Sally, who had actually doused herself in the rest of the Soir de Paris, made sure she sat in the front. The perfume was overwhelming and Bobby grinned as she saw the pilot open the top of his window to let in some air.

'Are you based on the south coast?' Sally asked him as soon as he started off down the driveway.

'Yep, we're all just enjoying this bad weather, it's giving us a much-needed break, so a good excuse for a party, we thought.'

Sally looked round at the three girls in the back and winked. 'We ATA girls like a good party,' she told the pilot.

'So I've heard!' he laughed.

The crowd of men in RAF uniform parted when the girls walked into the mess to let them through to the bar.

They were becoming used to causing a stir wherever they went and, it was obvious that word had soon gone around that some ATA girls were coming. There was a group of sulky WAAFs standing in the corner, anything but pleased that their crews were about to be commandeered by the 'glamour girls.' Their resentment was not helped by the fact that the ATA girls, as a civilian organisation, were in civvies while they were in their Oxford shoes and uniform.

The men rushed to buy drinks for their guests and Bobby found herself with a cider in each hand. She was laughing at the feeble attempts of two pilots to outdo each other for attention when another pilot elbowed his way through.

'Hello Bobby,' he said.

'Gus!' she exclaimed with pleasure. She suddenly felt the need to adjust her hair and she discovered she was nervous.

'I got your message. It was lucky I wasn't away flying,' she could not resist pointing out, a little put-out that he had not doubted she would turn up.

The other two pilots backed off, knowing when they were beaten and Gus signalled Bobby towards a table in the corner.

'I've been wanting to track you down but it's been a bit busy,' he said. 'I had a couple of days' leave and I thought there might be an opportunity to see you so I grabbed a lift and got them to send you an invitation. We needed to talk face-to-face, you know I can never say anything in a letter.'

He touched the side of his nose and she smiled, understanding. Secrecy was everything in this war.

She knew that air activity had been getting more and more intense and she could see by his strained face that the last few weeks had not been easy.

'So, how are you?' he looked piercingly into her eyes, as if trying to read the small print.

'I'm OK ... it seems everyone wants aircraft, lots of them and now.'

His face darkened for a moment. All around him, pilots were holding in the tension they were feeling, almost trying too hard to have fun. Tonight was a chance to let their hair down and many of the men at the bar were already beginning to show signs of having drunk too much. Gus fingered his own glass of beer. His latest trips to France had been a disaster. The one when his 'package' had been shot along with all the resistance fighters had been followed by two more ops when two aircraft and their pilots had been shot down. Something was going badly wrong on the ground in Normandy. The enemy were being primed and, looking at Bobby's sympathetic face, Gus had a sudden desire to offload some of the pressure that was mounting inside him. He sighed and longed for a normal conversation where he did not have to watch every word he uttered.

'Can you tell me what happened in France?' Bobby muttered through the corner of her mouth. She glanced up to make sure no one was listening.

'I can't say much, but we had a bit of a tricky time on a mission a few weeks ago and ended up rescuing this French guy. He asked if I knew Norfolk. When I said I did, he asked if I could take him to Salhouse Farm. He said Mr Hollis would look after him. I was a bit surprised, I have to be honest. Who is he?'

Bobby was wary, she could not reveal the truth behind Michel's relationship to her father. 'He's a distant relative,' she said, finally.

'Ah, I thought as much, he really does look like you, doesn't he? So that's why your father taught you French.'

'Hmm,' Bobby replied vaguely. 'But what can you tell me about his rescue?'

'Not much, we weren't there to get him, he just sort of ended up having to be brought out.'

Bobby thought longingly of the pre-war days when everyone could talk honestly and openly. *Both of us are hiding secrets*, she thought.

Sally's voice called over from the bar: 'Come on, you two, someone's unearthed the gramophone. We've got some jiving to do.'

Bobby and Gus both shrugged and got up. He grabbed her hand as the tones of Duke Ellington filled the wooden building.

Two songs later, Bobby was puffing and panting. Sitting in a aeroplane all day had not helped her fitness for dancing.

'Can we sit down?' she pleaded with Gus, but then the gentle strains of Vera Lynn's '(There'll be Bluebirds Over) The White Cliffs of Dover' came on the gramophone and Gus pulled Bobby close to him.

She suddenly realised how tired she was and relaxed her head onto his shoulder. He tightened his arms around her. As the last notes of the song finished, Gus leaned in and kissed her.

* * *

Bobby got into her bed quickly at the end of the evening. The room was freezing and from under the covers, she manoeuvred one arm so she could throw her skirt and blouse, slip and underwear onto the chair next to the bed and then hurriedly snuggled down. She found she was shivering, and pulled the counterpane further up around her shoulders. She stared into the gloom and frowned. She had been taken aback by Gus's kiss and especially about how her own stomach had turned over as their lips met. She realised she could still feel the imprint on her waist where his hand had pulled her towards him.

Bobby plumped up her pillow fiercely and tried to analyse the evening honestly. The kiss had been so quick she had hardly had time to respond, Bobby reasoned, reassuring herself that she had not led him on. She knew from the other girls' tales of romantic conquests that RAF pilots found it a heady experience being with an 'Attagirl' and the intensity of Gus's arm around her had worried her.

She also realised she had never felt such a strong physical attraction to a man before.

Chapter 14

It was another 'washout day' and all the girls were listlessly spending time in the restroom. The mail had been delivered and Bobby had a letter from her aunt and another from Harriet, who regaled her with the news of how she had ditched Gerry, been out with three new airmen in a week and it was only in a final postscript that she demanded to know how good a dancer Gus was and did Bobby swoon in his arms?

'Bobby, can I see you for a minute?'

Margot Gore, the commander at Hamble popped her head round the door of the restroom.

As she disappeared again, everyone looked at Bobby expectantly.

'I've no idea,' she said to the questioning faces of her fellow pilots, outwardly smiling but inside, quivering with nerves. 'I haven't broken any aircraft recently so it can't be that bad.'

Margot was always very friendly with the girls, but she was still the boss.

Bobby knocked on the door marked with a plaque bearing Margot's name and title.

'Come in, Bobby,' Margot called from inside but as soon as Bobby got through the door, she halted in surprise. Standing with his back to the window at the side of Margot's desk was Edward Turner.

He smiled at her and she feigned a smile back.

'Do sit down,' Margot said, pointing to the green leather-backed chair in front of her wooden desk. 'I believe you've met Mr Turner?'

Bobby gave a weak smile of recognition and sat slowly on the seat, clasping her hands together. She looked from one to the other and waited, completely perplexed.

Margot picked up some papers, banged them into shape on her desk and got up to leave.

'Bobby, Mr Turner would like to speak to you in private.' She glanced at Edward, who took over and Margot left the room, closing the door quietly behind her.

'Miss Hollis,' Edward had decided it would be easier to revert to formalities between them. 'I think you are aware there is a young Frenchman who needs to be returned to his country. I cannot say much more but there are problems over there and Michel Bisset is the person we need on the ground. His unscheduled visit here has given us a rare chance to brief a member of the Resistance in person, now we need him to go back as soon as possible. It is a crucial time.'

That revelation took Bobby by surprise. The last she had heard, Michel was being cosseted by her mother and was not capable of having a proper conversation, let alone leading a resistance network. So much had been happening at home while she had been having slow dances with Gus.

'I am not sure how strong Michel is,' Bobby registered with surprise how protective she felt about the young man who was, after all, her half-brother.

'We are aware of that,' Edward interjected, 'he's not confident about his new role. It's imperative that he has someone with him that he trusts during the journey to get him on and off that plane so, with your permission, we will arrange for you to have leave to do that. Obviously, as an ATA pilot, you are not at liberty to travel abroad so it will have to be on your own time, I'm afraid. I'm sure you understand we need a strong network over there and there is only Monsieur Bisset who is sufficiently aware of the problems from both sides. The knowledge his unexpected visit here has allowed us to impart, means he will now be able to reorganise and do some investigations for us. We have, as you may be aware, problems with radio communication in France since the Germans confiscated them all.'

Bobby looked at him in surprise. If she had heard him correctly, she was to fly with Michel over to France. It was unheard of but Edward Turner was adamant. There was no sign of the shy, blundering man she had met at the farm. This was a man used to being in control.

Edward went on, 'This is a top-secret mission and only a few people will be informed of it. You have undoubtedly already signed the Official Secrets Act, but this mission is especially important. We are using the same pilot who brought Monsieur Bisset out of France but we need someone he trusts to reassure him in his own language, someone who can communicate with the ground in French, plus, we need someone we can trust on the aircraft to operate equipment, the security of having a second pilot on board, and we can't risk involving anyone else. And that person, it has been decided, is you.'

The pause emphasised the stillness of the room.

'I don't exactly know Michel Bisset that well, Mr Turner,' Bobby protested, realising at the same time that that pilot would be Gus.

Edward raised his eyebrows at her. 'I believe you are related to the Frenchman, aren't you?' he replied. It was not really a question. 'This is a very delicate operation; we need to pre-plan every bit of it and we need Monsieur Bisset's complete co-operation. You will leave one week from today when you will receive your full briefing on rice paper at the airfield. You must read it thoroughly, learn what is necessary and then eat the briefing.

'I think, at this stage, we'll just leave it at that. Miss Hollis, you will dress in uniform and the rendezvous will be at 22:00 hours next Thursday to give you time to get to ... where you are going. A car will pick you up at 20:00 hours and a separate car will pick up Monsieur Bisset to avoid unnecessary risks. He will meet you there. I don't have to remind you of the secrecy of this operation. Your fellow pilots here must not be told anything.'

Bobby stumbled out of the room and leaned for a moment against the wall in the corridor. Questions were whirring around her mind. How high up was Edward? Was he not the lowly civil servant she thought? What the hell was she letting herself in for?

'Bobby,' Edward called from behind.

He caught up with her and put his hand on her arm, gently.

'There is danger in this mission. You can refuse to go, if you want to. You are a volunteer.'

Bobby looked into his deep, brown eyes and saw a genuine concern there.

'No, I may regret this, but of course I'll go.'

* * *

The following week, Bobby gathered up her overnight bag, her wash things and her gas mask and then stood next to her chest of drawers, undecided about whether she needed to pack anything else. All ATA pilots took an overnight bag in case they got stuck somewhere and could not get back, but she could hardly allow herself to entertain that possibility – the thought made her shiver – so she forced her practical side to the fore. She needed to be prepared for all eventualities. If, heaven forbid, they had to land in France, she hoped her uniform would protect her and entitle her to decent treatment under the Geneva Convention but it could be very cold in the air over the Channel, she had heard. She searched into the bottom of a drawer for a woollen sweater she could wear under her uniform. It was one that Aunt Agnes had knitted her. She hugged it to herself, suddenly longing for her aunt's common sense. Being an ATA pilot was one thing but flying behind enemy lines was a completely different scenario. Her stomach lurched. She felt as if she were drowning.

She was about to push the jumper into her bag but paused, fingering its warmth and thinking about her family. The strange, unnerving conversation with her father on the landing had left her wondering what would be behind the door they had opened up between them; her mother had finally shown signs of coming out of the shadows and her aunt's reliable practical common sense had given her strength. She felt a sudden need to hug them all.

She wondered whether this new need to reach out to people was because of Michel. From the first moment she met him, she had felt an urge to protect him, a feeling that had been completely natural. *Maybe that is why I'm prepared to take on this ridiculous mission,* she thought. *To be able to protect my little brother and start to recreate a proper family?*

The journey to the airfield took longer than she expected, although, realistically, she reasoned, she had no idea how long it should have taken. Without signposts, which had been removed years before to confuse any invaders, she had no idea where she was. She peered around her at the fields, pretty thatched cottages and the river that they were passing. The car suddenly pulled over to one side and Bobby looked up expectantly.

'Put this on, please, miss.' The driver's hand came over the front seat and he handed her a blindfold. She reached to take it, feeling slightly sick. The car drove on for about another twenty minutes while Bobby's mind – and heart – raced. They eventually stopped and she got out to be led by the driver. He took the blindfold off for her and she blinked. They were at an airfield and the first thing she saw was an Anson, glistening in the distance; it was like a foreboding shadow. Bobby was qualified to fly Ansons around Britain, ferrying ATA pilots between deliveries or back to base, so she breathed a sigh of relief, but she was not used to flying at night and had avoided going anywhere near coastlines, so she hoped she would not be called on to actually operate the controls. This trip was already terrifying enough.

A man in a pin-striped suit approached her as she got out of the car. The driver stood to attention and saluted him. Bobby half put her hand to her head as well and then dropped it, as part of a civilian organisation, she never had to salute anyone, but she had no idea who he was or what she was supposed to do. He took her into a nearby large brick barn where he handed her a parachute, a small satchel, a brown envelope and, terrifyingly, a cyanide pill. He told her to read the information inside the envelope and then destroy the notes. Before she had a chance to say anything he informed her she needed to be at the Anson in five minutes' time and then marched off.

Bobby stared after him and then realised she was wasting precious time, so she sat down on a concrete bench behind her.

The note was brief. She was flying over enemy territory and apart from sitting in the co-pilot's seat to operate the landing gear, her sole task was to get Michel to board the aircraft, keep him calm and endorse his new position as head of a local resistance network. She heaved a sigh of relief that she was not going to be expected to fly but she felt a shiver of alarm that Michel was going to have to take on such an important role. It sounded as if there might be opposition from the local network as well as from Michel, but it was going to be her job to reiterate to all that the highest authorities, both in the French Resistance and the British Government, were insisting that he had to be the person to take on the job. He had to believe in his own capabilities, and she was to use her influence to convince him.

She shook her head in disbelief. This was a huge responsibility and she felt that Edward Turner and the rest of the bigwigs were overestimating her influence on the young Frenchman. She touched her hair; it was getting her into more trouble than she had ever bargained for. The next words on the instructions chilled her heart.

In the event of an unforeseen landing, she was not to meet any other resistance fighters, she was not to go out and she was to remain hidden at all times until she was returned to the rendezvous point at 02:00 hours one week after arrival, when an aeroplane would pick her up. There would be no radio messages transmitted to the ground and no one would know anything about her. The cyanide pill could be used 'if necessary' to avoid giving the enemy any information, she read with an icy chill spreading over her body.

Bobby slowly chewed the rice paper, feeling she was having her last meal.

There was a sound from the far end of the barn. She got up from the cold concrete plinth and peered into the darkness, her pulse racing. In one corner, sitting with his head in his hands, was Michel.

'Michel,' she whispered. He jumped and shot to his feet. He stood with his hands by his sides and she immediately went over to him and put her arms around him, feeling him shiver. For a second, he clung to her, their two faces masked by a mass of auburn hair.

'*Je ne peux pas*, I cannot . . .'

Bobby looked at the figure in front of her. He was relying on her to have the answers. Bobby had never had anyone to worry about but herself and she was shocked to realise she was about to risk her life for this young man and that there was no doubt in her mind that that was exactly what she was willing to do.

'Come on, Michel, we both have to do this. We will be fine. *J'en suis sûre.*' She felt anything but sure but somehow her appearance of confidence did the trick and Michel reached back to grab his parachute.

Something really important was happening in France; things were hotting up, she knew that from the number of aircraft deliveries she was having to make, and it had not taken her long to work out there was a treacherous leak in the Normandy network. She went on.

'*Ne t'inquiète pas.* I've lost one brother, it isn't possible I should lose two. You've been brought into my life for a reason. We both have a job to do. I will help to get you safely into France. You will take over the network there and you will do a brilliant job. Everyone is counting on you. And then, when all this is over, we will meet up again as family.'

For a brief moment, their eyes locked and each took comfort from the familiar reflection that stared back at them. She took his hand like a mother with a small child and headed towards the Anson. They climbed in and

Michel sat down pathetically on one of the seats at the back, clutching his parachute like a man holding onto a lifeline. Bobby climbed into the co-pilot's seat.

'Hello First Officer Hollis.'

'Gus! It is you. I thought it might be. I'm so glad to see a friendly face.'

'Looks like it. Everyone ready? OK, let's get these checks done and then get going. To be honest, you're more used to an Anson than I am, we rarely use them, so I'll be relying on you in case of problems.'

What he means, Bobby thought to herself, *is that if he gets killed by enemy fire, I will have to take over.*

Bobby realised the authorities were not taking any chances with this mission.

This aircraft had to get Michel to Normandy.

Chapter 15

'Straps on,' Gus called back to Michel. Bobby hated being in the co-pilot's seat. Her hands were itching to touch the controls and she had to concentrate on the wheels to stop them twitching but she peered across at him noting his take off procedure to check it coincided with her knowledge of the plane. Gus may not have been used to an Anson, but his take off was smooth.

'This is low. We're only at 500 feet?' she said to him.

'I need to be able to navigate and it helps to avoid problems, you'll understand that,' he replied. 'Once we get over the Channel, I'll need you to find a river and a railway line that go southwest in a parallel line. Here's the map, I was told not to show any markings on it, so we're relying on my memory and our visual abilities but it's near Louvigny, a small town on the Rivière l'Orange or something. A message has been sent to say we're coming but they know no more than that. Once we get within sight of the landing field, we can use the 'S' radio but that's where we'll need your French. Mine is less than rudimentary and I won't understand a word these French chaps are saying.'

Another reason for me to be here, Bobby thought.

'OK,' she said, glad to have something to do. 'It looks almost a full moon, do you always fly when it's so bright?'

'Yes or a few days before or after a full moon, you'll find that helps with navigat—Dammit,' Gus suddenly called as they flew towards the south coast. 'Balloons.'

Bobby's heart leapt. *Not again*, she thought, they were becoming the bane of her life. They were being used more and more whenever there was a threat of a raid and she, like all ATA pilots, usually found another route to avoid them, but this aircraft had no choice but to go the most direct route to get there on schedule.

Gus skilfully dodged the cables, and she kept a constant look out for any signs of the enemy. She had to acknowledge Gus was an excellent pilot and was obviously very used to flying fast and low. Also, like her, he was used to flying without a gunner, which made pilots more inventive and very quick at manoeuvring, even in an Anson.

After about half an hour, Gus kept glancing upwards, scanning the skies. His face was looking strained as messages about enemy aircraft came in on the radio to be transmitted through Gus's headphones. Bobby, who never had a radio, began to think dire warnings over the airways were a mixed blessing as she watched Gus become more and more anxious.

'I think we might be OK,' he finally said to her, looking at the clear skies on each side of them.

Bobby gave a sigh of relief. They did not need an attack.

Just then, Gus swore and swerved to the left. Michel moaned as he lurched against the side of the aircraft and Bobby banged her elbow. She knew better than to interrupt a pilot's concentration but held her breath waiting to see what had happened to cause him to move so quickly.

Once he had righted them again, Gus said to her, 'A rogue bandit, coming our way.'

Bobby leaned forward – not being able to see the enemy was making her feel impotent. Just at that moment, a German Messerschmitt flew within feet of their cockpit. She could see the pilot. A young man with the whites of his eyes showing. She could not help herself, she waved at him, her auburn curls blocking Gus's head.

The enemy aircraft suddenly lurched upwards and then disappeared.

Gus burst out laughing. 'My God, I wonder why we got away with that. Maybe he was short on fuel or maybe he just wants to get home in one piece. Or,' he paused and then chuckled, 'maybe he was just too surprised to see a woman in the cockpit and thought you were an angel come to foretell his impending doom!'

She sat back in shock. She had never seen a German so close.

'Are we alive?' a weak voice came from behind her.

'*Oui, Michel, oui*, I rather think we are,' Bobby replied slowly. 'I told you, we will both die in our beds surrounded by our grandchildren.' She looked round to see him give a wan smile.

The rest of the journey passed quickly as she concentrated on navigating and Gus gave his full attention to looking out for the enemy and flying the aircraft. Then she spotted what they were looking for.

'There, down there,' she told Gus. The river sparkled in the moonlight and the tracks of the railway followed its banks. For a second, she felt a buzz of excitement; she was over France. She had never been abroad and had always longed to travel and see the world. But down below her were people who had been invaded, whose everyday lives had been turned upside down and, if the newsreels were to be believed, were constantly living under the threat of execution, prisoner of war camps and starvation.

Gus checked his watch and his compass. 'In eight minutes you need to look out for three flares on the starboard side. They will only be fleetingly lit, so we need to be quick.

She carefully checked her watch. After six minutes, she scanned the ground. 'They're there, they're there,' she called, pointing to a field to their right where there were three torches being flashed intermittently.

'What letter are they flashing?'

Bobby searched her memory for the Morse alphabet. She had learned it in training but rarely used it. 'M' she said finally.

'OK, talk to them on this radio.' He passed over a different transceiver to her. 'Here, they have a second receiver on the ground to this one. Tell them we have a special package for them that we had to pick up last month unexpectedly and ask if it's OK to land.'

'*Bonsoir*,' she uttered into the mouthpiece. '*Nous avons une livraison spéciale pour vous que nous avions dû récupérer le mois dernier de façon inattendue. Est-ce-que bon pour atterrir?*

She listened and then told Gus, 'We've got the OK to land.'

'Right, I only have minutes to land and less than 600 yards to do it in. I need to head towards the bottom of that 'L' shape. Michel needs to get out as soon as I get those wheels down and then I can make a U turn while he's getting out. There's no time to lose. Tell him to jump at the last minute. Someone will be there to meet him. We have very little time to take off again,' he paused. 'I can't think of anyone I'd rather have by my side.'

Bobby stole a sideways glance at his profile. *Oh dear,* she thought, *I wish he didn't make my stomach turn over.*

Bobby relayed all the information but Michel stood hovering by the door, his hands clinging onto the cold metal. He seemed incapable of opening it.

'You'll have to go and do it for him, we can't waste time,' Gus told Bobby. She unstrapped herself and went to the back to help. The door was stuck and she struggled to wrench it open.

Gus shouted back to her, 'Hurry up, there are some more lights coming out of the woods, I don't know if they're French or German.'

Bobby threw her whole weight against the door, but Michel just stood there, glumly staring into space. Gus was yelling something from the front, but she could not hear him. She stepped backwards and pitched herself at the door. It suddenly flew open and she fell out onto the ground beneath, with Michel tumbling out on top of her. Gus was already revving the engine, apparently unaware that she was no longer on board and then, to her horror, the aeroplane taxied off down the field, the wheels bumping along the clumps of grass. She stared after it, lying prostrate on the wet, muddy ground, too terrified to move. She spat out some bits of grass she had almost swallowed as she fell and stumbled back to her feet. It was a large field, surrounded by dark, foreboding trees. There were some dark shapes running from the woods towards them. She hoped they were French.

'*Bienvenue en France*,' a French voice hissed at her as Gus swept the Anson back up into the sky, talking to an empty space behind him.

Chapter 16

There was immediate consternation amongst the group of about five men around Bobby and Michel. While two of them hugged a static Michel in a Gallic embrace, chattering on in French, the other three looked aghast at Bobby. They were only expecting one 'package'. What were they supposed to do with two?

The men were dressed in dirty gabardines with belts pulled tightly around their waists. Three of them wore black berets and they all carried shotguns, slung carelessly over their shoulders. Their boots were covered in mud and every one of them had used that mud to darken their faces so they would not be seen in the moonlight. Bobby, with her shiny, pink cheeks felt that she shone out like a sunbeam in the darkness.

Bobby experienced a deep panic arising from her stomach; somehow, she had actually landed in France. She was furious with Gus. How could he have left her here? But even as that thought passed through her racing mind, she knew he was unaware that she, as well as Michel, had fallen out of the plane. Now the words on the briefing note that she had dismissed as being out of a theatrical melodrama suddenly seemed like a terrifying portent. These were real Frenchmen, talking rapidly and in a dialect she could not understand; she had no idea where exactly she was and even less idea what to do – and she was behind enemy lines. She looked round at Michel for help but he seemed incapable of speaking so Bobby started to speak, explaining as best she could, what had happened. There was a momentary pause and then she saw the famous French shrug from the tallest man amongst them as he moved to quickly propel her and Michel forward. There were no lights anywhere and Bobby was torn between being grateful to the moon above and being terrified that they were so clearly illuminated in its light.

She watched Michel lean down and automatically rub some mud on his face and bent down to do the same before stumbling after the men towards the woods in front of them. Glancing behind her, imagining German boots thundering towards them, she could just see the outline of a large house that seemed to be watching them through its closed shutters. It loomed, full of shadows and menace, and Bobby shivered.

A low whistle revealed two men hiding in the bushes about twenty feet away from them. They emerged, running, half-crouched to have a quick conversation with the tall man and her guides abruptly changed direction, turning away from the woods towards the gable end of the house. As they crept in front of it, Bobby warily glanced up at its faded grandeur and peeling pink-icing paintwork. Desperate to think of anything other than the situation she was now in, she tried to imagine its history. It looked ornate enough to be from a golden era full of crinolines and feathers and it occurred to Bobby that theirs was not the first clandestine group it had witnessed moving silently through its grounds during France's turbulent history. She hardly dared look up to notice its massive hipped roofs and decorative quoins but tried to crouch down as far as she could in an effort to make herself as invisible as possible. There were no torches, but these men obviously knew their way. Bobby mentally raced through every possible scenario she was about to face and then decided it was just all too terrifying so concentrated on the more immediate threat of not falling over instead. At the far end of the overgrown terraced lawn, the group entered some more woods and while Michel followed noiselessly with the practised manner of one used to creeping silently around the French countryside at night, Bobby's boots kept catching on leaves and roots.

'Silence!' a man behind her whispered in a French accent.

For the first time, Bobby knew what it was like to be in enemy territory. Her heart was racing and every tree shape looked like a German soldier. She had never been so terrified. Not even, she realised, when engine failure in a

Swordfish had caused the aircraft to drop like a stone for a few heart-stopping seconds before she was able to restart it. But now, all the fears she had experienced as an ATA pilot seemed like tiny slivers of glass rather than the huge shattered mirror she was facing here.

After what seemed an age, but in reality was probably only ten minutes, they arrived at a small row of about seven houses lined up on one side of the road, as if clinging onto each other in solidarity. On the other side, there was a small school building with a broken gate and a noticeboard covered in threatening posters with the familiar black spider-like swastika. Bobby felt a chill go down the back of her neck. The street was empty and all the houses were blacked out, like those in England, so all she could make out was a long line of shadows rather than cosy homes. The houses all looked the same, Bobby noticed as they got nearer. They all had rendered fronts with shuttered windows, now closed tight against the cold, the war and prying eyes. Every house in England had vegetables growing in every possible corner but here, the houses butted onto the street, with no pavement between and there was little sign of any gardens. A few window boxes remained but only the straggly residue of an occasional dead geranium tippled over their wooden frames. It was if the inhabitants of the houses had given up any hope of revival for their plants or themselves. Many of the houses had bullet holes in them, a chilling testament to struggles that Bobby did not even want to think about. The men pushed Bobby down into a crouch and led her along the side of the street, indicating to her to keep pressed in against the walls until they approached the house at the end when one man gave an owl hoot and a tiny crack appeared in the doorframe. It opened an inch at a time as they approached and after three low whistles from the man at the front of the group, it opened a few more inches. A woman in a checked pinny was holding the door ajar, rapidly scanning the horizon from side to side. They all sidled through.

A hurried conversation followed in which Bobby realised this was only a stopping-off place and that they would be on their way again. The woman led them to a cellar, first moving a worn rug and then lifting up a large wooden hatch to reveal some roughly hewn steps. The little group trooped down and then two of them started to move some vats of wine. Behind the vats was a doorway, hidden in the gloom. They opened it and signalled for Bobby and Michel to go through it. As they bent down, Michel looked her in the eyes. 'I am so sorry, Bobby, I had the panic and now, I put you in so much danger.' He gave her a quick hug and added, 'But I am not sorry that you are here with me.'

She gave him a squeeze and turned towards the tunnel behind him. Having a real, live brother was going to present its own problems, she thought, ducking her head to avoid the flimsy wood that shored up the passageway. The tunnel smelt freshly dug and was held up with rough wooden struts. There was no room to stand up and Bobby, at five foot eight, found it hard to crawl her way through and constantly banged her head on the roof. She heard scurrying and decided to close her eyes, just feeling her way with her knees rather than seeing what creatures shared this underground escape route with her.

After a few minutes, they emerged behind a barn at the back of the small hamlet. In the moonlight, Bobby looked from right to left. Here there was another street of about ten houses, some showing signs of artillery fire with pitted walls and damaged roofs. One of the men waved his arm to get Bobby and Michel to move quickly from doorway to doorway until they came to one of the houses on the left of the little street. They knocked twice, paused and then knocked again. The door opened a fraction and after the word '*Artistique*' had been uttered as an obvious password, it was opened fully to let the group in.

As the door closed quietly behind them, Michel fell forward into the arms of an older man in faded blue overalls whose large hands embraced the young man's thin frame, hugging him and saying over and over again, '*Mon fils, mon fils.*'

Their French was so rapid, Bobby could not follow it but then the older man stood back to scrutinise Michel from head to foot to see if he was in one piece. Then he turned to her, registering for the first time her auburn hair and similar features to Michel.

He stared and as a result, the other men stared too, for the first time, taking in her appearance.

Michel whispered something to his father and he scanned her face carefully.

The older man moved forward.

'We will speak the English, it is more ... secure,' he said, taking in the three bemused French faces in front of him. 'So, you are the daughter of the Englishman my wife tell me about.'

His face showed little antagonism and Bobby wondered how he could be so calm. His son was not his son and now, here was a girl who was another reminder of a family scandal he surely wanted to forget.

'We will talk in a moment,' he said quietly to her.

'Claudette,' he called into the kitchen from where a smell of rotting vegetables was emanating.

A girl in a faded print dress came into the room. She was around twenty-two and her dark hair was swept up into a bun. She fiddled with this bun now as she spotted Michel for the first time. A blush crept up her face but Michel showed no reaction, only smiling vaguely at her.

'*Bonsoir*, Claudette,' he said, adding the obvious comment, '*Je suis revenu.*'

She nodded. Yes, he had come back and still he did not love her.

The older man went on. '*Claudette, le café, si'il te plaît. Et quelquechose à manger pour Michel et notre invitée.*' The girl looked suspiciously at Bobby and then hurried back to the kitchen to prepare something for their guests to eat. The man turned back to face Bobby and he held out his hand to her. '*Je m'appelle Raoul.*'

She took his hand and shook it as firmly as she could to disguise the shaking. It was huge and calloused and engulfed her hand, but it was warm and gentle.

'*Je m'appelle Bobby.*'

He repeated the word slowly, trying to pronounce it but putting the accent on the last syllable to make it 'Bobbee.'

The other men were shuffling backwards, wanting to be away to fade back into the shadows of the woods.

Raoul led Bobby to an old armchair and then took the men out to the kitchen to see them through the back door.

Bobby called, '*Merci beaucoup,*' to them, not sure how such a normal thank you could offer gratitude to the men who had just risked their lives to bring them to this place.

Michel followed his father and once the door had shut, Bobby heard them talking in the hallway. It was very fast French, but Bobby heard her name several times. She realised Michel was filling his father in on all that had happened since he was scooped up by an English aircraft just a few weeks ago.

Bobby looked around her and sat down on the old, threadbare armchair that was near the fireplace. She found herself relaxing in that room, not because it was warm, it was not, but there was something that made it feel like a haven. It was a narrow room with the remnants of red gingham curtains bordering the black card that had been placed over the windows. The mantlepiece over the stone fireplace held precious items such as a chipped vase and a child's painting of a tree that was curled at the edges and had yellowed with age. Bobby looked at the ashes in the grate. They showed a tiny glow of red that put out hardly any heat. There were stubs of candles that had been lit, giving a tiny glow of light, but the Kerosene lamps on the walls were dusty and showed no evidence of having been used in ages. She tried to work out what it was that made it feel so safe when, in fact, she was in the worst danger she had ever been in. Sitting in the old, tattered armchair with wings that seemed to envelope her, she decided it was the feeling that the room resounded with echoes of this family with which she had somehow become entwined. They had lived here for generations and the ancestors' support emanated from the walls as the changing scenes had played out in the room—wars, peace, children, love and even death had all taken place here and because of that, the house had a permanence that gave her comfort. There was one rocking chair, standing like an oak tree in one corner waiting for its owner, equally as solid and rooted, a low stool and several hard-backed chairs around the table which had a torn lace tablecloth on it. The cloth was clean and, in its day, had been a beautiful piece of work but now its edges were frayed. On a small dark wooden table next to the fireplace was a picture of a beautiful woman with dark hair, curled around her face. Bobby knew it was Nicole. She beamed a smile that showed an openness of spirit that would have tempted the heart of any soldier far from home.

Raoul and Michel came back in and Raoul bolted the front door and then sat on the rocking chair opposite her. He seemed to melt into it and Bobby could hardly see where he ended and the wood began. Michel pulled a three-legged stool up from the other side of the room, but before he sat on it, he adjusted the cardboard that had been stuck on the window behind the faded gingham curtains. He seemed nervous and twitchy and his father put out his hand to help steady him onto the stool.

'There is always danger,' Raoul explained to Bobby. 'You need to be prepared. If anyone comes to the door, you must hide. We will show you in a minute.'

Raoul glanced towards the kitchen. 'We will speak in English so that Claudette . . . she is a good girl but it is better for her if she knows only a little.' The girl's back could just be seen but she had left the door open and Bobby was sure she was listening. Raoul sat down in the rocking chair that moulded to his large shape.

'This house is what we call a "*maison sûre*", a safe house, it is used by people . . . in need. We change them every month. You will stay in the cellar, you should be safe here. We pretend to work with the Germans.'

'Michel has told me a little of what has happened to him and how it is you are here. Now I need to know from you both what you have heard about the latest events here.' He turned to Michel, who looked from his father to Bobby and back again; he was clutching the edge of the stool with his fingers. Raoul stood up and placed a firm hand on the young man's shoulder, nodding to him in encouragement. Michel sat up straighter. He took a deep breath and spoke, haltingly at first but then his voice gained strength.

'I have a job to do. I know there have been problems. I have information for the . . .' he faltered, knowing the word 'resistance' was the same in both languages and glanced towards the kitchen door. 'Friends. There is much to do and I have been given the authority to do it.'

He stopped. He did not want to tell his father anything that would put his life in jeopardy.

'I will arrange a meeting, but what do we do about her?' Raoul sat down again and jerked his head towards Bobby.

'She needs to hide and stay hidden for one week. There is another plane that will come,' Michel replied, gaining confidence as the candles flared in the holders. It was as if being on home turf gave him a strength, or maybe it was the calm control of the man opposite them who had brought him up.

Bobby remembered the rice paper and thought now was as good a time as any to make sure there was no doubt about the importance of Michel's role.

'Your son,' she paused, blushing slightly, 'your . . . er . . . er . . . son . . . has been briefed by the highest authorities to take on this task. It is important for all of us . . . tout le monde,' she said haltingly, realising the French phrase actually meant all of us and, more literally, the whole world. There was a huge power in those three words. She stopped as Raoul leaned forward to gently put his hand on her shoulder this time. There was one issue this large Frenchman wanted to address and then to never mention again.

'Yes, Michel is my son. I know there was a man from England, a man who look like you too, I think, but this is my boy. My wife, she thought I was dead. I was missing for a long time. She tell me that when your father hear his son – your twin – die, they both needed comfort. Now Michel is my comfort.'

Bobby was overcome and felt a sudden need to burst into tears and sob on this strong man's shoulder, but she gulped and took another breath. Raoul's matter-of-factness over her brother's death was such a relief after a lifetime of tiptoeing around the subject with her own family. It was never mentioned at home, even Aunt Agnes avoided it and to hear someone talk about it as if it were a naturally tragic event was liberating.

At that moment, Michel almost fell off the stool.

'I am sorry, Papa. It is all so much . . .'

'Of course, of course, you must eat and then rest. Bobbee and I will talk later.'

He ushered them both into the kitchen where Claudette had placed two earthenware bowls on the table with two spoons. There were no windows except for a rooflight above that was covered with cardboard like all the windows in the house and a few candles were dotted around to relieve the gloom. There was a tiny piece of black, sticky bread placed next to the bowls and the soup looked thin, but there was a dusty bottle of red wine placed in the middle of the table with three glasses.

Bobby thought back to Mrs Hill's farmhouse kitchen full of garden vegetables, milk and fresh eggs. She knew that as a farm, they were able to squirrel away produce while the rest of the village were limited to one egg each a week, dried milk and dried potatoes, but this French kitchen was another story. She glanced at the shelves. There was a tin of chicory, three turnips and a few basic ingredients, but little else. She tucked into her soup but then looked up to see Michel push half of his bread across to his father. His father shook his head but Michel insisted. Bobby looked at the piece of bread she was about to put in her mouth and instead passed it back to Claudette, who looked across at Monsieur Bisset for approval. He gave it and she carefully split it in half, putting some in her pinny pocket to take home the following day for her sick brother and then greedily ate the rest. Bobby's heart sank. This was what occupation was like. She had moaned and groaned at home, but they did not have to expect a knock at the door any minute, have their food taken away from them or live on weak soup. She had a great deal to learn.

Chapter 17

The candle was getting low in the holder by the time the wine had been drunk. Raoul explained to Bobby that she would sleep in the cellar where there was a mattress. The table was moved to one side, a trapdoor was opened and Claudette disappeared down some steps with a rough blanket and a candle and some matches. Bobby wondered if all the houses in France had hidden cellars and hidden holes in walls. Claudette came back and fetched a porcelain chamber pot. At this point she told Bobby to follow her so she could show her to her 'bedroom'. The pot she placed on the floor, next to the mattress, and then put the matches next to the candle on the other side. She shyly left a nightshirt that Bobby suspected belonged to Michel on the top of the blanket, lovingly patting it as she spread it out. Bobby smiled to herself, thanked her and followed the young girl back into the living room. She thought longingly of the overnight bag she had left on the aircraft and it suddenly occurred to her that Gus would have been devastated once he realised he had abandoned her behind enemy lines. She wondered whether he would get into trouble.

Raoul was telling Claudette to go to bed. '*Tu peux aller te coucher maintenant, Claudette. A demain.*'

Claudette nodded goodnight to them all, resting her gaze for a moment on Michel, as if he were a miracle who had returned from the dead and then she climbed the stairs to her attic room. Raoul signalled to Michel that he should also go to bed and the young man wearily dragged his exhausted body up the wooden stairs to his own room.

Raoul settled back into his rocking chair to light his pipe.

'I have just enough tobacco for one pipe a day. It is my luxury,' he smiled at her. Bobby experienced a tingling feeling of being enveloped by his warm welcome.

'How do you speak such good English? It's better than my French,' Bobby asked, curling up in the armchair opposite him.

'I learn it when I am on, as you call it, the run? I was in the *armée*. I fought at Marne – you remember, the allies won that battle, but I was left on the battlefield, almost dead. A bayonet wound in my head, a bullet in my groin, it was only because some Belgian soldier heard me moan, he picks me up and takes me to a doctor in the village nearby. I am very ill with infection for many weeks. I receive treatment from a doctor in the village and, at last, I am a little better but by then, you see, I was a deserter. I could not go home or back to my unit and it was too dangerous to send a letter home – for me and the doctor's family. I hid in his loft. I learned medicine and English from him. He teach me many things and *peut-être*, also some names for the Germans that a lady should not hear.'

Bobby started to laugh but Raoul butted in, suddenly very pleased with himself.

'I think you should be my daughter. I am so used to the red hair for a child, it seems you are part of us here. I am glad you came, even though my son should not have made it happen for you. You are now in such danger.'

'I'll be fine,' Bobby reassured him with a confidence she did not feel. 'I am used to being frightened. I am a pilot for the Air Transport Auxiliary,' she added with a blush of pride.

And with a third of a bottle of wine warming her stomach, there was a comfortable silence between them. Raoul puffed away on his pipe as he took in this information and she watched the flickering of the candle. He did not seem surprised but then again, Bobby reasoned, there were women in France doing much more dangerous things.

'*Alors, ma petite*, tell me about why you fly,' Raoul finally said.

'I have to,' she replied simply. 'It is the only time I am . . . free.'

Bobby started by explaining to him about how she learned to fly so as to be able to spray crops on the farm and how, once the war came, the chance to join the ATA seemed like a dream come true for her. But once she began to talk about how it gave her a chance to show she was as good as any boy, she admitted she had actually done it to prove she could compete with a ghost – her own brother – and maybe earn the respect, if not the love, of her father.

Raoul lit another candle as Bobby realised that once she had started, she could not stop. She told him about Michael, her mother's nervous frailty and her father's remoteness. It seemed nothing could shock this rock of a man. He listened intently as she drifted between French and English and encouraged her with questions and understanding. He wanted to know all about her life in England and the farm where she was brought up. She talked about Agnes and Archie, the animals on the farm and Harriet and Gus. She described the little plot next to the barn and the moment she had shared with Michel there. She even told him about Boy, something she had never told anyone outside the family.

'You see, when I first saw a shadow, I felt something so strong I couldn't put a name to it, but it was as if my twin was there next to me. I was half a person but when I created Boy I felt whole again – as if it were not really my fault that Michael had died and I had lived. And then when Michel came to our house,' her eyes suddenly lit up, 'it's not quite the same, but somehow, I feel a part of *my* Michael has come back to life, just like my mother does. I have found a brother.

'And now,' she added shyly, looking over at his encouraging, sympathetic face, 'I don't know why, but I feel, I have found you too.'

To her embarrassment, she realised she had started to cry and then the tears flowed, her shoulders shook and it seemed that the guilt she had carried for years, the grief of the family and the responsibility for always being the strong one, slowly ebbed out to be absorbed by the man sitting opposite her, into the bare wooden floors, the peeling wallpaper and away up the cold chimney into the starlit night in the north of France. She felt liberated.

Raoul reached over and put his hand over hers. He got up, put his pipe down and said, 'You see, I was right, we are your family too. *Eh bien, ma petite.* You are so tired, you should rest.'

He picked up a candle and led her towards the wooden steps to the cellar. 'Call me when you are ready and I will bring down another candle,' Raoul said.

Bobby put on the nightshirt and flapped her arms up and down. She giggled at the absurdity of her situation. *That wine must have gone to my head,* she thought. She should have been back at base, maybe having a cosy drink with Gus in the local pub but instead she was in the north of France, an enemy-occupied country, being harboured by a key figure in the Resistance. It all seemed somewhat ludicrous and yet, she had to admit, exciting.

She called out to Raoul and he made his way down, holding a candle.

As Bobby lay down, suddenly exhausted, Raoul covered her with the rough blanket. He pushed her hair out of her eyes and for the first time ever, Bobby felt safe, secure and totally accepted. She closed her eyes, feeling his dry, rough hand gently stroke her hair.

* * *

Raoul stayed with her until he thought she was asleep then he moved towards the steps again. He paused to look back at the girl curled up on the mattress. He had seen men destroyed and sobbing on his kitchen table, he had seen his wife die in the bed upstairs and he had seen neighbours dragged screaming from their own doorways but the sight of that young woman, exhausted but so brave, brought him to tears quicker than he could have ever imagined.

He covered the trapdoor with a rag rug and pulled the table back over while he pondered on another war that again was bringing him so many unexpected experiences. He thought he had been through every possible emotion in 1918 at the sight of the red-haired child by his wife's side at the front door when he finally made it home. But after a week of Gallic anger, where he paced furiously up and down the yard at the back of the house, he tried to put himself in his wife's position. She had believed he was dead. The last she had heard was that he had 'died' on the field at the Battle of Marne and it had been a long silence before he had been able to tell her he was alive. Isolated in another country, Raoul's home life in Normandy began to feel like another world and while pacing up and down outside the house, it occurred to him that Nicole had been plunged into grief believing her husband had died and could perhaps be forgiven for reaching out to this man for comfort. But there was one more nagging memory that he could not, in all conscience, ignore. The young maid at the Belgian doctor's had been fascinated by the tall Frenchman and, one cold night, she had come to find him in the loft where he lived. Her warm voluptuous body had been too tempting to resist and there followed a liaison that continued for months until she contracted pneumonia. Raoul had sobbed his heart out the night she died, burying his head into the wet straw that served as a pillow during the nights of passion that he had shared with the young girl. He was never sure whether it was grief at her death or the final admittance that he had broken his wedding vows that made the tears flow so freely. He begged *Le Bon Dieu* for forgiveness but when he came home to find a strange little boy in his house, to begin with, he saw it as punishment for his betrayal.

His resentment was appeased by his wife's unbridled joy at seeing him again and once the boy was told that this strange man was his papa, the boy's adoration made him realise he had been granted a very special gift. Shot in the groin, he knew he had no chance of having any children, so Michel had been like an unexpected treasure to him and he decided he was not going to waste time in anger and bitterness. From that moment, he had never doubted he was, in all but creation, Michel's father. It was he who had nursed him through measles, he, Raoul, who had advised him on how to deal with bullies at school when they made fun of his red hair and it was he who had explained to the cringingly embarrassed young man, about girls.

Oh, yes, he thought, as he climbed into his rough, straw bed, it was he, not this cold man in England, who was the true father of Michel and now he had a young woman who was a part of Michel to wrap in his safe arms as well. He realised he was prepared to give his life to get her safely home to England.

Chapter 18

Bobby was woken by a loud banging on the door upstairs. For a moment, she could not remember where she was and there was no light in the cellar to help her, but then she felt the cold stone floor next to her and the events of the previous night came back. Her head thumped from the effects of the wine but not as hard as her heart as she listened to a loud voice above barking orders.

The voice was yelling something in German but Raoul answered in a calm, quiet voice. She heard heavy boots pounding over the floorboards above her head and held her breath.

She dared not move in case a noise gave away her presence. She heard some pots clanging in the kitchen and the boots march back over the floorboards above and then there was silence.

In a heart-stopping moment Bobby heard the rug being moved and the table scratching back. She closed her eyes and thought of her parents, safe in Norfolk and ignorant of her plight. They had already lost one child, surely they were not about to lose the other? She stood up, shaking, partly because of the cold and partly because of terror. Was this to be her last moment of life before she was dragged out into the street and shot?

'Bobbee, Bobbee, are you there?'

Raoul's voice came down the steps.

'Yes,' she replied weakly.

'It is OK, it is OK.'

Bobby's knees gave way and she fell back down onto the mattress, wondering how she could ever have thought this was an exciting adventure.

Raoul and Michel appeared, haloed in the light from the trap door as they peered anxiously down.

'Are you OK?'

'I think so. Is it safe?'

'Yes, he has gone,' Raoul said. 'They come regularly to take our food and we have to give them what we have, but it was good Michel was here, when he came last week, the soldier wanted to know where Michel was and I had to say he was ill with a fever. Something very catching,' he smiled.

'So you see, this week I am pale and thin and that is good,' Michel added, with a grin that lit up his pallid face. He went on, 'My father is a doctor so sometimes he is able to treat the Germans. It means they leave us alone.'

'Here is an old dress of . . .' Raoul paused, lovingly fingering the faded print frock in his hands, 'my wife's. You can get dressed and then you may come up for the breakfast. We have some bread hidden that the Germans do not know of,' Raoul added.

Their heads popped back out of the trap door and Bobby gave a huge sigh of relief, reaching for the clothes. This was going to be a very long week.

Minutes later, Bobby emerged from the cellar. Michel was standing by the window next to the front door, keeping guard, and she was ushered into the kitchen where no one could see her. Raoul drew in a sharp breath as he caught sight of Bobby in his wife's dress and then motioned to Claudette to serve the coffee.

'It is chicory, it is terrible,' Michel said. Claudette handed him a chipped cup. For a moment, the two young people shared a shy smile. Claudette let her hand linger for a second under his fingers but by now, Michel was looking with disgust at the weak liquid in the cup. She walked away with her shoulders slumped.

He pulled a face towards Bobby. 'We have – had – such good coffee. But now . . .'

'It will end, all this,' Raoul told him. 'We thought the last one would never end, and it did.'

'Yes, but will we ever be free again?' Michel asked.

It was a question that hung in the air between them.

Michel went back to his post at the window. His eyes narrowed when he saw their neighbour, Paul Cloret, walking up the street, glancing in windows. He drew back from sight but was puzzled. Monsieur Cloret had been a neighbour for years, he and his wife, Simone, had helped Raoul when Nicole was ill but recently, Cloret had been more withdrawn and become far too nosy for Michel's liking. Michel made a mental note to make some checks.

Bobby sipped on her coffee and munched on the tiny piece of stale bread, ignoring the hunger pangs in her stomach. She suddenly had a vision of hot porridge and a mug of tea, but such thoughts were not helpful, she crossly told her brain. Looking around the kitchen, she tried to imagine it when Raoul and Nicole were just married. Did he ever twirl her round the pine table in a waltz, she wondered? She could imagine the fresh-faced Nicole as being a good dancer and Raoul certainly looked like someone who would have had a romantic twinkle in his eye. The kitchen would have been a warm, cosy place, she decided, looking over at the now cold range in the corner. Bobby closed her eyes and thought of the kitchen at home, the most welcoming room in the house, with Mrs Hill bustling around and Aunt Agnes giving her mother instructions. A feeling of homesickness overwhelmed her, and she made a promise to herself that when, and if, she ever got home, she would make all her family face their demons and they would tackle the future together as a team; something they had never been.

In the meantime, she had six days to get through. She would have to occupy herself for hours in the house, but apart from a brief time out of the cellar for meals while Michel kept watch on the street at the window, she would have to stay hidden until after curfew. Never one to waste a moment, Bobby's brain was already forging a plan to mentally commit to memory every single aircraft she had ever flown and every aeroplane she was yet to fly to prepare for her next level of ability with the ATA. She also decided she would use the time to practice her French.

Claudette bustled around behind her, glancing from time to time between the foreign interloper and Michel in the living room. Bobby was not fooled for one minute by Claudette's lowered eyes and once Raoul had gone to talk to Michel, she decided she would tackle the girl's suspicions head-on. She took the tea towel from Claudette's hands and started to wipe up the dishes, smiling at her.

Claudette glared at her but Bobby started to chatter on as naturally as she could in her rusty French. She could not put the girl at risk so she avoided any details, but she could put her mind at rest that she was not a threat for Michel's affections, so she told her that she was related to him through a family in England and that he was like a brother to her. The young Frenchwoman's face cleared and she took a dried plate from Bobby's hand with a beaming smile. She did not question how the relationship came about, all she cared about was that this English girl was not a romantic rival after all.

By the time Michel and Raoul came back into the room, Claudette was chattering excitedly to Bobby like a long-lost friend.

'You must hide now, Bobbee,' Raoul said, steering her towards the cellar trap door.

Bobby nodded and went without comment.

Four hours later, she was bored to tears. She had mentally been through every dial and switch on five aeroplanes, translating them all in her head into French. Forced to use the porcelain pot, which she had tried to put out of sight in the corner of the room, she paced up and down and did some press ups to keep warm. It made her think of Christine, the athletic girl who always did exercises in the restroom in Hamble and she wondered what they would all think if they knew she was in France. The thought of Sally's indignation at being left out, in particular, made her smile. Bobby had been in France only a couple of days but already she felt a million miles away from her life as an ATA pilot.

She was about to start sit-ups, when she heard footsteps and a murmured conversation above her. As always, she stood looking up towards the rafters as if they would give her a clue as to what was happening above her but all she could do was wait.

Finally, she heard the rug being pulled back.

A small child was guided down the steps. It was a young girl of about eight with dark, lank hair. Her coat was torn and tattered and her shoes were muddy, but the first thing Bobby noticed was a big yellow star of David with the word '*Juif*' on the left-hand side of her coat.

Her stomach turned over. This child was a Jew.

Raoul came down the steps behind the child.

'This is Elizé. She is going to stay here for a while.'

Bobby smiled reassuringly at the child, who looked absolutely terrified.

'*Bonjour, ma petite*,' she said crouching down next to her.

The child looked at Raoul.

'It is OK,' he said in English. 'Bobby is one of us.'

'Does she speak English?' Bobby asked, surprised.

'Yes, her father was English. Her mother is French but she speaks both languages fluently.' He indicated with a shake of his head that she should not enquire any further and Bobby took his lead.

'So, we are going to be roommates,' she said to the little girl.

She took the child's hand and led her over to the mattress.

'Which side do you like?'

Elizé looked up through long, wet eyelashes. Her eyes were dull and lifeless.

'Well, never mind, you can choose later. I don't mind,' Bobby told her.

Claudette appeared at the top of the steps and an already familiar smell permeated the cellar. She held a dish and a spoon. Bobby thought she would remember the smell of turnip soup for the rest of her life. She moved forward to take the bowl and gently passed it over to the little girl, who paused for a moment and, ignoring the spoon, slurped it hurriedly straight from the bowl. Drops of it fell to either side of her mouth and she licked them eagerly.

Claudette came down with a valuable piece of bread, and slowly fed it to the child. Bobby moved over to Raoul, who whispered, 'Her father was shot as an alien in front of her eyes two months ago and this morning, her mother is taken. As she is herded onto the railway trucks, she throw Elizé into the arms of one of ours, a woman who put a blanket over the badge and claims she is her daughter. The child is all alone. We are trying to get her to safety but she has to stay here for a while.'

The hairs on the back of Bobby's neck seemed to stand on end. She looked over at the small, pathetic figure and clutched at her heart with her hand, as if trying to protect it from the piercing pain that Raoul's words had just inflicted on her. She remembered with a chill the newsreels suggesting that Jews were being sent to camps. It had seemed so far-fetched she had been sceptical but here was a child who was a victim of a regime whose brutality exceeded anything people at home could contemplate.

The rest of the morning, Bobby did everything she could to make the child feel more comfortable, but she had little experience of children and suspected she was doing everything wrong. She wished she had played more with Archie's nephews and nieces but in her determination to fly, she had had little time for anyone else. Bobby was beginning to suspect that this week in France was going to change her more deeply than anything she had ever done. All she had to do was survive it.

Chapter 19

Edward Turner was usually a very mild-mannered man, always courteous and kind, but for the past few days, Mavis Arbuckle, his secretary, had witnessed an impatience and, if she did not know him to be a consummate professional, she would say, an anger in his manner. Mavis listened to his brusque voice on the intercom and grabbed her pencil and notepad to go and knock on the panelled door to his War Office room on the corner of Horse Guards Avenue.

'Yes, sir?' she said, looking at the bent head in front of her. Edward was seated at his desk, fiddling with his tortoiseshell fountain pen. He was studying some papers in front of him, his forehead furrowed into a frown. He waved his hand at Mavis to get her to sit down and she sat with her pencil poised over her notebook, calmly waiting.

Several minutes of silence passed while Mavis studied the man she had worked for over the last four years. To begin with, she had thought him cold and, to be honest, a bit slow, but she very soon reappraised her opinion of him. The first month as his secretary had led her to believe he had been elbowed into a desk job to keep him out of harm's way but then she had seen him galvanise into action during the evacuation of Dunkirk and she began to discover that his role in the War Office was of a much deeper importance than many people knew. She also suspected that before his role in Whitehall, he had been an operative out in the field. He always looked so out of place behind a desk, like a coiled spring desperate to unwind. His decisiveness – and inventiveness – during that Dunkirk week had taken her by surprise. She knew from her years with the Secret Service that his knowledge came from personal experience of being on the ground. She also knew that Edward was frequently consulted by the Foreign Secretary, Anthony Eden, who would call him in when he wanted to know what might be happening with intelligence information. Once Dunkirk was over, Mavis Arbuckle was fully briefed about her boss's true role. From that day, Mavis had watched Edward from the sidelines and had finally acknowledged, she would follow him to the ends of the earth.

'Take a letter, will you, Miss Arbuckle, to be sent immediately,' Edward finally said. 'Obviously, it's top secret,' he added unnecessarily. 'To Group Captain Patrick Markham, you know the address. Dear Patrick, I have a particular interest in a mission that left T . . . on twentieth inst. under your command. I would be grateful if you could inform me of any developments. Please advise at your earliest convenience. Give my regards to Marjorie. Yours etc,'

Mavis waited but it seemed her boss had gone into a trance, staring out of the windows of the trapezium shaped Whitehall building at one of the four distinctive domes.

'Is that all, sir?'

'Yes, yes, sorry. Take it for coding if you would, and oh, a cup of tea might be nice.'

Mavis hurried out of the room. She kept her notebook with her for security while she made the tea but while the urn got back up to boiling point, she pondered what it was that was bothering Edward. She knew he was distracted and wondered whether it was simply the pressures of war work or whether there was something else troubling him. She had witnessed the young man flick off the attentions of women at the War Office parties and she had given up hope of ever seeing him succumb to the wiles of the female sex, but having watched her nephews grow up, her sixth sense picked something up in Edward's demeanour. She racked her brains to think which woman might have finally ignited his interest but there were no phone calls or letters that came through the office that might have given her a hint. She wondered whether the letter she was about to type held a key to Edward's distraction. She peered over her pince-nez at the cup and saucer in front of her and added the condensed milk. She might try to find him a nice biscuit, she decided.

Edward paced up and down his office. He glanced back at the pile of papers on his desk. Anthony Eden had asked for that report on the situation in Changi prisoner of war camp in Singapore by the morning and he had to study the deeply disturbing reports that were coming in from the areas near Auschwitz. He really needed to concentrate but his imagination was being fuelled by disturbing reports from France. The Special Operations Executive on the ground in Normandy had used the usual complex messaging network to inform them that a small Jewish child had been unexpectedly delivered to the safe house where he knew Bobby was being held. With the normal escape routes jeopardised, he was concerned about the increased danger that it put on the Bisset family and, of course, Bobby. He looked at the papers in front of him and focused on the ones marked 'Top Priority' but as soon as his office day ended, he raced back to his bachelor flat in Kensington to try to formulate a plan that might help.

He had played rugby against Malvern School where Patrick Markham was a pupil many times and they had since met at functions at Whitehall. The two men got on well and he had been invited to luncheon at the Markham's home on several occasions following the setting up of 161 Squadron, which was such a top secret exercise that many of his colleagues in the War Office did not even know of its existence. He knew that Markham had appreciated his input on the logistics and secrecy of the operation and there was a mutual respect that had grown between them to such an extent that when Markham had had a personal dilemma several years ago, he had called on Edward for some impartial advice. They now considered each other to be friends and Edward decided if anyone could facilitate him to help Bobby, it would be Markham. Edward was justifying his interest in the flight that took Bobby to France because of his job but he was disturbed to discover that his interest in her welfare was becoming anything but professional.

The troubled civil servant marched each evening along the London streets, thumping his highly-polished shoes on the tarmac. He was in a bad mood, unable to understand why he suddenly felt responsible for this woman. He had avoided all romantic entanglement into his early thirties, but for some reason, the sight of Bobby with head held high and a determination do her duty, walking slowly down that corridor in Hamble had unleashed an urgent desire to enfold her in his arms and hold her safe. There had to be a way he could call in a favour from Markham.

* * *

Three hours away by road in Bedfordshire, another young man was having equally troubling thoughts. Gus Prince was waiting for his orders for the next drop off and was having a cigarette outside the main building at Tempsford. He was increasingly busy delivering and picking up SOE agents, invariably known as 'Janes' and 'Joes' regardless of their code names. Many of them were young women and he felt sorry for them, knowing the clandestine life they were about to take up. One looked remarkably like that difficult girl from primary school, Marie, he thought, but he asked no questions and she offered no information. Some had family in France and they were all expected to speak the language fluently so they could uncover vital information and send it back to Britain. Every time he took one over, he looked at their pale, young faces and wondered whether they would ever set foot on British soil again.

The adrenalin kept him focused while he was flying but as soon as the concentration was no longer needed, he felt a knot in his stomach that would take him a moment to identify as worry. As a pilot, he had learned to be calm under pressure and he approached his job with professionalism, but that professionalism seemed to fly out of the window at three o'clock in the morning when he woke in a cold sweat envisioning a young woman with auburn hair facing an execution squad in a narrow French street. He had returned from the mission feeling a complete failure, knowing he had let Bobby down, but his superiors applauded his actions, more concerned about getting a pilot – and his aircraft – back in one piece rather than worrying about an ATA girl who, if she kept her head, would be picked up again in a week.

Unable to mention the incident to anyone, Gus reasoned that as he would be going back in a week – well, five days, four hours and ten minutes to be exact, he sadly realised he knew the precise time – there was no need to worry; she would be safe back in Blighty before anyone knew she had gone. Secrecy was so much part of the war that it had become second nature but that did not help his sleep patterns when all sorts of dire situations presented themselves to him in nightmares.

'Hello Prince,' Group Captain Patrick Markham came out of his office and was about to pass Gus when he halted. 'Got a light?'

'Yes, of course, sir,' Gus saluted and then leaned over with a match to light his commander's cigarette.

'You did the Normandy mission, didn't you?'

'Yessir.'

'I know we've done the debrief with you, but ...' Markham paused and looked round to check no one was listening.

'The girl you lost there, think she's capable of keeping her head?'

Gus winced at the word 'lost' and felt a huge guilt engulf him.

'I'm sorry, I didn't mean lost,' Markham said with a sudden wave of sympathy. He knew the circumstances had left Gus no choice. 'I just wondered whether you think she's got the balls to survive over there and not do anything stupid.'

It was a question Gus had turned over and over in his head but now, facing his commanding officer, he felt a huge pride for the girl he had known since childhood, the one who had dealt with the school bullies, saved Harriet from endless scrapes and had flown upwards of fifty different aircraft.

'Yes, I do, sir. If anyone can survive, it's Roberta Hollis, and she won't give anything away, either. She's the strongest woman I know.'

Markham looked sideways at the young pilot and smiled to himself. He had not been fooled for one minute by Edward Turner's sudden interest in an unplanned drop-off in Normandy. Now here was another one. She must be quite a girl if she had ensnared Prince and, if his suspicions were correct, his old friend Turner, he thought.

He stubbed out his cigarette under his heel. 'Well, let's hope you're right and she doesn't get in harm's way.'

Chapter 20

Bobby was getting increasingly worried about Elizé. The little girl sat for hours on the corner of the mattress, her knees tucked up and her arms huddled around them. She hardly spoke, ate the turnip soup without seeming to taste – which Bobby conceded, could be a blessing – and just swayed gently backwards and forwards.

The hours passed slowly. Bobby tried to interest the girl in every game she had ever played in her isolated childhood, but Elizé's eyes just looked through her. Eventually, after three days, Bobby gave up and went back to trying to make notes on British planes for her next test. She had asked for paper and a pencil, but she also kept the matches close to hand so she could burn her notes if there was any sense of a threat from upstairs. The last thing she wanted to do was to give the Germans information about British aircraft.

She was absorbed in her task, lying on the mattress, when she felt a shadow above her.

'What are you doing?'

She looked up in surprise to see Elizé staring at the diagram of a Wellington she had drawn on the paper.

'It's an aeroplane,' she said gently.

'It's big,' Elizé said.

'Yes, it's enormous. Let me show you.'

Bobby sat up and made a space next to her and the girl warily sat down.

'You see, it has wings that are bigger than this house and it takes six people to fly it. But because I deliver aircraft, I would fly it on my own.'

Bobby could not keep the pride out of her voice.

'It's called a Wellington, has huge twin engines and when they start up, you can't hear yourself think, it's so loud,' she went on, warming to her favourite subject. 'It's one of the huge bomber planes that are making such a difference to this war. Did you hear about the Lancasters that bombed the dams in the Ruhr Valley? It was when the bombs were made to bounce along the water and then into the dams.'

Elizé shook her head. Newspapers were controlled by the Germans and radios were banned in France.

'How?' she asked.

Bobby picked up her pencil and started to draw a diagram, explaining how the Mohne and Edersee Dams were breached, causing catastrophic flooding of the Ruhr Valley and of villages in the Eder Valley but the child had stopped listening. She was just looking enviously at the pencil in Bobby's hand.

Bobby looked at the child's intent face, then she turned the paper over and passed it to her. 'Would you like to draw?' The girl took the pencil and Bobby watched closely. Elizé bent her head and bit her lip in concentration. She drew a head and then put some hair round it, then gradually a woman's face emerged. Bobby took a sharp intake of breath; this child was seriously talented. She moved away to give her some space, curling up on the other side of the room on an old blanket to watch from afar.

She knew that Elizé had been born in about 1936 so most of her life had been spent as an unwilling witness to the second world war of the century. It seemed so unfair that her childhood was being devastated, particularly that her religion was putting her at such huge risk, marking her out as alien. The situation with the Jewish people had consisted mainly of just rumours in Britain, but there was a growing unease about what was happening to them. And now, in front of her, was an innocent victim whose life had been blasted by an intolerance that was so strange to Bobby. She had been brought up in the Church of England but on the farm, some of the farmhands were Catholic and Rachel, the maid, was Jewish. There had never been any problem as to which God everyone worshipped and for all her family's faults, Bobby thought, intolerance of other religions was not one of them and, as a result, this hatred of other people's beliefs was something she did not understand.

There had been few clues about the traumatic childhood Elizé had suffered so far but Bobby knew that she was witnessing a moment of a vital bond being recreated on paper between a daughter and her mother. She wanted to reach out to Elizé, feeling her isolation and loneliness and identifying with it but even she could not imagine the horrors that would haunt Elizé's sleep for the rest of her life. To see your own father killed and your mother dragged off onto a cattle train was so far removed from anything Bobby had ever experienced, all she could do was send waves of compassion across the dank cellar and hope that some of them reached the child.

Bobby had never been one to feel sorry for herself, even though she often caught Aunt Agnes, Archie and sometimes Mrs Hill and Rachel looking at her with pity, but she had always managed to exist as an entity, content with her own company and not needing anyone else. But the longing to help this little girl gave her such a strong feeling of empathy, it brought her up with a jolt.

It reminded her a little of her affection for Harriet, whose need for love had eventually broken through the barrier she had erected around herself, but this child was smashing that barrier into tiny little pieces and it left her breathless. She longed to envelop the child in her arms and protect her from all harm, which, she reasoned, considering they were both fugitives hiding in a French Resistance house behind enemy lines, was not going to be an easy task.

They emerged from the cellar once it was dark, the curtains were closed and the windows shuttered. Michel kept watch on the street outside while they had their meal. His private concerns about Paul Cloret had intensified and he was having him watched. To have an informer living next door was a risk the Bisset family could not afford to take. Michel peered up and down the road, but all was quiet except for the sound of Claudette's wooden shoes on the kitchen floor as she prepared the meagre evening meal. With a shortage of rubber, the French people had started to nail wood to the bottom of their shoes and Bobby had soon learned to recognise the clomp, clomp of the young woman's feet on the floor above her cellar bedroom and had even started to find it comforting. Everyone was limited to 1,200 calories a day but for once, there was some fatty meat on the table and it was a rare treat for them all. Claudette was struggling to find food with any nutrition in it so she had been growing rhubarb in a tub in the back yard but last week, the government had warned that it contained oxalic acid and should not be eaten, so she had been at her wits' end about what to give everyone, particularly with two extra, unexplainable mouths to feed. She would trail around the little shops in the village, queueing for hours, often in vain, but this morning, her patience had enabled her to buy some meat and black bread and she had even managed to cajole some pears out of an elderly neighbour with a depleted orchard. Claudette had returned triumphant and had been proudly slow-stewing the meat all afternoon to try to soften its sinewy flesh.

'We normally find some food on *le marché noir*,' Raoul explained, doling out the meat with pride, 'but while we have *des invitées*' – he grinned at his two guests – 'maybe not at the moment, huh?'

Bobby was being torn apart by guilt at the inconvenience and risks this family were taking on her behalf and looked across at him with a frown. She opened her mouth to speak.

'*Mais*, now I have my big family, and it is good,' he carried on, cutting across her.

'He's actually enjoying this,' she thought, suddenly taking in his beaming face as he looked from Elizé to Bobby, over to Michel and then at Claudette, who was proudly bringing in a large platter of rare potatoes she had been saving for just such a treat.

It occurred to Bobby that having all his charges to worry about had given Raoul a way to cope with the grief of losing his wife and that he welcomed his extra 'guests' after Michel's unexpected stay in England had left him and Claudette alone rattling around in this large, old-fashioned terraced house.

Raoul grinned around at the full table with satisfaction and reached for the salt dish before remembering it was not there. Salt was just one more treat they had to manage without. He shrugged.

Chapter 21

Edward had thought about asking for the War Office car to take him to Tempsford but he decided in the end to take the train and not to use a travel warrant but to pay for it himself. This was a trip that did not need to be traced in any documentation.

He told a puzzled Miss Arbuckle that he would be out for the day, tucked *The Times* under his arm, picked up his bowler hat from the hat stand and headed off to the station. He was not allowed to work on the train, that was too risky, but he was so looking forward to being out of London and maybe forgetting for a moment that there was a war on. It was late March 1944 and things were on a knife-edge in the battle against Hitler. Only yesterday, Edward had received details of an attack on Monte Cassino and the Allies had landed at Anzio but the death tolls everywhere were high, both in Europe and the rest of the world. The Allies were growing more determined than ever and there were plans for an invasion in June but Operation Overlord, as it was called, was giving him and all his colleagues nightmares, as they tried to work through probability factors more than three months in advance. Edward suspected it would all ultimately depend on the weather, but he had been putting all his concentration into making sure the logistics would work to get enough troops to land without the Germans realising they were there.

Edward rushed along the pavement, brushing his floppy fringe out of his eyes. He was completely discombobulated. It was a great word, he decided, and described exactly how he felt. Throughout Eton and Cambridge, he had been in complete control, focusing his sights on a future where he could make a difference. A tall, good-looking man, he was pursued by a succession of hopeful socialites. He dated some of them but never lost his heart. He joined the best societies and clubs and made important contacts. He toyed with the idea of politics but when he was approached by a man in a bowler hat at the entrance to the University Library, he knew he was being targeted for a career that would be fascinating but would mean he could never be completely honest with anyone again. He got an excellent degree, became a competent tennis player, a good sailor and could balance a crystal sherry glass on a small, hors d'oeuvres plate – all necessary attributes of a member of the Secret Intelligence Service who wanted to fit in with people of influence.

He had been sent out into the field as a 'special operative' and had spent some fraught pre-war years in Germany and the Netherlands. He had survived many serious situations, barely escaping with his life on occasions, but the adrenalin and the thrill was something he could not recreate in the endless strategy meetings he was forced to suffer back in London. His quick mind had allowed him a chance to rocket up the ranks in the War Office and he had found it quite easy to compartmentalise his thoughts and develop a slightly awkward persona so that people did not suspect how intricate his work really was. It did not concern Edward that people thought he was a slow, ponderous type in a pin-striped suit, it was a small price to pay for keeping his work secret.

But today was a day just for him. He was thirty-two years of age and his parents had despaired of him ever finding a wife, which is why his father and Andrew Hollis had dreamed up the ridiculous idea that he and some girl should get hitched. That, however, he acknowledged, was before Roberta Hollis, with her mane of glorious auburn hair, burst into his life. Not long after he had met her, he found himself completely blown off course and foundering on the rocks. The sailing analogies suited his situation, he thought, putting his head down against the bitter wind. He felt as if he was being buffeted through waves and tossed and turned in a maelstrom.

'I was doing fine in this war,' he muttered to himself, heading down to the Underground, 'and then she goes and gets herself dropped in the wrong place at the wrong time. Oh, for heaven's sake . . .'

A woman looked up at him in surprise.

'Sorry, just thinking out loud.'

She pointed to a poster that warned 'Careless talk costs lives' with a sanctimonious nod of her head at him.

'I know,' he said, smiling initially at the irony of the telling off – to him, of all people – but the moment shook him. He had always been so good at disguise and subterfuge, but this smouldering passion was shaking him out of his comfort zone. He was letting down his guard.

Once at Kings Cross, he bought his train ticket. Everywhere along the platform there were signs asking whether the journey was necessary. Edward felt he could not quite answer that question truthfully, so to salve his conscience a little, he immediately gave up his seat to a serviceman and stood, wobbling between unnamed stations on the rattling branch line, working out his strategy. With no identifying signs, like everyone else in the carriage, he had to concentrate to count the number of stations. He had organised to meet his friend, Markham, for an old pals' luncheon but he had an agenda all of his own. With a plan in his head, he went back to looking at *The Times* crossword but, somehow, he found it hard to concentrate.

* * *

'Edward, do come in,' Group Captain Patrick Markham got up from behind his desk and moved round it to greet his visitor. 'How are you, old chap?'

'Fine, fine thank you.'

The two men swapped niceties and then Markham closed his papers and looked at his watch. He had been in since five so he told his secretary he was taking a break and suggested they should retire to The Thornton Arms for a bite to eat.

Edward suddenly realised he was very hungry. Always a man with a healthy appetite, his stomach had been so churned up over the past few days that he had found it hard to eat. He cursed Bobby Hollis gently in his head.

The two men found a cosy corner at the back of the pub where there was no chance of being overheard and nursing their pints, they whispered intently, catching up with a judiciously edited version of each other's war in recent months.

Eventually, Markham put down his pint and faced Edward.

'So, lovely as it is to see you, Old Man, spill the beans. What is it you want?'

'Let's go outside,' Edward replied, the memory of the woman in the tube coming back to him. 'We can't talk here.'

Once outside, away from the pub, he blurted out, 'I want to go to France on the pick-up of the English woman.'

'You too? I thought so,' Markham replied mysteriously.

Edward looked up, a horrible suspicion forming in his mind. Was there someone else in Bobby Hollis's life?

'What do you mean?' he said sharply.

'Oh nothing, just that RAF pilot who did the drop looked just as forlorn as you. He was desperate to go back and rescue her too.'

Edward felt a searing jealousy rip through him. He thought back to the smiling photograph of the good-looking RAF pilot he had seen on Gus Prince's file. He had noticed they had been at school together but had failed to attach any significance to that fact. He cursed his stupidity. He was supposed to be trained in looking for possible scenarios and nuances.

'Anyway,' Markham was saying, 'you can't. It's absolutely impossible.'

'There must be a way,' Edward insisted.

'No, there isn't. What's happening to you Edward? Are you going mad?'

Edward pondered this for a moment. 'I think I may be. I can't sit here and do nothing.'

He looked so uncharacteristically pathetic that Markham patted his shoulder in an embarrassed show of affection.

'I'll order us both a sandwich at the bar. I think it's Spam – just for a change.'

By the time Patrick returned, Edward had pulled himself together and he stood up straight. 'Sorry, Old Boy, that was a ridiculous thing to say. Just forget I ever suggested it.'

'Yes, of course,' Markham replied with a smile. 'But only a man in love would think of it.'

Edward looked up with a jolt. 'In love? Don't be ridiculous.'

'Look, Edward, I've known you for a long time now. You saw me through that difficult business before I married Marjorie, and I've always known you to be a sober, sensible chap, but the Edward I'm seeing before me has been very rattled. It has to be a woman.'

Edward stared down at his shiny shoes. *Is this what it had come to?* he wondered to himself. *Have I taken leave of my senses? Would I have risked my career, even the security of a mission just to fly in like some knight on a white charger? Am I so eaten up with jealousy that I can't bear another man to be the one to save her?*

'I just needed to be the one to get her back to safety,' he said out loud to his old friend.

'Edward, I suspect you have more experience than even I know, but can you fly?' Markham lowered his voice but his tone brooked no argument. 'I mean, are you capable of taking off and landing without lights? Are you able to navigate at low altitudes in a foreign country – and avoid flak at the same time?'

Edward's shoulders slumped. He hated feeling this useless.

Markham relented. 'She will be safe in a cellar somewhere, being kept well out of harm's way. As long as she does nothing stupid, she will be safe. Let's go and get that sandwich and another pint.

Chapter 22

At that moment, Roberta Hollis was crouched in a Normandy street, trying to avoid capture by a platoon of German soldiers who were standing on a street corner, just yards away.

She had not intended to come out, but the house had been quiet for two days. She and Elizé were starving and there was no sign of Raoul, Michel or Claudette. The supplies of water and bread in the cellar had run out that morning and by two o'clock in the afternoon she decided she had to go and find something to eat. She had emerged, nervously, from the cellar, pleading with the frightened Elizé to stay put while she made some investigations. She found a kitchen that looked as if Claudette had tidied everything before she left but there was no food. Bobby was used to the men disappearing for hours on end without explanation, but they had been gone for so long. She was worried and could not even contemplate what she and Elizé would do if they did not come back.

'First things first,' she told herself and went as silently as she could from the kitchen to the outhouse where some supplies were kept. She was examining the paltry stores of food when she heard the front door click.

Bobby froze and then edged her way back into the house, looking anxiously into every corner, expecting to see German boots waiting for her. There was nothing except ... except, she realised with a panic, the cellar trap door behind her had been pushed back and left open.

She nervously peered over into the dark abyss below.

'Elizé? Elizé?' she whispered. There was no reply. With her eyes, she followed the route from the cellar to the front door and let out the first swear words of her life.

'Bloody hell, where's she gone?'

She peered out of a crack in the doorway to the street. It was all quiet. She looked from side to side and just glimpsed the hem of a child's dark brown dress heading round the next corner.

Bobby moved slowly along the street, dodging in and out of doorways. She was absolutely terrified, more for Elizé than for herself, but she also knew that she was putting the whole Bisset family at risk, never mind the local resistance network.

I can't think of that just now, she told herself, all her ATA training of calmness under pressure coming to the fore. *I just have to get Elizé back.*

She mentally thanked Claudette for having the fore-sight to cut off the 'Juif' sign and star from Elizé's coat. They had burned it ceremoniously on the second night. Elizé was a 'nobody' and hopefully, that would save her life, as long as she was taken for a random French child and did nothing to draw attention to herself.

When Bobby got to the end of the street, she spotted Elizé standing dumbstruck looking at the backs of a group of German soldiers by the marketplace. They were laugh-ing and joking and passing round a cigarette.

She was about to hiss a warning to Elizé when a blonde woman in a plaid coat swept past the Germans, swinging her hips. The soldiers all turned to look at her but she strode past them with her head in the air.

'*Monique, qu'est ce que tu fais là? Je t'ai perdue. Oh ma petite, rentre immédiatement à la maison.*'

And with that maternal exclamation, she gathered the bemused child up in her arms and headed back around the corner to where Bobby was cowering to keep herself out of sight.

'Move . . . fast,' she said out of the corner of her mouth as she passed the doorway where Bobby was crouching and for a split second, Bobby froze.

'I said "move", Roberta Hollis. *Now!!!*'

Bobby raced to catch up with them as the woman checked the street behind them before opening Raoul's door. They all burst in and then the woman shut the door carefully behind them.

There was a moment's silence while Bobby stared at the person who had just saved their lives.

'Marie, Marie McGill, what in heaven's name are you doing here?' Bobby spluttered.

'*Never* use that name. I am Adèle – do not use any other name, do you hear me?' She looked meaningfully towards the child but Elizé was so traumatised, she was oblivious, staring blankly into space.

Marie glared at Bobby with the same glare Bobby remembered from school, but then put her fingers to her lips and moved towards the open trap door. She shepherded the shaking child towards it and Bobby meekly followed.

Marie leaned up and closed the trap door over them. She knew the rug was rucked up on top of it, which would give away the hiding place if anyone came in, but the first priority was to get the two fugitives out of earshot.

She stood with her arms folded on the bottom step while Elizé ran towards Bobby, clinging to her and sobbing.

'*J'étais terrifieé*' the little girl said finally, her chest heaving. 'I didn't know where you were.'

'I know, I know but you're safe now.' Bobby murmured calming words while assessing the woman in front of her. She had not really changed since school and was definitely just as formidable.

Once Elizé had stopped crying, Bobby stepped back and the two women sized each other up.

'I might have known you'd cause trouble, I warned them when I brought the child.' Marie said. 'Weren't you told to keep a low profile? Can't you do anything you're told?'

Bobby could not keep up with the questions in her head but bridled with indignation at the accusations.

'Everyone has disappeared. I didn't know what had happened. I had to get food for the child and me. Anyway, how did you know I was here? It was you that brought Elizé? And . . . while I'm at it, M—Adèle, what on earth are you doing here?'

At that moment, the trapdoor re-opened and Raoul's head popped over the top. 'Are you all right, *mes petites*? *Je suis vraiment désolé.*' He suddenly stopped in the midst of his apology, seeing Marie. '*Oh merde!* What are you doing here?'

Bobby butted in. 'What the hell is going on, Raoul? And, A . . . Adèle, you still haven't told me what the hell are you doing in France and . . . how do you know Raoul?'

Raoul looked shocked and worried, looking from English girl to English girl. This was awkward. Marie looked at Bobby with disdain and said, simply, 'The less you know, the better for you.'

Marie had turned towards her and was about to say something when she just shook her head in frustrated anger and strode towards the steps, closing the trap door behind her.

Bobby and Elizé were left hugging each other in the dark while there were frantic whisperings coming from above and then the trapdoor opened again.

Raoul and Michel's heads appeared. Bobby was so relieved to see them safe that she ran up the steps towards them with her arms outstretched but Marie was standing in her way, next to Raoul's chair, one hand holding onto the back of it, her knuckles showing white with anger. She ignored Bobby and jabbered something very fast in French that Bobby could not catch and then made her way through the kitchen towards the back door to check the yard behind before vanishing.

Bobby stared after her for a second and then ran towards Michel.

'I thought I had lost you . . . lost you both,' she said, first hugging Michel and then Raoul.

'Non, non, we are here,' Michel said smiling but he caught his father's eye over her head. They very nearly were not. He turned to the window to keep watch and heaved a sigh of relief to be safe behind locked doors again.

Michel had gained his strength, his clothes were no longer hanging off him and the haunted look on his face had been replaced by a determined expression and an eagerness to get the job done. The pale young man who had turned up unexpectedly in Norfolk had been replaced by a more mature adult who his father hardly recognised.

Michel had taken charge of recent operations which were to sabotage the railways in readiness for Operation Overlord. He had spent the last week spying on his key suspect, but the informer was clever and covered his tracks well and the two men knew that, if it had not been for the young woman who had just left, the traitor would have won and a whole network of resistance fighters would have been wiped out.

A major operation to derail a supply train had been jeopardised by a message that had been intercepted by Adèle and at the last moment, the resistance fighters had fled leaving an ambush of Germans lying in wait for nobody. For two days, the men had dodged the furious enemy, hiding out in ditches and barns until they had been able to make their way home.

Raoul and Michel looked at each other, they had only just escaped the Germans to find a new danger in their own home.

Michel scanned the street from the side of the window to make sure the German patrol had left. The only people he could see were French townsfolk, hurrying to get their meagre supplies before the curfew hour but he needed to get Bobby out of sight. He signalled to his father, who ushered her back towards the cellar, taking a moment of pride to look back at the confident new leader of the local network.

'And Claudette? I couldn't find her either,' Bobby added, stopping in her tracks.

'No, when ... something ... happens, it is better that she is not here, we send her to her family,' Michel told her. 'I am sorry, we meant to be back but ... we could not. It was not safe.'

Bobby did not need explanations. She was still reeling from the appearance of her old adversary from school. She had a sudden desire to giggle, thinking what Harriet would say when she knew she had run into Marie, here in France, then it occurred to her that she would not be able to share her experiences with anyone for many years. She realised she was giddy from the tension of the last half hour and the relief that they were all safe and instead of going down the steps to the cellar, collapsed into the rocking chair where Raoul usually sat.

In his head, Michel was calculating the hours until he could get Bobby safely out of the country. She was not supposed to meet anyone, especially not a Special Operations Executive, and the fact that they knew each other put them all at huge risk.

He hurriedly pulled Bobby back up out of the armchair and ushered her back down the stairs to where Elizé was waiting nervously, promising to bring them food and water immediately.

The trap door closed over them and Bobby turned her attention to Elizé, who was still shaking. The last time the child had seen a German uniform it had belonged to the soldier who was using the butt of his rifle to push her mother onto a railway truck and, judging by the child's whimpering when she was asleep, Bobby suspected that that uniform appeared nightly on huge monsters in her dreams.

Bobby sat down on the mattress and cuddled Elizé close, rocking backwards and forwards. She started to hum a lullaby she suddenly remembered her Aunt Agnes singing to her.

That's odd, she thought, *I thought no one ever sang to me as a child.*

Chapter 23

It was Bobby's last day in France and for the first time she understood the term 'de-mob happy.' She would soon be home, able to carry on with her wonderful job, see her family, who were improving in her estimation by the minute and see Ed . . . Gus . . . she stopped, stumbling over the name Gus. She realised she had hardly thought about him since she had watched his Anson fly into the distance. She tried to remember his face but the one that had popped into her mind was Edward's. She sat back on her heels on the cold concrete floor in surprise.

'Now, where did he come from?' she said out loud.

'*Qui?*' Elizé said.

'*Les hommes,*' Bobby replied. 'I've just got too much time to think, *ma petite.*'

Elizé gave the knowing smile of an eight-year-old, which warmed Bobby's heart. Pulling the blanket around her on the mattress, while Elizé drew on her paper at the bottom of it, Bobby took stock of how much she had started to look forward to the evenings with Michel, Raoul and Claudette.

The last week had opened up a different side to the war and while it had been fraught with danger and tension, it had also been a very special time for a girl who had never had a cosy home life. Bobby had luxuriated in the evenings spent round a tiny fire with a bottle of wine and the comfortable chatter of Raoul and Michel, Claudette fussing round them. Elizé, too, would sit sleepily on a small stool next to Bobby, waiting for bedtime. Putting her hand affectionately on the child's head, Bobby often wondered whether the walls of this house were having the same effect on Elizé as they had had on her, creating a haven that seemed sacrosanct. Once Elizé was in bed, Bobby curled up in the armchair, ready to hear Raoul waxing lyrically about the charming life in a small French town before the war and the horrific reality of how that idyll had been smashed to smithereens by the arrival of the Germans.

But, with the evening when they could escape their confinement still several hours away, Bobby shivered and decided it was time to do her exercise routine on the cold cement floor. She started to hum to herself and knelt down on the space in front of her. Elizé looked over with a puzzled expression. Sometimes, these English people were very strange.

'Come and do some press-ups with me, it'll warm you up,' Bobby called over.

Elizé wandered slowly over and, copying Bobby, knelt next to her. She did not even flinch at the coldness of the floor on her bare knees and started to do what Bobby did.

They pumped up and down but then Bobby fell down onto her elbows, exhausted. Elizé fell on top of her and they both started to giggle. Once they started, neither of them could stop. To hear the child's tinkling laughter was such a joyous sound that Bobby started to cry.

'What is the matter?' Elizé asked her, catching herself mid-laugh.

'I'm just so pleased to hear you laugh.'

Elizé sat back on her heels, considering this comment. 'Is it all right to laugh? It feels so wrong when Papa is . . . and Maman . . .' she asked simply and Bobby reached out her arms and enveloped the child in them, hugging her tightly.

* * *

Bobby had been wondering all week what was going to happen to Elizé, so when they emerged from the cellar to have their last evening meal in France, she decided to tackle the subject head on.

'*Alors*, Raoul, Michel . . . what about Elizé?'

Raoul looked across at Michel, who stepped forward and coughed in embarrassment and said, 'We have organised the pick-up for you for tonight, after midnight. It is still a good moon. And, we . . . we have arranged that Elizé will go with you? Maybe to your house?'

He said it as a question, not wanting to assume that Bobby and her family would take the little girl in as one of their own but Bobby's response filled him with relief. It was a suggestion that had come down the wire from some high-up official in London who seemed to know Bobby, and Raoul had been doubtful whether it was asking too much of a man who probably hated everything to do with the Bisset family.

There was another reason why they had to get Elizé out of the country. They knew the Germans were planning house-to-house searches following the failed sabotage attempt and, aware that they used 'reprisal' executions as a way to terrify the locals into betraying their neighbours, they wanted the two girls safely out of harm's way.

'*Naturellement*,' she said with a smile, putting her arm round the girl's shoulder. There was nothing else to be said but inside, she was filled with a huge feeling of a complete joy she had never experienced before. She knew she could not have got on the aircraft without Elizé.

All through the meal, Elizé kept looking shyly up at Bobby with an adoring expression. Bobby beamed back.

Is this what maternal love feels like? she wondered. Throughout her life, she had kept her heart firmly locked up in a steel casket and now this child had found the key.

Raoul took the cork out of the wine and poured a glass for each of them, even a very small one for Elizé. He called Claudette out of the kitchen to join them then he stood up and cleared his throat.

'So, my "daughter", you leave for England. You will leave a big hole in our house and in our hearts. You brought my son back to me and now he is taking control here, I am very proud of him.'

He saluted Michel with his glass and they all raised their wine to toast Michel. Michel, who was looking so much healthier and stronger than when he arrived, blushed. Claudette beamed at him with pride.

'You take with you our little Elizé, who is now my granddaughter,' – he really did enjoy adding to his family – 'and hopefully, her war is over. We pray to *Le Bon Dieu* that she will once again be reunited with her *maman* but for now, we trust her to our Bobbee, who will be her mother until that day.'

Bobby wondered whether he had started the wine early, he was certainly warming to his role as organiser of his new, extended family. Michel had not seen his father this happy since before his mother was ill, and he grinned indulgently.

'We drink this wine and eat this food, thank God for this evening and for all of us being together,' Raoul went on. 'It is a very special evening in our lives and one we will repeat when this terrible war is over, which I am beginning to think, *peut-être, grâce à Dieu*, oh, and also to the Allies,' he smiled, 'will be soon.'

Claudette glanced across at Michel. Brushing a stray hair back from her face, she thought of the day she would be able to wear a new pretty, floral dress and then he could no longer ignore her. Bobby spotted the look and reached across to put her hand reassuringly on the French girl's red raw one. There was one thing she could do before she left, she thought.

Michel looked at the old grandfather clock in the corner and nudged his father. 'Ah *oui*, we have a small job to do before we go tonight,' Raoul said. He led Bobby and Elizé back to the cellar for the last time. Bobby looked around at the dank room that had been her home for a week. It was a week she would remember forever. She changed into her uniform, which seemed from another life, and settled down to tell Elizé a story, hoping the little girl would get some sleep before their adventure.

Bobby was drifting off herself when she heard a commotion in the street above. There were scuffling footsteps, and then the sound of a woman sobbing before the quiet closing of a door. Bobby sat up quickly, her heart thumping. She looked up at the firmly-shut trap door above them and thought how the word 'trap' appropriately summed up when you were stuck underground with nowhere to go. She held her breath, waiting for sounds and debated whether to wake Elizé but then decided the little girl was better being left for as long as possible in a world of dreams.

After an agonising ten minutes, the trap door opened and Bobby froze, waiting to see who would peer into the gloom. She automatically put her arms out to shield Elizé but it was Claudette who peered down.

'Bobbee, Bobbee, *dépêchez-vous.*'

Bobby hurriedly gathered up Elizé and glanced around her. She had destroyed both their drawings, hoping that Elizé would be able to re-do the ones of her parents. She had come with nothing and now she was leaving with nothing, except one small Jewish child.

She followed Claudette through the kitchen and out of a scullery door to a wall behind.

'*Il faut grimper,*' she whispered. '*Je vais vous passer Elizé.*'

Bobby looked at the wall in front of her. She was glad her ATA trousers allowed her to climb properly and all those lessons on tree climbing from Archie were about to pay off. She clambered up and then reached down to take Elizé, who had such a mask of terror on her face that Bobby was worried she would scream. She put her finger to her lips and Elizé nodded slowly and bit her lip.

Claudette whispered to her to go two streets down, find the large tree on the corner and hide behind it until Michel came for her.

Bobby reached down her hand to clasp Claudette's. She had not even had time to help her friend's lovelorn cause so as she swung her legs over the other side of the wall, she whispered urgently to her, '*Dites-lui*, Claudette, tell him how you feel.'

Claudette grasped her hand tightly for a brief moment and then pushed her away, anxious she should flee as quickly as possible.

Bobby and Elizé bolted down the street. Bobby did not register the houses they passed, nor did she look to see if they were being followed, it was past curfew and anyone found in the streets could be arrested, let alone a woman in a pilot's uniform and a small Jewish child. She found the tree and the two of them crouched behind it, wrapped in each other's arms, trying to look as small as possible. After what seemed an age, Michel suddenly appeared at Bobby's shoulder.

'*Vite, suivez-moi*,' he said in a low voice and went off down a small alleyway. The two girls followed, Elizé cling-ing onto the bottom of Bobby's jacket. They dodged from doorway to doorway, trying to make their footsteps as quiet as possible. Bobby hoped the people in the houses were too experienced at ignoring noises in the street to want to investigate.

They reached an area where there were some trees and a common with a pond. On the edge were some ducks with their heads tucked under their wings. Their undisturbed slumbers seemed incongruous while such drama was unfolding around them.

In one corner of the common, Bobby spotted a small group of men carrying a dark shape. It looked like a body. Another one had a spade. Bobby pulled up sharply with a cry. She immediately shielded Elizé's eyes but hissed at Michel. 'What? Who?'

'The informer,' Michel replied bitterly. 'There will be no trace. *La justice*, she is done.'

Chapter 24

Gus had been pacing up and down all day.

'For Christ's sake, sit down!' Walter Jones, one of the other pilots, called across the room. He had watched Gus do nothing but go around in circles since he came on shift in the late afternoon and it kept distracting him from his letter to his sweetheart.

'You're making me dizzy. What *is* the matter with you?'

A third pilot, Rob, looked up from his newspaper. 'He's been watching the weather all day. We've all got missions tonight. Why are *you* in such a faff?' he asked Gus.

Gus stopped pacing, only now registering anyone was talking to him. 'What?' he asked the two pilots.

'Oh, we may as well leave him alone, it's hopeless,' Walter said. 'He must be in love,' and went back to his letter. Rob shook his head and concentrated on his crossword.

Gus kept glancing out of the window. It was dark but he could see the clouds were gathering. His last trip, when he had had to leave Bobby in France, had been three days before the full moon and they only had tonight before it waned, negating any chance of flying. Without the light from the moon, the pick-up would be postponed and he could not bear a delay.

He could not believe how nervous he was. Would she be there? Was she OK? And finally, would she be so pleased to see him, she would fall into his arms?

Gus gave a wry smile. That was in his dreams, he thought.

Markham came in the door.

'Flight Lieutenant Prince,' he called, beckoning.

All three pilots stood to attention. Gus immediately followed him out of the room, leaving Peter and Rob looking after him, but trained not to ask questions, they both shrugged and carried on with their tasks in hand.

'Close the door,' Markham said as Gus followed him into his office. 'At ease. Now Prince, the Met Office say the weather is clearing so your mission should go ahead.' He heard an audible sigh of relief from the pilot in front of him.

'You will fly a Lysander but there is a passenger, a child. She will have to be secreted in the drop tank. It will be an extremely uncomfortable journey for her. First Officer Hollis will be in the cockpit, just behind you in case of problems and must be ready to take over if necessary.'

Gus knew better than to show any surprise, but his mind was racing. Why was Bobby being accompanied by a child? He had spent the week creating endless scenarios about what was happening in France and none of them were good but certainly none of them included a child.

Markham was continuing. 'I'm assuming you remember the coordinates because you won't have any written instructions and we don't want you to use the radio. They know you're coming but speed will be of the essence. It's been a bit of a busy night over there and the pick-up will have to be very fast and efficient.'

He paused. He had just received an encrypted message that suggested that the night raid to Nuremberg involving more than 700 bombers was going disastrously wrong for the Allies.

'There is a chance the Jerries may have caught up with developments that have been happening over there tonight and the mission may be aborted at the last minute, so we're not using the usual Morse code. Listen to the radio but don't respond unless there's an emergency. The code word for you to pull out is "Dover". If all is A-OK, then it's "Paris". Got that?'

'Yessir!' Gus replied with a confidence that was ebbing with every minute.

'Righty-ho, then dismissed. Take off is in one hour. Send in Flight Lieutenant Jones, will you?'

Gus spent the next half hour checking the batteries in his reading light for navigation, the Met Office reports and the maps that he would need to get to his destination but, in reality, he had done this trip in his head several times over the past few days and it was etched in his memory.

Finally, he headed out to the airfield. The Lysander, with its dark paint to disguise it from the enemy, glistened every time the moon appeared from between the clouds. He looked anxiously upwards, there was still some cover which made flying at such a low altitude without lights a real problem, but by the time he had done his pre-flight checks, he was relieved to see that the sky had cleared and the stars were twinkling innocently as if mayhem were not happening in the world below.

He revved up and taxied the short runway and took off into the dark skies. A vision of Bobby looking expectantly at the sky, waiting for him, came before his eyes but he firmly dismissed it. This was a time to be a professional pilot not a lovesick schoolboy. He flew east to avoid the south coast as it was a prohibited area during the spring of 1944, so he knew nothing of the huge amount of activity taking place there with ships, tanks, armoury and landing craft preparing for Operation Overlord.

He flew low and fast across to Normandy, thankful it was the north of France he was going to and not some-where hours to the south. The skies were unusually quiet, he registered with relief. He was totally unaware that while the moonlight was allowing his mission to go ahead, it also meant the enemy was taking advantage of its bright light to pick off bomber after bomber on the ill-fated mission to Bavaria's second city, Nuremberg. The Germans had no time to worry about one small aircraft flying low over the Channel.

As he approached the pick-up spot, the radio sputtered into life. It was very crackly, but he could make out the word 'Paris' and breathed a sigh of relief. It was going to happen; he was going to rescue Bobby and take her safely home. He felt he could have flown without an engine.

Chapter 25

Bobby and Elizé were both shaking with cold. They had been led silently out of the village but were now on the edge of some woods that Bobby thought she recognised from the first night.

'We will be OK,' she whispered into the child's ear. 'Soon, we will be safe in England and I will show you the farm where I was brought up. Mrs Hill will look after you and Aunt Agnes will read you stories at night.'

She struggled to envisage her strait-laced aunt cuddling this small child as she dropped off to sleep but then she remembered the lullaby that had emerged from her own memories and thought that perhaps there was a side to Aunt Agnes she had forgotten existed. Bobby started to describe the farm, and as she recalled the images of corn-fields, cows chewing the cud and hens running in the yard, she gradually felt both her and Elizé's shivering bodies calm down, but then Michel wheeled round to face them, placing his finger on his lips.

The two girls froze.

In the distance, there were some dark figures coming through the trees.

Michel pushed them both behind a large, gnarled trunk, where they crouched down amongst the early spring flowers that had furled up for the night. Bobby looked at them enviously – if only she could furl Elizé and herself up too and disappear into the undergrowth. The approaching group made no sound and Bobby and Elizé held their breaths.

Michel gave a low owl hoot. There was a moment's silence and then a replying hoot.

He emerged from the tree and greeted with relief the three men who had approached them.

They spoke in rapid French, but Bobby understood that because of Michel's activities in the village that night, there had been a change of pick-up location and that they were to go to the west of the woods, not the east. Her French had definitely improved, she thought.

Together, the group changed direction and headed the opposite way until they reached a clearing where Michel pushed both the girls into a ditch.

'The pilot could not be told of the change,' he whispered to Bobby, we have to get his attention. Is there one word we can use so he know it is you? Our friends have led the Germans to the wrong place but now we must act quickly.'

Another man came up beside him with a flashlight. They both looked expectantly at Bobby. She searched her mind, but it was a blank.

Then she had a vision of her and Gus Prince locked in regular fierce combat over a school desk while he tried in vain to beat her at their favourite game and she blurted out, 'Arm-wrestling!'

Michel looked at her in puzzlement but then started to flash the letters out in Morse with the lamp. She hoped with all her might that it was Gus who was the pilot or else those words would not make any sense at all.

Up above them, Gus talked out loud to an empty cockpit. 'What . . . ?' he exploded.

He checked and re-checked the message that was being flashed to him from the wrong side of the woods to the expected coordinates.

'Arm-wrestling? Arm-wrestling? What the hell?'

He worked through the possibilities rapidly in his head. At first, he thought the Germans had laid a trap for him but then it was repeated over and over.

Then it dawned on him. This was a message only he would understand when there was no time for a code to be established.

He burst out laughing.

'Of course, Roberta Hollis,' he told the dark woods below him, 'still making the most of your victories, are you? You always won, damn you. OK, have it your way. Ah, there you are, my lovely. Gus Prince to the rescue.'

He turned the plane left and then swept it down like an avenging angel guided by the torches being waved in the air by the resistance fighters.

Bobby heaved a huge sigh of relief. Either the Lysander was being flown by Gus or it was some other bemused RAF pilot who was taking an enormous risk by following gibberish messages.

Michel nudged her to move towards the flat part of the field. She had just a brief second to hug him.

'I will see you . . . when all this is over.'

'*Mai oui*,' he replied, clinging to her. 'We are family now and it is for all-time.'

'And Michel,' she said quickly over her shoulder as she left, 'Claudette is very beautiful, you know.'

He just had the chance to look at her quizzically before he remembered he was supposed to be pushing her and Elizé towards the plane. Bobby spotted the ladder on the side of it and propelled Elizé up it, following just as the plane started to taxi for take-off.

She and Elizé fell into the belly of the aircraft.

'That can only be Roberta Hollis. Are you OK?' The voice was so familiar that Bobby let out a huge sigh of relief.

'Oh Gus,' she called to him, 'I've never been more glad to see anyone in my life!'' Gus so wished the aircraft could fly itself so he could come to the back to hold her in his arms, but he had no choice but to tightly grip the controls, his fingers hurting with the intensity of his grasp.

'The child has to go in the bottom there. Can you see it?' he asked. 'It's not comfy but it's safer.'

Bobby looked around in the gloom as the aircraft pitched left and right to avoid the trees. She and Elizé kept falling against the side of the plane. She grabbed hold of the little girl and gently levered her down into a coffin-like space that had been moulded out of the underneath of the Lysander. Elizé gave little sniffs as she tried not to cry so Bobby smiled reassuringly at her.

'We are going home, *ma petite*. Not long now. Just close your eyes if you can, and *et voila*, we will be in England.'

Gus was concentrating on getting them safely out of danger.

After a few minutes, Gus called back.

'Are you all right back there?'

'Yes, we are, well, I think we are. That was a bit hairy.'

'Is the child all right?'

'Yes, well, if you can manage to fly this aircraft without bobbing about,' Bobby said in her usual commanding voice, 'she could perhaps get some sleep.'

Gus laughed. It was so good to hear her voice.

'That's typical,' he replied. 'I come all this way, risking life and limb. I have to change the pick-up, you send me some ridiculous message and now I'm here in the middle of the night, dodging enemy flak just to take you home.'

They both laughed this time.

As they approached the north coast of France, the search lights were scanning the skies.

'This could be a bit bumpy,' he warned her. 'There's some sort of raid going on tonight, the Jerries seem to be on full alert.'

Bobby sat back, clutching her knees, thinking how ironic it would be if she got wiped out here and now, after surviving a week in enemy territory, being harboured by a family of resistance fighters.

Gus flew lower than ever, almost skimming the tops of the trees as he approached the Channel. He took a calculated risk that the searchlights would be looking higher up and not expecting an aircraft to fly directly over their heads. It was a risky strategy but once he saw the French coastline in the distance, he believed it was one that had paid off. But just as he approached the coast, he heard gunfire from below and arched upwards in an almost vertical move. Bobby fell backwards.

'Sorry,' he called backwards, 'just taking some avoiding action'.

Elizé woke up and called up to Bobby. '*Que s'est-il passé?*'

'Nothing, *ma petite*, go back to sleep. Gus is just showing off.'

She looked nervously towards Gus, who was doing anything but showing off, he was performing the most amazing aerial feats she had ever witnessed, avoiding flak.

She waited until the Lysander righted itself again and then spoke. 'OK, Prince, you win. I might be better at arm-wrestling, but that was quite a manoeuvre. I'll grant you that.'

He chuckled back to her. He just loved being Roberta Hollis's knight in shining armour.

Chapter 26

It was still dark when they arrived back at Tempsford. Bobby uncurled her aching back and helped Elizé out of her uncomfortable cot. She stretched and yawned. Bobby hugged her and led her down the steps. For a moment, Bobby paused in the cold March air and breathed down to her stomach. England had never looked so good or so safe. To be able to walk down the streets and not be in fear of a German order being yelled or the butt of a rifle being pushed into your back was a privilege she would never take for granted again. Now she really knew what they were all fighting for.

'Is this it? Is this England? Are we really here?' The questions poured out from Elizé's little rosebud mouth, which had started to quiver.

'Yes, *mon ange*, we are really here and as long as we keep Mr Hitler on that side of the water, we will be safe.'

The child looked exhausted and Bobby also felt a wave of fatigue wash over her but then Gus jumped down from the aircraft behind her and ran towards her. He was about to sweep her up in his arms when he heard his commanding officer's voice behind him.

'All OK, Flight Lieutenant Prince?'

He saluted and stood to attention. Bobby stood up straight, suddenly remembering she was back on English soil and an ATA pilot.

'Yessir.'

'Dispersal now, then straight back to barracks,' Markham said, taking a curious look at the woman who had inspired two men to heroics. He had to admit she was quite a sight for sore eyes in the cold early hours of the morning with all that glorious hair, even with a pinched, pale face that told of an anxiety-filled week, but this was not the time or place to allow a romantic huddle. Markham smiled at his efforts to enforce a professional approach, knowing that Marjorie would have accused of him of deliberately sabotaging any affection between the two adults in front of him as a mark of favouritism towards his friend, Edward. The far too attractive RAF pilot gave an apologetic look towards Bobby and reluctantly marched off.

'You too,' Markham said to her.

Before Bobby and Elizé had a chance to move, the drone of another aircraft came behind them. Again, a Lysander was lurching out of the dawn sky. The pilot was struggling and both Markham and Gus ran towards it as it bumped to a shaky halt on one side of the runway. Markham signalled to the ambulance and fire vehicles and then both men moved quickly out of the way to let the emergency team do its job. It would not do to be too close to an aeroplane that could burst into flames at any moment. The cockpit opened and Walter Jones half fell out. He was clutching his shoulder and blood was streaming down his uniform. From the ladder at the back came a familiar blonde girl. She did not see Gus or Markham but in contravention of all the rules, strode straight across towards Bobby as Walter was helped into the ambulance.

'You are a bloody idiot,' she whispered furiously to Bobby. 'First you put the whole network at risk by landing when you shouldn't have. Then you put my job and all my contacts in jeopardy so I have to be sent home on a night when the whole German airforce is on the lookout for Allied planes and then to top it all off, they take a pot shot at my pilot.'

With that, she marched angrily towards the cottages on the edge of the airfield. Bobby stared after her.

'Who ... is ... that?' an ambulance man next to her asked.

'She's an old schoolfriend of mine,' Bobby replied.

* * *

Bobby followed Markham and Gus over to the cottages on the edge of the airfield holding Elizé's hand. It felt cold and it grasped hers firmly. Bobby looked around her; had it really only been a week since she had flown over to France with Michel? It seemed like another time, another universe.

A woman with a welfare officer's uniform came out to greet them.

'Does the child speak English?' she asked Bobby.

'Yes, I do,' Elizé piped up, indignant at being ignored.

'Oh, I'm sorry, my dear,' the officer said, leaning down towards Elizé. 'I didn't realise. That's wonderful. Well, First Officer Hollis has to go and talk to some people now, so we've got a nice breakfast prepared for you. Why don't you come with me and then you can meet up with her again later after you've had some sleep?'

Elizé looked scared and clung onto Bobby's hand tighter.

'*C'est bien, ma petite.*' Bobby bent down on one knee to face the little girl. 'I have to do this, but you are perfectly safe now and I bet they have a lovely omelette waiting for you. I won't be long and then after a little nap, maybe we can take you home?' She looked questioningly at the officer, who smiled blandly without commitment. Elizé finally let go of her hand and glancing back at her all the way to the cottage, allowed herself to be led away.

Bobby walked behind the officer and entered the room indicated to her. When she opened the door, she gasped.

'Edward! What are you doing here?'

For one brief second, Edward moved forward as if to hug her, but then he stopped, embarrassed. There was another officer in the room, so Bobby immediately stood up straight. It unnerved her how tempted she was to fall into his arms and sob with relief; he looked so solid and strong, like a welcoming port in a storm. She looked again – he did look terrible, however, really pale and drawn.

Edward coughed and took command. 'I happened to be in the vicinity,' he lied. 'So, I thought I would check you got back safely.' He stared at her, hardly able to believe she was there in front of him. He took a deep breath. 'I was hoping to be in on your debrief but I've just heard I have to leave immediately to get to London, so I will leave you to my colleague who will do it on my behalf. You will undoubtedly have information for us that will be extremely useful, so I am going to leave you to get on with that and I will catch up with you soon.

'It's good to see you back, Bobby,' he added quietly. He looked straight at her and his whole face softened. Bobby saw the depth behind his dark eyes and it occurred to her that it was because of this man that she was back on English soil again with Elizé at her side. He not only intrigued her, but every time she saw him, she was beginning to develop a need to be enfolded in his safe arms, she realised with a jolt.

Bobby looked closely at him as he brushed back his unruly fringe in embarrassment but before she could say anything, the other officer signalled her towards a hard-backed chair next to the desk. He sat, waiting for Edward to leave.

Edward closed the door behind him but then his hand reached out to grab the wall for stability. He had spent the last few hours pacing up and down outside the cottage, scanning the skies. Reports of heavy activity on the coast of France overnight had left him with a churning stomach and for the first time in his life, he had felt completely out of his depth and out of control.

This damned war, he thought angrily.

*　　*　　*

Bobby's debrief took ages while Edward's colleague took her through intensive notes. She described conditions in France, the way the network was operating and the situation with the informer. In return, she was left in no doubt of the fact that her little sojourn behind enemy lines had to remain a secret from everyone, including her family and fellow pilots. Elizé was to be explained as an orphan who had connections with her French family and needed caring for and nothing more. By the time Bobby was released to the care of the welfare officer, there was no sign of either Edward or Gus and to be honest, she was too tired to care. She asked where Elizé was and they told her she had been found a bed in the room next to hers and was tucked up fast asleep.

'You could probably do with a rest, too,' the small, dark-haired welfare officer said. 'You can have a few hours here but that's all. There is a bed here you can use. Even though you are ATA, on this occasion you will be given a rail warrant to take this child to your home, where I believe she is to be cared for and then you must return to Hamble. You have forty-eight hours.'

Bobby nodded. It all seemed so normal, but no one had really told her how she was going to explain the arrival of a small Jewish child in England.

She had just taken her boots off and was about to climb under the covers when there was a tentative knock on the door. She called 'come in' and there standing in the doorway was Gus. His hair was ruffled and his face anguished. Bobby rushed forward and put her hands on his shoulders.

'Gus, whatever is it? You look in such a state.'

He didn't speak but reached forward and put his arms around her, kicking the door closed behind him.

'You shouldn't be in here, Gus, what the hell are you doing?'

He took her face in his hands and looked intensely into her eyes.

'I can't tell you what I've been imagining these last days while you were stuck in France.'

She gently led him towards the bed to sit down. 'I don't know what to say,' she said.

'Don't say a word,' Gus muttered into her hair and then he moved his head round to kiss her. His lips were soft and Bobby tilted her head up and hesitated for a moment before kissing him back. The tension of the last week flooded through her and she found a glorious oblivion in that moment. Gus moved to gradually push her backwards onto the bed, running his hands over her body.

She murmured, welcoming his desire for her and he climbed on top of her. He started to undo her shirt, taking her breasts in his hands and then leaned down to kiss them.

Bobby's knowledge of intimacy had been limited to some unsatisfactory fumblings in the haybarn with a rather attractive cowhand, but no one had told her how pleasurable it could all be. She moaned with delight and arched her body towards him. Gus was expertly touching various parts of her body, moving her uniform out of the way slowly to reveal her white skin. He leaned his face towards her and whispered, 'I think I may be in love with you, Bobby Hollis.'

'What?' she said, suddenly sitting up and pulling away from him.

'I don't know; I just know you drive me mad.' He tried to gently push her back down but Bobby wriggled out from underneath him to stand up. She rearranged her uniform and started to do up her buttons.

She needed time to think.

At the age of twenty-nine, she realised this was the first time she had actually been kissed properly. It was all happening too fast and she had a sudden need to ask Harriet what to do.

She looked up, guiltily, feeling his disappointment, but Gus's stricken face suddenly made her laugh.

'Oh, I'm sorry, Gus, but you do look so sorry for yourself. I really like you, but love? I'm just not sure.'

Gus turned to grab the jacket he had discarded on the floor and shuffled to his feet, avoiding her gaze.

'I'm sorry too, I just want you so much. I was so worried something had happened to you over there.'

He started to back out of the door.

'Gus, I . . .' Bobby started to say but he shook his head and opened the door before disappearing into the corridor.

After a moment, she turned towards the bed, and climbed in. Had she really been about to make love to Gus Prince? She was not sure what had stopped her but the last vision she saw in her mind as she drifted off into a troubled sleep was the face of Edward Turner. The next thing she heard was a knock at the door.

'Yes?' she said sleepily.

'Want a cuppa, sir?' a voice came through the closed door.

'Oh, yes, please.' She sat up and pulled her fingers roughly through her hair. She was still in uniform and she pulled the jacket straight under the covers. Her boots were discarded on the floor next to the bed. Bobby quickly scanned the room to check there were no signs of her earlier visitor.

An orderly came in carrying a cup and saucer. He had been told it was an ATA pilot but he had nearly dropped the tray when he heard a female voice. He put the tray down shakily on the small wooden table next to the bed.

'It's a bright morning, s . . . ma'am. I prefer cloud myself, less chance of any little packages from across the Channel.' He pulled the blackout blinds back to reveal the bright morning sunshine and turned to go.

Bobby nodded. She had almost forgotten how the danger had always come from the skies in Britain, rather than the street outside your front door. She sighed. It was good to be back.

The door pushed open a little more and Elizé's face appeared.

'Are you awake?' she whispered.

'Yes. There's no need to whisper,' Bobby laughed. 'Come in.'

She pulled back the covers so the little girl could climb in next to her and put her arms around her.

'Bobbee. Bobbee . . . are we really safe here? Am I safe? Is it dangerous here to be a Jew?'

'No, well, some people might not like it,' Bobby admitted, thinking of the people who had thrown insults at a Jewish family in Norwich in the early days of the war and of some of the comments Rachel had received in the market. 'But,' she added hurriedly, 'they won't do anything about it, you're safe here.'

Elizé leaned back and thought of her mother. She looked sideways at Bobby, considering that if only this guardian angel from the skies had come just a few days earlier, Bobby might have been able to save her too.

'Do . . . you think Maman . . . is still . . . alive?' she said the words haltingly, as if saying them out loud might put a jinx on the possibility.

Bobby pulled her tighter towards her. 'I don't know,' she admitted, 'but if we can find her, we will.'

She had no idea how she was going to do that but she felt a need to give this child the precious gift of hope.

* * *

Bobby had no time to work out a strategy as she and Elizé embarked on the journey to Norwich. The child's nervousness was palpable. Her hand gripped Bobby's all the way to the station and when she saw the train on the platform, she froze.

The guard was waiting with his whistle poised but Elizé would not move, her eyes staring at the guard's van with its iron-barred window. It brought back the most horrific memories for the child.

All around them there were service people pushing and shoving to get on the train but Elizé stood transfixed, her eyes staring at the guard's van.

She suddenly turned to Bobby and screamed.

'*NON, non, je ne vais pas, je ne vais pas.* I WILL NOT GO!'

Bobby went down on her knees and hugged her close.

She talked softly into her ear, ignoring the curious stares of the people around them.

'Do you trust me, Elizé?'

The child nodded slowly.

'I am going to take care of you. This is England, there are no Germans here. I promise you will be safe. This train is just going to take us home, home to Norwich, I will be with you.'

Elizé eventually allowed her to pick her rigid body up and carry her onto the train, ignoring all the heads that had poked out of windows to see what the commotion was. She bundled Elizé into the carriage in front of them where a kindly-looking woman reached out and helped them both to climb aboard.

Once in the carriage, the guard blew his whistle and the train started to move off.

Elizé had her face buried in Bobby's shoulder. The carriage was packed but an elderly man stood up to let them both sit down.

'There now,' a woman with a wicker basket on her knee said in a broad Norfolk accent. 'You see, pet, it's all right.

Your mummy won't let anything bad happen to you. Here, I've got a nice jam sandwich. You tuck into that. You'll soon feel better.'

Elizé peeped out from Bobby's collar. She saw a carriage full of kind faces, all smiling at her and she slowly began to relax. She reached out her hand and took the sandwich, biting warily into it. It tasted good and she started to munch it.

'Thank you,' Bobby said. 'She's had a tough time.'

'I know, I know,' the woman said, patting Elizé's knee. 'But you're all right now, aren't you, duckie?'

The woman kept up a steady chatter that lulled Elizé to sleep as the train's clickety-click wheels sped them across the country.

It was late in the afternoon when they arrived at Norwich. Bobby thanked the woman, who had favoured the carriage with the story of her entire life during the journey. Bobby had welcomed the lack of pauses and said very little.

She tumbled out onto the platform, pulling Elizé behind her and started walking towards the bus stop.

'Bobby, Bobby,' a voice called from behind her.

'Archie! What are you doing here? How did you know?'

'I didn't, just here to pick up some supplies.' He pointed at the two boxes in the back of the cart. 'They're some seed we needed. Came in on the last train. I can't believe it's you, lassie, what on earth are you doing here?' He paused and then added, 'You're looking a bit pale.'

He peered into her face, assessing every strained muscle and tight sinew. Something had been going on. Then he spotted Elizé, who was hanging back, looking in awe at the large, solid man in front of her who seemed to treat her heroine as a child.

'And who's this, then?' Archie asked.

'This is Elizé. She's ... she's with me.' Bobby had no idea what more to say. She was going to have to do better than this. Fortunately, Archie had spent his life watching the Hollis family from close quarters and was quite used to keeping his thoughts to himself.

'Right you are, well, in the cart both of you. You'll just be in time for supper.'

Elizé's eyes grew bigger. She suddenly realised she was very hungry indeed.

'Welcome to Norfolk, young miss.'

His strong arms swept Elizé into the back of the cart and she leaned against the seed bags. He went to help Bobby but she was already sitting in the passenger seat.

He frowned. It was not like Bobby to concede the chance to drive. This was all too peculiar.

'So, how are you, Bobby Hollis?' he asked casually.

'Fine, Archie, just fine.'

'Hmm, if you say so,' her old friend muttered, glancing sideways at her.

'Sorry, Archie, I just need to think for a minute.'

'Yes, of course. You just sit there and see how a proper driver deals with this mutt.'

Bobby smiled at him and then leaned her head on his broad shoulder as they drove along. She needed to work out what she was going to say to her family. She had to give them some explanation.

Chapter 27

Mrs Hill was busy in the kitchen, taking the potato pies out of the oven with a singed oven glove. She had given up trying to follow the butcher's wife's suggestion to use Vaseline as a fat after an article in the paper claimed it could cause bowel cancer. A traditional cook, she was almost relieved to go back to the sparse potato recipe she had used over the last few years and was assessing the cooked pies with a professional air, prodding the crimped edges. Bobby came in the back door and sniffed the air gleefully; there was no sign of turnip soup here.

She crept up behind Mrs Hill and put her arms around her. The cook jumped and then spun round.

'Bobby Hollis, you gave me a fright. Where on earth did you spring from?'

'Happened to be passing, just thought I'd pop in.' Bobby tried to sound as casual as she could.

'Wonderful, you're just in time for supper,' Mrs Hill exclaimed, too busy working out in her head how many portions of pie there were to express surprise at Bobby's sudden appearance. Then Elizé's head peered round from behind Bobby, her eyes popping at the warmth and bustle of the kitchen.

'And who's this little mite?' Mrs Hill asked, wiping her hands on her pinny.

'This is Elizé, she's going to be staying here for a while.'

Mrs Hill looked sharply at Bobby, who gave her a warning look.

'Of course, poppet. How lovely. I bet you're starving, aren't you? Rachel, take our little . . . Elizé?' She waited for confirmation, 'into the morning room and give her some milk and some of those nice carrot biscuits you've made. She looks ravenous.'

Elizé's eyes grew even larger and she looked round the kitchen taking in the fresh eggs from the hens, the vegetables from the garden and the pies that were being prepared. It was too much for her and she started to sink to the floor.

Bobby swept her up in her arms and looked at her watch. It was six o'clock and her family would probably be about to start eating.

'I think she'd prefer some pie if there is some. Maybe we could take it with us into the dining room? Is everyone in there?' she asked Mrs Hill.

'Yes, of course, lovey, you'll want her to meet everyone. You go in, we'll bring something in for the pair of you.'

Bobby stopped outside the oak-panelled dining room door knowing that once she had opened it, she would have to have something sensible to say.

But at that moment, the back door flew open and a familiar voice boomed from the kitchen.

'Hello, Mrs Hill, thought I'd pop in and say hello. Just on my way back to barracks. My mother sent these apples. Everyone in the dining room? Shall I go through?'

The whirlwind that was Harriet Marcham put Bobby into a tailspin. She knew her vague explanations would not be accepted as readily by her friend as by her family.

While she hovered in the hallway, the door from the kitchen burst open at the same time as the dining room one was opened. Bobby, with Elizé in her arms, was standing in the middle of the hallway looking in both directions while her friend emerged from one side and her aunt came out from the other.

'Bobby!' they both said at the same moment.

There was a stunned silence as they took in the bedraggled state of Bobby and the wan child in her arms.

'This is Elizé and she's really hungry,' Bobby stated.

Deciding that confidence was the best weapon, she marched into the dining room to find her parents sitting at the table.

'Hello, Mother, hello, Father. How are you?'

Aunt Agnes swept into the room and Harriet, not wanting to miss a moment of this unexpected drama, followed close behind. She had made herself at home at the farm since she was little and had never stood on ceremony, but then she remembered her manners and was the first to speak.

'Good evening, Mr and Mrs Hollis, I hope you're well. Sorry to intrude, but my mother sent you some apples.'

Bobby's aunt turned to sit at the table next to her sister, taking a moment to assess the situation. Her niece had constantly surprised her during her young life but turning up with a small, and, if she was not mistaken, Jewish child, was an unexpected scenario that was going to take some explaining.

'Bobby, it's good to see you,' she finally said, 'and you, Harriet. The child may sit here next to me. Would you all like something to eat?' She did not wait for a reply. 'Rachel, could you set for three more please?'

Bobby had a burning desire to giggle. It was as if she were the vicar calling in for afternoon tea, not a daring escapee from France with a child in tow.

Elizé was staring open-mouthed at the typically English scene in front of her. Her father had told her about life in England, but she had never expected it to look like the scene from the lid of the old shortbread biscuit tin her mother kept in the pantry. The flowered curtains were held in place by plaited ties, the backs of the tapestry chairs had lacy covers on them and on the sideboard were crystal goblets and a decanter. It was like she imagined the king's palace to be.

'So, Bobby,' the scary, tall woman in the grey dress was speaking. 'Are you going to keep us in suspense or are you going to tell us who this young woman is?'

Elizé suddenly shrank backwards, willing the large swirls on the rich carpet to swallow her up.

Bobby reached down and took her hand. 'Aunt, Mother, Father, this is Elizé. She is part French, part English ... and she needs a home for now.'

Put so simply, there was no argument.

'Of course,' her father said immediately. He had seen children like Elizé standing at the roadside in France during the Great War. At the time, he had wanted to gather them all up and bring them home but somehow when he got home to his own child, he could not find any of that paternal feeling to lavish on his own daughter, only ever seeing her as a reminder that he had lost his son. But seeing this little girl standing forlornly in front of him, he was shocked to feel a wave of emotion he had not experienced for years.

His wife jumped out of her chair and unexpectedly gathered the child in her arms. Here was a chance for her to show her husband she could be a good mother.

Bobby looked in surprise at the unexpected change in the woman in front of her. For a second, she felt a pain in her stomach as she thought of all the times as a child that she had longed for such a hug from her mother but then she saw the smile on Elizé's face and felt ashamed of herself. This child had lost everything and deserved a hug so much more than she had ever done.

Aunt Agnes looked quizzically at Bobby trying to prompt her into sharing some more information but received a blank stare back. The full story was going to have to wait, probably until the end of the war, Bobby wearily realised.

'Oh well, that seems settled then. Here, child, have some milk.' Agnes reached behind her to take a glass from Rachel and gave it to the little girl. 'Rachel, could you prepare the small, spare room for Elizé, please?'

Elizé sipped at a little of it, realised it was real milk and gulped it down.

'We're lucky,' Bobby explained gently to her, 'We have our own cows and although most of it has to go to the Government for rationing, we do pinch a little for ourselves. They don't miss it but don't tell them.'

Elizé had spent so much of her young life being hounded by the authorities, the thought of not obeying the rules was beyond her comprehension. Even though she spoke English like a native, she felt like a foreigner in this strange land.

Harriet broke the tense silence that had emerged. 'So, Bobby, what have you been up to? What's the news?'

She looked meaningfully at Elizé but Bobby determinedly ignored her.

'How's Coltishall?' Bobby returned.

Always easily distracted, Harriet launched into a description of a dance she had gone to the previous Saturday where there were some new GIs from a nearby RAF station flaunting their wealth.

'They get so much more money than our lads, you should have seen the girls flocking round them. Our chaps were livid. They couldn't compete.'

'And what about you, Harriet?' Agnes butted in. 'Are you in love with the Americans like all the other girls?'

'Not me,' Harriet laughed. 'I prefer homegrown gorgeous men. Although,' she paused, her head on one side, 'if they could get me some nylons, I might be tempted.'

Mr Hollis's right eyebrow raised in disdain. Bobby and Harriet looked at each other and grinned.

'How long have you got, Harriet?' Agnes asked.

'Long enough to catch up with all Bobby's gossip,' she said, meaningfully.

Harriet looked at Bobby's parents and aunt and then at Bobby. She jerked her head towards the garden.

Bobby gave a slight nod, not actually sure whether she wanted to have a tête-à-tête with her friend or not but then Rachel put plates of food in front of them both, which gave her time to think.

'Just let's eat first, Harriet,' she said.

Mathilda Hollis looked delightedly around the table. During the past few weeks, she had been having long chats with the new local doctor. He had read her file with interest and she had found it easy to explain to his kindly face how she had been living in a confused world where shadows and ghosts became muddled in her mind. He gave her some small, white tablets, organised an hour of help with a kindly older man called a psychiatrist every week and it was as if a fog was beginning to clear. For the first time since her husband had come home from the war, she decided she would speak out and asked the question everyone had been longing to voice.

'So where's Elizé come from, then?'

Agnes looked proudly at her sister while Bobby sat transfixed. Her aunt had written to tell her of her mother's new confidence but she had not realised how much things had changed since her last visit home. Aunt Agnes nudged her niece to carry on. After taking a deep breath, Bobby launched into the story she had fabricated in the hallway three minutes earlier.

'She's the niece of Ellen, one of the girls at Hamble. She's got family in France, some of them managed to get out but Elizé's mother is still there and the child needs a place to stay. Ellen's home is in Scotland, which was far too far for Elizé to travel, so I brought her here. It's OK isn't it?'

She sat back in relief. She had thought of something vaguely plausible. Agnes caught Harriet's eye. They both looked sceptically at Bobby but she was cutting into the pie in a determined fashion.

Elizé stared with surprise at Bobby on hearing about her newly-invented family, but she shrugged and got on with the milk and delicious pie in front of her. She desperately wanted to stay in this wonderful house with these strange people and was prepared to be anyone Bobby wanted her to be if it meant she could stay here. She looked at Bobby's mother, who reminded her of her lovely grandmother, who had died two years ago. Mathilda reached out her arm and clasped the child's small hand in hers. For the first time she could remember since the horrid war began, Elizé felt safe.

After supper, Bobby put her arm around Elizé's shoulders and said she would take the little girl up to show her to her bedroom.

When Bobby opened the door to the chintz-wallpapered room with a view over the garden, Elizé clapped her hands with delight and ran around the room, examining every nook and cranny. She could not believe she was going to have this lovely room all to herself. At home, she had been crammed into a corner on a mattress opposite her parents' bed. But then, suddenly the room looked too big and she felt a sharp pang of loss and her face crumpled.

Bobby patted the bed. 'Come and sit down, Elizé, I have to talk to you.'

Elizé frowned. She did not like the seriousness of Bobby's tone.

'It's all right, I know it's all strange, but you have to be very brave.' Bobby held her close. 'You can stay here, but tomorrow I have to go back to work. Everyone will look after you and I will come when I can. Will you be all right?'

Elizé looked doubtful, but then Mrs Hill bustled in, carrying an old, scruffy teddy bear.

'I'm sorry to intrude, Bobby, but I thought Elizé might like this. It belonged to my niece, before she got too big for it. I thought Elizé could look after him, his name is Mr Ted.'

Elizé hugged the bear, who looked so comfortable and friendly, she felt sure she could tell him her secrets when she felt lonely.

Bobby looked gratefully at Mrs Hill, who stood with a benign smile on her face. There was a noise behind her and Mathilda peered round the door.

'I've got a lovely ribbon, here. I thought it would look wonderful in Elizé's hair.' She edged into the room and sat down to thread it through the child's long, wavy strands. Elizé leaned back, like a kitten being groomed by its mother.

An embarrassed cough came from the landing.

'I've got to go to check the stock in a minute,' Bobby's father called. 'I wondered whether Elizé might like to come with me before she retires for the night.'

Bobby was stunned and even more so when Aunt Agnes appeared behind her mother and said, 'Here, let me help with that ribbon.'

She stood up and looked gratefully round at her family. Somehow, without her even having said a word, they were prepared to accept the story behind Elizé's appearance at the house. The table lamp shone behind Elizé's head, throwing a glistening ray through her brown curls. Bobby drew a sharp breath, wondering whether things were finally beginning to change at Salhouse Farm; was this child an angel sent to dispel the ghosts that had pervaded the house since her brother Michael had died? Time would tell, but she suddenly felt more optimistic than she had ever done.

Harriet broke the spell. She charged into the room and took hold of Bobby's hands.

'I have to go soon, can we have a few minutes to catch up, do you think?'

Without waiting for a reply, she pulled her friend past everyone and dragged her downstairs and out of the back door, leaving the family and Mrs Hill to fuss over Elizé.

Chapter 28

Harriet turned to face Bobby, her hands on her hips. 'Don't think you can just march in here with a small child and get away with it. What exactly is going on?'

Bobby looked behind her to make sure no one was listening and pulled Harriet further towards the barn to sit on some straw bales. She suddenly felt nervous that her friend would see into her innermost thoughts and decided to distract her with the intrigue about Elizé.

'Oh, Harriet, I have such a story to tell you, but I can only share a little and you cannot tell a soul. Do you hear me, Harriet Marcham, not a soul?'

Harriet made a little cross over heart like she had done when they were children. 'Cross my heart and hope to die.'

Bobby quickly ran through some thoughts in her head. She had signed the Official Secrets Act and had been left in no doubt that her activities in France could not be disclosed. She told Harriet she had been 'somewhere' and unable to get back and that Elizé had been under threat and had to escape and that, unbelievably, it had been Gus

Prince who had piloted them out of danger. She hesitated over her story, but her friend was too stupefied to notice, ignoring the missing details and grasping onto the one piece of information that was of most interest to her.

'So, you were rescued by Gus Prince? That's unbelievable!'

Bobby laughed self-consciously. 'Yes, our hero!'

'Oh, how romantic. I would have swooned in his arms, but I bet the moment was wasted on you,' she laughed.

Bobby halted for a moment while she dismissed a vision of Gus's face close to hers on the bed but then said quickly, 'There was no time for any swooning,' and deflecting the attention away from herself she went on, 'But next time, I'll tell him to come and rescue you instead. Maybe from all those GIs?' She looked at Harriet's enraptured face and was suddenly serious.

'Harriet, do you mind that I seem to keep bumping into Gus Prince? Do you still have feelings for him?' Bobby hesitated but then went on, 'It's just that, well, I have to admit, I do find him attractive and I don't know what to do about it.'

Harriet grasped Bobby's shoulders with delight. 'That's fantastic, Bobby, I've been waiting years for you to notice men and Gus Prince must be gorgeous now, he was certainly good looking when we were younger. Look, he has to marry one of us,' she said giggling, 'and I would love it to be you. I mean if he can't see what a fantastic catch I am then he doesn't deserve me.' She flicked her hair back like a movie star and giggled. 'Oh, I don't know, Bobby, he was just a childhood crush, it didn't mean anything. Of course, if you want to flirt outrageously with him and then drop him, I'll pick up the pieces when he's lost and broken-hearted and that's just fine by me.'

Harriet examined her thoughts honestly. She had forgotten all about Gus Prince until Bobby mentioned she had met him in Scotland. Then, by chance, last week, she had bumped into his mother in the greengrocers. Mrs Prince had been delighted to see Harriet, who was always a favourite of hers and had regaled her with news of her pilot son, hoping the young woman's eyes would light up with interest. Harriet did not want to confess to Bobby that since then, she had found herself scanning every pilot in blue uniform, hoping he might turn up on her base. She looked sideways at her friend. Somehow, she just could not picture her and Gus as a couple and she decided there would be no harm in daydreaming about how she was the heroine of the story, not Bobby. Such imaginings would, she knew, keep her occupied for hours during the long, tense nights on duty when she was waiting for crews to return.

Bobby was released from any more feelings of guilt by Harriet's rapid switch of subject to her exhausting shifts.

The news from Coltishall was grim; as a telephone operator Harriet was often on nights, struggling to bring home crews that she had shared breakfast with hours before. Some of them were prised out of the plane, too injured to care, other planes never returned. It was a relentless round of drama and she felt emotionally drained. She tried to think of something positive to tell Bobby. 'Oh, we had a visit from Ralph Reader's Gang Show and we all sang along to his signature tune – you know, "We're riding along on the crest of a wave,"' she sang, completely out of tune.

'Oh, I do miss you, Harriet,' Bobby laughed, reaching over to put her hand over her friend's mouth to stop the rendition, 'but I don't miss your singing.'

Harriet looked quizzically at Bobby. 'You've changed,' she announced, suddenly worried. 'You said you found Gus attractive; you're not in love, are you?'

'Yes, I think I am . . . but, no, Harriet, not with Gus – or any man for that matter.' She ignored the merged picture of Gus and Edward that had suddenly popped into her mind and failed to notice the relief on her friend's face.

'But I am in love with life, Harriet. For the first time . . . I've realised . . . well . . . how precious it is.'

Bobby lowered her head and slowly carried on, almost talking to herself. 'I've never allowed myself to feel much because somehow I didn't think I deserved love, but now,' she paused, glancing towards the house, 'that little girl has shown me how it's possible to reach out – despite everything that's happened to her – and what it's made me realise is that if you trust people, they will take you to their hearts.'

Bobby was silent for a moment. She envisaged Gus's face, expressing love for her. That was followed by the scene back in France when she remembered Raoul beaming and recounting, for the umpteenth time, amusing stories to his new extended family. Then there was Michel with a serious expression planning his next pick-up points while the long-suffering Claudette bustled around the kitchen. And finally there was her own family, offering ribbons, teddies and trips round the farm.

'Why have I never noticed the goodness in people before?' she asked Harriet.

'Because your heart was locked up in that mound of earth over there,' Harriet replied in a matter-of-fact manner. 'Look, Roberta Hollis, you had a strange childhood, that's for sure, and you're definitely a strange girl.'

Bobby pushed her gently and they both laughed.

'But,' Harriet said, more seriously, 'I do think there's something I've heard about. It's called being a twinless twin. You've always felt guilty you survived and Michael didn't, but now you need to start to live for two.'

Bobby started to pluck at the straw under her fingers. There was a long silence filled only by the caw of the rooks in the nearby trees.

'Would you give me five mins, Harriet? There's something I have to do. Don't go anywhere.'

Bobby got up and walked slowly towards the square railings by the barn. Harriet watched, her eyes pricking with tears, feeling this was a crucial moment in her friend's life.

Bobby stood with her back to her friend and to the house and spoke to Michael, as she had many times, but this time, it was different, she felt his presence like she had never done before.

'Michael, I need to have your permission to live for both of us. I've discovered over the past few weeks that I may not be the self-sufficient, driven girl who only needs flying to survive. I'm beginning to see changes in me and in our crazy family and now I've got Michel and Elizé to protect as well. But I need you to know that I haven't abandoned you. But I can't go on feeling this terrible guilt so will you . . . please . . . let me go?'

She ended her one-way conversation by reaching down and putting her hand gently on the angel's head and wiping her eyes. It felt strangely warm, even in the early evening March air and she was sure it was smiling more than usual. Her fingers stroked the top of the marble and she closed her eyes. For the first time in her life, she felt at peace.

She turned and looked at the house that had always filled her with foreboding, but now, she ran towards it, pulling at Harriet's hand on the way past.

'Come on, Harry, we need one of Mrs Hill's scones, and we need one now!'

Chapter 29

It was as if Bobby had not been away. She sat in the large armchair at Hamble and tried in vain to reply to the letters she had received from Gus and Edward. The difference in the tone of the letters summed up the two men. Gus's were casual and chatty, as if nothing had happened between them, whereas Edward always had some excuse to write to her. Something to do with advice on which trains were likely to be cancelled or which foodstuffs were going to be scarce. She inevitably ended up writing something non-committal to both of them – a little like the postcards she always sent when she went away on holiday as a child – telling them both the same things, without going into detail.

When she had returned to base, it was quite normal that no one questioned her absence. There was no time to check on each other's movements. Being an ATA pilot could be an isolating experience for a group of girls who raced around the country, only passing each other occasionally in a NAAFI or on an Anson and after her experiences in France, the companionship of Elizé and the unexpected warmth of her family, Bobby was feeling lonely. She needed to fly to take her mind off the events of the previous couple of weeks. It had all been too much for her to process and the swirling fog outside did nothing to help her clarity of thought. The girls chatted around her, swapping stories of boyfriends, aircraft differences and the best RAF base to grab a bed in but Bobby's mind was racing. She was fretting about Elizé and whether she was settling at the farmhouse, she worried at night about whether Michel and Raoul were safe and now she knew what Gus's role was in the war, she knew all too well what risks he was taking. And then there was the incomprehensible role of Edward in all that had happened. Incapable of concentrating, she threw down the notepaper in frustration.

'You all right, Bobby?' Patsy asked. Patsy had passed all her exams to be able to fly most types of aircraft. She often had her head in a book learning the controls, insignia and capabilities of everything from a Moth to a Wellington and had a single-minded attitude to her job that Bobby had always tried to emulate.

'Yes, I'm fine,' Bobby lied. 'Just fed up with being stuck here. I need to get up there and feel the air underneath the wings of the plane.'

Patsy unexpectedly reached over and touched her hand. 'I know, there's so much going on out there and we're stuck here, waiting for the fog to clear.' She stared through the window. 'You know, Bobby, this fog sums up the war.

It's like living in a world where none of us can see straight. We hear one bit of good news and then one bit of bad that seems to cancel out that glimmer of hope. We're such a small part of it all. I think the whole country is waiting for the confused picture out there to suddenly clear and reveal a blue sky to victory. It's no wonder you're feeling a bit at sixes and sevens.'

Bobby looked at her and nodded gratefully. That was exactly how she was feeling. Their role was such a small part of the bigger picture, she had not recognised how small their part was until she had gone to France. All over Europe, the world probably, she realised, there were little pockets of people doing tiny amounts to try to preserve their freedom while in Germany and Japan, their people were also fighting for what they believed they were entitled to.

'Do you think there will ever be a blue sky?' she asked Patsy, suddenly needing reassurance.

Patsy smiled. She pointed to the headline in Bobby's newspaper. 'Allies invade Holland by air', it proclaimed.

Sally was holding court as usual, regaling them all with details of a party at The Ritz in London she had gate-crashed the previous weekend. Patsy went over to help Sheila with her sewing and Christine was doing jumping jacks by the window. It was all far too normal.

Bobby went back to her letters, fingering one in her left hand from Gus and one in her right from Edward.

Really, these men are becoming a bit of an issue, she thought. *I like them both, but they're so different. I know Gus is interested in me, but, Edward?* She blew out a sigh. She had no idea how he felt about her. She tried to imagine her life with one of them and the vision always merged in her head. One appealed to her sense of fun and the other was such a safe, reliable option but, she suspected, with hidden depths. In all honesty, though, she was not sure he had even noticed her.

Edward was an enigma that was beginning to keep her awake at night and while he was certainly solicitous and polite, there had been no sign of anything other than a friendly concern. She suspected, he, too, was furious with the attempt to force a relationship between them. If she knew anything about Edward Turner, it was that he was a man who made his own decisions. On the other hand, Gus's declaration had completely unnerved her. She had no idea whether their relationship was anything more than a physical attraction? Did he know her at all? Was he enough for her?

In the end, she was saved from writing to either of them by the loudspeaker, which went off to announce that the weather was clearing and the 'chits' were about to be handed out.

Bobby was due to go take her exams soon to be able to fly the twin-engined big bombers like Manchesters and Wellingtons. It was a huge opportunity for her to rise to the lofty heights reached by only a few men and even fewer women and she wanted to make sure she did nothing to blot her copybook, so she stood eagerly in line by the hatch, waiting for the sheets to be spread out in front of them.

'I'm off to Scotland,' Theresa said with a groan. She was a tall girl who was married to a male ATA pilot; they were always trying to fix their deliveries so they could meet up en route. Charlie, her husband, she complained was scheduled for Cosford, so their rendezvous was going to have to wait. She knew that with good weather, the trip to Scotland could take three hours or if the fog persisted, it could be four days before she got back to Hamble so her face formed a pout and she turned away from the hatch clutching her 'chits'.

'I'm for Bognor, Abingdon and Ronalds . . . way,' Alena, a Polish girl said slowly. 'Where is Ronalds . . . way?'

'Oh, that's on the Isle of Man, you'll love it,' Patsy told her, laughing. With her longer experience in the ATA, she always had titbits of information about every runway. 'The land appears in your port window at the last second before you think you are about to ditch in the sea. And the weather there is always much worse than here. I'm off to good, old safe Speke and Redhill. Should be back in time for a drink.'

Bobby scanned her sheet. A Hurricane to Brize Norton, an Anson to Lee-on-Solent and then, a Spitfire to Upper

Heyford. She would have to get a move on with marking her maps, they had already lost a couple of hours of the morning.

Once all her pencil marks were sketched onto the maps, she raced to the Met Office to check the latest weather reports, then to the signals room to get the latest barrage balloon reports and finally to the locker room to pick up her overnight bag and her parachute. Bobby checked her overnight bag for the maps, toothpaste and brush and bit of Pears soap, makeup and night things. She zipped it back up and grabbed her white scarf that went everywhere with her, then she tucked a £1 note for an overnight stay and the bar of chocolate for glucose into her handbag and walked onto the runway.

The first two trips went smoothly; they were both routes Bobby had done before and she felt a moment's pride when she brought the Anson in smoothly in strong crosswinds. Without an automatic wheel drop system, she needed help to wind them down and had been assigned Luke, a young flight engineer who scowled all the way at having to be second in command to a woman all the way from Brize Norton. He had prepared so many complaints about her piloting skills but when they landed at Lee-on-Solent, he nodded at her in reluctant approval. His approbation was wasted on Bobby, who was too busy looking for her next delivery, a Spitfire to take to Upper Heyford. It was a route she was not familiar with and had to concentrate on but once she had spotted the airfield with its round Nissen huts, she skilfully brought the aircraft to a standstill on the tarmac near the control tower. Bobby looked around her. There were Wellingtons everywhere, it was a busy training station and its young pilots would soon be moving on to an operational Bomber Command airbase elsewhere.

She looked with envy at the high turrets of the Wellingtons and the impressive engines that propelled these huge aeroplanes. Her exam to raise her to a Class IV was in two weeks and on Monday, she was due to go to White Waltham to train for it. Her stomach turned over. The prospect of flying one of those great beasts was immensely exciting – and terrifying.

'Hey, it's one of those female pilots,' a voice called.

She turned around, a little fed-up with the ribaldry that always followed such a call.

'Gus!' she squealed with delight and then pulled herself up, suddenly embarrassed. 'What are you doing here?'

'More training, more sprogs,' he said, delightedly grasping her shoulders and giving her a hug. He could not believe his luck. Without a full moon to fly agents by, he had been drafted in at the last minute to cover for a pilot and he had been really bad-tempered about having to leave his post at Tempsford to go and spend three days with rookies in Oxfordshire but it seemed the fates were with him. Since Tempsford, he had been cross with himself for rushing things and had decided all he needed was time and Bobby would be his.

'How long have you got, any time for a cuppa, a drink, dinner, a lifetime?' he laughed.

She looked at her watch. It was too late to fly back to Hamble before dark.

'Do you know what, Gus Prince? You may just be in luck. I might have to stay over.'

Gus sent a silent prayer of thanks to the darkening heavens.

She arranged to meet Gus later and then left him dealing with his pupils to go and sign in. She also talked a welfare officer into assigning her a bed for the night.

Maybe this was a sign, she thought, as she swilled her face. Perhaps she was fighting fate and it was written in the stars that they should meet up. It occurred to her that it could be that fate was taking a hand because she could not.

'Stuff and nonsense,' she muttered through her tooth-paste. A practical girl from a child, Bobby had always felt like the master of her own destiny, it was just that, at this particular moment, she did not know what that destiny was.

She paused as she was about to put the toothbrush back in its bag. A disturbing vision came to her . . . that of Harriet's pretty face. She glared at her own reflection in the mirror in disgust. No matter what Harriet said, somehow, Bobby had always been convinced Gus was destined for Harriet.

* * *

That evening, when she and Gus were sharing a couple of drinks and a bag of crisps in The Bell, Gus pointed up to the beams and told her about The Bluebell in East Kirkby where RAF crews left their pennies to buy a round when they returned from a mission. It was a tradition that young pilots at Upper Heyford had started to emulate but, even here, a number of coins had started to build up, patiently waiting for their owners to return. His face clouded for a moment. He had witnessed too many crashes by inexperienced pilots who never even got the chance to fire one shot in anger at the enemy.

Bobby felt a chill in the back of her neck and suddenly looked at Gus in panic. It had never occurred to her that he might die, flying low over the fields of France every time there was a full moon. The thought made her examine her heart. Did she really care for this man? How would she feel if he was hurt?

She put her hand to her head and ran her fingers through her hair.

'Are you OK, Bobby? You seem a bit distracted. Is my conversation not scintillating enough for you?'

'Yes, I'm fine, sorry, it's been quite a month, I don't know whether I'm coming or going.'

She looked intently at the man on the other side of the table from her. He was so attractive but for some reason, he felt more like a friend than anything else. She had often thought about the episode at Tempsford but had never been able to imagine anything deeper happening between them. She looked across at him as he launched into yet another amusing anecdote about a pilot who was so arrogant about his flying ability that his crew tied a blindfold around his eyes before take-off. His bumpy ascent nearly cost them all their lives, Gus told her, but the pilot never boasted again. Finishing triumphantly, Gus looked up for admiration. Bobby studied his face closely and examined her feelings. She liked Gus but in her heart of hearts, she sensed that his easy charm and excellent sense of humour would never be enough for her and that her fierce independence was not the adoring audience he needed. Edward was another matter, she thought. She knew she had hardly skimmed the surface of his character but felt, somewhere deep inside, that he would listen carefully to every nuance of what she was experiencing and would be able to give her the support she needed. Bobby realised that, even without Harriet in the frame, she and Gus were not meant to be.

*   *   *

Bobby was quiet for the rest of the evening and Gus went to bed perplexed. He was getting a little fed up with this game. He felt a fierce attraction for Bobby but it always felt as if he were chasing a moonbeam. He tried to examine his feelings. Gus had almost found it too easy to be successful with women and had found the challenge of Roberta Hollis irresistible. He always had done but as a grown man, it occurred to him that he might be enjoying the chase too much. What he did not want to do was ask himself how he would feel if he ever really did catch her.

Chapter 30

The following morning, Bobby was sitting in the guard room at Upper Heyford waiting for her 'chits' for the day. She was not feeling at her most patient and was getting irritated at the length of time she was having to wait. She started to drum her fingers on her trousers. There was a golden-haired WAAF sitting next to her, trying hard not to gaze at the gold-winged insignia on her tunic.

'Hello,' the girl said. 'I'm sorry for staring but are they really pilot's wings?' She pointed at the wings.

Bobby smiled at her. 'My name is Roberta, Bobby for short.' Slightly embarrassed, Bobby pointed to the insignia and leaned over to explain. 'I'm in the ATA, that's the Air Transport Auxiliary, I deliver aircraft .'

The girl's mouth dropped open. She had heard about these mythical creatures but had never imagined she would meet one.

'My name is Lily,' she stammered. Then she came out with a torrent of questions. How did she get to be an ATA pilot, what did she fear most, how did she deal with all the male prejudice, which aircraft was the best to fly and . . . and . . . ?

'Whoa,' Bobby said, laughing. 'One question at a time.'

'I'm so sorry,' Lily said, blushing. 'I've just never met a woman pilot before and it's just . . . amazing.'

Bobby looked at the naked adoration on the girl's face. It was so different from the sceptical comments she got from men and often, the blatant jealousy of women. This girl was just an open book of interest and approval.

Bobby explained to her about how she was the only daughter of a farmer in Norfolk and how she had watched her father and Archie drive, mend and repair the machinery. She paused and then added in a matter-of-fact manner that her male twin had died at birth so no one had even noticed she was a girl and she had learned lots of things a girl would not be expected to know.

Bobby stumbled over the words, realising how difficult it was, even now, to discuss Michael with a stranger but the girl was too absorbed in her story to notice. Bobby took a breath and carried on. She explained that once her father extended the farm, he had started, at Bobby's suggestion, to look at the way they sprayed crops in America and decided it might be a good investment to let her have flying lessons.

'What's it like up there?' Lily asked breathlessly, breaking in on Bobby's thoughts.

'It's incredible, Bobby admitted, suddenly released from her usual reticence. Acknowledging Michael's death was giving her a freedom she had never experienced before and it felt good.

She closed her eyes and then opened them to glance across; Lily had her eyes shut too.

'I feel the controls in my hands, the throb of the engine under my feet and I look towards the runway knowing I can whizz over it in a matter of seconds and then that moment when I lift the wheels up . . . there is nothing like it in the whole world. I feel as if I am an angel, taking wing and flying off into the unknown. I feel as if nothing can touch me – although I know I'm at risk from the enemy, faulty machinery or the weather, just like any other pilot, for some reason, I never worry about that. I am in control and nothing can hurt me.'

'Is this what you were waiting for?' The desk officer was standing in front of Bobby holding out a sheet of paper.

'Oh, thank you,' Bobby said. Lily looked up in surprise to see someone else standing there. Bobby stood up and turned to face the young WAAF.

'Goodbye, Lily, it's been nice to meet you.' She turned to go and then turned back.

'Go for your dreams, Lily, no one can deny you the chance to try.'

She then told Lily about the ATA's Ab Initio pro-gramme, which was now allowing people who had never flown to apply. She saw the girl's face light up.

Bobby swept out of the guard room. Behind her was a young woman who had no idea what she could achieve.

She felt a tap on her shoulder.

'How do I find out about this programme?' Lily asked breathlessly.

Bobby told her to ask her superiors.

Lily thanked her and then suddenly gushed, 'We may never meet again but I want to say you are the most amazing woman I have ever met and you may have changed my life. I will never, ever forget you.'

Bobby stared after her. She had been so wound up with everything that had happened to her she had forgotten how important her small part in this huge war machine was and how the role of women in the ATA could be seen as a beacon for women in the future.

'Thank you, Lily,' she whispered to the back of the disappearing girl.

* * *

The 'chits' were finally handed out and Bobby headed out to the Anson taxi she was to fly to Gosport where there was a Spitfire waiting for her to be delivered to Cosford and from there, she was to take a Mustang to Bognor Regis. She hoped there would be a car waiting to take her to the station from there as it was only a grass Advanced Landing Ground and not a full tarmac runway so there would be no chance of a lift in an Anson home. She glanced at her watch. With any luck, if there was a car, she would make it back to Hamble in time for supper.

This time she had a flight engineer called Walter who was waiting for her, looking just as churlish as Luke had the day before. Being second fiddle to ATA pilots was not the most appealing shift and the fact that this one was a woman had already made him the butt of jokes in the NAAFI that morning.

'Let's go, Walter, I've got pilots waiting to be ferried and four more deliveries today,' she said distractedly, not hearing his muttered reply that he preferred to fly with male pilots.

They took off with six passengers. Two of them Bobby knew but the others she did not.

'Hi, Dolly, Phil. How are you both?' she asked.

Phil leaned over to two other male pilots who were looking suspiciously at Bobby.

'Don't worry, she's a good pilot,' Phil confided. 'One of the best actually.'

They all settled onto the double row of seats in the back.

'It might be a bit bumpy,' Bobby warned. 'Find something to hang onto. There are some cross winds.'

As they approached Gosport, she circled, wondering how she was going to land at such a small airfield. She struggled to hold the controls, battling against the wind, which had picked up more than ever. The chatter in the back had stopped and there was a tense silence.

After pitching and tossing from side to side, Bobby finally brought the aircraft to a halt, right outside the control tower. When she climbed out, the airport's CO came out of the tower towards them. He looked completely startled. His own squadron was grounded due to the strength of the wind, he informed her, and yet the only aircraft flying was being flown by what he had just called 'A flaming slip of a girl.' He was not pleased, but Bobby was and strode past him and a stunned Walter to sign in at the control tower. Then she went to find the NAAFI for a well-deserved cup of tea. She was beginning to be less in awe of these men in uniform.

The canteen was quiet but a steady buzz of conversation was going on in one corner. Two male ATA pilots that Bobby did not know had their heads together, speaking in hushed tones.

She took her cup of tea over to them and stood, waiting to see whether they would welcome the intrusion of a female pilot. They looked up, almost guiltily as if caught in an unsuitable conversation and then one of them got up and pulled a chair out for her. She was surprised, it was not often that women were accepted so easily by their male colleagues.

'Bobby,' she said, reaching over to shake their hands.

'Paul, and this is Harry,' one of them replied. 'Just got in have you?'

'Yes, Anson taxi from Upper Heyford.'

'We saw you come in, quite some flying that,' Paul begrudgingly acknowledged. He paused for a moment. 'If you're just in, don't suppose you've heard, have you? About Patsy Collins?'

Bobby's insides turned over. 'What?' she falteringly asked, remembering the restroom at Hamble the day before when Patsy had talked about going to 'good old safe Speke and Redhill.'

'Goner,' was the stark reply. 'She misjudged the runway at Speke and the wind got her. Took her straight into the gas works. It was lucky only the aircraft went up in smoke, could have wiped out Speke.'

Bobby stared down at her cup of tea. Reflected in the liquid, she saw Patsy's face, laughing at jokes, sniffling with a cold and grinning in the taxi on the way to the Gosport party and her own eyes blurred. It seemed impossible that such a good pilot could have had such a tragic accident but she, herself, had experienced that day's strong winds and knew how the gusts would sweep relentlessly across the exposed Liverpool industrial areas. She took a deep breath to control the tears that threatened to fall. Losing a pilot was a disaster that affected them all, including the two men in front of her and they all looked glumly into their cups. These men had both lost ATA pilot friends, like Bobby had, and it made no difference what sex they were. Bobby stirred her tea fiercely.

'Not good to lose this many pilots,' Paul said. 'Especially women. You've all been doing a great job.' He reached across and put his hand on her shoulder, giving it a squeeze.

Bobby was surprised to hear him speak so warmly of female pilots and thanked him with a nod, unable to speak.

'It's all right, I've worked with some damned good women pilots,' he said, pouring more condensed milk into his tea, 'and I doubt any man could have just brought that Anson in better than you just now. We're all at the mercy of the weather, your friend was just unlucky.'

They all sat in silence and then Paul got up to go. 'I'm getting the train back, so I'm off. Don't take off until these winds have subsided,' he urged Bobby.

She looked up, surprised at his concern.

'It's a habit. I've got three sisters,' he said, putting on his jacket and grabbing his helmet and parachute. Bobby took herself off to the toilet, where she leaned back against the cold, white tiles before letting the tears flow. It took time for her to compose herself enough to be able to go to the Met Office to check if the winds really had subsided. An ops manager advised her that the Mustang to Bognor Regis was cancelled but that she should be OK to fly the Spitfire to Cosford.

Hamble was subdued when Bobby finally got back, and every time she looked around the restroom, she would hear Patsy's laugh. The whole group was devastated by the loss of a friend and fellow pilot but they all reacted differently.

Some wanted to talk well into the night, sharing memories of the girl from Lancashire who had made them laugh on so many occasions while others, like Bobby, took themselves off to bed early to pull the bedclothes around themselves and gently reflect on a war that did not seem to know the normal rules that stipulated young people should survive to old age.

The following day, Bobby tried to put all thoughts of Patsy out of her head and concentrate on packing for No. 1 Ferry Pool, White Waltham, for her big bomber training. She could not believe how guilty she felt that her life was moving on while arrangements for Patsy's funeral were being posted on the noticeboard. She was due at Transport for ten o'clock so she ran past the wooden board, only pausing in the corridor for a second while she took in the time and date of the service. She sent a fervent prayer to the heavens that she would be able to get time off to attend the funeral.

Chapter 31

Roberta Hollis leant over her book in the classroom at White Waltham. She had her ruler across the page, testing herself on the next paragraph. She was enjoying the total concentration of the intensity of the training. It was like going back to school with disciplined days and concentrated study time and after Patsy's funeral, she particularly appreciated how hard work blocked out other thoughts. The funeral had been such an emotional event with Patsy's large family from Lancashire filling the front pews. Not all the Hamble girls had been able to make it, but there were enough of them to form a guard of honour as the coffin passed, their heads held back stiffly to honour their friend. The patient engineering instructors at White Waltham had also heard about the female ATA pilot and it made them work even more tirelessly to make sure that the young people in front of them would never be unsure about which instrument did what, how to deal with different weather patterns and how to cope with unforeseen problems. One, a tall man in his fifties, called Reg, constantly warned the young women in his classroom about the risks of flying dozens of different aircraft at a moment's notice in all conditions. A veteran instructor, he had seen too many names being posted of people who had sat in those very desks in front of him now. His words resonated in particular with one young pilot in the front row with deep auburn hair who still cried every night for her dead friend.

'You never put your personal safety at risk, fly in fog or fail to prepare adequately,' he told them for the third time that week.

'You never fly in anything but a completely professional manner and you never think you know better than the Met Office. Take your time to do your navigation plan and at the first sign of danger, find somewhere to land.'

He sighed and set them their next task, which was looking at how the transmission worked on a Wellington.

Reg was an experienced pilot himself, but he knew that being an ATA pilot was a particularly dangerous career and one that was exacerbated by the hectic schedules they had to follow and the range of aircraft they had to fly. He had a daughter in the Navy in Portsmouth and as he looked at the bent heads of the young women in the classroom, he decided he might go through the safety checks one more time before tea with them.

* * *

Later that night, Bobby was going through her notebook. She studied the bewildering set of notes about fuel and oil systems, speed propellers, gauges, flaps and undercarriages, which were different in every plane. She decided she would go to the library after dinner to find out more about how the American aircraft systems, with more electrical systems, could be de-mystified. She had to learn them so thoroughly that, even under pressure, she would be able to carry out a strict cockpit drill before taking off. There were terrifying stories about rushed engineers leaving spanners in the cockpit, which ended up under a rudder pedal, and that could be fatal. It was drummed into all of them that one mistake or a hurried departure could cost them their lives.

The test flights on the twin bombers always included the pilot being able to fly with only one engine in case of failure or an enemy hit and most trainees struggled to keep the huge wingspans level without two operating engines.

'A Wellington has a wingspan of eighty-six feet and two inches,' Reg told them all the following day during a practical session on the runway.

'No wonder they won't stay straight,' Audrey, the girl Bobby was sharing her digs with, whispered. 'it's like trying to fly with twenty eagles tied to each other.'

The group looked up at the huge beast that was towering above them.

Reg continued, 'It is seventeen feet high, so obviously you'll need a ladder to climb up, not swing yourselves in like on a Spit.'

He then went on to explain how the catch on the door opened two ways and how you had to remember the correct way to push it. He then asked for a volunteer, but before anyone could speak, he turned to Bobby, who was immediately on his left and pushed her towards the ladder. 'You'll do. Up you go.'

He told Bobby to sit in the front seat and then pushed the catch so that the hatch was open. Bobby suddenly dropped out of the bottom of the plane, into the arms of a waiting engineer, who was primed for the moment and was already laughing when her backside appeared above him.

'And that's what happens if you get it wrong,' the tutor said with a certain amount of satisfaction to the giggling crowd.

Blushing with embarrassment, Bobby brushed herself off and stood next to the engineer. He was young and rather good-looking, she noticed, feeling it might have been less embarrassing if he had been fifty and ugly.

'Fourth one today,' he said triumphantly. 'The others were a bit heavier though, and not as pretty. Maybe I could buy you a drink tonight?' he said quietly into her ear.

'Sorry, I've got the practical exam tomorrow and need to be on my best form,' Bobby replied reluctantly. Maybe after all the tension she had been under, a night out with a good-looking engineer was exactly what she needed, but she had last-minute cramming to do and she wanted to get to bed early. 'Maybe tomorrow night?' she suggested.

His face lit up. 'Sounds good to me, we can celebrate your success.'

'Yep,' she replied, 'or commiserate.'

Audrey winked at her. 'Think you've made a hit there,' she said to Bobby. 'Looks like you've fallen for him!'

Bobby grinned and took hold of her arm as they walked to get a well-deserved cup of tea.

Bobby spent the evening in the library, going through all her notes and imagining all sorts of problems that she could face as a pilot of a huge twin bomber. There were so many it was daunting. When she had started flying over the farm, she had never imagined she would get to this stage and a shiver of excitement went through her.

*　*　*

The following day's test went well and Bobby's examiner nodded approvingly when she performed the prescribed manoeuvres, making notes on his clipboard. Fortunately, the weather was kind to her but there were some sudden gusts as she came in to land. She kept repeating the mantra she had developed over her years in the ATA to herself. 'As cool as a cucumber, as cool as a cucumber.' Imagining the chilled salad vegetable had always, for some reason, taken the heat out of the situation for her and she knew that to panic always caused disaster, so she calmly veered the aircraft more into the wind and came to a standstill on the tarmac, looking a great deal more at ease than she felt.

'Congratulations, First Officer Hollis, you are now qualified to fly Class IV aircraft,' her examiner told her.

She could have kissed him but she managed to just smile gratefully and, apart from her shaking hands that struggled to get her out of her straps, there was no hint of what was going on inside her trembling body.

By the time she got back to her digs, she was skipping, humming a song.

Mrs Wilberforce, her hostess at White Waltham, was waiting and came out to greet her. 'Did you pass, my dear?'

'Yes, I did, Mrs Wilberforce,' Bobby said, with an enormous grin.

'Well, I'm sure that's very good, dear. Well done.'

Bobby suspected that Mrs Wilberforce was not convinced by these young women doing men's jobs, but at that moment, the young pilot could not have cared less.

'I have had a telephone call,' Mrs Wilberforce went on as they mounted the steps to the house.

'A Mr Edward Turner is going to call round. He would like to take you out for dinner. He will be here at seven o'clock. 'He sounded very commanding,' she added.

Bobby stopped in her tracks. She had arranged to meet the nice engineer, whose name she could not remember, but there was not a moment's doubt in her mind. She wanted to meet Edward.

Audrey was in the bedroom waiting for her. She was tense with excitement. In her hands she was holding her own qualification – she had passed that morning – but she held it behind her back until she saw Bobby's face. As soon as she saw the huge smile that reflected her own, she relaxed and waved the piece of paper in the air like a Union Jack. Bobby did the same and they both collapsed in giggles onto their beds.

'We did it, we did it!' Audrey chanted, suddenly jumping onto the bed and bouncing up and down.

'Shhh, you'll have the force of Mrs Wilberforce on us,' Bobby chuckled, and then paused. 'Audrey, you could save my life. You know that nice engineer . . .'

'Do I ever? He's gorgeous.'

'Well, tonight's your lucky night,' Bobby told her. 'Something, or actually someone, has come up and I can't go on the date. Would you be my complete heroine and go out with him instead?'

Audrey pretended to look doubtful. 'Well, I don't know, it will be a real favour, obviously, but we Class IV pilots have to stick together. So all right, reluctantly, I'll do it.'

Bobby threw her pillow at her.

The next hour was spent in the complete luxury of having fresh towels brought by the maid and being able to wash their hair in almost enough hot water.

'I'm so grateful to Mr Wilberforce for dying and not needing bathwater,' Audrey giggled. The two girls swapped the dregs of their lipstick, debated which outfits to wear and planned how they were going to sweep the unsuspecting men off their feet with their glamorous appearances. It reminded Bobby of pre-war days with Harriet. They seemed like a lifetime away.

'I could get used to this,' Audrey admitted, helping herself to two of Bobby's hair slides. 'A maid, fluffy towels and not having to rely on Eau de Cologne for my greasy locks.

'Oh, and,' she added, 'a lovely young man to go out with. At Cosford, there are only women and sometimes I feel female solidarity is a somewhat overrated thing.'

By five to seven, Bobby was ready and waiting in the hallway, with her coat on. She suddenly felt really nervous. This was the man her father thought she was going to marry. She was shaking again, she realised, but was not sure whether it was due to her success in her exam or the fact that Edward was coming to see her. She was almost giddy.

Edward, too, felt more out of control than usual. He had been to Reading for a meeting and could not resist making a detour to White Waltham to see Bobby, whose anxiety about her exam in her letters had made him long to take her in his arms to give her confidence. He knew he was taking a risk and that if she had failed, she would not be in the mood to share a relaxing meal with him, but as soon as he drew up in his black car outside her digs, she ran out with her arms outstretched.

Edward's mother had never hugged him in his life and his father was a distant figure, but the spontaneity of this wonderful woman in front of him made him bolder than he had ever been and he gathered her in towards him. She drew back, suddenly realising her exuberance was a little excessive, but it was too late, Edward was not going to let go.

'Edward . . .' she said gently, after a moment.

He immediately dropped his arms and shuffled backwards, his head down in embarrassment. 'Sorry, sorry, I just . . .'

'It's all right, it was a nice hug and I deserve it,' she finished with a flourish, 'I passed, Edward, I passed.'

The awkward moment was over and he was able to gather his wits and shepherd her towards the car. The driver was smiling to himself, seeing this high-up civil servant in a new light. He could not wait to share this information with his mates back at the transport depot.

Edward took Bobby to a country house hotel just out-side Reading; he did not want to share this evening with any other ATA pilots in a local pub. It was much posher than anywhere Bobby had ever been, in fact, she acknowl-edged, as her family never ate out, her experience of fine dining establishments was very limited.

Edward took her coat and handed it to the waiter. He pulled out the plush, red chair for her and she sat down, suddenly feeling like a schoolgirl.

He took command of the wine list and ordered a claret. 'Is that all right with you, Bobby?'

She nodded, speechless. She had spotted the obligatory five-shilling menu introduced in 1942 by Lord Woolton at the entrance but the whole place shouted opulence none-theless. Apart from the price of the menu, there was no sign of war deprivation here.

The waiter placed a white napkin on her lap with a flourish and stood to attention by the table.

He leaned forward and whispered in Edward's ear, 'I believe we managed to bag some pigeon today, sir. Would the lady like that, our chef does it with a particularly lovely sauce.'

Bobby nodded, looking around her. It was as if the war was not on and the unbidden vision of the Bisset's kitchen with its turnip soup made her stomach suddenly lurch.

'Oh Edward,' she said, leaning forward to whisper, 'this isn't right. All those people with no food and we have all this,' she waved her hand expansively.

For a moment, Edward was horrified. He had so wanted to give Bobby a treat and now his plan was in danger of backfiring.

'I just wanted you to have a break from the war, after all that you've been through,' he stuttered.

'Oh, that is so sweet of you, it's just hard when I know what others are going through.'

He leant across and brushed a stray hair from her face. 'Our being here cannot change what is happening out there and we are both doing our bit to try to help this war come to a satisfactory conclusion, but I wanted tonight to be special. I wanted to spoil you.'

For one panic-stricken moment, Bobby thought he was about to whip out a diamond ring and go down on one knee but he carried on, hurriedly reverting to a professional stance.

'We know how hard France was for you and the office wanted to thank you.'

She breathed a sigh of relief that this was a semi-business arrangement and then realised her next feeling was one of disappointment. *Oh dear,* she thought, *I don't know what I want, let alone what he wants from me."*

During the meal, the conversation flowed as fast as the wine and Bobby felt a little tipsy, so that when Edward came up with his next idea, she was more than receptive.

'I have to go back to London tomorrow,' he said. 'I am staying tonight at the pub in Marlow but I know you have two days off before you have to be back at Hamble and I was wondering whether you would like to come with . . . me.'

He stopped, realising how his proposition sounded.

'Obviously, you would stay in a hotel, courtesy of the Foreign Office.' He saw her face relax and then, he could not be sure, but maybe a look of disappointment? 'But there are some sights I could show you.'

Bobby had never been to London and the thought of going was a thrilling prospect, especially with Edward, she realised, but then she hesitated. She was not sure where either of them wanted this road to lead.

Eventually, the combination of the wine and the success of the day won and she heard her voice saying, 'Yes, I'd love to!'

Chapter 32

Gus was furious. He marched up and down the mess. He had just made his weekly telephone call to his mother, only to be regaled with the latest gossip from Salhouse, which she could not wait to share with him. She had heard, only this afternoon at the Red Cross meeting, that that independent miss, Roberta Hollis, was going to be married off to some civil servant called Edward Turner. Gus's mother had failed to notice her son's sudden silence until he abruptly told her he had to go, slamming down the phone, and leaving her staring at the receiver in surprise. A prompt call to Hamble told him exactly what he did not want to know; that First Officer Hollis had just that minute left with someone in a large black car to go to London.

There was only one person who could have persuaded her to go to London and that was this Edward 'Toff' Turner, he fumed. He winced as he thought of Bobby and some faceless bureaucrat character strolling up Pall Mall together. He felt he had been doing so well and then this pin-striped character had turned up on the scene. He could not believe it and banged his cigarette out noisily on the ashtray.

'You OK?' Walter asked, pausing on his way to get a cup of tea.

'Yes ... no, oh Walter, women! Don't they drive you nuts?'

'Constantly, mate, constantly. That's why I need a slice of something sweet with this tea. I've been stood up for tonight. Maybe we should go to the pub and see who we can chat up there?'

Gus turned to face his friend. 'Yep, that's exactly what we'll do, who needs 'em. We've got missions tomorrow, let's enjoy ourselves.'

* * *

By that time, Bobby was having the time of her life. Edward was an excellent, informed guide and he revelled in being able to take her round some of the sights. They both went quiet as they passed the ones that had been bombed and Bobby struggled to imagine their former grandeur. They strolled down The Strand towards Fleet Street and Ludgate Hill and eventually to St Paul's Cathedral. She was completely overawed at the story of how firefighters had struggled for hours to keep St Paul's free of the flames that threatened to engulf it from nearby St Paul's Churchyard.

'Churchill demanded it should be saved,' Edward explained as they stood looking up at its huge dome.' He looked at his watch.

'Come on, I need to call in somewhere. I'm hoping for some news you might be interested in.'

Bobby was getting used to the mysterious nature of this tall man next to her, but his next words took her by surprise.

'You remember that you've signed the Official Secrets Act?' He looked sharply at her. He just needed to remind her.

'Yes,' she replied, 'of course.'

'Good, let's go then.'

He took her arm and marched her off down Embankment towards the House of Commons, empty and forlorn after the government relocated parliament to Church House. The Blitz had done its damage to the Mother of Parliaments.

They arrived at a small door in St George's Street. Edward knocked on the door and a marine opened it slightly.

'Afternoon, sir, good to see you again.'

'Afternoon, Lieutenant, I have a guest with me. She's got clearance but needs to sign in.'

Bobby was taken to a desk where the Lieutenant, with a blush, pushed to one side a piece of embroidery he was doing to relieve the boredom. He gave her a pen and she signed her name and rank in the huge ledger that was there but had no idea what she was signing or where she was. The marine gave her a badge. Edward took his own out from his top pocket.

He gave her a boyish grin and motioned for her to walk down the corridor in front of him.

She glanced from side to side, seeing small rooms with desks, and walked past people in uniform scurrying backwards and forwards. It was an underground rabbit warren.

Edward led the way and every time he strolled through a corridor, people stood to one side to let him pass. *He's certainly well known here*, Bobby thought.

He took her into a room with maps and a row of telephones in the middle. She looked at the maps; they had pieces of coloured wool connected by drawing pins. In front of her was the whole world and the enormity of the war suddenly struck her. There were pins from Norway to Russia, from Japan to Australia and from Paris to London. This was a strange place and seemed like a hive of activity but she had no idea what it was all for, and Edward did not tell her that this was where Churchill, the prime minister, and his advisors had moved to in order to run the war from a place of safety.

The phones rang constantly and men in uniform rushed to answer them, but Edward ploughed on, through corridor after corridor. She passed one room with a toilet vacant/engaged sign and wondering what that could be, she peered in to see a telephone on a desk.

'That's a transatlantic line,' Edward whispered to her, mysteriously. Intrigued, Bobby longed to ask more but Edward had moved on. She felt she was watching a film at the pictures.

As they moved along the next corridor, she distinctly smelt the odour of a cigar.

'Is that . . .?' She stopped, dumbfounded.

'Yes, probably. He's in here most of the time,' Edward replied as if it were the most natural thing in the world to have just passed down the same corridor as Churchill.

'If you hear three taps on the pipes, you'll know he's gone for his nap and we all have to be quiet until we hear two taps to say he's awake,' Edward whispered with a boyish grin. He pushed on towards a small room with one desk and a telephone. In it was a civilian who sprang to his feet when Edward pushed open the door.

'Can I help you, sir?' he said.

'Yes, hello Matthews,' Edward replied. 'I'm looking for the latest information from the Normandy network. Do you have it?'

'Yessir. It's just come in. I think you've been expecting it.'

He handed over a piece of paper to Edward, who studied it with a frown. Then his face cleared.

'We think we may have traced where she went,' he announced triumphantly.

Bobby looked at him questioningly.

'It's Elizé's mother, we've got a trace on the train that took her. We believe we may know where she is,' he said, with a satisfied smile.

Bobby put her hand over her mouth, to stop herself squealing with delight.

'Is she . . . is she all right?' she nervously asked.

'We don't know, but there is a possibility she may still be alive,' came the reply.

Bobby immediately envisaged little Elizé's face when she told her.

Edward read on and his face clouded. She may have gone to Aincourt, the report said. He knew that prisoners from that camp were usually handed over to the Gestapo and then they would transit to Drancy internment camp and from there would be moved to extermination camps. It sent a shiver down his spine.

'We can't get to her, so don't get Elizé's hopes up,' he said, trying to sound reassuring.

He thanked the officer and shepherded Bobby out.

As they emerged into the spring sunshine, she breathed the clear air with relief. Edward took her arm. He felt chilled. He had so hoped to give her some positive news.

'Come on,' he said, 'let's find somewhere to have a drink. I could do with one.'

Bobby looked at his face and recognised the deep concern that she found there. She knew he had wanted to give her an optimistic update and she tucked her hand into his arm and gave him a squeeze.

'I know you're doing your best, Edward. It's all any of us can expect.'

She leaned forward and gave him a kiss. He immediately responded and she found herself dissolving into his arms. This time there was no hesitation.

Chapter 33

Edward was not sure what was happening to him. He felt giddy, like a schoolboy. His two days in London had left him breathless. After that kiss outside the War Rooms, Edward Turner's personality threatened to light up like a sparkler. It was as if he had escaped his self-imposed crusty chrysalis to find a world full of beautiful butterflies.

He had started to wonder whether the boring persona he had adopted was beginning to convince everyone a little too much – even himself. But that was before Roberta Hollis.

Bobby was having a different problem. She was having such a good time with Edward, who had suddenly blossomed into a charming, fun companion, that it had taken her by complete surprise. The serious, halting man she had first met had vanished with their first kiss and Bobby found herself touching her lips, memorising the tender, yet intense caress. She had no idea what was going on inside herself and she longed to talk to someone but did not know who.

Once she was back at work, however, Bobby put all concerns about her private life on hold as usual. There were aeroplanes to fly.

It was 5th June 1944 and she was due to fly a Hurricane to Hawarden and then a Wellington from Hawarden to Shawbury but had been told to check the weather throughout the day as it was likely to change. When she arrived at Hawarden, she managed to grab a cup of tea in the NAAFI. There were four airmen on the table next to her who looked at her with interest.

She smiled at them. 'Afternoon,' she said cheerily. 'You flying from here?'

'Yes,' the tall, thin pilot replied. 'We fly bombers.'

Bobby nodded and gave a slight smile.

There was a pause and then one of them, who looked too young to be in uniform, said, 'What are you doing here, then?'

'Just going to Shawbury, with that there,' she said, pointing to the Wellington that was waiting by the control tower for her.

The young man spat out his tea over his cup and saucer. 'You're doing what?'

'Delivering that,' she repeated.

'Never. On your own?' the pilot butted in.

'Apparently so,' she said, resisting the urge to sound superior.

'For God's sake, it takes at least five of us to fly a Wellington and you're telling us that you, a girl, do it on your own?'

'Yep.'

Bobby finished her tea and gave them a cheerful wave. The four men watched her go with a mix of astonishment and admiration and then turned back to the overriding conversation of all pilots, that of the impending briefing everyone had been talking about for weeks. The pilot glanced at his watch, it was not long to go before they would be called in and he suspected their fate – and that of the nation – would be sealed.

The confidence waned a little as Bobby hauled herself up the ladder into the main hatch on the lower surface of the aircraft's nose. She pulled the ladder in after her and clambered her way into the cockpit of the huge machine, having a good look around her as she went before sitting in the cavernous cockpit, which was used to housing more crew than a solitary young woman. Bobby meticulously carried out all her test checks and then took a huge breath and started up the enormous Merlin engines. They roared into life, almost making her jump out of her skin. This was a different animal to the nifty Spitfire. She started to taxi down the runway ready to take off at exactly eighty miles per hour, noticing with alarm that her every move was being watched by the RAF men she had met in the

NAAFI. They were shielding their eyes against the late afternoon sun and she could not help but notice they had their mouths open just like those airmen in a field in Lancashire two years before.

By the time she reached the edge of Shropshire, the weather had closed in and the clouds were getting lower and lower. Bobby knew she was going to have difficulty flying this aircraft at a low level and urged it to get on the ground before the winds and visibility worsened.

'So much for "flaming June" she thought, glaring at the grey clouds that were threatening to engulf her.

* * *

In London, Edward was standing with a group of civil servants behind the Prime Minister, who was puffing his cigar at double speed. They were watching from the sidelines in the War Rooms, as the meteorologists and strategic experts still argued about the weather for the D-Day Landings. The debate seemed a waste of time to Edward, and he suspected to Churchill too, as the convoys had already set off across the choppy seas. The Allied Forces were already committed. He remembered the way the wind funnelled between England and France and how, as a keen, young sailor, he had longed for strong winds to get the full exhilaration of the day's sail but he hoped they would not get them today. Edward was exhausted but no more so than the men around him. Hardly any of them had had any sleep during the last week and put-up beds had appeared all over the underground rabbit warren that was the hub of the war's strategic planning. A tea trolley appeared and there was a general buzz of excitement. Extra biscuits had been unearthed by the matronly figure of Mrs Webb, who bustled around the tea urn, handing out cups and saucers. She manoeuvred purposefully amid the leaders of the country, making sure they all had a plate and then, believing there was nothing like a bit of sweet biscuit to revive the spirits, she handed round the orange drop cookies. Scanning the room to make sure everyone had got one, she turned her trolley round, patted her pinny in place and retired back to the tiny kitchen, feeling that she too, had done her bit during this tense moment in world history.

* * *

In France, Michel and Raoul Bisset were standing in their front room, gazing through the window in undisguised glee at the RAF aircraft above them. The streets of their hamlet were eerily quiet but they could hear the distant sounds of gunfire and could see the smoke. They had been working non-stop to put a resistance plan in place to harass the Germans from the south of the Département de Calvados to keep them away from the coastline. The two men had no idea where the troops had landed but from the direction of the wind and the sound it carried, Raoul was delighted it was in the opposite direction to where German troops had been heading earlier that week. The Allies had fooled the enemy and the two Bisset men could not have been more pleased. Raoul put his hand on Michel's shoulder saying, '*Vive la Libération*.' Then they both put on their boots, grabbed their rifles from the cellar and headed out to help the Allies achieve just that.

* * *

In the skies above Shawbury, the liberation of France was the last thing on Bobby's mind. She was having far too much trouble keeping the huge wingspan of the Wellington on an even keel. It was her first delivery of this aircraft and she desperately wanted it to be right but there was a strange noise coming from the fuselage. She checked all her gauges and dials, everything was in order but the noise was getting louder. She tried to put down the landing gear, but there was a sickening crunch as it reached the halfway point. This was a newly-repaired aeroplane and her experience had taught her that the rush to get craft back in the air sometimes meant that problems were not automatically solved before they were released. She had two choices, either to circle with one hand while she tried to free the wheels with the other or to attempt to land. The first option was too risky – and difficult – so she had no choice. Bobby knew the control tower was watching her closely and hoped she would get the plane, and herself, down in one piece. She saw a green flare being shot off, which showed they had spotted her difficulties and were ready for a forced landing. The ambulance and fire engine moved into position.

Bobby gulped down the panic that had risen from her stomach into her throat. There was no time for that. She had to use all her training and experience to work out the best way to get this huge aircraft – and herself – onto the ground in one piece. She looked down at the airfield below. The obvious route onto the tarmac looked hard and uninviting but there was a large stretch of grass to one side of it. She decided the softer earth was her best hope. Checking all the instruments, she made sure the nose of the Wellington was turned upwind to help her get a straight approach, then closed the throttles and tried to get the aircraft in the best position for landing, using her rudder to keep it into the wind. Her flaps had to be reduced in proportion to the wind strength but she needed all their strength to help her slow down and on top of all that, she was not sure the wheels were going to cooperate with the controls she was pushing with all her might. There were some loud noises that seemed to reverberate through the whole aircraft, making it – and her – shudder but then she felt the wheels touch down, banging, rather than gliding onto the ground.

This was the moment she had dreaded the most – keeping the wings level and slowing down gradually, but with damaged landing gear. The sooner she could bring the aircraft to a standstill the better. She slowed even more, trying to keep control but then the aeroplane listed to starboard as one wheel refused to go fully down. Even so, the fact that she was on the ground gave her just enough time to adjust the landing to cope with the wind from the other direction.

It was not a text-book landing but ended in a sudden, jolting shudder as the plane skidded to a stop in deep, muddy ruts. Bobby was flung forward against her straps and her foot was caught under the rudder pedal, which had buckled in the impact. As soon as the aircraft came to a halt, the emergency vehicles raced over but Bobby could not move. She found she was shaking and her left ankle was throbbing.

'You all right in there?' a disembodied voice called from the hatch below.

'Yes,' Bobby whispered, her voice a squeak. 'Yes,' she repeated louder.

'Come on, then, out you come.'

Bobby eased herself out of the seat and put her foot down, yelping in pain as she did so. 'I think I've hurt my ankle,' she called.

'It's a miracle if that's all you've hurt,' the man's voice came back and then his arm appeared to help her down.

She half fell down the ladder to land in a heap on the grass, crying out in pain.

'My God, that was quite some landing,' the short, tubby Erk said to her. 'I've never seen anything like it.'

'And I never want to again,' Bobby said shakily.

Chapter 34

The country was in a state of quiet satisfaction. The D-Day Landings had taken the Germans by surprise but the Allied losses had been great. There were few details released to the general public but the startling figures were on a piece of paper on Edward's desk. He looked at them over and over again. He struggled not to equate those stark numbers with the unbidden images of the telegraph boys on bicycles all over the country, delivering their dreaded cargo to families who had hardly dared to breathe since Tuesday 6th June began. His immediate job was to coordinate the Resistance's work with that of the encroaching Allied troops, who were fighting hand to hand across Normandy, and it was proving to be more than a challenge.

He pressed the intercom button. 'Miss Arbuckle, would you come in a moment, please?'

Mavis Arbuckle patted her permanent wave into place and picked up her notebook. She walked into the office and stood opposite Edward, her pencil poised. 'Yes, sir?'

'Do sit down, Miss Arbuckle. Could you please contact our French translator and get him to come in this afternoon?'

She nodded and made a note.

'Secondly, could you see if there's any news on Drancy internment camp? There was an escape from there last week, could you see whether anyone has been picked up – by either side?

'And finally, Miss Arbuckle, can I ask, how would I know if a woman is in love with me?'

Mavis Arbuckle had been schooled in not betraying any of her own thoughts or emotions but this last question took her completely by surprise.

'I'm sorry, sir, what was that?'

'I just thought, well, you're the only woman I can talk to discreetly and I know you would never discuss anything said in this room with anyone else.'

She sat quietly, with her hands in her lap, clutching her pencil and notepad and wondered how on earth she was going to reply. She stared at the clock on the wall, begging it to stop while she came up with the right answer.

Edward waited patiently, not even acknowledging the oddness of the non sequitur that he had just uttered.

'I think you should ask her,' she finally said.

'Thank you, Miss Arbuckle. That will be all.'

Mavis went back to her desk and immediately telephoned the French translator. She then put a telephone call in place to find out more about Drancy, but finally, she allowed herself a moment to sit back in her chair.

'I was right!' she thought triumphantly. She knew there had been something different about Mr Turner and now she thought about it, there had been signs. His desk had become a muddle, he had let his floppy fringe get out of hand and his voice had been softer. She had actually heard him chuckling to himself on occasions.

She clasped her hands together in glee. She adored Mr Turner like a maiden aunt with a favourite nephew and it had been her private daydream over the last few years that one day a woman would also look beyond that civil service front he had perfected and find the exciting, caring and fun man underneath.

At ten past six that evening, both Mavis and Edward Turner were still in the office. Edward had been concerned about the news from just north of Louvigny where there had been some reprisals committed by the retreating German army and there were reports that some resistance fighters had been among those executed. The village where the Bisset family lived was less than two miles from Louvigny. He and the French translator had spent the afternoon trying to get a telephone call through to the network but there had been no response. He had contacted Adèle, the SOE who had been on the ground there. She had been kept busy with translations at her parents' home in Norfolk since her emergency evacuation the night that

Bobby and Elizé had been brought back but was due to come to the office at 6.30.

Mavis telephoned her neighbour to feed her cat, Tiddles, so she did not have to rush home. She knew a young woman was coming into the office and she was not going to miss the chance to meet her, wondering whether she was the one who had put her beloved Edward Turner into such a tailspin.

At one minute past half past, a tall, young, blonde woman strode into the office, peremptorily demanding to see Mr Turner. Mavis's heart sank and she hoped fervently that this was not the one.

She showed the visitor into the office and looked carefully at Edward to see his reaction. She was delighted to see there was no particular warmth in his greeting. The woman's code name was Adèle but Bobby would have recognised her as Marie McGill.

'Miss Arbuckle, thank you for staying,' Edward was saying, 'would you mind very much getting our visitor a cup of tea? And if the urn is still hot, maybe I could have one too?'

Mavis bustled off to the kitchen, but for the first time in her professional career, she longed to be a fly on the wall in that office and not the reliably discreet secretary she had been since the age of twenty-two.

'So Adèle, you are due to go back to France tomorrow, I believe.' Edward was saying.

'Yes, sir. Tomorrow. It's a crucial time for the Resistance and they need all the help they can get.'

'Yes, and so do we,' Edward replied. 'Our comms are down; more radios have been confiscated and we are concerned there have been reprisals. You managed to hide a radio before you left, I believe?'

Marie nodded but had gone pale, thinking of her family in Louvigny and her friends in the Resistance. She knew how ruthless the Germans were and in retreat, they would be merciless. Her grandmother had been in ill-health and confined to bed in her nightie when Marie had been forced to flee France, so she was in ignorance of the existence of the radio Marie had quickly hidden amongst her grandmother's smalls in the old armoire. It had been a huge risk and put her grandmother in jeopardy, but Marie had had no choice, that radio could not be found. She hoped the fearsome reputation of the old lady would deter any soldier from conducting a search of her grandmother's underwear.

'I'm due to go back tomorrow night, sir. The Allies are making headway but not enough, I believe. No one knows about the radio as far as I know and if it's still there, I should be able to get information to you by the usual channels. Sir, you do know it was not my choice to come out, don't you?' she added hesitantly.

'Yes, yes, of course,' Edward replied, uncomfortably aware it had been his decision to bring Adèle out of France. Once she had met Bobby and had helped a Jewish child, she was in mortal danger of being identified as a spy and they had lost two of those in the last month, just when they needed as much information as possible. Once the informer had disappeared, they knew that the Germans would carry out extensive searches and they could not risk their SOE being found, but now they needed her back on the ground. They were taking a huge risk sending her back in, but they needed that radio communication.

'We may need you to get Monsieur Bisset and his son out of there,' Edward said. 'If they have not already been identified by the Gestapo, they soon may be, and the Germans are taking every possible revenge they can before they're forced out. There is an escape route in place but it is dangerous, we dare not do it by air, all the radios have been destroyed except your and we can't get a message to them so we need you back in there to lead them to safety. Is that OK?'

Edward looked carefully at the confident face in front of him. He was in awe of these young women who were carrying out the most perilous tasks, isolated in a foreign country where they could not trust anyone. Most of them lasted no more than six weeks. His heart went out to her.

'Of course, sir. I've been wanting to go back ever since I was forced to leave,' Marie said, tilting her chin up.

'You will have to be extremely careful,' Edward added and as she got up to go, he said, 'Good luck, mademoiselle, your country is proud of you.'

Chapter 35

Gus was swinging the Lysander from left to right but he could not lose the Messerschmitt. It was tailing him with a dogged determination. He had delivered a 'Jane' to France – that cocky blonde he had brought out a few months earlier who he had now recognised from school, but he kept that information to himself. He was on his way back, but had had to divert north towards the Norfolk coast to avoid heavy fighting in the Channel. He was relieved to be away from the action and was feeling pleased the drop had all gone well when he suddenly felt his cockpit being shaken by gunfire.

He looked all around and then spotted the Messerschmitt behind him.

'Damn,' he exploded.

He was in the direct line of fire and needed to use all his skills to try to avoid a direct hit. He veered the aeroplane from one side to another, doing anything other than what the German might expect, but the Messerschmitt was not giving up.

Peering through the window, he reassured himself that he could not see any damage and checked his fuel gauge. Enough to get him to somewhere but not Tempsford. To lead an enemy aircraft to such a secret location was not an option. Most of the RAF did not even know of its existence.

'Bugger, bugger, bugger,' he shouted to the skies.

He opened his transmitter and said the words that might give him a ray of hope.

'Hello Darky, Hello Darky, Hello Darky, this is F- Freddie, this is F- Freddie, this is F-Freddie. May I land?'

The word 'Darky' was used as a codeword to alert airfields that there was a aircraft in need of urgent assistance. In emergencies, the nearest airfield would pick up the signal and help them find their way home. It was a last resort system that had saved many airmen's lives and Gus listened intently for a reply. He hoped he was near enough to an airfield for his message to be picked up.

But in the meantime, he had to lose this aeroplane that was mirroring his every move.

Gus went down as low as he dared, letting his wing tips almost touch the water to try to outmanoeuvre the enemy who was homing in on him. At that moment, he felt a huge shudder go through the aeroplane. He was hit.

He looked from side to side to see where the damage was. The gunfire had clipped the end of his starboard wing tip but there were no flames. Feeling strangely calm, he swung the aeroplane downwards again and found that the shattered wing tip actually gave him an advantage as the aircraft suddenly tipped to the port side. He was celebrating his unexpected luck when he looked up, just in time to see the Messerschmidt circling around to come in for the final kill.

Gus felt a searing anger – an anger that was directed at the pilot coming towards him, at the decision to take the machine gun off Lysanders to reduce weight, leaving him with no defence and finally, at a crazy war that, in just a few seconds time, would snuff out his life at the age of twenty-eight. He was just weighing up the odds of ditching into the cold, grey water below when he spotted two RAF Spitfires heading his way, aiming their fire at the German aircraft. While he concentrated on surviving the next few seconds, the two Spitfire pilots were weaving in and out above him, putting themselves between him and his foe. His concentration was divided between watching with a calm fascination and dealing with an aeroplane that was flying at a dangerous angle.

Above him, there was a burst of gunfire and the Messerschmidt broke into bits, like a china plate hit by a coconut at a fairground. It plunged into the water that only moments earlier, Gus had thought would embrace him in a wet shroud. He whooped with delight and waved his arms in triumph at the British pilot behind him. The Spitfire passed him and gave him a 'thumbs up' and then gave him a salute to acknowledge his brave tactics in trying to throw off the enemy. He watched the two aircraft head back south to where they had several more hours of providing protection to British shores and whispered his very weak but heartfelt thanks towards the tailfins of his saviours.

He had little time to feel any satisfaction as his own Lysander started to tilt and waver and he had to put all his efforts into flying with a lopsided aircraft. It was a tricky manoeuvre and although he had practised it in flying school, the reality of flying with a damaged wing under pressure was much more difficult than in practice.

The radio burst back into life. Somewhere, there was a WAAF who was doing her utmost to bring him in. He heard her calm voice telling him a station with a code he recognised as Coltishall was ready for him and giving him instructions for landing. Gus reached out and touched the transmitter in gratitude and replied.

'Hello, I am coming in.' He tried to keep his voice as calm as hers. Gus could hardly hear the reply but was determined to do everything he could to follow her instructions and get down in one piece so she would not have nightmares about the aircraft — and pilot — she had lost.

He limped over the coast, spotting Hickling Broad and then Barton Broad below him like welcome beacons on his starboard side. He was getting nearer but he was losing fuel. His fuel tank must have been hit.

Scanning the horizon, he spotted an airfield and checked his map. He sent a second message telling Coltishall that he was losing fuel.

'Hello F-Freddie, we are ready for you.' The WAAF then repeated the coordinates slowly, she was bringing him towards the airfield with her patient but insistent code that gave nothing away to a listening enemy. He knew she would have cleared the airfield of any other aircraft and would have the emergency services on standby. He was about to put his life in the hands of a young WAAF and the waiting ground crew.

The airfield was like a mirage and he concentrated on steadying the Lysander to bring her in. It wobbled towards the runway and then he suddenly realised he was bleeding.

His left leg had been hit and there was blood pouring from it. He looked at the dark stain in surprise; he had not felt any pain.

As he lurched onto the tarmac, he suddenly felt a searing pain from his leg. It was badly hurt and he was not sure he could stay conscious long enough to finish the job.

Gus's aircraft bounced along the ground, veering off at the last minute onto the grass and he knew he was completely out of control. His survival now depended completely on his own skill and a great deal of luck.

He struggled to slow down, breathing a sigh of relief that the brakes were still, thankfully, in one piece and for an agonising few moments, he watched the control tower speed past his window. He struggled to decrease the speed until, at last, the plane shuddered to a halt and at that moment, he passed out.

The emergency vehicles raced to the Lysander to get there before it burst into flames. It was an aircraft that was particularly prone to sudden ignition, so the fire engine started immediately to douse the aircraft while the ambulancemen struggled to break open the Perspex with hammers, to get the pilot out.

Above them, in the control tower, as the sun rose, a WAAF was watching anxiously. After three nights of being on Darky watch, aware of action further south, she had jumped as the machine next to her burst into life. She had immediately felt the panic of the young pilot over the North Sea and had done her utmost to get him back safely, alerting the ground crew and directing the coastal defence planes towards his coordinates while continuously and firmly sending information so he could find her.

'Please let him be all right,' Harriet Marcham pleaded with God.

'LACW Marcham, you should be off duty now.' The voice of her superior penetrated her thoughts and she hurriedly signed off and left by the 'out' door just before the next shift came in through the 'in' door. They were not allowed to meet so that any disasters of the previous shift were not passed on to the girls who still had eight hours of tension to deal with.

It was as she was making her way to the locker room that she heard the orderlies racing along the corridor in her direction. She automatically stood aside and then looked with disbelief at the features she had gazed at adoringly for so many of her schoolgirl years. She gasped as she realised the bloodied, unconscious figure on the gurney was Gus Prince.

'Gus,' she whispered, 'Gus.'

She reached out her hand to take his, but the orderlies pushed past her, anxious to get their patient to the infirmary.

His eyes were closed and she could not tell if his chest was moving up and down. Harriet clasped her hand to her mouth to stop the scream that threatened to emerge. She had imagined their reunion so many times of late, but she had never imagined this.

She leaned back against the wall and slowly sank to the floor.

Chapter 36

Edward was exhausted. He spent his days doing his normal work and then, once the clock had struck six, he would start on the seemingly impossible task of trying to help causes closer to his heart. He hardly went home to his own flat, preferring to bed down on the leather sofa in his office. Mavis had secretly taken his shirts home to wash and carefully iron before bringing them back the following morning. It was only after three days that Edward realised that the cupboard where he kept one clean shirt was constantly being replenished with fresh ones.

He went out to her find her at her desk. 'Miss Arbuckle ... Mavis,' he said, making her blush. 'You are an absolute gem. I don't deserve you.'

'Yes, you do, sir,' and emboldened by his relaxation of formalities, added. 'And may I say, sir, you also deserve the love of that woman, whoever she is. I hope she appreciates you.'

Edward smiled and reached out his hand to put it gently on her shoulder. 'Thank you, Mavis. I'm still working on that one.'

He got back to his desk and looked again at the letter from Bobby, telling him about her accident. She was anything but sorry for herself, just furious that her ankle prevented her from flying at this crucial time. The letters between them were becoming more relaxed than any conversation they had previously had, and Edward found it was easier to be himself when there was a Post Office between them.

*　*　*

Bobby was surprised at this new, chattier side to Edward and began to wait eagerly for his letters. They provided a welcome relief amid the dramatic – and terrifying – letters she had been getting from Harriet, proclaiming with a mix of triumph and terror that she had been the one to bring Gus Prince's stricken aircraft home but that her last sight of him had been on a stretcher.

Bobby was stuck at home. Her ankle was badly broken, she could not put any weight on it for two weeks and she was not a good patient.

'Aunt Agnes, could you get me the atlas please?

'Mother, I could just do with that yellow cushion.'

'Rachel, can I have a pen and paper? I need to write to Harriet and Gus.'

Mrs Hill raised her eyebrows to heaven while she listened to the constant list of jobs for them all to do. She had known this girl since birth. It was time for action.

'Roberta Hollis,' she said, rubbing her hands on the kitchen towel and marching into the pretty lemon-painted morning room, 'you are being a pain in the neck. We're all doing our best to look after you, but Elizé and I have all the summer fruits to bottle, Rachel is out queueing at the shops to try to get a bit of scrag end, and your mother is taking an old jumper apart to re-knit it. Now, here's a jigsaw, don't speak again until it's done.'

Bobby grinned shamefacedly and took the box from her. 'I'm sorry, Mrs Hill. You're absolutely right. I just can't bear being stuck here, unable to move. I feel so useless.'

Mrs Hill gave her a warning look and turned on her heels. Bobby resigned herself to her task and started to turn all the pieces the same way to find the edges.

An hour later, Bobby had most of the framework done of the idyllic English village scene, but was bored. Then she heard the welcome sound of Harriet's voice at the back door. She twitched with excitement at the prospect of a visitor and getting some news but Harriet seemed to be having a lengthy chat with Elizé and was in no hurry to come through to the morning room.

'Harriet Marcham, are you coming in to see me or not?' she called loudly through the doorway.

Harriet's face appeared and Elizé peeped round her skirts.

'I told you she was being very naughty,' Elizé said, grinning.

'I'm not, I'm just fed up.' There was a definite childish pout to Bobby's face.

'Well, I'm heading to see Gus in the hospital next and I really don't know what she's moaning about compared to what he's going through,' Harriet told Elizé.

She went over to the chaise longue where Bobby was lying and sat down opposite. Elizé perched on the end.

'This piece is in the wrong place,' Harriet said, picking one of the cardboard pieces out of the jigsaw.

'Never mind that, tell me what's happening. How's Gus?'

Harriet's face clouded. 'Not good, to be honest, Bobby. You know I told you that he's in and out of consciousness. I go as much as I can, but I don't get a great deal of time off. I'm only here today because I've done three nights at a stretch. I'm going on to the hospital after this.'

'I so want to go and see him. Does he know you're there when you visit?'

Harriet thought for a moment. She was thoroughly enjoying being the person at Gus Prince's bedside. She had felt a guilty pleasure that Bobby was unable to join her.

'I don't know to be honest, but I want to be there when he does wake up.' She looked so pathetic that Bobby put her hand out to cover hers.

'Oh Harriet, what are we going to do with you?'

'Mademoiselle Marcham can kiss him like in *La Belle au Bois Dormant*,' Elizé piped up, remembering her mother telling her the fairy tale where the princess lay asleep for one hundred years.

'Elizé, we're ready for the jars,' Mrs Hill called from the kitchen and the little girl got up in excitement to go.

'She seems to have settled in,' Harriet said, watching her skip out of the room.

'It's unbelievable,' Bobby remarked. 'It's like *this* place was the castle in *Sleeping Beauty* and she's woken them all up. She's still getting nightmares of course, but Aunt Agnes often takes her into her bed with her and cuddles her till she calms down.'

'Aunt Agnes?' Harriet said in disbelief.

'Yes, and it's not just her, my father has started taking her on his rounds on the farm. Elizé's struck up a particular friendship with one of the Land Army girls, Hannah, I think her name is. Even mother seems to have found a new mission in life as a '*grandmère*' and has finally accepted that Michel is not her son come back to life but – oh, I don't know, any connection with Michel seems to galvanise her into action.

'I don't suppose you've heard anything from him, have you?' Harriet asked.

'Nope, you know what comms are like but I believe Edward may be onto it and I trust him.'

Harriet felt a little quiver in her stomach. As soon as she had seen the bloodied and battered body of Gus Prince, all those feelings that she had had as a child had flooded back but this time, she was a grown woman and this was not some playground game. Gus was fighting for his life and his frail and damaged figure in the hospital bed had unearthed an compelling need to protect him and bring him back into the world – a world where she would be waiting for him. She felt destiny had brought her to this moment and that this was the reason why, at the age of twenty-eight, she was still not married; no one else had ever made her feel like this.

Harriet looked sideways at Bobby, trying to read her emotions. She had stupidly handed Gus to her friend on a plate but then Bobby's confidence in Edward gave her hope. It occurred to her that if Bobby got involved with Edward Turner, it could leave the coast clear for her with Gus.

Gus is just a typical male, she thought to herself, *blinded by a mane of gorgeous hair and the fact that she can fly. He'll grow out of it. I just need to make sure I'm there when he does.*

The visit was short, but it boosted Bobby. Once Harriet had gone to race off to the hospital, she made herself concentrate on the jigsaw until someone had time to offer her a cup of tea. Gus was in hospital; Harriet was exhausted with endless night shifts and all over France there were soldiers fighting yard by yard to expel the enemy. Bobby felt ashamed of herself.

* * *

Gus woke with a start and panicked. He did not know where he was. He tried to sit up, but a gentle hand stopped him.

'Stay still, Gus, it's all right. I'm here,' Harriet whispered to him.

He looked confused but immediately felt calmed to see such a familiar, sweet face looking down on him. He tried to focus.

'Harriet Marcham, is it really you? But you're so . . . what are you doing here? Where am I?'

'You had an accident. I was the WAAF who brought you in.'

Gus frowned. He remembered German gunfire and a wonderfully calm voice leading him to safety.

Gradually, the whole story came back to him and he leaned his head back and groaned.

Then he felt down to his leg. It was still there, he realised with relief, but he could not feel it.

'My leg?' he said, anxiously. 'Harriet, tell me, will it be OK?'

'I'll get the nurse,' Harriet said, not wanting to answer.

She looked over to the consulting room where Gus's parents could be seen through the glass window. The doctor was sitting behind a desk, Gus's father was pacing up and down, his mother was clutching a handkerchief to her face.

Chapter 37

Marie was hiding in the same doorway where Bobby had crouched earlier that year. She checked her watch. It was four o'clock in the morning, just before dawn and only a few hours before the hastily arranged rendezvous for the two French fugitives and the small boat off the Normandy coast. She was completely alert but getting nervous, they were running out of time before daylight. Marie mentally checked her arrangements one more time. They had had to be changed late last night when a platoon of German soldiers turned up to billet in the hamlet, exhausted from hand-to-hand fighting across Normandy and the urgency to get Raoul and Michel to safety had intensified. The Gestapo were going through villages, picking out anyone they suspected of having a connection with the Resistance. She did not know whether the Bisset cover had been blown or not, but several resistance fighters had been captured, and torture for information was a natural progression. Leaving them at large for one more day was certainly not an option.

She had retrieved her radio, relieved that her confused grandmother had not even noticed that Marie had not been there for several weeks. Choosing her time to send messages was crucial, they had to be short and incomprehensible to anyone listening in. The penalty for possessing a radio was death. She had transmitted faster than ever before, sticking to the codes she had agreed with Edward and once the message had been sent, she buried the radio next to the privy in the back garden, perilously close to the long drop of the toilet. There had been no time to alert the baker, whose van was due any minute now to pick up Raoul and Michel, and he would be in complete ignorance of the added threat of the soldiers. She scanned the street from her position. There were two German guards, dozing in the doorway down the street outside a house where a platoon was, she hoped, sleeping soundly.

She suddenly spotted Michel and Raoul dodging into doorways down the street. Marie held her breath. At that moment, Monsieur LeClerc's baker's van drove into view, waking up the two guards who grasped their rifles, ready to challenge the vehicle but then relaxed again when they saw it was the regular bread delivery. It was time for Marie to act out her part to distract the soldiers from the sight of two men sliding into the van.

She slid out of the doorway towards the soldiers, giving them her sexiest smile. She was veering from side to side, looking, she hoped, very drunk. It was an offence to be out during curfew and she was taking a huge risk.

Behind her, Monsieur LeClerc was unloading his bread, not the baguettes he loved to bake but the stodgy, tasteless brown loaves that had become the norm during the war. He was desperately hoping the Allies' landings would result in some white flour. However, this morning, the condition of his bread was the last thing on his mind. He was horrified to see the soldiers and for a second, hesitated, but then he heard the passenger door quietly opening and he knew his cargo had arrived. He had to carry on.

'*Bonjour, mes beaux soldats,*' Marie said slurring her speech. '*Je suis perdue. J'ai passé une telle bonne nuit avec votre commandant et maintenant, je dois aller chez moi.*'

She hoped that telling them she was lost after spending the night with their commandant would strike enough alarm in the men to make them nervous of carrying out their duty.

She sidled up to one of them, she was counting on the fact that the smell of the wine she had gargled with would suggest an alcohol-fuelled night.

The two men looked at each other. Their commandant was a fearsome man and well-known for his liaisons with women.

One of them, the smaller of the two, looked up as the baker's van went slowly down the street. They had been in France long enough to know that there were two things that the French would not forgo just because there was a war on. One was their wine and the second was their bread but the appearance of this woman just as the van arrived was just a little too coincidental.

He grabbed Marie's arm. He was going to take her to the commandant and check out her story. He nodded towards the van, saying something to his friend in German.

Marie had to think fast.

She retched and doubled over, putting her finger down her throat as she did so.

She was sick all over the soldier's shiny boots. He pushed her away from him in disgust.

She took her chance and wobbled off down the road as casually as she could, her heart racing, not sure whether she had got away with it until she turned the corner where she broke into a run, preparing to vanish back into the shadows.

The van disappeared over the horizon. Inside, Michel and Raoul had hidden themselves under the sacking that held the bread. They had no idea of the drama they had left behind, but they knew they had nearly forty kilometres to go and then a tight schedule to coordinate with a tiny boat that they hoped would be waiting off the Normandy coast for them. They had told Claudette nothing, but in two hours she would get up to prepare breakfast for them. They hoped she would not worry too much and would spot the tiny silver spoon they had left on the sideboard.

It was a signal they had agreed on in case of the need for a quick escape. She was not to sound the alarm but to pretend they were still there for as long as possible—hopefully until the Allies got there. It was a huge responsibility to ask of her, but she had welcomed the chance to do something to protect the two men she loved most in the world.

Chapter 38

It was only like the hum of a motorbike but when the pilotless planes sounded over the fields of Norfolk, the local people, including the Hollis household, held their breath. It was safe as long as they could hear it but once the hum stopped, that heralded the moment when it was ready to bomb the ground beneath and they would all dive for cover. Germany was using the V1 bombers relentlessly, as if to remind the British that one small D-Day victory on the northern coast of France was a drop in the ocean in this global war.

There had been many occasions when the Hollis family had ducked under the dining room table, only to hear the buzz of the aircraft disappear into the distance. After several embarrassing occasions when they all emerged, patting their clothes into place, they, like many English people, became somewhat blasé and would just look skyward as if they could puff their cheeks out and blow any planes away to a harmless end in an empty field.

Bobby was propped up on the chaise longue in the dining room. She strained her ears; there was that familiar eerie sound. She still found it difficult to move but if she leaned towards the window, she could glimpse the sky. There it was, heading their way.

Her mother hurried in. 'Bobby, get under the table, quick. It's one of these darned things.'

'Oh, for heaven's sake, mother, stop fussing, it'll pass over.'

But then the hum stopped. Mathilda Hollis grabbed Bobby and pulled her with her under the relative safety of the huge oak dining table. Bobby cried out in pain from her ankle but then immediately shouted to the kitchen for them all to take cover. She could not get to Elizé to protect her and her heart started to thump.

Two seconds later, a huge explosion rocked the house, sending plumes of dust everywhere.

There was a chilling silence and then a commotion broke out. Everyone was calling to each other. Mrs Hill came running in to the dining room, her face covered in flour.

'Are you all right?' she asked urgently, pulling them both out from under the table.

'I think so,' Mathilda replied. 'Bobby?'

'Yes, I'm OK but everyone else . . . ?'

Mathilda and Mrs Hill ran towards the back door, fearful of what they might find outside. Bobby hobbled behind, not caring whether she put her foot down or not.

The barn was in flames and there was hardly anything left of the buzz bomber apart from splinters of plywood that had scattered in all directions.

Men ran from everywhere, carrying buckets. At the front of them was Archie, his face was grey.

'Agnes . . . Agnes,' he called, rushing towards the barn. Two men tried to stop him but he wriggled free and disappeared into the flames.

Mrs Hill said to Bobby in a chillingly quiet voice, 'Miss Clarke went into the barn to get some hay for the haybox.'

Elizé appeared behind Bobby. She had been playing with her toys in her bedroom, fortunately away from the window that had shattered. Bobby clutched her in her arms but looked towards the barn with alarm.

Andrew Hollis raced over from the stock enclosure, shouting to the men to get a chain of water buckets going, but they were already in place, chucking bucketful after bucketful onto the fire. He joined the line, desperate to douse the flames. The fire had taken hold and black smoke from the winter feed was spiralling towards the blue sky.

From one side of the farm a group of Land Army girls ran to join them and from the other, a group of German prisoners of war who were interned at the farm, raced to help. The English officer was in front of them, shouting instructions.

'There's my friend, Hannah, and her friend, Karl!' Elizé shouted above the noise to Bobby. Furious that she could not help, Bobby just sent a silent thank you to the two enemies who were working side by side in front of her to try to save her aunt.

At that moment, an ash-covered figure staggered out of the barn. He was holding the inert figure of Agnes.

Everyone rushed forward except Bobby, who staggered, trying to hold onto Rachel's shoulder.

'She's not breathing, she's not breathing,' Archie said in short panting breaths. He looked frantically around at the crowd of people who had given up trying to contain the blaze and were standing helplessly, clutching their empty buckets.

'I can help,' a German voice said.

A young Land Army girl stepped forward. 'Let him help, he's a doctor.'

Elizé ran over to her and took her hand, saying proudly, 'This is my friend, she's called Hannah.'

Archie was eyeing up the prisoner with suspicion but Andrew Hollis lurched forward.

'No, you bastard, you will not touch her.'

He grabbed the prisoner's rough jacket and tried to push him away but Archie got there first.

'Move away, Boss. He's our only hope.'

Andrew Hollis was shaking. He hated having these prisoners on his farm and avoided them at all times. His memories of the Boche charging at their trenches with their bayonets fixed still haunted him and he shivered with hatred every time he came across one. He stood up tall to square up to Archie, but then realised that Archie's face was smeared with tears. Slowly, Andrew stepped to one side and reluctantly motioned to the German to help Agnes.

Archie was staring, stricken, at the woman in his arms. For years, paralysed by shyness, he had watched Agnes go off every week to a remote spot in the woods, clutching a small posy. He was the only person who knew that it was where she had buried the burnt remains of the telegram telling her that Peter Martin, her fiancé, had been killed at The Somme. He also knew she took the flowers to place reverently on the ground, causing walkers to pause and wonder at the small burst of colour amongst the cracked leaves and that sometimes, she would pound her fists on the oak tree next to it, sobbing her heart out. That weekly pilgrimage had broken his own heart. The tall officer moved forward and gently prised Agnes from Archie's arms, laying her carefully on the ground. Archie protested when the man loosened Agnes's top button to expose the top of her chest but this time, it was Andrew who laid his hand on his shoulder to stop him.

'Give me something to, how you say,' the doctor rolled his arms to demonstrate.

The girl, Hannah, immediately took off her green jumper and handed it to him, giving him an encouraging smile.

Bobby felt there was a frisson between the two but transferred her concentration back to the doctor, who was turning Aunt Agnes over then rolling the jumper up to put it under her stomach. He moved her forearms to put her head on them, and then pushed Agnes from the base of her spine. The whole group was holding its breath. The POW turned her still body over onto its back and motioned to Archie to hold her hands above her head. Archie looked down at the pale face and tears started to fall freely from his bloodshot eyes. The doctor went on to push forward with his thumbs from below Agnes's ribs. Suddenly, Bobby's aunt spluttered and started to cough. Archie could not help himself, he gathered Agnes up in his arms and gently rocked her back and forth and then carried her triumphantly into the house. The German sat back on his knees in relief.

Andrew Hollis looked at Archie's love-stricken face in shock. His wife gave a secret smile and squeezed Bobby's hand in satisfaction.

'Archie's waited a long time to claim that woman,' she whispered to Bobby. 'I think it's finally time.'

Andrew went over to the doctor and after a moment of staring into his eyes, reached out his hand slowly. The German took hold of it and shook it firmly. Mathilda's eyes clouded with tears. Ever since Elizé had arrived Mathilda had seen glimpses of the kind man she had married and now, here he was, shaking the hand of his enemy.

Bobby looked over at the little family graveyard to the side of the barn, it was more visible now from the house. A late afternoon sunbeam was lighting up the white marble of her brother's grave. She followed its shaft and blew a kiss towards the blue sky above her.

Chapter 39

Gus looked at his parents in horror.

'What do you mean, I won't be able to walk?'

His mother looked at his father. He coughed and said gently, 'You may be able to walk, in time, but it's not going to be easy.'

'What about flying?' Gus asked quietly.

There was a dreadful pause and then his father said, 'Fraid not, son, not unless this terrible war goes on for years.'

Gus lay back on his pillows. He had nothing else to say.

Day went to night and back to day. Gus lay for hours staring at the curtains around his bed without seeing them.

After several days, Bobby hobbled into the ward. She was leaning on her crutches, finally able to put her weight down.

Gus was turned on his side, staring at the wall. She spoke softly, 'Gus, Gus, can you hear me?'

Gus did not want to turn to face her. She was the last person he wanted to see. To win Roberta Hollis, he felt he had to be a whole being, not a broken body and a fragile mind. From their days at school, he had somehow thought of the two of them as examples of what young people should be: athletic, able and confident – the sort of youngsters who made heads turn. It was not a conceit, just a confidence that came of being admired by classmates and being the best at everything. He tensed his body, he felt ashamed of how it had let him down.

A nurse followed Bobby to the bed and drew up a chair for her, which she flopped down onto thankfully. The nurse looked at Gus and gave a little shake of her head like a teacher of a naughty pupil.

Bobby did not know what to say. The last time she had seen Gus, he had been so full of confidence, almost to the point of being cocky. This shrunken figure in front of her was like someone she did not know.

'I'm sorry to hear about your leg,' she started. 'It must be terrible for you.'

It suddenly occurred to her how she would feel if she had been told she could not fly again and she reached out her hand to touch him, but then withdrew it.

'What happened to your foot?' he asked flatly.

'Broke it,' she replied. 'It seems we're still trying to compete with each other.'

Gus did not smile and then muttered something.

'I'm sorry, Gus, what did you say?'

He turned over and looked at her.

'I said, I'd rather have died in that plane.'

Bobby put her hand to her mouth in horror. 'Oh, please don't say that,' but part of her knew what he was talking about. A life spent in a wheelchair was something she could not contemplate for herself or for the man she thought she knew in front of her. She had no solution, no hope to offer him. Being anything less than fit and able was a prospect neither of them could cope with.

They were so alike, she realised. They needed the bravado, the glamour and the exhilaration. That was what had given their burgeoning relationship such a tingling excitement. Without that, they were both just a sham. Their relationship was as thin as the lightest clouds in the sky.

She sat for a few more minutes but could not think of anything to say. After an agonising silence, the nurse came back and told Bobby she needed to take his temperature.

Bobby reached for her crutches in relief and stood up with a wobble. 'I'll come again, Gus, you take care of yourself.'

Gus stared after her. Her golden auburn hair seemed to have lost its lustre.

As Bobby went shakily out of the ward, she knew a bond had been broken between them. Gus knew it too and turned back to the wall.

* * *

Edward Turner dug out his old sailing boots, lifejacket and sou'wester from the stowage in the cockpit. The weather was going to be terrible and he was going to need them on his beloved forty-five foot motorsailer, the aptly-named 'Challenge', a name that summed up what lay ahead of them. Since the war had begun, the boat had been commandeered to pick up downed Spitfire pilots off the English coast, but tonight this powerful little vessel was going to rescue two resistance fighters who were being brought halfway across the English Channel on a small French boat. It was Edward's pride and joy and he wanted to be the person to helm it.

He had received a coded message from Adèle just twenty-four hours earlier to say that the pick-up had been brought forward and had picked up the telephone to organise a rendezvous with his contacts on the south coast, but then his finger paused over the dial and it only took a brief moment for him to persuade himself that, as a covert operation, he could organise the pick-up much better if he went to Portsmouth in person. As soon as he got to the boat, he found John Blake, his sailing friend and mentor fast asleep in the bunk, surrounded by empty beer bottles. He grinned with delight at the fact that, really, there was no choice, he was going to have to make the journey himself, which was, in all honesty, exactly what he had hoped.

Edward hugged the unexpected opportunity to himself. He had been getting fed up with being office bound in a suit and this was his chance to taste the excitement and thrill of danger, which had been lacking in his life recently. Sailing had always provided the excitement he craved and tonight, with an important mission to undertake, his whole body was quivering as a testament to his belief that he was, for once, doing something important that did not involve endless strategy documents. It also occurred to him that by doing something heroic, he might in some small way be able to compete with an RAF pilot at Tempsford.

He checked the safety equipment and the rigging and set off from Gosport, dousing all lights. He started the engine but winced at the noise and immediately switched it off. He looked at the stretch of water in front of him and was just considering how he was going to take his boat noiselessly through it on his own when a gruff voice yelled, 'What the hell's going on,' and then a tousled head of grey hair appeared in the hatch.

'Turner! What in God's name do you think you're doing?'

'We're going on a fishing trip,' Edward replied with a grin, looking at the man who had taught him to sail as a boy.

John Blake looked around at the horizon and spluttered.

'Fishing? At this time of night and in these waters?'

'Well, we're fishing for a couple of men,' Edward told him. 'It's a mercy mission now come and help me and take the wheel, we can't put the engine on."

John Blake shook his head and then regretted the move. It reminded him of how many beers he had actually consumed the previous night but still grumbling, he silently took the helm as a member of a well-practised crew while Edward sprang into action and jumped onto the deck to haul and let the sails out, breathing that familiar sigh of satisfaction as the wind caught them. They kept quiet as they left the town of Gosport behind and headed into open water.

The winds were increasing. Edward trimmed his sails and set his compass towards the rendezvous point half way between England and France. The waves were beginning to hit the deck, but he knew his boat inside out and had faith in its sturdy construction. It was a ketch with a beautiful mahogany wheelhouse and he was confident it was a capable and seaworthy craft. Edward checked his timings; at six knots it was going to take eight hours to get to the coordinates. He yelled to John Blake to start up the engine to supplement the sails, he was going to need every bit of power he had to compete with the waves.

Standing next to the mast, Edward had never felt more alive and wondered, not for the first time, how long he was going to have to remain stuck behind a desk all day.

He was grateful there was hardly any moonlight in the cloudy skies but it meant he had to be constantly on the lookout for lightless naval patrol boats crossing his path. He did not want to be spotted by anyone. The slow, ponderous civil servant was unrecognisable as Edward leapt about the deck, adjusting sails. He was a naturally nimble man and he had sailed in far worse weather.

He did not even struggle to stay awake. He was completely alert. Once they had settled their course, he went back to the wheelhouse to take over the helm.

'Evening John, good to see you. Now, be a good chap and go and put the jug on, I'm parched and you look as if you could do with a hot drink.'

Captain John Blake longed for a strong coffee but had to settle for tea, which was all they had on board. He did not argue with the man he had known for years, who was having the time of his life. John clung on to the side of the hatch against the pulsing hangover that was making him unsteady and went to light the gas on the gimbled cooker. The two men had been firm friends from the first day when a young lad in neatly-pressed shorts had turned up for a sailing lesson. John had watched with pride as the shy, gawky Edward blossomed into a capable, likeable young man with an unexpected wild streak. Young Edward proved to be not only a willing learner but also an hilarious companion. The two spent comfortable weekends in each other's company exploring the south coast, battling with the elements and sharing stories over a campfire on shore. Away from the confines of a stifling upper-class household, Edward discovered an adventurous side to him that was as joyous as a lark suddenly finding wings and John Blake was as proud of him as any father.

Blake got out the two metal mugs and the tea and muttered about how he had always known that the pin-striped suit was a disguise and that, in fact, the man at the wheel was as mad as a hatter, albeit a damned good sailor.

'Taught him everything I knew,' the older man said to himself just as a large wave hit the side of the boat. 'Just as well, looks like we're going to need all the help we can get tonight.' They were being tossed around like a cork.

Hours later, the waves had subsided, along with John's headache and the boat was zipping across the water. In the distance, Edward focused his binoculars on a small vessel coming towards them.

'Bloody Nora, I hope that's them,' Blake said. 'I don't want to explain to any authorities what the hell we're doing here.'

Edward peered out carefully, checked his compass bearing and then beamed.

'It's them, there are four of them and one of them has got a black beret on. You can't get more French than that.'

'I just hope he doesn't smell of garlic,' John replied. 'My stomach couldn't take it.'

'Maybe we should get the jug on again, Blake, they'll be in need of a cup of something hot. Heaven knows what sort of hairy escape they've had to get here.'

'We've only got tea, and they'll hate that,' John told him, but went anyway.

Edward threw a line and the two boats briefly came alongside and a remarkably sprightly Raoul and Michel jumped across. They gave a grateful wave to the French fishermen who had brought them and turned around to face their new rescuers.

They grabbed each of the Englishmen's hands and pumped them up and down, babbling in French, very little of which Edward understood. John Blake looked blankly at them both.

'I apologise, we speak English now,' the older man said with a huge smile. 'It is England that is to be our home until this war is over, no?'

'Yes, it is,' Edward replied. John reached across them with two mugs full of hot tea. They took them gratefully but winced with distaste when they sipped the tea.

'I'm sorry, it's English tea,' Edward told them, 'it's all we've got.

'Come below and I'll go through the arrangements with you. John, take the helm, would you?'

Chapter 40

Harriet had been on a week of nights but as soon as she was able, she went in to see Gus. She knew what the doctors had said and she knew what his parents had said. She also knew what she was about to say.

She marched towards his bed. He seemed to have shrunk into his body and he looked listlessly towards the window.

Harriet pulled the curtains round the bed and stood with her arms folded. She waited.

'What? What do you expect me to do?' Gus finally said, furiously.

'I expect you to deal with this and not give in,' she said. 'You've got a long way to go but you will get there. Do you know how many times I've waited for crews that didn't come back at all? And the ones that do often have disfigured faces or have to have amputations. You've just got to teach your legs to walk again.'

She looked at his crestfallen face and added with a smile, 'Besides, I'm going to marry you Gus Prince and you are going to stand at that altar on your two legs as I walk down the aisle.'

Gus looked at her in astonishment and then burst out laughing. The vision of this pretty, dimpled girl in front of him looking fierce and determined was the first thing in days to pierce his misery.

'Who says you're going to marry me? I haven't asked you. I might be in love with someone else.'

'Poof, an infatuation and you know it. We've been destined for each other since we were at school. You're not going to escape me, especially now you can't walk too well,' she grinned.

He lay back on his pillows and gave her a wry smile.

'We'll see, Harriet Marcham, we'll see.'

Harriet called the orderly who was passing with the meal trolley and said imperiously, 'He'll have some supper now, thank you.'

She sat down next to Gus and tucked a napkin into his pyjama top. He looked in indignation at her.

'I don't need feeding, thank you very much.'

'Good. Well, here, there's nothing wrong with your hands, take this knife and fork and eat up. You're looking a bit pasty and your mum's worried about you.'

Gus resignedly put the first morsel of real food he had tasted in days into his mouth.

While he was chewing, Harriet took the opportunity to lecture him further. 'You're being pathetic, sitting here feeling sorry for yourself,' she told him. He tried to retaliate but she held up her hand to stop him.

'I've seen men learn to walk with false limbs, you have to believe you can walk again. It all comes from up here,' she said, prodding his forehead with her finger. 'Your dad's spoken to the doctors and they say you have a fighting chance of not being in a wheelchair but it's going to take time – and effort – and I'm not going to let you give up. I'm going to be with you every painful step of the way.'

She looked threateningly at him.

'OK, OK, I hear what you're saying,' Gus said. He put down the fork and stared at his plate. He felt tears prickling his eyes.

She softened her voice. 'Come on, Gus, you can do better than this. You're a strong, healthy young man with your whole life ahead of you. You have nothing to lose by giving it your best shot. Your mum, dad, brothers and me . . . we can all help you. You just have to stop feeling like you need to be perfect and accept you're an ordinary human being. It's OK to have frailties you know.'

He could not speak but reached out his hand toward her. She grasped it, trying to pass on her strength to him.

'Now, where's that sponge and custard?' she said, looking round for the orderly.

That night, as Gus went to sleep, he felt as if a huge weight had been taken off his shoulders. He had been feeling guilty about his need for perfection since Bobby had been to see him. Disturbingly, it had brought reminders of Hitler's Aryan race to mind and he had been disgusted with himself. Harriet had somehow given him permission to be a normal human being and her belief in him had given him the kick up the backside he needed. He smiled when he thought about the telling off she had given him but then a vision of her dimpled cheeks and soft smile came into his head and he felt a strange tug on his heart.

When his parents came in the following day, turning the corner towards his bed with dread, they saw their son sitting up in a chair with his hair brushed.

His mum rushed forward and hugged him. 'Oh, Gus, you look so much better! What's happened?'

Gus smiled sheepishly at them both. 'I've had the Harriet Marcham treatment.'

His father looked puzzled but his mother nodded knowingly.

'Ah yes, Harriet. Don't ever underestimate that young woman.'

She had always loved Harriet, finding her so much more approachable than Roberta Hollis, who she had begun to suspect her son had fallen for. She hated the way that girl strode into church on Sundays as if God were lucky to have her there and felt a little frisson of excitement at the thought of the delightful Harriet as a daughter-in-law, imagining swapping cake recipes with her and fussing round a little dimple-cheeked grandchild in a bonnet.

The visit was spent discussing Gus's treatment. He had agreed to have experimental therapy and sounded almost excited at the possibilities. A specialist physiotherapy unit had been set up locally and he was going to be at the forefront of some new equipment that could strengthen his muscles enough to allow him to walk. The previous reliance on bed rest was being challenged in America and Gus had volunteered to try the new techniques.

Gus looked around him and for the first time noticed that the curtains on the screens around his bed were blue.

Chapter 41

Mathilda Hollis was all of a dither. The visitors were due in an hour and she had not put the flowers in their rooms yet. Her husband had not come out of the study all morning. After some softening of the relationship between them, he had been very quiet for a week now; ever since Edward Turner had telephoned them with a very difficult conundrum. In his study, Andrew stared out of the window, looking calm but inwardly, his stomach was churning.

Agnes knocked on the door and walked straight in. Andrew turned to face his sister-in-law and, just like every occasion that he had seen her since the fire, he marvelled at her bright eyes and slightly flushed face that was haloed by her grey hair, singed in places by the fire. He had delighted in the change in her over the past few weeks and for a moment, the frown on his forehead eased.

'Hello Agnes, what can I do for you?'

'I wanted to know whether you'd decided where the Frenchmen are to be housed. I presume Michel will go in the room he had on his last visit but what about his father?'

This was exactly the quandary that Andrew had been battling with for several days now. He had been stunned when Edward Turner had told him they had carried out a rescue mission to get the two men out of France and his wife had excitedly taken over the phone call to insist they both came to stay at the farm. Too chilled to speak, he had backed away from the receiver, for once, grateful that she had taken the lead.

The thought of having Nicole's rightful husband under the same roof with him prompted emotions that Andrew thought he had buried in the Normandy fields, along with nearly all his troop of soldiers.

He was so angry with himself. He had been in control for many years, managing to deal with a wife with overwhelming grief, concealing his own feelings about losing his son and cutting off any affection for the remaining daughter, but then all that changed when Michel burst into their lives and he had been forced to face his demons. Now the biggest demon of all was coming to stay in his own home.

'I don't know, Agnes,' he admitted. 'What do you think I should do?'

Agnes looked surprised to be asked for her opinion and took a moment to think.

'Well, from what Michel has told us, Raoul sounds like a forgiving man and if you meet him halfway then I think it might be all right, and he'd be quite comfortable in the front bedroom.

Andrew nodded. 'All right, put him in there, then,' and uncharacteristically, he added with a grin, 'but if he floors me, you'll have to come to my aid.'

As this was the first time in more than twenty years that Andrew Hollis had joked with her, it took a little while for Agnes to respond but emboldened by her new relationship with Archie, she replied, 'I'll have the Germolene ready.'

They smiled at each other, ready to enjoy this new rapport between them, knowing they made good allies.

For the next hour, the house became a hive of activity and when the clock struck five, the toot of a car was heard coming up the drive.

Andrew took a huge breath and went to join his wife on the porch. Agnes stood behind him, remembering another welcoming party on the porch in 1919. She felt it was a shame that Bobby was not there to share in this moment and resolved to store up every detail to recount to her in a letter that night.

The car door opened and a chauffeur went to the back doors to let the occupants out.

Rachel, who was peering from inside the hallway marvelled at the shininess of the car and the smart-looking man in a peaked cap who was now standing to attention next to it. This Edward Turner certainly came from another world, she thought, if he could organise a car like this in times of petrol rationing.

Michel almost fell out of the back seat, filled with enthusiasm to be back in what he now thought of as his second home.

Mathilda rushed forward towards Michel but her path was blocked by Raoul, who rushed round from the other side of the car to envelop her in such an enormous hug that he lifted her off her feet. She giggled with delight and it was only when he put her down to stride up to Andrew, that she was able to run to greet Michel.

Andrew stood stiffly but Raoul immediately grabbed him by the shoulders and gave him a loud kiss on each cheek and then pumped his hand up and down.

'I am so, so pleased to meet you,' Raoul said, beaming from ear to ear. 'It is so kind of you to welcome us into your home.'

Agnes looked sideways at her brother-in-law and could not help but smile at the look of astonishment on his face. He had never been kissed by a man before.

Raoul then spotted her and marched up to grab her by the waist and swing her round. 'And this must be the wonderful Tante Agnes. I hear so much about you.'

She clutched her chest to get her breath and laughed.

Raoul stood back and looked around him with delight.

'Ah, but it is exactly as Michel described. What a beautiful house, wonderful countryside and such beautiful people.' He clapped his hands with excitement.

Michel came up to Andrew and shook his hand firmly. 'Thank you so much, sir, you are too kind to invite me and my father here. It seems we are, once again, in your debt.'

Mathilda proudly took control and ushered everyone into the drawing room, which, Agnes suddenly felt, looked brighter than it usually did.

Mrs Hill arrived with a large tray of tea and freshly-baked scones, which had used the week's rations all in one go. Rachel followed behind with the teacups, loving every moment of this bizarre family reunion.

There was not a moment's awkward silence during the rest of the afternoon. Michel filled them in on how they had escaped the clutches of a vengeful, retreating army and they all listened intently. He stopped when he got to the point where he needed to tell the family the real story about Elizé. He took a breath and began. 'You need to know that little Elizé was brought to us after her father was shot in front of her and her mother was taken on a truck to a camp. We then had to get her out of France. I think now, you have heard about these camps?'

He looked at Andrew Hollis, who nodded gravely but in fact, his mind was recalling the day Elizé had been brought to the house. He had always suspected Bobby's story about Elizé was a fabrication.

Michel hesitated and glanced at his own father. They had discussed with Edward Turner how much they could tell this family.

Raoul took over.

'We are unable to tell you too much but you need to know your daughter was very wonderful in Elizé's rescue, in fact, she was *incroyable,* and although we may not say more, you should be very proud of her.'

Agnes and Andrew exchanged glances. They had no idea that Bobby had done anything of the kind. Both their minds raced with possible scenarios but, well-schooled in war-time secrecy, they had no choice but to draw their attention back to the present, leaving a plethora of questions unanswered.

Andrew found himself feeling ashamed of never having noticed before what a strong young woman his daughter was. He was going back over the details of her last visit and started to realise there were gaping holes in her story. He suspected she had an impressive tale to tell, that somehow involved the Bisset family. It occurred to him that, however implausible it would sound, she might, somehow, have gone to France and met the large man in front of him and for the first time ever, he experienced a fierce pride in her and then realised with a jolt that she was, in fact, just as good as any son. He just needed to tell her, he thought.

Raoul was chattering happily when he suddenly mentioned Nicole's name. It was the moment Andrew had been dreading and he stiffened.

'So, because of Nicole, we have so much in common, you and I.' Raoul announced to Andrew. 'We share the same love for Michel and,' he gave a wickedly conspiratorial wink to Andrew, 'we have both loved and now I will love all your family, who feel like my family already.'

At that moment, the back door slammed and Elizé flew into the room and flung down her school satchel to race over to Raoul, whooping with delight.

'Now it is perfect. Well it would be,' her face clouded, 'if only Maman – and Papa – were here.' Her little face threatened to crumple but then Raoul lifted her high above his head and he tickled her. She giggled and their laughter resounded throughout the room. Michel went over and grabbed her in a huge hug as soon as his father put her down.

For a moment, Andrew Hollis looked at this huge Frenchman with envy. He wondered how Nicole could ever have forgotten the larger-than-life Raoul enough to fall in love with him. He felt like a pale shadow next to Raoul and was unnerved by his unsolicited connection with this extraordinary French family. He was still not sure how to deal with the bizarre situation and in the meantime, he had to learn to face Raoul at breakfast every morning.

In addition, there was his sister-in-law's wedding to his trusted friend and foreman to prepare for.

Chapter 42

It was the autumn of 1944 and Edward poured himself a whisky from the oak cabinet in his office. He felt sick. The report in front of him had made for harrowing reading and while his first reaction was one of incredulity, he knew that the source who had compiled it was a calm, measured man who could be relied on to tell the truth.

Mavis knocked on the door to tell him she was leaving for the day. She had her coat and hat on and her handbag on her arm, but she stopped short when she saw Edward's anguished face. 'Are you all right, sir?'

He took a moment to register she was there and then looked up. His face was grey.

She put down her handbag and went over to sit on the hard-backed chair in front of the desk. She reached out her hand to cover his, which was stone cold.

'Oh sir, whatever is the matter? Can you tell me?'

'It will be in the papers tomorrow so yes, I suppose I can, but first you may need to join me in a whisky.'

Mavis Arbuckle would normally only drink a small sherry before her luncheon on Sundays but as Edward passed over the document to her, she read: 'French Resistance Report on Release of Drancy Concentration Camp – Atrocities, Deaths and Survivors.' She nodded and held out her hand to receive the crystal glass.

The two sat in silence for a while as she scanned the first few pages. Edward watched her face drain of all blood and reached over to take the document back.

'Don't read any more, Mavis, it's unimaginably horrendous. Those poor people . . .'

Her reply was faint. 'I read about these camps but I never really thought the reports were true.'

'I wish they weren't, Mavis, I wish they weren't.'

He took a gulp of his whisky and went on, 'There may be some good news though. They have liberated some survivors but we'll have to wait and see. Heaven knows what state they'll be in.'

They sat in silence, both thinking of the people who had met their fate at Drancy. Mavis offered up a prayer for them all. Edward was thinking more on a practical level of how he could help anyone left alive.

When the telephone rang, they both jumped. Mavis reached over to pick it up.

'Edward Turner's office, how may I help you?' She passed the receiver over to Edward.

He listened for a moment and then his face cleared and he smiled. 'Of course, I'd love to be there. Thank you so much, goodbye.

'That's just what I needed,' he told Mavis. 'I've been invited to a wedding.' He chinked his glass against hers and they both took a sip.

* * *

Bobby, fully recovered and back at work, was flying a Tempest from Aston Down to Redhill. She knew the route but had to concentrate on the mist that was threatening to descend rather than think about all the arrangements that had to be made at home for Saturday. Fortunately, it was the end of her roster this weekend and she had two days' leave, which meant she could get home in time for the wedding. She had received a letter from her mother, which had told her all about how Michel and Raoul were conspiring to add a French tradition to the day but were delighting in keeping it all a secret. Another had arrived this morning letting her know that her father had invited Edward Turner.

Bobby had been astonished at how that news had turned her stomach upside down. She had not seen Edward since their weekend in London and although his letters had been regular and very chatty, showing a drop in his guard, the prospect of seeing him in person again had thrown her into an uncharacteristic confusion and she did not need her father putting pressure on them both.

She landed the Tempest and sat for a moment gathering her thoughts before climbing down onto the tarmac to sign in. There had been a strange feeling of loss since she had seen Gus at the hospital and especially when she read the glowing, excited letters from Harriet about his progress. She had felt quite distant from him, as if he were a character in a dream she had once had.

Edward was another matter.

'Hey, Bobby!'

Audrey appeared from the other side of the airfield. The two girls had not met since they had been on the training course together for the heavy bombers.

'Audrey! How lovely to see you. How's Cosford?'

'Full of women!' she laughed, 'but, Bobby, wait till I tell you. I've got such exciting news. Have you got time for a cuppa?'

Bobby checked her schedule. She needed to call in at the Met Office but said she would meet Audrey in the NAAFI. The forecast that morning had suggested the weather was set to improve if she delayed her next flight slightly so once she had verified that fact, she picked up her maps to take a Fairchild to Hawarden, then an Anson back to Hamble, thus gaining half an hour before she had to do her pre-flight checks.

She found Audrey holding two cups of tea and two biscuits.

'I decided we deserved these,' Audrey said. 'But we'll have to talk fast because I only have an hour.'

'I have less than that, so spill the beans. What is it you have to tell me?'

Audrey leaned forward to whisper. 'You remember Freddie, the guy that you handed on to me at White Waltham? Well, we're going to be married!' She sat back in triumph to wait for Bobby's reaction.

'Married! That's amazing,' Bobby exclaimed, remembering the good-looking engineer who had caught her as she fell out of the Wellington during training.

'He was a good catch,' she joked.

'Oh, Bobby, he's gorgeous. After that first date, it just got better and better and he writes to me every day. We're just waiting for this stupid war to finish and then we're getting hitched. But what happened with you and that . . . what was he called . . . Edward? The one you dropped my lovely Freddie for.'

Bobby felt the sudden need to offload all her thoughts to someone who was not involved with her complicated life and she explained quickly and vaguely about Gus, and then about Harriet and finally Edward, hesitating as she got to his name.

'Hmm, sounds like you've got yourself in a bit of a pickle,' Audrey said. 'So how do you feel about Gus now?'

'Oh, I don't know, he's great. Attractive, lively company but, now my friend Harriet has decided she's completely head over heels about him that's taken any choice out of it. He didn't ever really want me, I think I was just a distraction from . . . whatever it is he does. And to be honest, I've never connected with him on the same level as I do with . . .' she tailed off.

'So tell me about Edward then,' Audrey said, nibbling her biscuit.

Bobby took a deep breath. 'He's a bit of a conundrum. I feel there's such a deep man there but I can never quite grasp it. I thought he was shy and awkward when I first met him, but he isn't.'

She thought back to walking along the Mall with him in London when he tucked her arm through his, and then she remembered the way everyone in the War Rooms stood back in respect to let him pass. Finally, she remembered his kiss and unconsciously touched her lips.

Audrey took a sip of her tea. 'This war is making actors of all of us. I mean, I was a teacher in a primary school. Who would ever have thought I'd be flying aircraft all over the country? Do you fancy him?'

Bobby was taken aback. She had never thought about it. The physical attraction between her and Gus had been really strong but with Edward, she had been so busy trying to work him out, she had never thought about whether she was attracted to him.

'There may be something between us,' she admitted, realising that he had been constantly in her thoughts since

London and that her stomach had tied in a knot just thinking about him. 'But I don't feel I know him and now he's been invited to my aunt's wedding this weekend and I know my father will be putting pressure on us both. He wants me sorted and settled by the time the war is over so I can go back to the farm with a man to take over and look after things. But I don't want that sort of relationship.'

Audrey looked intently at her, then nodded. 'I know, things have really changed over the past few years for us women, especially us in the ATA. We've done something no one thought we could and we've done it well. I agree with you, I know I'll find it hard to go back to being the little woman at home again. Maybe I should warn Freddie – or maybe not,' she burst out laughing. 'Perhaps I'll leave that until I've got him down the aisle!'

Bobby had a great deal to think about but by the time she had started up the Fairchild, the wind had picked up and in her usual professional manner, she put every other thought out of her mind while she piloted the aircraft up into the sky towards Hawarden.

Edward Turner would have to wait.

Chapter 43

Agnes Clarke had taken a few moments on the day before her wedding to go into the woods. She placed the rosehips amongst the burnished leaves and went over to lean on the tree next to where she had buried the charred remains of the telegram announcing Peter Martin's death. She closed her eyes for a moment but then heard footsteps crunching through the undergrowth. She opened them to see Archie standing in front of her, his eyes soft with love.

'Eh lass, you needn't fuss, I'm just here if you need me.'

She moved forward to be clasped in his arms and they strengthened around her.

'You've always known about this place, haven't you?' she said in a muffled voice from his shoulder.

'Yes, I have and it's all right. You can still visit if you need to. I'll not interfere.'

She looked up and then all around her. 'No,' she said in a decided manner. 'No, I don't need to. I'll dig up the spring bulbs I've planted here and put them in our garden; there's only the cinders of that stupid telegram here. I'd rather remember Peter from a chair in my own garden full of blooms.' And with that, the couple walked slowly back towards the farm, Archie's arm around Agnes's shoulder.

*　*　*

The following day dawned bright, but cold, even for October. Mrs Hill and Rachel had been up till the early hours of the morning, preparing the limited wedding breakfast. They were struggling to feed so many mouths but delighted villagers had kept popping round with an odd cake or a plate of biscuits to add to the limited rations for such a special occasion. Mrs Hill stood back to check the table. She tutted, but was actually quite pleased with what they had managed to achieve. No one would be able to say that the Hollis family were not able to put on a good wedding breakfast.

Agnes and Mathilda were alone in the bedroom and Mathilda was fussing round her sister, trying to put some saved rose petals in her hair.

'Do stop fussing, Mathilda,' Agnes said, pulling away. 'I'm a woman in her fifties, not a blushing young bride.'

'Well, you look like one today,' Mathilda said, beaming happily. The family had been through so much and now, here was her sister, finally finding some happiness. It was more than she could ever have hoped for.

Elizé burst through the door. She had a new dress on, made from fabric unearthed from the attic. Rachel had stitched it with love and care, completely captivated by this little girl who thanked God so fervently every Sabbath for bringing her to Salhouse Farm, always adding an extra prayer for her beloved mama and papa.

'I'm the bridesmaid, I'm the bridesmaid,' she said, twirling with delight.

The two women took a hand each and danced with her around the room. It was a moment of pure joy for all three of them.

Downstairs, a door slammed and Bobby called up the stairs. 'Anyone home?'

They all raced to the landing to look down towards Bobby and then her mother tutted in horror.

'There's only an hour before the wedding, you'll have to get a move on. You look a sight and you can't go to church wearing those boots.'

'OK, mother, just give me a moment, father insisted he wanted to see me.' Bobby said, ignoring her mother's relentless attempts to make her into a lady.

She had a moment's trepidation standing outside her father's study. *What hair-brained scheme does he have in mind now?* She firmly knocked on the study door and went in to find her father gazing out of the window.

'You look very smart, Father,' she said, noting his best suit and the piece of heather in his buttonhole.

'Well, I'd like to say the same about you,' he smiled, 'but you do look a bit windswept.'

'Just come in on a Tiger Moth, I managed to get a landing at Coltishall,' she replied, adding with a tentative smile, 'Admit it, I look like the wreck of the Hesperus.'

'Well, yes, now you mention it . . . Roberta, I need to say something.'

Bobby's heart sank. Whenever he called her Roberta, it was serious.

'I want to talk to you about Edward Turner.'

Then Bobby's heart stopped for a moment. She did not need this. She was having enough trouble working out how she felt without her father interfering.

He went on.

'I made a mistake.'

She looked up in surprise.

'I had no right to try to force you into a marriage with him. It has to be your choice. I shouldn't have thought I could manipulate you.'

He looked intently at her, as if seeing her for the first time.

'After all, you are my daughter and that brings with it a stubbornness that I, of all people, can't criticise.'

Bobby went to move forward but he put his hand up to stop her.

'I haven't finished,' he said. 'I haven't been a good father to you, no, I'm not denying it. You've deserved better.' He was thinking of Raoul but then shook himself to get back to the subject.

'But, I do take credit for the fact that you are standing in front of me today, an ATA pilot, a woman who, I suspect, has done some amazing things. I am intensely proud.'

Bobby could not speak; she was so overwhelmed.

Her father moved forward as if to hug her but then stopped and put his hand on her shoulder instead. He gave it a squeeze.

'There's something else,' he went on. 'I've been talking to the people at Coltishall. When this war is over, they've offered you a job as a pilot trainer at the airfield. Nothing definite at the moment, but they're very impressed with your flying and, of course, you'll be able to help out with the running of the farm as well. Yes, well that's all,' he finished, exhausted with his emotional outburst.

He brushed past her and went out of the room, leaving her stunned and alone.

At that moment, Edward Turner arrived and was shown into the study by Rachel. He found Bobby looking shocked and tearful and immediately moved towards her.

He so wanted to take her in his arms but she waved both hands in front of her and fled from the room. An emotional encounter with Edward would be just a step too far.

Later that morning, a group of schoolgirls were gathered outside the farm's front porch. Each one was clutching a white ribbon that they were twirling excitedly up in the air but once Agnes, dressed in a pretty, dusky pink dress, appeared in the doorway on Andrew's arm, they all lined up to stretch the ribbons across the pathway.

Raoul was grinning from ear to ear. He handed a pair of scissors to Agnes as Michel struck up a lively French tune on a violin from his position in front of the children.

'You see, Miss Clarke, you must cut through these ribbons. That will be how you cut through any obstacles and then, *et voilà*, you will have the perfect marriage! It is something we French like to do. It is a good custom, no?'

With a flourish, he waved Agnes and the family through, winking at Bobby, and Michel played joyously all the way to the church where Archie awaited his bride, nervously twiddling with his Sunday tie.

Bobby sat in the front pew, wearing a tweed jacket with the plain white blouse and navy skirt she had changed into as a concession to her mother. On her head was the plain, blue felt hat she had unearthed from behind the tennis racquets in the understairs cupboard. Her compromise was completed by some leather gloves, to the approval of the gossips in the village who had despaired of the tomboy, Bobby, ever looking like a lady. They were all out in force to see Miss Clarke finally walk down the aisle. There were a few who muttered about Mrs Hollis's sister marrying a foreman but most people, full of respect for the middle-aged couple, were smiling indulgently at the scene in front of them. Even Peter Martin's sister had tried not to think of how her brother should have been the one waiting at the altar for Agnes and had sneaked into the back of the church to watch.

Bobby rested her hands demurely on the hymn book, but her fingers were clasping the cover a little too hard. She could feel Edward's eyes on her from the back of the church and then when the vicar was asking the couple to say their vows, she felt as if she were repeating them under her breath to try them out for size.

She had never seen Aunt Agnes look so radiant, she thought. Gone was the grey, high necked dress and instead she wore a fetching, fitted dusky pink crepe outfit that reflected in her eyes, which were shining with happiness. There was a small posy of rosehips and autumn leaves from the woodland pinned to her left chest and a similar one on Archie's lapel.

Archie was shifting from foot to foot. He hated being the centre of attention, but his face softened every time he looked at Agnes. Bobby felt a tear running down her cheek and reached in her handbag for a handkerchief. She looked round the pews. To one side were Harriet and her family. Harriet was looking misty-eyed too, and Bobby suspected she was imagining walking down the aisle to Gus.

'I do hope he isn't in a wheelchair,' Bobby thought as a pang of guilt hit her in the ribs. She had hardly thought of Gus these past few weeks. She hoped he had not thought about her either.

Behind Harriet were Mrs Hill and Rachel and then in the next pew were Raoul and Michel. Her mother and father were seated to Bobby's left with an excited Elizé between them. The little girl could hardly keep still and was constantly shifting in her seat. Bobby's mother had a beatific smile and put a restraining hand gently on Elizé's arm. Elizé looked up at her and clasped Mathilda's hand with her own. They looked like a grandmother with her adored grandchild. Raoul's voice boomed over everyone else's during the hymns, he did not know the words but had a rich baritone voice and managed to pick up the tunes easily so sang lustily. Michel looked so much better, his cheeks were a healthy colour and he had put weight on. Bobby started to cry again, thinking how far they had all come since Michel burst into their drawing room that night. It occurred to her that since she had unleashed her own emotions, this crying was becoming a bit of a habit.

As the wedding party strolled back to the house in the October sunshine, Edward made his way through the throng towards Bobby. He touched her arm and she reared up as if struck by a red-hot poker.

'Edward,' she said, awkwardly. 'It's so lovely to see you here. How are you?'

'Well, thank you. And you?' He was polite but distant. Both of them were embarrassed by the shadow of their fathers' arrangement hanging over them. It was as if being at the farm put their relationship on a very different footing from the one they had started to develop away from family pressures.

'Bobby, about what our fathers discussed . . .' Edward thought it was time they took control of their own destiny and was about to say so, but Bobby interrupted.

'I . . . I've been offered a job teaching pilots at Coltishall when the war finishes,' she blurted out.

Edward looked shocked. In the familiar guise of a pin-striped Civil Servant, he did not give himself a chance to examine his own thoughts on the subject but found his mouth opening to voice the opinions of his parents, colleagues and the Edward Turner everyone thought he was.

'But surely, as a woman, you wouldn't want to do that?'

Bobby looked at him as if he were speaking a foreign language.

'Not want to do it? Of course I would, it's my dream,' she asserted, raising her chin.

Too late, Edward Turner realised he had made the biggest mistake of his life.

Chapter 44

Bobby was burning with indignation. She had spent her life proving herself to her father and now she was facing similar outdated attitudes from Edward. She had expected more of him. She tried to explain her feelings in a letter to Harriet but her friend's reply was unequivocal.

Dear Bobby,

I can't believe you are thinking of working all your life. Why wouldn't you want a man to take care of you? It's your job to look after a home and family, you know that. That's what we women do – and we're very good at it. I can't wait for this war to be over and we can all go back to cooking and looking after a house. I've really missed it. I don't want to compete in a man's world – they're welcome to it. I like Edward, he has an inner strength that I admire and he obviously adores you. I've always put you on a bit of a pedestal, Bobby, to be honest, but I think it's time for you to give up your goddess status and come down to earth a bit!

Seeing as how you asked – or didn't! – I am strug-gling with the shifts at the moment, I'm so tired. Every moment off I have, I'm at the hospital. Gus is doing really well but it's slow progress. Sometimes he is full of optimism and then he plummets back down into despair. I'm doing everything I can to keep his spirits up but all he talks about is flying. The doctors are really pleased with him but it's going to take a long time and he's not very patient! It's a good job I adore him, he's a complete grumpy guts sometimes.

Anyway, as soon as Edward goes down on one knee, you just grab the opportunity. Maybe we could have a double wedding!! Wouldn't that be exciting?

Must go, crews in peril to save!

Lots of love,

Harriet.

Bobby looked at the letter in disgust and threw it to one side but it was so hard to be cross with Harriet, she was irrepressible and just bounded back every time you rebuffed her, and in her words, Bobby heard the opinions of women up and down the country. She had never been able to understand why she had always felt she had to be different.

Sighing with frustration, Bobby stalked off to get her 'chits' for the day. A Typhoon from Kemble to Lasham and then a Tempest from Aston Down to Dunsfold. That did not seem too arduous, she thought, picking up her parachute. There were loads of Canadians at Dunsfold, Bobby thought.

Maybe I should find one to go on a date with, that would show Mr Edward bloomin' Turner.

By the time she got to Dunsfold, the weather had closed in and it was almost dark. Bobby had had a moment of concern as she realised she was only just going to get to the airfield before blackout so she was relieved when she touched down. She was going to have to stay the night.

A lovely Canadian twang greeted her in the NAAFI. 'Hello, little lady, you look as if you could do with a hot chocolate. Permit me to get you one.'

Bobby turned round to see a tall pilot with brown hair and twinkling eyes.

'Well, if you insist,' she said, settling herself in at the nearest table. 'I am bushed.'

He introduced himself as Adrian from Montreal and he immediately launched into regaling her with endless tales of his bravado. She smiled as she listened. *What is it about men that they think we're going to be impressed if they tell us they're like one of those new comic heroes?* she thought while seeming to nod with interest at his story.

She would have loved to have told him about flying behind enemy lines and getting stuck in France but she had put her signature on that dotted line of the Official Secrets Act. It did give her a moment of quiet satisfaction to think about it though. How surprised he would have been.

When he asked her to join him for a drink that night, she was too tired to argue and agreed, but first she had to find a bed for the night. The only place she could find was in the boiler house on a mattress but at least it was warm. She left her overnight bag, swilled her face in the ablutions block and went to meet her date.

The evening was a disaster. Firstly, Bobby thought that Adrian was probably married. It was the knowing looks and sly comments that his friends at the bar made as they passed that fuelled her suspicions. Secondly, she was not prepared to play the 'little girl in a man's world' game any more. His determination to impress this young woman with his tales of heroism and bravado fell on deaf ears. She had nothing to prove. He could only fly one type of aircraft. She could fly dozens.

When he tried to kiss her at the end of the evening, she just longed for her bed and made a quick getaway, dodging under his arm and waving her goodbyes from a safe distance.

She lay on her mattress and wondered how she would ever find anyone who would respect her independence.

* * *

Edward was pacing up and down in his office early in the new year of 1945. Churchill and Anthony Eden had gone to Athens to try to reconcile the warring factions. The

Home Guard had been stood down but the war was still far from over.

He pressed the intercom to ask Mavis Arbuckle to come in. She grabbed her pencil and pad and went to sit with her hand poised ready to write.

Edward had a list of things he needed to deal with but the main task was to try to help the Dutch, who were starving after the failed Operation Market Garden. The Germans and the weather were conspiring against the people of the Netherlands and Edward suspected the situation on the ground was dire, but he needed more information. He dictated five memos, all of which would need coding and sending over to agents in Europe. Since the liberation of Paris, it had been easier to get messages through to France but communication with other areas of Europe were almost impossible. The mercy flights were planned with a delicate agreement that if the Germans did not shoot at them, the allies would not bomb German positions. Edward, however, was not taking any chances and had volunteered to organise a back-up plan of trucks to go into the Nazi-occupied northern areas as soon as possible. It occurred to him that Churchill and Eden might, after all, have the easier task.

'That's all for now, Mavis, thank you.' He looked at his watch. She should have gone home by now but as she hovered, he added, 'Mavis, do you have a minute?' She sat down again with an encouraging smile.

'Mavis, I'm afraid I need your advice again. I'm not doing very well as a potential suitor. Do you mind me asking: how much independence do you think women will want once the war is over?'

She thought for a moment, realising how significant her answer was going to be in her beloved boss's life.

'Well, sir, this war has certainly changed things. I mean, I'm a single woman, so, since my father died, I've never had to answer to a man, and I must say, I'd find it very hard to give up that independence now. I like making my own decisions and I'm used to my being my own woman. I'd never want to give that up.'

'Oh, that's a shame,' Edward joked. 'I was hoping to introduce you to an old friend of mine, a sea captain. He's a confirmed bachelor and needs taming.' The thought of Mavis Arbuckle with his friend, John Blake, almost made him laugh out loud but he coughed to control himself.

'I'll just stick to taming my Tiddles,' Mavis tittered, but then her flushed face became serious again. 'I think, sir, if you don't mind me saying, that times have changed and women have discovered that they're as good as any men in so many areas. They're not going to want to go back into the kitchen.' She stopped, weighing up his reaction and then decided to speak her mind fully.

'The point is, sir, in your case, if a woman is going to be interesting enough to entice you, then there'll be little point in trying to make her conform to normal conventions. She's going to need to be able to fly.'

Edward smiled at the irony of her comment. 'As ever, you're absolutely right but I think I may have already messed it up. How am I going to make her believe that I'm open-minded enough to let her do that?'

He looked so forlorn, Mavis longed to give him a motherly hug.

'If I can suggest, sir, that if you can just be yourself and stop hiding behind the mask of this high-ranking civil servant,' she waved her arms to encompass the impeccably-dressed figure in front of her, 'then she'll realise you're able to see her as an equal.'

He nodded in agreement, so she went on, 'But, sir, you must mean it. Any woman worth her salt'll be able to see through it if you're not sincere and for a man brought up as traditionally as you have, it's not going to be easy.'

With that, Mavis Arbuckle got to her feet and moved around the desk. For once, she towered over her employer and put her hand on his shoulder. She could only guess at the internal battle that was going on in Edward's head. She suspected he was two people, the first, she knew was bound by convention but the second? She had glimpsed another Edward at times, one whose eyes twinkled when a task seemed impossible or when he had been out of the office on a mission that only he knew about. What he got up to on those occasions, she had no idea, but he always came back looking reinvigorated and full of mischief. There had been that occasion recently, she recalled, when he had gone to the south coast and come back with those Frenchmen.

'I've got the feeling there's an exciting young man who masquerades in this pin-striped suit,' she said, 'and that, given your head, you embrace adventure like a rock-climber. Don't be afraid of a woman who's the same. It means she's worthy of you.'

She blushed and grabbed her notebook.

'Goodnight, Mavis. Where would I be without you?' Edward said as she closed the door behind her.

Chapter 45

The daffodils were out and for once, the sun seemed to herald a warmth to the spring of 1945 that had nothing to do with the weather.

Bobby noticed their nodding heads as she made her way to the restroom at Hamble and nodded back at them, feeling a shared optimism. She was acting as a taxi pilot and although it was giving her more regular hours and less stress, she would be glad when this month was over. Flying the same aircraft over and over was less of a challenge and Bobby needed a challenge.

The winter months had been quieter, with fewer fighters needed, but also because the terrible weather meant that landing areas were reduced to little more than muddy strips in fields. Even so, she had hardly had time to get home. She knew that Michel and Raoul were making themselves useful on the farm, that the newly-married couple had moved into Archie's little cottage and that her mother was actually thriving on the new responsibility of being the woman in charge of the household. Her aunt's description of her mother was like reading about another person. The psychiatrist had been delighted with her progress and with Raoul and Michel to fuss over, she had discovered a new confidence that had taken them all, especially her husband, by surprise. Bobby could not wait to go home and see for herself. She received regular letters from Harriet describing, in interminable detail, how Gus was doing with his new treatment and how she had done him a schedule of achievement goals.

Bobby smiled, thinking of Gus being bombarded with Harriet Marcham and her determination to get him walking again. She had received an occasional letter from Gus and an even rarer one from Edward. Both were perfunctory towards her, but she was pleased to note the warmth in Gus's descriptions of Harriet.

'Hi Bobby,' Sally followed her into the restroom. 'Haven't seen you in ages. How are you?'

'OK . . . bit bored. On Ansons.'

'Poor you,' Sally said. She flopped down in the armchair next to Bobby and tilted her head back. 'Is it all over yet?' she asked plaintively.

Bobby threw a cushion at her. 'Nearly, but not quite. We're almost in Berlin, I heard on the wireless today.'

'Oh hell, I'm running out of time.'

Sally's determination to find a husband before the war was over had been thwarted by a series of doomed relationships and she was getting desperate.

'I don't know what I want,' Daphne said from across the room, voicing the opinions of all of them. 'Part of me just wants it all to be over and the other part is terrified. I couldn't bear to go back to where we were before the war. I'm a pilot now and I love it. How the hell am I going to tell my dad I don't want to go back to that boring admin job?'

'Well, let's see what we can do about that,' Sally was suddenly galvanised into action. 'I heard there's an Embassy do tonight at the Savoy. I think I can get us an invite. Are you both up for that? We should have enough time to get the train and get back if we get a move on.'

Bobby and Daphne perked up. A night out was just what they needed.

* * *

The sumptuous foyer was full of people in either uniform or evening dress and the three girls hung back for a moment until Sally spotted her cousin, a tall man with glasses. The Savoy had been too opulent for a Blitz-torn London but once the Americans joined the war, it had received a huge boost and was enjoying a revival as one of the poshest places in the capital. Even so, the menus on the A-frames next to the restaurant pronounced that they, too, were keeping to the maximum meal-cost of five shillings, which meant that many service people were able to eat there for the first time in their lives.

'Reggie!' Sally called, moving towards him as he turned around.

'Sal, you came! And these must be your friends,' Reggie said, steering the trio towards the group he was with.

He signalled to a waitress passing with a tray of drinks and each girl took a glass, grateful to have something to do with their hands. They had all put on their best frocks, which were, frankly, looking a little worn after years of rationing, but their hair gleamed, and Bobby and Daphne had borrowed Sally's lipstick when she was out of the room.

The group of men turned to greet the new arrivals and Reggie introduced them with a touch of pride in his voice that he knew three gorgeous ATA pilots.

Bobby clutched the stem of her glass tightly. One of them was Edward.

They had not met for months and their last meeting had been re-played over and over in her mind, the embarrassment worsening every time.

'Hello Bobby,' he said, quietly. Outwardly, her unexpected appearance seemed to have no effect on him but inside, his heart was thumping.

'Ah, you know one of these lovely ladies, do you, Turner? I might have known!'

Sally immediately turned her attention to a tall, older man with a monocle. His distinguished looks suggested a large fortune. She turned triumphantly to the others, giving them a wink. Daphne was commandeered by Reggie and Bobby was left facing Edward.

'How are you, Edward?' she said, twirling her glass in her hand.

'Fine, thank you. And you?'

Bobby muttered something but she knew her cheeks were aflame and the words that came out were mumbled.

He took her arm gently and steered her away from the group.

'I've been wanting to contact you but it's been a bit difficult – so much happening at the moment. Is there any chance you might be home a week on Saturday?'

Bobby looked puzzled but searched mentally through her roster. 'I think I could be, why?'

'I may have something of interest to you and your family. It would be good if you could be there.'

This man was so mysterious, she just could not work him out.

'Good, I'll see you then,' she said. 'But for now, why don't we go and have a dance?'

The lights swirled above the pair as they took to the dancefloor. She was amazed he was such a good dancer and not stiff like the men around her, who looked like penguins, she thought with a giggle. That drink must have gone to her head.

His arm encircled her waist and his hand on her back seemed to burn through her dress.

The band was playing Glenn Miller's 'Little Brown Jug' and their feet had to move very fast. They both burst out laughing when Bobby stumbled and fell into Edward.

'I'm sorry,' she said, 'I'm out of practice.'

'No, it's me and my clumsy feet,' he gallantly replied, taking her in his arms once more.

The band did not draw breath before launching into 'In The Mood' and the slower tempo made them each suddenly aware of the proximity of the other. Bobby closed her eyes for a moment and the room spun.

'Bobby . . .' he started, 'I want to apologise.'

She looked up and waited.

'I am such a fool,' he blurted out. 'I don't think I sounded enthusiastic enough about the chance of you having a job at the airfield when all this is over.'

She stood back and looked him squarely in the face.

'No, Edward, you did not. I've never pretended to be anything other than what I am and, believe me, I'm not the woman for you if you think I could ever be content with just being a housewife preparing cucumber sandwiches for Embassy suppers.'

The vision that invaded Edward's mind made him burst out laughing. 'No,' he said, with a grin, 'I don't suppose a pinny would suit you, would it?'

'Not one bit,' she retorted, starting to smile. 'Look, I don't think tonight is the time for any deep discussions, let's just dance and have a bit of fun.'

'That's fine by me, work is just not allowing me a minute to think at the moment, and,' he said, pausing to acknowledge her career too, 'I don't suppose yours is either.'

It was step in the right direction, Bobby thought.

Chapter 46

It felt good to be heading out into the field again, Edward thought, automatically filling his bag with only the bare essentials. He needed to leave as much room as possible for some supplies for his friends. He felt the familiar calm confidence he loved so much when he was about to face the unknown. Edward had been moved from Whitehall to Baker St where the Special Operations Unit was based to focus on the work being done by this top secret organisation, but his prowess with Dutch and German and high level clearance meant that he was to be flown to Holland to coordinate the Dutch Resistance emergency food projects. He needed to get it up and running, aware that it was already too late for thousands of civilians in the Netherlands who had starved to death after the Germans had blocked supplies and flooded the land. The Dutch railway workers' strike was intended to make life as difficult as possible for the enemy but between the weather and German retaliation, the Dutch were thwarted in their attempts to plant food in the waterlogged fields and the nation was suffering from an horrendous 'Hongerwin-ter'. Frozen canals meant no barges could make winter deliveries and the population was now trying to survive on between 320 and 580 calories a day.

Edward checked his notes. Flour had already been airlifted in from Sweden and there were two follow-up relief efforts planned – Operation Manna and Operation Faust. One was going to air drop food over German-occupied territory and the second was hoping to use 200 vehicles to truck food into Rhenen. Both areas were still occupied by the Germans and he sighed, know-ing how much subversive coordination by the resistance networks would be needed to ensure all three operations got food through.

During his time in the field in the run-up to the war, Edward had spent some time in Holland and spoke both Dutch and German well. He was a valuable asset in the complex negotiations. He was also hoping he could further another cause while he was there.

He took the train to Lincoln and then a car was wait-ing to take him to RAF Scampton, where plans were being made for Operation Manna which would, as the Bible had described, drop food from the heavens.

He was given a tour of inspection to examine the makeshift hammock-type arrangements that were to be attached to the undercarriages of Lancaster bombers so that 'blocks' of food could be carried across the Channel and he watched bemused pilots being sent out on low-flying missions without knowing why or what they were being trained for.

A reconnaissance aeroplane was being sent over the Netherlands that night and it had been arranged that Edward would go with it. He did not feel any anxiety about being dropped so close to enemy territory. Edward Turner only felt nervous when dealing with women – landing near enemy-held territory just elicited an excited grin from him.

The pilot was more on edge. Only two weeks before, nearly 200 Luftwaffe pilots had carried out a suicide mission, using their propellers as scythes and cutting into American bombers. A young man in his mid-twenties, Philip Howes had survived three tours and even though the gossip in the mess was that the attacks were a last-ditch effort to subdue the Allies, he was worried that his luck was in danger of running out, just before the war finally ended. He felt he was living on borrowed time.

Helping Edward climb up the ladder at the back of the Lysander, Philip Howes looked at the civil servant with disbelief. There was no evidence of a slight tremor of the hands or a tiny twitch in his cheek – both signs he had regularly seen in men about to land in war-torn Europe. This man seemed to have a child's enthusiasm for the task ahead.

'More fool him,' Philip thought, believing naivety to be the reason for his passenger's phlegmatic approach.

Edward smiled at Phillip and signalled to him to pass his bag up, but Philip paused, weighing it in his hands.

'What on earth do you think you've got in here?' he asked crossly, 'the Crown Jewels?'

'Worth more than the Crown Jewels to the people I'm going to see,' said Edward, leaning across to take the bag from him, but Philip held it back.

'Not on your life, sir. You can only take essentials. The landing is too soft, we need as little weight as possible.'

He pointed to Edward to go back down the ladder and Edward had no choice but to obey. He took out some tins, milk and flour from the bag, just leaving some chocolate hidden under his smalls.

Philip picked up the bag again and nodded, motioning Edward into the plane.

'Sorry, sir, but I can't risk your life for a few supplies. It seems you're too valuable.'

Edward sat silently in the rear of the plane, relieved that at least his flight was going to be followed so soon by the food drops. Philip flew low over to the Netherlands, sticking firmly to the areas that had been liberated by the Canadians. From the high position in his cockpit, he was able to get good photographs by moonlight of the land below. Edward peered out of the side window to see the shadows of ruined buildings and devastated landscapes. He remembered the colourful bulb fields and the gently-turning windmills and felt a huge sadness for the nation that had made a young man feel so welcome in the 1930s. The landscape looked ravaged – by nature and by man. Cities were flattened and proud buildings destroyed. Edward had seen Coventry and London but somehow, even in the reflection of the moon, this country below him looked more forlorn and desperate – as if the heart had been ripped out of it.

It had been arranged that Edward would be dropped near to the finally-liberated Arnhem. He had to get as close as possible to his rendezvous point as there was no petrol for cars and the Germans had confiscated all bicycles. Everywhere was eerily quiet below him but occasionally he spotted a few bedraggled people, dragging one exhausted foot in front of another, on a desperate night march. They hardly had the energy to look up to check whether the plane above them was friend or foe, almost as if they were hoping an enemy plane would put them out of their misery.

Edward scanned the map. 'There', he shouted forward, spotting the place he knew as Easter Meadow. 'The Germans haven't left much standing, but that's the place, I'm sure of it.'

'You'd better be,' Philip replied. 'It's a long walk if you're wrong. OK, I'll circle, get enough height and then we can go in. I'll have to be quick; I can't risk getting waterlogged.'

The pilot waited until he saw the signal, a powerful beam flashed the letter 'X'. Once the lamps were turned on, Philip went down and touched at 'A', the first light, as he passed 'B' he noted that the colour of the ground had changed and he knew the meadow had been ploughed recently. He squeezed the brake lever as hard as he could, almost making the Lysander stand on its nose.

'Please be as quick as you can, sir,' he called back, but Edward was already out on the ladder and calling his thanks to his pilot.

The aircraft immediately did a 'U' turn and taxied to take off, bumping along the furrows.

Edward turned around to be greeted by a man in a traditional cap who ran out to meet him.

'Hans!' Edward exclaimed, taking a moment to recognise his friend before clasping his hand. He was shocked to see the man's sunken cheeks and dark-rimmed eyes. He looked like a walking skeleton.

'Edward, it's good to see you. How are you?'

'Better than you, I suspect.'

Hans and Edward thanked the men with the torches, who turned to go back over the field to the village of De Praets and then Hans said abruptly, 'When will food be coming?'

'In two days,' Edward told him, reaching in his bag to hand over the two bars of chocolate he had managed to stuff in the bottom.

'Give this to Maria and the children,' he said. 'I'm so sorry I couldn't bring more.'

'Maria and Lotte are gone,' Hans said in a voice devoid of expression, 'only Markus and I are left now.' There was a pause. 'They found a bicycle hidden and they shot them. They knew that would be worse for me than to be shot myself. Markus was whisked away to safety by my friends but those bastards made me watch.'

Edward did not know what to say. He reached out and hugged his friend, who held himself stiffly.

'Come,' Hans said, pulling back. 'We go, they are waiting for us.'

As they walked to a half-destroyed house, Edward thought how little the typing on a report had been able to express the hardships that the Netherlands had suffered. Everywhere, there were muddy tracks of refugees, fleeing from the enemy. The fields were invisible under several feet of water on either side of the dykes and the village of De Praets had nothing left except the apexes of houses pointing upwards like icebergs in a sea of rubble.

They were greeted by five men, all looking as emaciated as Hans. They welcomed Edward enthusiastically with hope in their eyes. He was a herald of the longed-for Manna Operation. They stood in a circle; there were no chairs anywhere but someone produced some chipped cups and poured out weak, black tea for them all and they sat down on the floor.

It was several hours later that the meeting finally broke up with all the distribution plans in place. Edward realised he was starving but that any food would stick in his throat. He only had another day to wait before he could be picked up and taken back to Britain, these men would have to wait a further twenty-four hours after that.

Hans and Edward walked to Hans's house; it was partially destroyed but the front room was still intact. The house was cold and Edward was struck by the sparseness of the rooms, with no sign of the coloured rugs that used to adorn its floors and walls.

Edward remembered evenings spent laughing and joking over a bottle of wine with Hans and Maria, with the two little ones tucked up in bed in the loft above. He looked round for their little dog, Otto, but he was nowhere to be seen.

'I'm sorry, we have to sit on the floor,' Hans explained. 'We had to burn the furniture. We even had to eat the dog; we have nothing left to give.' He turned urgently to Edward. 'Make it stop, Edward, make it stop.'

Chapter 47

The sun was shining when Edward woke the next morning. He stretched and groaned. His body felt wrecked from the bare floorboards but with the sun shafting though the skylight, it did feel like spring and brought an optimism he had not felt since he had arrived. Starting tomorrow, 141 sorties of bombers would fly low over the Netherlands bringing sugar, dried egg powder, margarine, potatoes, tinned meat and other essentials over a ten day period to the starving people below. He just wished it could be today.

Hans was already up. He proudly offered Edward some dark bread that he told him with excitement, had been made with Swedish flour that had finally got through to the village late last night. He and the rest of the villagers had been up at dawn to queue outside the baker's, revelling in the glorious smell of freshly-baked bread. Edward tried to refuse the bread but Hans insisted, pushing a still-warm piece over to him. It was his proudest moment of the last few months and his delight in being able to offer a guest something to eat was too palpable to deny.

The small amount of food seemed to inject an energy into Hans and he grabbed hold of Edward's arms.

'Markus has gone to school. I was able to give him some breakfast. It's almost like before,' he said gleefully, but then his face darkened again as the reality of his shrunken family hit him in the chest.

While Edward munched on the dry bread, Hans told him, 'We must go now, I've heard we have your little friend's mother and that she is safe.' With that, he ushered Edward out of the door.

His neighbours were all out on the streets, still looking wary about being able to walk around freely. A few Allied soldiers were on the corner, leaning against their trucks. They were disobeying orders and were handing out their own rations to the crowds of people who were clamouring against the vehicles.

Edward and Hans made their way to the path alongside the river. The ruins of Arnhem could be seen on the other side, a grim reminder of the two battles it had taken to reclaim it. The rendezvous was arranged for ten o'clock. Edward scanned the horizon. In the distance, a handcart was being pulled along the towpath by two men. In it, there was a woman in a tattered brown coat. As the cart approached, Edward felt nervous. He had received news only a week ago that Elizé's mother had been among those freed with the liberation of Drancy, just hours before she had been due to be transported to an extermination camp.

The rescue plan he immediately put into place was a tricky and dangerous one. She had had to be taken through the network in France and into the Allied-occupied part of the Netherlands and he had no idea what physical or mental state she was in.

As the cart got nearer, Hans moved forward. He reached his hands out to help the woman but she sat, transfixed, unable to move from sheer exhaustion.

'Come Madame Waters,' Edward said gently. He too reached out his hands and she looked frantically from one man to the other, terrified to trust anyone.

'We are going to take you to Elizé,' Edward told her.

At her daughter's name, Rebecca lurched forward. Hans was used to emaciated bodies but Edward looked in horror at the thin sticks that served as her legs and arms.

Hans and Edward thanked the two men who had pulled the cart ten miles that morning and they nodded in acknowledgment, then turned around to go back, but not before Hans gave them some bread, which they ate greedily.

Rebecca could hardly walk and Edward was glad he had asked Mavis to organise a few days' recovery time in an English convalescent home before he took her to Salhouse Farm.

Edward checked his watch. They did not have much time before they were to meet the plane back at Easter Meadows and he took Rebecca by one arm, signalled to Hans to take the other and they made their way back to the flat landing area they had come from. The sun had mercifully dried it out a little, Edward realised, noting that his feet did not squelch quite as badly as they had the day before.

The plane was already approaching so Edward hugged Hans by his bony shoulders and promised he would return to see him when the war was over. He thanked him from the bottom of his heart for his help and reassured him that, as from tomorrow, the Hongerwinter was over. Hans nodded, unable to believe his country's nightmare was nearly at an end.

The Lysander slowed but Edward had to get Rebecca on board fast so quickly helped her up the ladder. It was like pushing a feather. Philip Howes's head popped out from the side window of the cockpit and he threw out a bag.

'Just a few things I managed to smuggle on board without your friend's weight,' he told Hans with a wink. The bag split open and out dropped tins of Spam, dried milk and egg powder. Hans ran to pick up the scattered items and with his arms full, he turned his face upwards, towards the departing plane. There were tears running down his cheeks.

Edward showed Rebecca the undercarriage where she would have to go, recognising that the confined space would certainly not house his six-foot-two inch body but would easily fit the tiny frame of the woman. He put a parachute under her head, hoping they would not need to use it and she lay down without a murmur.

'Are you all right, Madame Waters?'

'*Oui*,' she replied weakly.

'You are safe now,' he told her, laying his hand on her head gently.

Her wide eyes blurred over with tears and then she started to sob convulsively until the aircraft had almost reached the coastline, when she finally fell into an exhausted sleep.

'Bit of flak coming,' Philip called from the front.

'Damnation,' Edward muttered, looking worriedly at the sleeping woman. They did not need this.

The aircraft began to veer from left to right as the coastal defences of the enemy fired at them, prompting bursts of fire on either side of the wings.

Edward Turner was not a particularly religious man, but for the next few interminable minutes, he prayed in desperation for someone or something to protect this vulnerable woman who had already seen her English husband shot, had been forced to abandon her daughter to a stranger, and had suffered goodness knows what horrors in a concentration camp.

There was a loud noise and the Lysander suddenly lurched to one side.

'We're hit but I think we'll make it,' Philip shouted. 'It's the wing but at least they didn't get the fuel tank.'

For a moment, Edward imagined the dangers Bobby had faced every day on her own in the cockpit of so many different planes and felt a profound guilt that he had not afforded her the admiration and respect she deserved. He hoped he would be granted the chance to live long enough to rectify that.

The aircraft was now approaching the English coast, which looked glorious in the April morning.

'I've radioed ahead, we're landing at Halesworth. It's full of Yanks but hey ho, we can't be fussy. Right, I just need to concentrate to get this bugger onto the ground. Fortunately, it's a slow prop and the engine will run slow.'

Edward peered out of the window, the wing on his side was charred and had pieces of twisted metal shining in the sunlight.

'It's going to be bumpy, you'd better prepare her,' Philip said.

Edward looked down at Rebecca, whose eyes had opened. There was no fear just the resignation of someone who had faced death too many times. Edward clenched his teeth; this woman was not going to die if he had anything to do with it.

'Not sure the landing gear's going to work, brace yourselves,' Philip said in a tense voice.

Edward took off his own parachute and tucked it around Rebecca, struggling to keep his balance in the rocking plane, then he flung himself onto the floor over her to use his body as protection against any shattering metal that might come her way.

The wheel mechanism grated and ground but gradually, the wheels clicked into place.

'Stand by, this is it,' the pilot shouted. 'We're supposed to make a three-point landing but we may go over.'

Edward knew he meant that all three wheels were supposed to touch down together, it was that manoeuvrability that gave these planes the edge on quick take offs and landings, and he held his breath.

The plane juddered onto the runway and then skidded. It lurched over onto one side and Edward wrenched his shoulder trying to keep his position. The Lysander seemed to go into slow motion until it finally came to a standstill, but at the last moment, the hatch above them shattered and Edward was showered with shards of Perspex.

'Get out now!' Phillip yelled. 'We're on the fuel tank.'

Edward quickly got up and dragged Rebecca with him. She had gone limp and he feared she had been hurt. His shoulder was killing him, but he used every ounce of strength to use his other shoulder to push the rest of the Perspex out and projected her in front of him, hoping there was someone to catch her below.

He followed and fell onto the tarmac. Two men scooped Rebecca up and then a voice came from the distance. 'For God's sake, man, run! It's going to blow.'

He hurriedly got to his feet and ran as fast as he could but was suddenly hurled into the air by an explosion that resounded in his ears as the aircraft burst into flames.

With a cry he landed on his damaged shoulder on the tarmac with a cry and three burly firemen picked him up like a rag doll.

'Is she all right?' he said to them faintly.

'She's OK, mate, we've got her,' one of the men replied, just as Edward passed out.

Chapter 48

It was April 1945 and the country was celebrating the suicide of Hitler. Everywhere Bobby looked, people seemed brighter, more optimistic. She grinned at the ground crew who were laughing and joking next to the Anson she was flying in to Coltishall.

'You won't be flying these for long,' one of them pronounced with satisfaction as he watched her climb the wing. 'It'll be back to a normal life for you girls.'

Bobby looked at him in horror, she had not contemplated what the end of the war would mean for her and all her ATA friends. At Coltishall, she borrowed a bicycle to ride to the farm where she found everyone in a state of anticipation and all thoughts about the future were banished from her head. Her mother greeted her at the door, looking rosy-cheeked and excited. Bobby hardly recognised her.

'I'm so glad you could get here, Bobby. Do you have any idea what's going on?'

Bobby shook her head.

Her mother went on. 'A very efficient Miss Arbuckle telephoned. She said she would be accompanying Edward to see us this afternoon. I don't know why either.'

'Nope, he just asked if I could be here. What is that man up to now?' Bobby replied.

Her aunt came out of the kitchen and gave her a hug. 'I must say, Bobby, I do find him rather exciting, don't you?'

Bobby looked at her aunt, who had a conspiratorial grin on her face. A quiet watcher of people, Agnes had long ago made her mind up about Edward. It had not taken long for her to suspect there were hidden depths to him and she had started to believe he was just the right partner for her headstrong niece. At the breakfast table in their little cottage that morning, she had told Archie she was going to do everything she could to encourage the relationship between Bobby and Edward Turner.

'Aunt Agnes, I'm surprised at you', Bobby said 'You've become quite mischievous since you got married, haven't you?

'I know and it's really good fun. I think Edward Turner's enough of a challenge for any woman, maybe even you.' And with that pronouncement, she turned on her heel with a satisfied smile and went to check the scones, which were in the oven for afternoon tea.

Elizé came hurtling into the hallway. She flung her arms around Bobby.

'We've got potato scones for tea,' she said jumping up and down. 'I helped make them. Aren't I clever?'

Bobby swung her up in the air, making her giggle. 'Yes, you're very clever, *ma petite*. And I'm sure they're better than mine. Archie always called mine rock cakes, very rudely, I thought!'

'Hmm, yours are terrible, mine are scrummy,' the child said, laughing.

A car came up the gravel drive and Bobby stole a quick look in the mirror. It was too late now, she thought with regret, seeing her tangled hair, and quickly ran her fingers through it, trying in vain to inject some style.

Andrew Hollis came out of his study, put his hand on his daughter's shoulder in greeting and went out onto the porch.

A black sedan had drawn up and a lady in a maroon tweed suit with a matching hat and cream gloves emerged from the back seat. Mavis Arbuckle stood taking in the scene in front of her. Her eyes immediately pinned on Bobby and she peered at her through her pince-nez. Edward, sporting a sling on his arm, got out of the front and went around the car to the other side to help out a tiny, frail woman dressed in a dress and cardigan that were both too big for her. Her hair was combed into a slide and her eyes were bright.

Elizé burst from behind Bobby. She ran, then stopped, clamped her hands to her mouth, then ran again.

'*Maman, Maman. Oh c'est vraiment toi!*'

She almost knocked the frail frame of her mother over in her enthusiasm, unable to believe it was really her. The thin, emaciated woman and the little child clung to each other and both started to sob.

Everyone on the porch was stunned. Mrs Hill and Rachel had sneaked out from the kitchen and Rachel uttered a squeal and reached out to squeeze Mrs Hill's arm. She had heard so much from Elizé about this woman and then, by some wonder, she was here in Norfolk. Mrs Hill stood transfixed but then felt her arm going numb so gently removed Rachel's fingers, one at a time. At that point, the two women hugged each other and jumped up and down.

Bobby and her parents moved very slowly forward as Edward took a step towards them. He looked very pale.

Bobby ran towards him. 'Edward, what *have* you done to yourself, you look terrible,' she placed her hand on his arm.

'Well, that's not the welcome I had in mind,' he replied with a laugh and then winced at the pain from his ribs. Bobby looked him up and down to check for more damage but was relieved to find that, otherwise, he seemed to be in one piece.

He greeted Mr and Mrs Hollis and then turned to introduce Mavis Arbuckle, who was having the time of her life. At last, she believed she had met the woman who had turned Edward Turner upside down and, assessing Bobby's trousers, boots and untamed hair, she nodded her approval.

Elizé called over between sobs. 'Bobby, it's *ma mère*. You see, I told you she was alive and oh, *elle est ici*, she is here . . . she is . . .'

She buried her head in her mother's skirts, unable to speak any more. Elizé's mother clasped her thin arms around her daughter and bowed her head so that the two heads intertwined.

Andrew Hollis went to over to the pair and said gently, '*Bienvenue*, madame. We are so, so pleased to have you here,' and he slowly led her and the clinging child towards the house. He noticed that Elizé's mother could hardly walk and that her strength was being eroded with every painful step and he felt an emotion he had not felt for years. To see this tiny woman, who was the living embodiment of the ravages of war, pierced his heart like nothing he had experienced since he walked up this path from the Great War. Mathilda proudly led them all into the drawing room, just as Raoul and Michel came through the back door. They had been helping on the farm and only stopped to take their boots off before following the commotion.

They looked in wonder at the woman.

'She's Elizé's mother,' Rachel whispered to them. They looked incredulously at the slight figure and then Raoul, for once, cowed into silence, clasped his son's hands.

'*Un miracle, Michel, un miracle!*'

Mrs Hill burst into life. 'Tea and scones, I think. Now, Rachel, now!' Rachel bustled off to the kitchen while the rest of the party settled into the chairs. Everyone waited expectantly, looking at Edward.

From the first moment he had entered the farm, so long ago, it had somehow become a natural expectation for him to take the lead. Even Andrew sat silently, waiting.

'Rebecca – Madame Waters – was in a camp,' Edward said.

There was a moment's pause while everyone made the connection between the rumours and the reality of the painfully thin woman in front of them.

'We managed to get her out, and here she is.'

With those few words, he deflected any questions and Mrs Hill handed out the scones.

* * *

Edward had left the drawing room to get some fresh air. He went outside and lit a cigarette. He was in a great deal of pain but his relief that his plan had all come together made it all worthwhile.

'Edward.' Bobby's voice came from behind him. He whirled round but then grimaced with pain.

'Are you all right, Edward?'

'A bit battered and bruised but yes, I'm fine.'

She had moved forward, and put her hand on his lapel. He leaned down and softly kissed her.

Mavis Arbuckle had been to organise the timings with the chauffeur and was on her way back to the house when she spotted the couple. She tightened her hands on her handbag to stop herself from clasping them together in glee.

She had been delighted when Edward had asked her to come on this trip as female companion to Madame Waters. She had immediately suspected that this 'over and above' mission her boss had undertaken would lead to a woman and as soon as she had sized up Roberta Hollis, in her boots, standing with her arms folded, she had been hoping this was the end of the rainbow and that this striking young woman was the pot of gold Edward had been searching for all his life. She hurried past the pair of them, giving them a wide berth, her head lowered to hide her beaming smile, but neither of them even registered she was there.

'Bobby, can we start again?' Edward was saying. 'I think, after Hitler's suicide, we may soon, finally, be able to get on with our own lives . . .' He stopped for a moment, looked at the gravel beneath his feet and decided a bended-knee proposal would be scorned and anyway, he was not sure his injured body would be able to get up again.

Bobby waited and then broke in. 'Well, if you're about to ask me to marry you, you'd better get a move on, Edward Turner, or all the scones will be gone!'

They both burst out laughing and Edward knew he had found a woman who would defy conventionality like him and embrace life as an adventure.

They went arm in arm back to the house but then Edward stopped in his tracks. 'So, if I were to get down on one knee and ask the question, what would you say?'

'You know you'd never get up,' she grinned, adding, 'I'm not sure what I'd say. You're still on probation, but maybe one day, yes, maybe one day I will say yes,' she teased, squeezing his sore arm. He didn't feel any pain.

Chapter 49

Hamble was not the same place once VE Day had triumphantly heralded victory in Europe. The urgency to get planes to waiting pilots around the country had diminished and the ATA girls were spending far too much time playing backgammon or sewing. The tensions in the restroom were fraught with frustration and Bobby was one of the worst offenders.

'I can't bear it!' she said finally, throwing down the needle and cotton she had been using to mend a blouse. 'I'm so bored, I feel like just kidnapping an aircraft and taking off.'

Sally nodded, she had played three games of patience and had not managed to get rid of all the cards once. Daphne, too, was looking forlorn.

Christine bounded over. 'Come on, you lot, let's go for a brisk walk around the camp.'

They all groaned. Daphne threw a cushion at her.

'We've been on three already this week, I'm beginning to know every blade of grass,' she said.

The door opened and an ops manager came in. 'I need someone to take a Spitfire to Cosford, one of the last ones. Anyone want to go?'

They all jumped up but Sally grabbed the cards and put her hands out to stop them all.

'We're going to do this fairly,' she announced. 'The highest card wins,' and she shuffled the pack. The little group held their breath as the cards were handed out.

'Wait,' Daphne said, her downturned card in her hand. 'Is ace high or low?'

'Well as we're all pilot aces, I think it should be high!' Sally laughed.

Bobby slowly turned her card over. It was an ace. She triumphantly held it aloft, and then had a momentary feeling of guilt that she had won, but the girls crowded round her and clapped her on the back, enjoying her triumph. She felt overwhelmed and hugged them all.

'Well, I couldn't have gone anyway,' Sally was saying. 'I have a date with that Lord we met at the Embassy do and I'm not giving that up for anything. Not even a Spit.'

'You enjoy every minute of it,' Daphne added. 'I flew one yesterday, so I've sort of said my goodbyes. Anyway, I'm just dying for that march around the camp with Christine!' and she went over to grab a delighted Christine's arm before heading towards the door.

When Bobby walked over to the plane, she was astonished to see a guard of honour from the Erks who had
lined up, ready to salute her as she passed, her parachute
over her shoulder as always. She laughed as they burst into
applause and then gave them all a final sharp salute before
swinging up onto the wing.

Bobby tried to make the flight happen in slow motion.
She did every check twice, lovingly touched the instruments and verified her route several times. She was not
going to waste a moment of this last trip.

The Spitfire took off and she soared into the blue sky.
There was no feeling like it in the world and she felt grief-
stricken that she might not be able to fly these wonderful
machines again. By the time she got to Cosford, she was in
tears and had to sit in the cockpit for a moment to regain
her composure. She put her hand out to touch the panel in
front of her and bowed her head in reverence to a machine
that had helped so much in saving Britain from defeat.

In a desperate bid to make the moment count, she
got out her pen and on the underside of the dashboard
in front of her, wrote her name and the date, wondering
whether any pilot in the future would spot it and wonder
who Roberta Hollis was.

It took a moment for her to realise that flying planes
like this one had also helped *her* to discover who Roberta
Hollis was. The girl who had joined the ATA all those
years ago had been completely self-absorbed, a state that

had evolved out of necessity, and since then she had found her family, friends, a purpose and maybe, she thought, someone she could love.

* * *

The day of Harriet and Gus's wedding started off dull but then the blue skies broke through and it promised to be a perfect day.

It was early August and although the war in Europe had ended, the battle for the East was still raging. Edward was not privy to the information that Hiroshima and Nagasaki were about to be subjected to the most devastating weapon the world had ever seen, so he was able to look forward to the day's celebrations in ignorance.

Bobby had been delivering military aircraft without much enthusiasm since VE Day and without the urgency of getting planes to pilots for important missions, the days seemed long and tedious. So when Harriet's letter had arrived pronouncing that she was chief bridesmaid along with two full pages of things she needed to organise, Bobby almost welcomed it. Two months later, she wearily restricted herself to only reading one of Harriet's relentless letters every day.

Finally, the day had arrived and Bobby was in her bedroom, brushing her hair. She took a long, hard look at herself in the mirror and put the brush down on the walnut dressing table to consider her own future. The last Spitfire flight had left her feeling bereft and the tedious military aircraft deliveries that had followed meant that her days had lost any real purpose. Hamble was closing and many of the girls were wondering what their future held. Bobby picked up the brush again and rigorously carried on brushing and gave herself a good talking to. She was going to see Edward's father in the morning to discuss her role at the airfield in the future and her own father had promised to go through the farm's accounts with her. As long as she could still fly, life would be bearable, she thought, and then there was Edward . . .

She was wearing an old, pretty, floral dress that she hated, but Harriet had insisted she should wear to match the one Rachel and Rebecca had made for Elizé. Harriet also wanted to ensure that there was nothing grey, plain or war-like about her wedding. After VE Day, Harriet had issued Gus with an ultimatum that either he married her or she would confiscate his crutches. He had paused for a split second, taking in the pretty face in front of him. She had been at his side for months now, alternately shouting at him and giving him encouragement. She knew him like no other, understood him and loved him like no other and he realised he was about to make the best decision of his life. He reached out from his wheelchair to take her in his arms, but she jumped onto his lap and planted a huge kiss on his lips.

'See, I always knew you loved me,' she said triumphantly. 'It just took you a bit longer to get there.'

He hugged her closer. From that moment, Gus Prince
could not wait to make Harriet Marcham his wife.

* * *

Michel and Raoul were due to go back to France but had
delayed their departure until after the wedding. Michel
was keen to get back to Claudette and get the answer to
the question his last letter had posed. Until last night, they
had assumed Elizé and Rebecca would be going back to
France with them so it had taken them by surprise when,
at the dinner table, Elizé announced to the Hollis family
that she and her mother would like to stay, if the family
would have them, as the only memories her mother had
of France were very, very bad ones. Elizé's mother stared
down at her clasped hands in her lap. Andrew Hollis
immediately unearthed some homemade marrow brandy
from the back of the cupboard, overwhelmed with joy. He
handed glasses to the little gathering in front of him and
proposed a toast.

'I want to welcome Madame Waters ... Rebecca ... to
our family. This has been Elizé's home for some time now
and we are all delighted that you both want to stay. We would
have been devastated to lose you both.' Rebecca looked up
and for a brief moment, a wan smile lit up her face.

Andrew looked round with irritation to establish where the sniffing was coming from but then realised that all the women . . . and Raoul . . . were in tears. He gave up and put the glass to his lips. He put his head down and then gave a little sniff himself.

* * *

As the hour of the wedding approached, the party gathered outside the church, chattering excitedly. Archie was fiddling with his tie but Agnes pushed his hand out of the way and straightened it for him. He grinned at her. Mrs Hill and Rachel were exhausted after helping Mrs Marcham prepare the wedding breakfast and there was little time for them to get ready before the pies came out of the oven. The flustered cook grabbed her hat at the last minute and raced to the church, red-faced but content that the potato pastry was the best she had done in years.

Andrew Hollis looked proudly at his wife, whose own dimpled cheeks were a soft shade of pink. She was dressed in a re-made blue dress and hat that he remembered from when he had first met her. He put his arm around her shoulders and she beamed up at him, also glimpsing the young man she had fallen in love with so many years before. She, Andrew and Bobby had taken a little posy of late summer flowers to the family graveyard early that morning. It was Mathilda who had, in a poignant moment, ceremoniously placed them on Michael's grave. It was the first time she had been able to visit the grave since that grey day in 1915 when Archie had almost carried her collapsed frame away from the freshly dug mound of soil, but on this day, she stood up straight, held her head high and insisted on being the one to place the flowers gently next to the headstone. As her parents walked slowly away, arm-in-arm, Bobby stepped up to the cross and, like always, put her hand on it to feel a connection with the spirit of her dead twin.

'Oh Michael, what a family we have!' she whispered. 'I'm so proud of them, they've come a long way. We miss you every day but, Michael, you need to know – I finally feel a whole person. I know you'll always be in here,' she pointed to her heart, 'and I will carry you within me.' She paused and wiped her eyes then started again.

'Now, I'm going to live your future for you, for both of us. And do you know, Michael, we might finally have a future. It's been a tough few years. Oh, and one more thing, Michael, I think I have found someone to share my life with. You'd like him. He's not easy to read but that's what makes him interesting and I think, a partner for me. As you know, I'm not easy but I think he'll cope with that.' She laughed in the sunshine and patted the cross.

'And now, my lovely brother, I have to go to my daffy friend's wedding. I love you' she added, blowing a kiss to the sky.

* * *

A cart arrived with Gus on the back. His mother moved forward to pass him his crutches but while his parents anxiously looked on, he reached for just one of them and hauled himself off the duckboard at the back to stand unsteadily. Raoul burst out clapping and everyone else followed his lead. Gus moved forward gingerly into the church. Mr Prince handed his wife a handkerchief and told her to keep it.

Michel went back to lead the dance to church, as he had done for Agnes, but Harriet was already coming down the path, running from side to side to cut through the children's ribbons one after the other. He laughed and struck up a jig. Harriet started to dance her way to the church, with Bobby shaking her head in despair after her.

Waiting at the side of the aisle, behind the first pew, was Edward. He looked so tall and handsome, Bobby thought. She suspected so much about his role in, firstly, Michel and Raoul's rescue, and then in Rebecca's journey back to her daughter, but there would be years to wheedle the truth out of him – or maybe she would never know. To have her suspicions was enough. She looked down at the third finger on her left hand. It suddenly looked empty.

She smiled to herself. She had never thought she could feel as much love as she felt for that first Spitfire but Edward Turner came a very close second and she realised she probably would say yes – if he ever did get round to asking her properly.

Acknowledgements

This is my second novel and I have been in a bit of an appropriate tailspin over the research! My experience of flying is limited to sitting in the rear of an aircraft, looking sternly towards the cockpit door, daring them to do anything other than take me up into that scary airspace and back down again safely. That meant that when I decided I just had to write a story about the Air Transport Auxiliary and those wonderful women who flew dozens of different types of aircraft, I panicked, and could not have managed without so many people who, hopefully, helped me to get all the techie stuff right.

I visited the wonderful Maidenhead Heritage Centre with its inspiring ATA exhibition. Richard Poad from the museum was extremely kind in pointing me towards Mary Ellis, the famous ATA pilot, who was unbelievably generous in inviting me to her home on the Isle of Wight and patiently answering all of my questions about what it was like to be an ATA pilot. It was moments like those that have made writing this book so very special and I want to particularly thank Rosemarie Martin, her niece-in-law, who organised the visit and was so welcoming to me, an unknown author. I will treasure the memories of that lovely afternoon in Mary's conservatory. I certainly could not have written this book without spending that time with Mary. I felt so privileged to meet her and hope she would have approved of *Bobby's War*.

I also want to mention Bernie Kuflik, who is a volunteer at the Maidenhead Heritage Centre. He took all my queries to a group of other pilots and sent me amendments and suggestions to make sure I was writing authentically.

I particularly want to thank the wonderful Helen Mills, a former WAAF plotter who agreed to meet me at the Battle of Britain Bunker in Uxbridge. She has been a brilliant early reader for me and has saved me from making errors about life in the 1940s. Her insight, knowledge and interest has been a huge help to me and her life as a plotter may yet be inspiration for future novels, so watch this space.

As a former journalist, I do get anxious about getting facts wrong, so I am grateful to the Facebook group, Anything to Anywhere, in particular historian, Nick Sturgess, who was so happy to help over the uniform.

That website led me to Sally McGlone, ex RAF and now an MRes (Aviation History) specialising in the ATA. She kindly offered to pre-read it for me and her careful reading and encouragement really gave me confidence. I can only say a sincere thank you to her.

This last year, I have got to know Kate Barker, my agent, and Claire Johnson-Creek, my editor at Bonnier Books UK, so much better and I am very much in their debt for their help, guidance and positive criticism. Their professionalism and knowledge has, I know, made me into a much better writer and *Bobby's War* a better book – I am so grateful to them. I'd also like to mention Ellen Turner, whose publicity expertise has really helped to put me 'on the map'. To Laura Gerrard, my copy-editor, and Gilly Dean, my proofreader, I say a huge thank you. Your beady-eyed skills have prevented mistakes in everything from timelines to repetitions. The author, Clare Harvey, has been, as she was with *Lily's War*, incredibly generous with her comments and I feel so thankful that there are experienced authors like her out there happy to support newbies like me.

I have such a wonderful groundswell of support from people in my small Derbyshire town who are forced to listen to my angsts and doubts, and their belief in me has been humbling. Again, I want to thank fellow author, Tricia Durdey, who has been so generous with her time, loyalty and encouragement – her experience of being published has been invaluable – and Carol Taylor, who has unstintingly given her time to help me with talks, even a Zoom one during lockdown in the Coronavirus pandemic. Marie Paurin was my wonderful French 'consultant' and Peter Walton, a former RAF pilot, was incredibly helpful in guiding my aeronautical knowledge. I especially want to mention our lovely friends, Barry and Flora Joyce and George and Pippa Mansel Jones, who have encouraged me and fortified me with a glass of wine when necessary. Sarah Price has, as ever, been such a wonderful friend and without her reassurance and common sense, I doubt I would have ever got to this point.

And then there's my wonderful family. My husband, Kevin, who has willingly trailed around air museums with me, grateful that I don't write novels about hairdressing; my sister, Hilary, who shares in all my triumphs and disasters with unqualified support, humour and common sense; Gareth, Jonathan, Michael and Alex, who get as excited as I do about my journey, and Teresa, who searches out brilliant research books that she thinks I might be able to use. I look forward to the day when little Clara moves on from books about Thomas the Tank Engine to ones about Spitfires!

But my last thanks must go to our two daughters, Jayne and Sarah. Sarah listens tirelessly, helping to sort out plotlines and angles and giving me valuable journalistic advice. She and Jayne wholeheartedly share the moments when I feel completely overwhelmed. Jayne is also my wonderful marketing expert, who has now forbidden me from pressing any buttons until I check with her. I'm still not there with working out how to use social media but she – and Sarah – are constantly trying to save me from disaster.

They have become the sort of women I know Mary Ellis would have been proud to pave the way for.

Dear Reader,

It's so lovely to be back again with my new book, *Bobby's War*. As soon as I heard about the women who flew for the Air Transport Auxiliary, I just knew I had found the subject for my second novel. In *Lily's War* I'd learned how women had escaped the kitchen to do important jobs and how they had taken men on at their own game, but for women to become pilots, delivering all different types of aircraft all over the country, was a role I had not really been aware of. It was so groundbreaking, it completely inspired me. I visited the ATA exhibition at the Maidenhead Heritage Museum and they kindly put me in touch with Mary Ellis, one of the last surviving ATA pilots in the world, who at that stage was 101 years old. I was so thrilled that she invited me to visit her that it was only as an afterthought I asked where she lived. Getting to the Isle of Wight by public transport from Derbyshire proved to be a bit of an adventure and when I finally arrived at her house in the pouring rain, with my little wheelie case, I was drenched. Cool as a cucumber, she welcomed me into her home, ignoring my feet, which had gone black from the fabric of my new shoes, offered me a place to put my dripping waterproof and showed me into her conservatory. Following her, I hardly felt like a professional author but I had no doubt I was in the presence of a professional woman. Wearing smart navy slacks and a white blouse, I could easily envisage her clutching her Blue Ferry Notes, undaunted by either a huge Manchester bomber or a Spitfire. I knew immediately that nothing would faze this woman. We were joined by her niece-in-law, Rosemarie, who helped me by prompting Mary with anecdotes she had heard her talk about and throughout the afternoon Mary patiently answered my questions. I knew I was going to write a fictional book which would not in any way compete with the biographies that had been written about her but the little snippets of information that she shared with me were a wonderful insight into the incredibly pressurised lives these women lived. Her memory was astonishing, and she listed planes and places, remembering amazing details of each, even to the point of which airfields were the most difficult ones to land at and why. As ever, the minute details of everyday life were the ones that entranced me, the ones that aren't in any of the history books and I felt privileged that she shared them with me. I was so fascinated, I had to constantly remind myself to take notes; I could have listened to her all day.

There were some moments when I asked her about letting her hair down when I got the look; the one that let me know firmly about how professional these women had to be. Unrecognised by some, condemned by others, there was not a moment in Mary's career when she had been able to forget the heavy responsibility she bore. One

mistake and the reputation of women ATA pilots, as well as her own life, would be in danger.

Returning from the Isle of Wight I struggled to rationalise the storyline. I was going to take my heroine further than Mary might have approved of, but then I reminded myself, this is fiction so I have taken a few liberties that I hope you will forgive me for.

It was six weeks later that I read the obituaries telling me Mary had died. I was torn between being deeply upset that the world had lost this amazing woman and relieved that she had been so fit and able almost to the end. I felt incredibly privileged to have met her and will always remember the mischievous chuckle she let out at the end of the interview when she insisted on a photograph with me.

My visit to the Isle of Wight prompted a succession of visits to air museums and airfields including the wonderful Shuttleworth Collection. We arrived at a campsite in our camper van and the man who owned it immediately started to talk to my husband about how much he would enjoy the museum. The expression on his face when it was explained that it was me who was particularly interested in it rather than my husband gave me an insight into the natural prejudice that women like Mary had suffered and, I have to confess, elicited a little triumphant smile from me.

I hope you enjoyed *Bobby's War*. I loved writing it, creating the characters and developing the storyline. I am in awe of the women who were in the ATA; their ability to juggle frantic schedules, fly so many different types of planes and find their way around the country without radar or a radio. As someone who struggles to travel five miles without Sat Nav, their ability fills me with awe. They were real trailblazers and their determination, dedication and, I'm afraid to say, in some cases, their sacrifice, has made my generation's passage into equality an easier path and to the women like Mary, I would just like to say a huge heartfelt thank you.

If you haven't had the chance yet, I'd love you to read *Lily's War*, which is available now, and *Hannah's War*, which will be my next book. It is about Lily's friend, Hannah, who works as a Land Girl during the War. If you'd like to find out a little bit more about me, the books I write and upcoming news, do sign up to Memory Lane, Bonnier Books UK's community for lovers of heartwarming and moving stories about women's lives, featuring wartime, family and romance ◨ MemoryLaneClub.

Best wishes,

Shirley

Mrs Hill's Scone Recipe

First and foremost, I am going to hold my hands up and confess, my scones are like Bobby's – more of a rock cake with a gargoyle face. Mrs Hill, of course, was an experienced cook and working on a farm, was able to find an extra drop of milk or maybe even some churned butter, but even she was limited in her supplies, especially when all those extra guests kept turning up, so she had to be careful about what rations she used up. One person was only allowed 2oz of butter a week but 4oz of margarine, so I do remember my mother's residual hatred of margarine that lasted her whole life. This recipe uses lard, which seems to be out of fashion these days, but I know there are real cooks who swear by mixing a bit of lard with a bit of butter, so maybe play with this recipe a little and see how you get on. The dates provided the sweetness when they were so short of sugar. Do let me know what your results are like.

Ingredients:
5oz flour
2oz lard
1tsp baking powder
2oz dates, chopped
1 beaten egg
A little milk

Method:

Rub the lard into the flour with your fingertips. Add the baking powder, then the chopped dates. Add the beaten egg and a little milk and then leave somewhere cool for about 10 minutes before cutting them into round shapes. Bake in a hot oven for about 12 minutes and do remember, wartime cooks would never just cook one thing in the oven at a time, they would batch cook and then store them in the pantry in a sealed tin to maximise oven heat.

Of course, there would be days when there would be no supplies of dates or even sultanas but there were plentiful supplies of potatoes, so maybe these potato scones might have been on the menu too. I got this recipe from the wartime recipes in the wonderful book, *The Old Rectory: Escape to a Country Kitchen* (2017 Endeavour Press) by Julia Ibbotson.

Potato Scones (potato cakes)

225g (8oz) mashed potato
225g (8oz) flour
2.5ml (0.5tsp) baking powder
Salt and pepper

Mix potato, flour, baking powder, and salt and pepper together with enough milk to make a stiff paste. Roll out to about 5 mm. (0.25 in) thick, cut into rounds. Fry in a little oil until golden brown. Serve hot with butter if available.

I hope you enjoy these two recipes; I'd love to hear whether they are a teatime hit in your family. I'm certainly going to see if I can use them to improve on my scone track record so far.

Watch out for Shirley's next book . . .

Hannah's War

It's World War II and Hannah has joined the Land Army. A city girl from birth, she only joined because her beloved grandad taught her how to grow vegetables in his market garden in North Wales.

But when Hannah arrives at Salhouse Farm she is way out of her depth. Hard work, muddy hands and a shared dormitory lie before her, and soon she realises this is not going to be the cosy life in the countryside that she imagined . . .

Available in ebook September 2021 and paperback March 2022

Read on for an extract

Chapter 1

Hannah flung herself back against the wooden struts of the stall in the stables. In front of her, a huge black shire horse was rearing up, its eyes wide with fear. The new recruit to the Land Army brought her hands up to protect her head but that seemed to make the horse worse. The bucket of hay she was trying to feed it had already been strewn across the stone floor, its contents scattering in all directions. The light from the doorway was blocked by the massive flank of the animal and Hannah knew she was trapped. She looked round frantically to see whether there was anything she could use to protect herself; this stallion was completely out of control and she had no idea how to calm it down.

'Shhhh, it's all right, it's all right,' she said as reassuringly as she could, but the horse was whinnying so loudly, her voice was lost in the commotion. She tried to reach up to get hold of its head collar but it reared up again, banging its hooves against the wooden edges of the stall and trying to turn around in the limited space. Hannah was pinned to the wall, then, suddenly, it seemed to register she was there.

There was nowhere she could escape to and the horse's eyes, wide with panic, looked down from its great height, straight into hers as if she were the enemy it had been trying to wreak revenge on all its life.

'I'm going to die, I'm going to die,' Hannah whispered out loud. This had been her first attempt at dealing with this enormous animal and she had done something terribly wrong, but she did not know what. She cowered back in the corner, sank to her knees and put her hands over her head to try to protect herself. She started to cry as the horse came towards her. *This is going to be the last moment of my life,* she thought.

A gentle voice came from behind the horse. 'Das ist gut, Das ist gut, mein Kleiner kommt mit mir, tut es sanft. Ja, das ist gut, das ist gut.'

Hannah peered out between her fingers. A tall, young man with blonde hair was taking hold of the leather strap on one side of the horse's mouth. With his other hand, he was carefully propelling the animal's rear around so that it faced the door of the barn.

'Put your wrist down, your watch is catching the sun in his eyes,' he said quietly to her. He then gently started to stroke its nose, turning its head towards the doorway. Lulled by the rhythmical movement and, sighting a way out, the horse calmed slightly and gradually allowed itself to be led away from the stall. Hannah put her head down, hugged her knees and rocked backwards and forwards, making whimpering noises.

After about five minutes, through the gap in her knees, she saw German boots walk along the floor towards her. She peered up slowly, terrified of what she might see next.

'It is all right,' a German accent told her. 'You are safe now.'

Hannah jumped to her feet, glared at the man in front of her and started yelling. 'Safe, safe? You think I'm safe. You're a German. The bloody enemy. How in hell's name can I be safe?'

And with that, she ran, sobbing, out of the barn.

* * *

Hannah Compton was nineteen years of age. Tall with dark, curly short hair and brown eyes that very occasionally flashed with anger, she was an only child, used to being ignored by her father and suffocated by her demanding mother. Only her grandfather listened to anything she said and joining the Land Army had been a rebellion against the invisibility that threatened to define her life.

She ran across the yard, past one-legged Jed, the creepy under-foreman who was essentially her boss, past the young lad who always blushed with embarrassment every time he had to deal with one of the Land Army girls and past Andrew Hollis, who may have been the owner of Salhouse Farm, but was a man who walked around with his shoulders bowed as if he had one of the enormous sacks of grain from the store on them.

They all stared after the young girl and Jed was about to shout after her when Andrew Hollis put his arm out to stop him. The girl was out of danger and he had seen the terrified horse being led to the field. He wanted no more fuss and it was almost the end of the day anyway. He was already angry enough that one of the German prisoners of war had been allowed out of the compound to be the one to lead the animal. Having not even acknowledged the existence of twelve of his enemy from the Great War since they were forced upon him by the government, he was certainly not going to appear grateful or even interested.

Jed shook his head in frustration. He was supposed to be able to work this farm on the outskirts of Norwich with a couple of Land Army girls who knew nothing, some lads too young to shave or too old to climb a stile, and a boss who was a closed book that only Archie, the head foreman could read. And now, he had to deal with the bloody Krauts as well. He shuffled off, dragging his false leg behind him, surreptitiously taking out an aluminium flask from his gaberdine pocket and swigging its contents.

Hannah ran into the brick barn where she was billeted, through the dark dining room and up the wooden stairs in the corner. She hurled herself onto her side of the bed she shared with the other Land Army girl, Dotty, and cried non-stop for twenty minutes.

She hated this life, she hated the farm, she hated sharing a double bed with a stranger and she wanted to go home.

Chapter 2

'What happened to you?' Dotty said, roughly pushing the bedroom door open. 'Are you all right? I heard you had a set to with Hercules. He's a tough one, you should never turn your back on him.'

She sat on the bed and looked keenly at Hannah, noting the tear-smeared cheeks and her defeated expression. Dotty reached out her hand to cover Hannah's cold one.

'Seriously, Hannah, are you OK? I heard from that young lad,' she said, 'you know, the shy one, well, anyway, he told me you'd met one of the POWs. What was he like? Did he look like a monster? Are we all to be murdered in our beds?'

The memory of her saviour was coloured by her anger at having to speak to a German, but Hannah did have a vague disquieting memory that he seemed kind, which challenged all her preconceptions. She gave a non-committal answer to Dotty, unsure of what to say.

She tried to pull herself together, angry with herself, as always, that she could not let the words out that were forming in her head. Hannah sometimes looked in the mirror and wondered who the girl who looked back at her was. She wearily acknowledged that her new younger roommate, Dotty, was already behaving like an older sister; everyone always seemed older and wiser than she was. Hannah repeatedly tried to think of the future like her schoolfriend, Lily, did – as an adventure. But thanks to her mother's anxiety, Hannah had always been taught that adventure was not for her. She had joined the Land Army, determined to change that.

It had only been forty-eight hours since she had put on her new uniform, worth a whole thirty shillings, and as she put her khaki overcoat over the green jumper and brown breeches and placed her brown hat on her head, she finally felt she had a value in this war. Walking away from her terraced house in Talbot Road, Stretford, she left behind her mother, clutching her handkerchief and her father staring into space as usual. As soon as she was out of sight, she actually skipped along the pavement, feeling the apron strings of her mother stretch and break as she neared the bus stop. The determination that this was going to be the turning point she had promised herself for years, gave her footsteps a firm tread.

It was a taller, straighter Hannah with a spring in her step who had arrived at arrived at Norwich Station, ready to take up her posting at Salhouse Farm, about seven miles from the city. The young girl pushed her way along the platform at Norwich Station, carrying her battered leather suitcase in front of her like a suit of armour. To celebrate her arrival, she bought a postcard at the kiosk near the entrance to the station which she wrote and stamped to send to her mother as proof that she was strangely capable of finding her way without getting lost, being raped, murdered or arrested en route. She could not resist a smug smile when she popped it in the letterbox, delighted that all her mother's dire warnings had been in vain.

Her satisfaction did not last very long. She entered the gates of the long gravel drive at Salhouse Farm to be startled by a loud horn behind her and was forced to jump to the side, almost colliding with the huge stone pillars that guarded the entrance. A large grey truck swung into the drive and as it passed her, she gasped. In the back, peering out from the tailgate were a group of German soldiers in brown overalls. She recognised the prisoner of war uniform from Pathé Newsreels shown at her local Stretford cinema. Their uniforms were a far cry from the neat, pristine ones the German propaganda films portrayed and these men looked as grey and defeated as every British person in January 1943 could ever have wished but to Hannah, the sight of those men were enough to send her newly-found confidence reeling.

Dotty was sitting on the bed, waiting for more information but Hannah was still processing the fact that she had only been on the farm twenty-four hours and had already had a terrifying encounter with a shire stallion of more than six feet high and weighing nearly two thousand pounds. She had also had her life saved by a German officer. She wondered what else her new life could throw at her and felt tears welling up again.

'Come on, Hannah, you'll have to do better than this,' Dotty told her, sternly. Although only seventeen, she had been in service since the age of fourteen and she was beginning to realise just how naïve and timid her new roommate was.

'I don't think I can do this, Dotty, I just can't.'

Dotty looked surreptitiously at her watch. Time was ticking on and the cows would not wait.

'OK, we're going to have a talk about this, but not now.' She leaned over and gave Hannah a quick hug and went to the door. She sighed with exasperation at the dejected figure on the bed and went downstairs. All Dotty's optimism at being told she was going to be joined by one, maybe two more Land Army girls was vanishing. This one was already infuriating the hell out of her.

Hannah leaned back on the pillow and stared up at the ceiling. It was an attic room with peeling plaster and one metal skylight. The window in the roof had an iron bar down the middle and a black out curtain pushed to one side, held in place by an elastic band. The room had originally been painted a mustard colour, but the walls had faded to a dirty brown and although it was quite large, it was sparsely furnished, suggesting only the bare essentials in life were really necessary. An oval tarnished mirror hung opposite her reflected a couple of small side tables, three stools, a jug, china bowl and some wall hooks.

She turned over on the bed and pulled the bolster in towards her, curling her knees up. This was the bolster she had really wanted to put between her and the stranger on the other side of the room when she arrived at the farm last night. An only child, Hannah's dismay at having to share had been obvious but then Dotty had jumped fully-clothed into her side of the bed. For a moment, Hannah had wondered if she was shy too but then Dotty had reached down and one by one, flung every item of clothing out onto the floor next to the bed, before pulling a nightie over her head. In a matter-of-fact manner, she then advised Hannah to do the same thing if she wanted to avoid freezing to death and with that pronouncement, had turned over and immediately gone to sleep.

Her mother's fears were right, Hannah thought, she would not be able to deal with life in the Land Army and would have been much better staying at home and looking after her parents.

Then she heard Lily's voice. Friends from the age of five, Hannah and Lily and their third friend, Ros, had been through primary school first and then onto Loreto Convent and, somehow, Hannah never knew how it happened but she became the one to step back and let the other two take the lead.

As usual, Lily was characteristically blunt, even in her head.

'You joined the Land Army to escape that oppressive house, you know you did,' the voice told her. 'The reality is you're terrified of stepping away and being your own person. But now is the chance for us girls to really find out what we're made of and you may find you're made of tougher stuff than you think.'

Hannah grumbled into the bolster. She hated it when Lily was right.

* * *

By the time Dotty came back from milking, Hannah had fiercely washed her face and brushed her hair and the two girls headed downstairs to the large, cavernous room that was their dining room and sitting room. With its brick walls it was freezing but it had a few old armchairs with faded fabric dotted around the sides and a couple of occasional tables between. In the middle was a long wooden table and a variety of hard-backed chairs. At the far end, a trestle table along the wall held plates, a jug containing cutlery and some water glasses tipped upside down in neat rows. There was a polished metal urn fronted by pale green cups and saucers.

Their meals were brought across from the farmhouse by a girl of about sixteen. Rachel's hair was pulled back into a ponytail and she walked with a limp, the result of childhood polio. She put an enamel dish covered in pastry in the middle of the table and gave Hannah a warm smile. The meal was a vegetable pie and taking a first taste, Hannah was pleasantly surprised that food was actually edible. She was also very hungry, she realised. The hot food and Dotty's relentless chatter was calculated to take Hannah's mind off the drama of the day and finally, Hannah felt her shoulders relax slightly.

'You know, when I turned up here two weeks ago,' Dotty said, grabbing some bread from the plate in the middle, 'honestly, Hannah, I can't tell you how relieved I was.'

She went on to describe her life before Salhouse Farm, which involved being a skivvy in a large, freezing cold house outside Stratford on Avon. She talked in factual terms, but her words gave Hannah a chill at the back of her neck.

'I hardly ate,' she said, lifting her fork to her mouth with relish, 'I was always starving and oh, Hannah, the garret I was in was absolutely perishing. I only had one thin blanket *and*,' she stressed, 'we had to work fourteen hours a day.'

She sat back, satisfied that Hannah's mind had finally been distracted.

For the first time, Hannah focused her gaze, really seeing the young girl in front of her. She had been so wound up with her own thoughts, it had never occurred to her that there were any other stories to be told.

Dotty waved an enthusiastic arm around the cold, empty room. 'This, I'll have you know,' she said with a grin, 'is just pure luxury.'

Hannah looked dubiously around her and tried to see it with Dotty's eyes. To her, it was still a room devoid of any warmth, character or homeliness, but listening to Dotty, she made a real attempt to see it differently.

'My home,' Dotty scoffed at the word, 'is back-to-back in Birmingham. There's five of us, I'm the oldest. I shared a bed with two of my sisters and our two brothers slept on the floor. My mum just works herself to death doing people's washing, and my dad . . .' her voice faded. She was not ready to share her whole life with Hannah yet. 'Anyway, I've been in service since I was fourteen.'

Dotty's sallow complexion and red, raw hands bore testimony to the hours of hard-graft labour she had put in at her previous position as the lowliest member of a well-off household. As soon as she could, she had volunteered for the Land Army, the only wartime occupation she could join at the age of just seventeen and she was excited about the skills she was going to learn, believing they might prevent her from ever having to go back into a scullery. She told Hannah that the farm seemed a sad place, but she did not know why. She then leaned forward conspiratorially: 'I've checked out the locals for you,' she said with a grin, 'but it doesn't look too promising. Most of them are so old I'm not sure the last war wanted them, never mind this one.

'And then here on the farm, there's Jed, as you know,' she said, pausing for a moment, 'just watch him, Hannah. I'm too scrawny for him but I know his type, he reminds me of one of the footmen at my last job. I always had to make sure I was never alone with him in the boot room; you make sure you're never alone when Jed's around either.'

Hannah was absorbing Dotty's words when the door to the yard opened, letting in an icy blast of air and the farmhands walked in. There were three men, much older than the girls and a younger, fresh-faced youth. The older ones looked with disdain at the two young women, too experienced in farming to ever believe that young slips of girls could do the hard, physical work a farm demanded. One of them tossed his head back and made a dismissive snorting noise.

Dotty immediately spoke up. 'You mind your own, William Handforth. I'm doing as well as any of you and don't you suggest for one minute that I'm not and Hannah here will work hard too.'

The group of experienced farmhands muttered their disapproval and moved along the table to the other end as usual where they sat down waiting for Rachel to come back with their meals. They glared at Hannah and Dotty but then Dotty pulled out her tongue at them.

'Less of your lip,' a man with pox-marked skin called Albert said to her. 'I've told you; we don't want you here, you're no bloody use and you'll just make more work for us. Girls . . . Land *Army* . . . God help us if you lot are an army. Hah!'

'Ignore them,' Dotty whispered to Hannah, who was looking at the men with horror. She had never come across so much ill-feeling from strangers. She felt a sudden wave of homesickness and swallowed hard.

As soon as supper was finished, the girls went up to their room. Hannah was too exhausted to talk and flopped onto her side of the bed. It occurred to her she had just experienced the worst two days of her life.

Don't miss Shirley Mann's inspiring
debut novel . . .

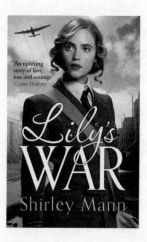

World War II is in full swing and Lily Mullins is determined
to do her bit for the war effort. Her friends and sweetheart
have all joined up and Lily's sure there must be a role for her
that goes further than knitting socks for the troops!

When she decides to volunteer for the Women's Auxiliary
Air Force, Lily soon discovers that she has a talent as a wireless operator. Helped along the way by a special gang of girls,
she finds strengths she didn't know she had and realises that
the safety of the country might just be in her hands . . .

Available now